PAUL BRADLEY CARR

1414°

Published by Snafublishing LLC
New York, San Francisco, London

Copyright 2021 by Paul Bradley Carr
All rights reserved.

To contact the author or for information about
special sales, please email hello@snafublishing.com

Cover design by Jamie Keenan
Interior design by Euan Monaghan

ISBN: 978-1-7375897-0-9 (Print)
ISBN: 978-1-7375897-1-6 (Ebook)

"We'll spend a million dollars to hire four top opposition researchers and four journalists. They'll look into your personal lives, your families. Nobody would know it was us." **EMIL MICHAEL, HEAD OF BUSINESS, UBER**

"The more cunning a man is, the less he suspects that he will be caught in a simple thing. The more cunning a man is, the simpler the trap he must be caught in." **FYODOR DOSTOYEVSKY, *CRIME AND PUNISHMENT***

THE FOLLOWING IS A WORK OF FICTION.

JOE CHRISTIAN WAS missing his eyebrows.

Missing them with an intensity that caught him quite by surprise.

What, in Fate's grand scheme, was a couple of tufts of hair in the unspeakably painful life and looming death of Joe Christian? A stubbed toe in a cancer ward. A set of house keys mislaid on the gallows.

And yet. As Joe stared into the smoky mirror, index fingers tracing the angry red bumps where his eyebrows once sat, he felt loss of the most profound sort. Even after he'd been forced to shave his head bald to evict the lice, and the angry purple rash had spread from his back to his chest to his neck, face, and scalp, he had at least been able to look in that mirror each morning and recognize the man who stared back. Now, bereft of eyebrows, Joe was a stranger to himself.

"No!" Joe slammed a blistered palm into his reflection. "No! No—no—no—no," the words emerging as a bestial chant. *I am still alive. I am still Joe Christian.*

It had been five days since Joe had last slept, but somewhere deep in his brain, his once fiery intellect still glowed: *The mood swings. The despair. The pain. None of it is real. It will pass. You're not dying. Just a few hours of good sleep, then you'll be able to think clearly. Everything is going to be fine.*

Joe's tears burned their way across the open sores on his cheeks and splashed into the sink, cleaving a channel through the pool of blood and mucus and toothpaste still struggling down the plughole. Because of course he *was* dying. The only question was what would bring the final cut: the insomnia, the madness, the infection. Or perhaps Fate would do it the old-fashioned way: a distracted bus driver, a frayed electrical cable on his homemade cell phone charger—

The little glass bottle still stood on the shelf below the mirror, its Chinese lettering (Joe assumed) echoing the warning from the man in the stained white coat: "Try this on hidden skin first. You understand? Wait a week before applying it on face." The doctor was just covering his own ass, Joe had later reassured himself, as he slathered the foul-smelling liquid over his scalp, forehead, ears, and eyebrows.

The same man had prodded Joe's sores through two sets of latex gloves, and for a moment his mask of bemused bonhomie had slipped. "You really should see a doctor."

"Aren't you a doctor?"

"Sure sure," the man had replied. "I doctor. I rich and famous doctor, look at my beautiful wife!" He gestured toward a large plastic cat slowly waving from the top of a pile of cardboard boxes.

Joe had played along, because the man was his only hope. His health insurance—once fully paid, once best in class—was long gone. Even CPMC's emergency room in the Tenderloin—the one his own money had helped to build—would no longer treat him; not until the bacteria spread to his heart or liver and the law forced their hand.

"No." This time the word came out as a distant whisper, as if the reflection in the mirror had been the one saying it. Joe had been waiting for months for Fate to reveal himself—waiting for some clue as to the ransom payable for an end to the torture. But each sunrise only brought a new day more exponentially bleak than the last. Each catastrophe only bloomed into a dozen more, like some perfectly vindictive fractal.

Now, along with Joe's eyebrows, went the last of his hope. There was no sign coming, and no escape. Fate would be satisfied only when Joe Christian was completely and painfully dead.

Well, OK, then.

Pressing the balls of his bare feet into the slimy carpet, Joe hobbled the ten paces from the sink to the Murphy bed that served as his living room, dining table, and office. He pulled back the yellow polyester comforter, exposing the bare mattress and a single limp pillow. From the recesses of the pillow, he extracted a black notebook, bookmarked with an orange ballpoint pen. Fate could access his laptop, or read his text messages. He could even, Joe was certain, monitor his heart rate via the ambient Wi-Fi signals from the backpacker hostel across the street. But the black notebook was Joe's alone.

He flipped to the marked page and, in the left of two columns, wrote the date in neat block capital letters: 9TH APRIL. Then, in the right column, he wrote the word "Eyebrows," before carefully crossing it through with a single line.

Joe stared at the journal entry, orange pen still hovering over the page. Even now, he was still an engineer, a man of science. He knew if his journal was to have any research value after he was gone . . . if his former wife and his estranged friends were to find the black notebook and finally see what he had spent months trying to make them understand . . . that none of this was his fault, that he was the victim of something far more sinister than karma or divine retribution for his crimes . . . If his suffering was to have meaning, he had to be absolutely sure of his data.

Joe closed his eyes and mentally retraced the events of the past week. Even if Fate had nudged him toward the Chinese doctor and his corrosive balm, Joe's decision to ignore the man's warnings and smear the poison over his face was all his own, wasn't it? Could he say for certain that Fate was *directly* responsible?

No, he could not. Correlation was not causation. And so next to the crossed-out "Eyebrows," Joe added a small question mark. His daily ablutions concluded for the final time, he closed the book and returned it to its fetid sleeve.

THREE BLOCKS SOUTH, in the newsroom of the *Bay Area Herald*, Lou McCarthy glared at the prompt flashing on the screen of her computer terminal.

Are you sure you're ready to publish? Y/N

She silently cursed whichever software engineer had programmed such a moronic question.

In the past five years, she'd keyed maybe five hundred stories into the *Herald*'s aging "news management system" and always hesitated over this last step. Can any journalist truly be *sure* they're ready to publish a story? Of course not. There are always more sources to chase down, more quotes to confirm, more on-the-ground reporting to do, more all-nighters to pull, more shitty instant coffee to drink. News is called the first rough draft of history for a reason: at some point you have to publish what you have and let the chips tumble.

This morning, three gallons of Kirkland House Blend down and no sleep for twenty-six hours, the question took on an even more weighty significance.

Are you sure you're ready to pick a fight with the most valuable private company in Silicon Valley history? Y/N

Are you sure you're ready to take a woman's worst trauma and turn it into public property? Y/N

All on the basis of a single leaked document from an anonymous source?

Are you out of your fucking mind?

Y/N

Lou glanced up at the IBM schoolhouse clock on the wall: 8:26 a.m. She might not be out of her mind, but she was definitely out of time. In precisely four minutes, Stephen Camp would crash through the news-room door, briefcase overflowing with papers, unnecessary umbrella wedged in his armpit, cursing the slowness of the elevator and the fresh crop of idiots he had encountered on BART, and Lou's window of oppor-tunity would pinch closed forever.

She read back her headline, still visible behind the dickish pop-up window.

RAUM EXECUTIVE ACCUSED OF RAPE

A fine headline. No hyperbole. No ambiguity. Just the bare facts, as laid out by her source.

But at the same time it was almost comically understated. Alex Wu was an executive at Raum in the same way that Neil Armstrong was an engineer at NASA. As the inventor of the Raum Band, Wu was widely considered to be the most powerful man in all of Silicon Valley. Not the richest—that would (soon) be his equally repugnant boss, Raum's CEO, Elmsley Chase—but certainly the most influential.

It was Alex Wu who, as Raum's chief technology officer, decided how quickly your vRaum car arrived, or your RaumService food delivery, or your RedRaum hookup. It was Alex Wu who, as inventor and custodian of Raum's top-secret algorithm, could with a single line of code fill a mil-lion stomachs, create a hundred thousand marriages, or bring an entire city to a standstill on polling day—as several antagonistic lawmakers had learned the hard way.

And now it was Alex Wu who, according to the draft lawsuit that had dropped into Lou's inbox last night, had modified that same algorithm to locate and track young women who matched his own sick victim profile, using the alcohol sensors in their Raum Bands to notify him when they were alone and intoxicated. Who, two months ago, had offered a paralytically drunk twenty-two-year-old college student (listed in the suit only as Jane Doe) a ride home in his Tesla Model π.

In an ideal journalistic world, Lou would have spent weeks reporting out the facts of a story like this. There would have been hours-long conferences with Stephen Camp, her editor of a half decade, followed by days of meddling from the *Herald*'s lawyers. To publish so inflammatory an allegation—let alone one based on an unverified lawsuit from an anonymous source—was a huge risk. To do so without even showing the draft to her editor was certifiably insane. Lou knew that. Obviously she fucking knew that.

But here's what else she knew: Alex Wu, the most powerful man in Silicon Valley, was a serial predator. Either Lou could try to stop him, or she could be complicit in every other rape he committed: tonight, tomorrow, and forever.

She had been chasing down rumors of Wu's behavior for months. Whispered stories of young women found wandering the streets, sobbing and bleeding. Secondhand tips about secretly administered drugs and sudden flashes of violence. Lou had spent countless nights trawling Stanford student bars and upscale hotel lobbies on Sand Hill Road, trying to find just one source willing to go on the record about Wu's crimes. She'd gotten close a couple of times: Sophie Aker—Wu's girlfriend at Stanford who wept as she told Lou how he'd once tried to strangle her with his belt—and Mei Lynn Xi—a young venture capital associate who'd complained to her boss that Wu had attacked her at a holiday party, only to be fired the very next week. There were plenty of other rumors from Wu's days at Stanford—including a persistent one, repeated by numerous former students, that he'd assaulted another classmate; an attack covered up by the faculty to protect the school's reputation. But every single time, hours before publication, Lou's sources were suddenly rendered mute, or struck down with amnesia.

Another rumor Lou hadn't been able to prove: While other startups had revamped HR policies and jettisoned executives in response to scandals, Raum had recruited a platoon of crisis managers to cover up bad behavior by the company's "senior leadership." The team's duties included smearing victims, threatening journalists, and even—Lou had heard—occasional housebreaking to retrieve physical evidence of criminality. But their preferred weapon was the secret payoff. According to local property records, Sophie Aker had taken possession of a new condo less than a month after Lou had first contacted her for comment about Wu. Similarly, a source at Experian had confirmed to Lou—off the record—that Mei Lynn Xi's credit card debts had disappeared overnight. What she couldn't figure out was how Raum actually made these payments. If the company spent investors' money paying off victims, that would certainly be a breach of fiduciary duty—possibly even a crime. But, despite weeks poring over Raum's financials and SEC filings, Lou couldn't find even a hint of this multimillion-dollar slush fund.

Now she finally had documentary proof of Wu's crimes, sent via an encrypted messaging app by her anonymous deep throat inside Raum. The same source who had sent her more than a dozen previous story tips, every single one of which had checked out.

Lou took another sip of cold coffee as she mentally cycled through her list of prepared excuses. At exactly 399 words, not counting the fifty-page lawsuit embedded as a PDF, the story was technically just a "newsshort," which meant she didn't need her editor's approval to publish. Also, the tip had arrived late and she hated to disturb Camp at home, especially with the new baby . . .

Lou shook her head. It was all such transparent bullshit. But any excuse was better than the truth: that she had worked all night, racing to finish the story before Camp arrived at the office, because she didn't trust her tired, defeated milquetoast of an editor not to sabotage it.

"Work with Tommy Paphitis on this," she could hear Camp saying. "He has strong sources at Raum." Funny how, for all his "we're all on the same team" lectures, Camp never ordered Tommy to share *his* story drafts with her.

Fuck that. She couldn't risk letting Camp delay this story, not today. In a few hours, just six blocks from the *Herald* building, Raum was throwing a revoltingly extravagant party to officially open its new headquarters, Raum One. Officially. But the whole business world knew the party's real purpose. Tonight, under the shimmering glass roof of Raum One, Elmsley Chase would announce his company's much-anticipated initial public offering.

A Raum IPO would be the largest and most lucrative public stock flotation in Silicon Valley history—a so-called "liquidity event" that would convert Elmsley Chase's personal shareholding into close to $100 billion of actual cash. The IPO would also refill the company's depleted financial coffers, allowing it to expand its services into dozens more countries. Post-IPO, Raum would be unstoppable, its overgrown-frat-boy execs even more untouchable. The mere announcement of the thing would trigger a tsunami of salivating press coverage; certainly enough to wash away something so mundane as a senior Raum executive accused of beating his victim so badly that she lost the sight in one eye. Lou knew if she published her Alex Wu story after tonight, Jane Doe's lawsuit would, at best, be dismissed as a smear campaign by jealous rivals. Probably it would be ignored entirely.

One final reason not to wait: Lou's source had given her a heads-up that Miquela Rio at the *Wall Street Journal* had also gotten hold of a copy of the lawsuit and was preparing to publish. Rio was a reliably shitty writer, and deeply in the tank for big tech and venture capitalists, but she was the only other reporter in the Valley with Raum sources even remotely as good as Lou's, and the *Journal* had a trillion times the readership of the *Herald*. If Lou didn't want to be scooped, she had to publish right now, while Rio was still tangled up with editors and lawyers.

Lou minimized the news management system and clicked over to her inbox. No new emails. She hit refresh. And again.

The silence was deafening, and frightening. Twenty minutes earlier she'd sent a watered-down summary of her story to Raum's press office for comment. The *Herald*'s ethics handbook was clear: except in extreme circumstances, the subject of a story must be given a reasonable amount of time to comment prior to publication. Typically that meant a full day, or at least a few hours.

Except in extreme circumstances. What could be more extreme than exposing a rapist who used his own company's technology to target victims? A company that was about to announce the biggest IPO in tech history.

Lou hit refresh a third time. She imagined her email bouncing from attorney to attorney inside Raum One. Before the clock struck nine a.m., battalions of PR people would be issuing statements, rebutting the story and attacking Lou's professional credentials. By ten, telephones would be ringing in the town houses of federal judges, dragged from their breakfasts to consider the company's plea for an injunction against future reporting. Raum's crisis-management team would be gearing up for battle: tracking Lou's phone to unmask her source, planting smears on friendly blogs, creating sock-puppet Twitter accounts to spread lies and innuendo about Jane Doe. Then would come the stans and the trolls and—inevitably—Claude Pétain. Ugh. She shook her head, then her entire body, to Etch a Sketch away the thought of the most grotesque and dangerous troll of all.

She had been through this a hundred times before, on a hundred different stories; surfed the same fucking wave of fear, followed by anger, followed by determination, followed by terror, followed by acceptance, punctuated at some point by a lecture by Stephen Camp and the lawyers about how, if only she'd written the story a different way or asked for just one more quote, Pétain's "Men's Lives Matter" scumbags would have stayed home that day and left her alone.

Be fair to the rapists; don't feed the trolls; investigate the victims; don't spook the advertisers; if in doubt, stay quiet . . . this was how investigative journalism worked now, as codified by the *Herald Ethics Handbook*.

It was a fight Lou could never win. There was no ethics handbook inside Raum One.

Was she kidding herself to think that a 399-word newsshort might finally slow Raum's hitherto unstoppable rise? Normally, yes. But maybe today . . . How could a technology company announce its IPO on the same day its top engineer was exposed as a rapist? Surely the markets—already jittery about Raum's stratospheric valuation—would never tolerate that kind of risk. Alex Wu might never see the inside of a jail cell, but at least he'd have to be fired. Replacement chief technology officers don't grow on trees. There would need to be a full security audit of Raum's systems to ensure that no other executives or employees were targeting vRaum users as Wu had. Taking down a predator, and cutting off the supply of victims. Surely that was *something*. Would change *something*.

Something worth losing your job over?

Y/N?

Something worth getting publicly mauled, privately smeared?

Y/N?

Death threats? Doxxing? Three pounds of human shit mailed to your desk?

Y/N?

She heard Stephen Camp's voice echoing in her head. *You're making this personal, Lou. It's not our job to take people down.*

No—*since you ask, Stephen*—a journalist's job is to publish the truth. Without fear, without favor, and without worrying what it might mean for her career, her safety, or her social life. An editor's job, meantime, is to protect reporters from all of the above. Or at least it used to be, before the Silicon Valley press corps was taken over by gadget bloggers and slathering fanboys who see journalism as a way to get close to their brociopath tech idols.

Lou looked at the printout of the lawsuit, clipped next to her monitor. So what if she *was* taking it personally? Wasn't it personal to Jane Doe? Wasn't it personal to Sophie Aker, who, ten years after graduation, was still in trauma therapy for what Alex Wu did to her; or to Wu's unnamed classmate who never got the chance to graduate; or to Mei Lynn Xi, who, last Lou had heard, spent her nights volunteering at a shelter for survivors of domestic abuse? Wasn't "taking it personally" just another way of saying "having a shred of fucking empathy for your fellow human beings"? Was taking down lying, abusive men really such a terrible goal? Lou kicked her bare foot against the box of printer paper under her desk.

She knew what Camp really meant. He meant her apartment. Or rather, her former apartment—the rent-controlled $650-per-month sublet that she'd found the week after she moved to San Francisco. The apartment with three roommates packed into two rooms, the lovable family of rats in the bathroom, and the asbestos kitchen tiles, which, nevertheless, had allowed Lou to defy the laws of financial gravity and survive on a journalist's salary in a city where rents now averaged $6,000. The apartment—*her* apartment—that now lay as rubble; obliterated along with a dozen others to make room for the construction of Raum One.

Lou was angry—but it wasn't like she lay awake at night fantasizing about pushing Elmsley Chase under a train, or dreamed of poisoning Alex Wu with ricin sent in the mail, or of taking a machine gun to the entire Raum board and tossing their bloodied corpses onto a bonfire along with all the other rich monsters roaming Silicon Valley with total fucking impunity. She had never once wondered if it might be possible for a sniper's bullet to reach Raum One's executive floor from her office window.

Hers was a productive anger. An anger always channeled back into her work, for all the good it had done. On the day the first of her neighbors were due to be evicted, she filed two full pages for the *Herald*'s print edition, dispassionately telling their stories. It was the most difficult piece

Lou had ever written, more grief counseling than journalism. She'd had to beg her neighbors to speak to her on the record; had urged them to understand the importance of using their real names and faces. Because only by humanizing the building and its residents—only by naming Mrs. Gee and her four children about to be thrown onto the streets, or by having Mr. Kowalczyk describe the debilitating emphysema symptoms that had rendered him housebound—could they possibly shame Raum into backing down. *Trust me,* Lou had told them. With the implied *I know what I'm doing.*

Then came the uniquely Raum-ian kicker: two hours after Lou published her story, Raum sent a statement to every journalist in town, denouncing Lou and her reporting. She still remembered it word for word.

> *Contrary to sensationalist reporting by the* Bay Area Herald, *not a single person has been made homeless by the compulsory purchase of 680 Market Street. All homeowners affected by the development of Raum One were paid a generous relocation bonus, many times above market rate, to ensure they would have no difficulty finding alternative housing. It's regrettable that the* Herald *continues to sow divisions between the tech community and other San Francisco residents, rather than celebrating the continuing success of the city's largest job creator.*

All homeowners . . . were paid a generous relocation bonus. The statement was as disingenuous as it was cruel. There were no *homeowners* living in Lou's building, just renters and subletters like herself and her neighbors, none of whom had been paid a dime for "relocation." Perhaps the *owners* of the building—one of the many faceless Delaware corporations and absent foreign landlords that now owned much of the city's rental property—had been adequately compensated by Raum. Probably somebody somewhere had gotten rich off the deal. The distinction was lost on most readers, and the world quickly forgot about the battle for 680 Market Street.

But Lou would never forget. Just as Mrs. Gee and Mr. Kowalczyk would never forget how she'd promised them her story would make a difference. Was that ever true? Had she believed it when she said it? Or was she just as much of an asshole as everyone else in this town?

Then came this lawsuit. Lou had no idea who Jane Doe was; hadn't even heard about the case until a few hours ago when her source had sent her an encrypted message with the document attached. The details of the case, if they went to trial, would soon become part of the public record. Raum's smear artists surely had the document too, and were already working to track Jane Doe down and silence her—or rather re-silence her: according to the lawsuit, Alex Wu had already succeeded in crushing her larynx and fracturing the hyoid bone in her throat. Nothing in Lou's story could possibly make things worse.

Are you still a journalist, Lou?

Y/N?

Or are you done?

Lou was pulled back to reality by the distant whir of an elevator beginning its descent toward the lobby. She had maybe forty-five seconds before it returned, carrying Stephen Camp and his stupid umbrella. She reached for her coffee, but found only an empty paper cup. Without turning her head, she pitched her arm back over her shoulder and heard a satisfying *tang* as the cup landed perfectly in the trash can. Somehow that felt like a sign.

Are you sure you're ready to publish?

Y/N?

4

STILL SLUMPED ON the edge of his bed, Joe Christian concentrated on the small glass bottle clenched between the fingertips of both hands. He couldn't remember having retrieved the Chinese balm from the bathroom shelf, or untwisting the safety cap. He must have performed both of these feats, though, because there was the bottle, held prayerlike against his chest, its acrid smell threatening to do for the hair in his nostrils as it had already done for his eyebrows.

Joe closed his eyes and let the sounds of the SRO fill his ears. Down the hallway a Mexican soap opera droned and shrieked, and a twenty-dollar hooker screamed at her john; and beyond the building's walls, the few remaining people even less fortunate than Joe yelled and clanked their shopping carts filled with aluminum cans through the Tenderloin. Funny to think now. Barely two years earlier, Joe and Amelia had hosted a fundraiser in their Palo Alto home to help get those self-same unfortunates off the streets outside his office and into single-resident-occupancy rooms just like this one.

He thought about Amelia, and about Linus and Nikola—unnaturally handsome, even at five and seven—heading off to school, dressed in their freshly dry-cleaned uniforms, clutching their matching red lunch pails. Did the boys even remember they had a father? Joe saw his wedding day, and the night Linus was born. He'd missed Nikola's birth thanks to an investor meeting in Dubai, but still vividly remembered the joy he'd felt as he watched streaming video of the delivery on his red-eye flight home, until the stewardess—mistaking the footage for something altogether less wholesome—had demanded he shut his laptop.

Amelia had never forgiven him for his absence, but neither had she ever complained about the lifestyle Joe's success afforded their family:

the homes, the vacations, the spa treatments and preemptive cosmetic surgeries. Nor had she protested when his relentless work schedule had sent their children to the best private school in Marin.

Joe's hands were trembling even more than usual as he brought the tiny bottle to his lips. In these final moments, he found himself again grasping for the reassuring certainty of science. Was the Chinese balm an alkaline? he wondered. If so, would it react like bleach, burning his esophagus and dissolving his stomach as he screamed and vomited himself toward merciful death? Or would it behave more like a neurotoxin—a tetrodotoxin or botulinum—inhibiting the signals to his brain that instructed his lungs to breathe and his heart to beat? Either way, his death would be excruciatingly painful. It was really just a question of burning or drowning; of timing and mess.

Joe willed his hands to tilt the bottle farther; just one last jerk of the wrist and a healthy gulp and—after ten minutes of agony, at most—blissful relief. Fate could never hurt him again.

Except Fate could do anything.

A series of angry beeps jolted Joe back to reality and sent the bottle tumbling from his fingertips onto the floor; the liquid glooping and seeping harmlessly into the carpet. On his bedside table, the drugstore cell phone that had been sitting jerry-wired into the radio alarm clock was vibrating its way toward the brink.

Joe grabbed the device and felt the prickle of an electric shock. That jolt, though, was nothing compared with the one that followed when his eyes were able to focus on the tiny screen.

Joe squinted at the unfurling digital text, barely comprehending what he was seeing. Could it possibly be true? He scrolled farther. Yes. There was the man's name and his photograph—another jolt, this time of recognition—and below it a headline, just published on the website of the *Bay Area Herald*.

RAUM EXECUTIVE ACCUSED OF RAPE

To anyone else, the headline would be depressingly banal—just another breathless, exaggerated faux scandal published in a failing tabloid rag. Another scorned woman trying to take down another powerful, successful man, aided and abetted by another desperate, virtue-signaling hack.

But suddenly Joe knew better. He continued to stare, not at the words of the story, but at the photograph accompanying it.

It must have been two years since Joe had last seen Alex Wu. They were at the same conference—Wu speaking onstage, and Joe in the audience. Joe had stared up at Wu, with his piercing green eyes, his thick black hair gelled back across his scalp, and the muscles of a competitive kite surfer rippling below his Raum T-shirt, and felt his own ego buckle against the onslaught.

In this newspaper photo, though, Wu struck a pathetic figure: emaciated, his Raum T-shirt loose over his shrunken frame. His obnoxious hair lank and thinning, his smug eyes distant and frightened. He was smiling, but with his lips tightly shut, as if trying to hide his teeth and gums. The copyright notice on the photo said it had been taken almost a month ago.

Joe took it all in: Wu's gaunt expression, the sunken eyes, the blotches on his cheeks artlessly concealed behind layers of what looked like stage makeup. His eyebrows. Or rather his lack of eyebrows.

Tiny silvery specks appeared at the edge of Joe's vision—an ophthalmic migraine triggered by a hundred trillion synapses exploding back to life. He scrolled back to the headline: the five words that surely spelled professional and personal ruin for the most powerful man in Silicon Valley. More synapses, this time transporting him back more than a decade to the very first time he'd heard the name Alex Wu.

Oh. My. God.

The fact that the alert had arrived at that precise moment, on that precise phone—a phone to which only Fate could possibly know the number—removed any doubt from the equation. The two realizations hit Joe Christian at the exact same time . . .

I know who Fate is.

And I know why.

Then, an instant later, a third thought.

Alex Wu has to confess. Then all of this will stop.

5

NINE FIFTEEN A.M. Lou McCarthy stood in the hallway outside the *Herald* newsroom, shifting her weight from foot to foot. She'd been standing there a full ten minutes, since Stephen Camp summoned her with two fingers and a face like thunder. Now she watched as her editor paced back and forth, ancient red Nokia clamped to one of two gigantic ears, silent but for the occasional "uh-huh" and "I understand" and "with respect, we don't agree with that interpretation" spoken into the elderly plastic handset.

Lou couldn't decide if Camp looked angry, concerned, or frustrated. Mostly he just looked tired, the dark bags below his eyes resting on his cheeks, and his thin graying hair lying flat over his forehead, giving him the look of a world-weary yokel. New fatherhood, aged forty-nine, had not been kind to Stephen Camp.

Eventually, he ended the call, pocketed his phone, and turned his attention to Lou.

"I guess my question would be . . ." Camp rubbed his forehead, and then took another swing at the sentence. "Why don't you tell me, in your own words, what exactly I read on our site this morning?"

"I'm sorry, Stephen," Lou launched into the first of her rehearsed explanations, "I only got the document from my source late last night and I know—"

"Lou, stop." Camp raised his palms in mock surrender. "You can spare the rehearsed speech. We've all heard it before. A huge scoop. Couldn't possibly wait. Also, just a newsshort. Blah-de-blah-wah-wah. Your contempt for the editorial process, this newspaper, and me personally are all duly noted and understood. What I'm struggling to comprehend is why you would drop a goddamned nuclear bomb on your own career."

"Was that Raum?" Lou nodded her head toward the pocket where Camp's phone now rested.

Camp laughed, somehow without smiling. "Yes, Lou, that was Raum's general counsel. Funnily enough, he was somewhat anxious to discuss the story in which you accused his CTO of rape on the eve of their IPO announcement. Specifically, the phrase he used was 'criminally defamatory' and 'a textbook case of actual malice.' Which, by the way, is what pisses me off the most: you've forced me to agree with Raum."

Lou knew she should probably be terrified at the prospect of a career-ending defamation suit filed by the most powerful and vengeful company on the planet, but in that moment her prevailing emotion was anger. "Why didn't you bring me in on the call?" That was standard practice at the *Herald*: When the subject of a story calls an editor to complain—which they *always* do—the reporter is invited to listen in, ostensibly to clarify any questions of fact or process, but really to demonstrate to the angry subject that both editor and reporter are firmly on the same team. An unshakable defensive wall. "I mean, Jesus Christ . . ."

If Camp was shocked by the insubordination, he didn't show it. "Oh-ho-no, don't even think about getting pissy with me for keeping *you* out of the fucking loop. You're not the one who walked into work this morning to find that one of his reporters had just published the fucking allegation of the century against Raum without consulting a single fucking editor."

In five years at the *Herald*, Lou had heard Camp swear maybe once. To hear him drop a triple fuck bomb in a single breath was the end of fucking days.

"My source is good. You know that."

"Actually, Lou, I don't know that. Mainly because I don't know who your source is. And neither do our readers. I have to assume at least *you* know who your source is. You'd have to be suicidally stupid to publish a story like this based on an anonymous tip. And I know you're not that."

Lou said nothing. She felt her own cheeks flushing red now: some combination of rage and embarrassment.

"What I do know," Camp continued, "is that Raum has a sworn affidavit from the attorney named on the Jane Doe lawsuit. He says the document you published didn't come from his firm. He's willing to say under oath that it's a forgery."

"That's bullshit . . ." It had to be. Lou had emailed Raum for comment only a half hour earlier—there was no way their lawyer could have obtained a sworn statement refuting the lawsuit that quickly. Not unless the document was genuine, and Jane Doe was real, and Raum already knew about both and had its rebuttal ready to go. Or . . . or what? Somewhere in the depths of Lou's brain, a horrifying possibility was beginning to assemble itself.

"He's sending us the affidavit. It's probably in your email already. Oh, and it gets better. The general counsel says the company has proof that Alex Wu wasn't even in the city the night your unnamed source claims he was attacking some equally unnamed girl. They have vRaum receipts showing he was at a restaurant in Woodside with his elderly mother, celebrating her eightieth birthday. The mother's ride receipts confirm it."

"Oh, come on, Stephen. Raum can fake the ride receipts, and the affidavit. They can fake all of it. That's what they do." Lou could hear her voice cracking. A familiar tang was building in the back of her throat, but she'd be damned if she was going to give Camp the satisfaction of seeing her cry. It never ceased to infuriate her that the first instinct of guys like Stephen Camp was still to believe the perpetrators, not the victims.

Camp gave one of his pained smiles, as if checking his teeth for spinach. "So, our defense is that Raum routinely fakes documents, so nothing that comes from inside Raum One should be trusted?"

"You disagree?"

"I don't disagree, Lou. So just out of interest, where did you get this definitely authentic lawsuit? Was it by any chance from someone inside Raum One?"

Lou opened her mouth to respond, but the words wouldn't come. The realization, now fully formed, hit her like the twist at the end of a horrible movie, except in this case the movie was her career and the twist was so obvious that she wanted her money back. By putting out a fake document about Alex Wu and then exposing it as a fraud after publication, her so-called source inside Raum had discredited not just Lou and her story but any future story about Wu, published by any reporter.

It was worse than that. If Raum sued the *Herald* and won, the cowards at the *Times* and the *Journal* would have the perfect excuse to spike any story that might upset a Raum executive. There was just too much reasonable doubt. Raum's IPO could proceed full steam ahead, investors safe in the knowledge that nobody would dare mention the discredited rumors about Wu. That's why they hadn't responded to her request for comment: they actually *wanted* her to publish. It had all been a fucking trap. One last punch in the gut to make sure she was truly down and out.

"Motherfuckers."

"Yes, Lou, they are. Famously so."

"I can try to call my source . . ."

"No, you can't," Camp sighed, loudly. "I guarantee if you do, the number will be disconnected, or will redirect to some pervy sex line. Or maybe just an endless recording of Elmsley Chase laughing his ass off at how easily we got played. Hell, I wouldn't be surprised if Chase turned out to be your mysterious source."

Camp must have seen the defeat on Lou's face. "For what it's worth"—he shrugged—"I don't think they'll sue. First off, the judge would likely throw the suit out on anti-SLAPP grounds. Second, even if they found a friendly court, our attorneys could subpoena all of Wu's ride receipts, emails, and text messages. Wu might not be a rapist, but you can bet there's plenty that Raum doesn't want us to see in those. Chase already has what he wants: the promise of a retraction, the rumors about Wu discredited, and your credibility shot to hell."

Lou swallowed her urge to remind Camp that Wu definitely was a rapist, which was precisely why the company was so desperate to discredit her reporting. "So now you want me to write a retraction?"

Camp shook his head. "I've asked Tommy to do it. I don't want you thinking another word about Raum for at least a couple of months, until we know there's definitely no lawsuit coming."

"And then?"

"Then we'll see."

Lou felt a flicker of surprise that she wasn't getting fired. Then the anger returned. Of course Camp had asked Tommy Paphitis to write the retraction—everything Tommy wrote read like a fucking retraction.

"What do you want me to do in the meantime?"

Camp rubbed the back of his neck. "What I need you to do right now is collect all your notes and give them to Tommy. Once he's done writing the retraction, he's going to report out the lawsuit properly and figure out if there's even a shred of truth to this shitshow. After that . . . frankly I don't give a damn what you do as long as it doesn't involve Raum or Alex Wu or Elmsley Chase or anyone else who might sue us into oblivion."

"So, Tommy is taking my story."

"I'll tell you a secret, Lou." Camp leaned forward and Lou could smell tobacco on his warm breath. "Everyone in this newsroom hates Raum. Elmsley Chase and his gang of crooks lie, they cheat, they steal, they cover up for rapists and abusers. Like you always say in story meetings, they're the modern Philip Morris."

"Standard Oil."

"What?"

"They're the modern Standard Oil."

". . . but unlike you, the rest of us don't see every anonymous tip as an opportunity to take them down, or end someone's career. Sometimes that happens as a side effect of what we do, but it's never the aim." Camp was standing so close now that Lou could see the little sprigs of hair escaping each of his nostrils. Why did so many men confuse looming with bonding? "You're not going to like this, Lou, but you could learn a lot from Tommy. You might—*might*—be a better journalist, and you're damn sure a better writer. But unlike you, Tommy doesn't let his . . ." Camp stopped short of using the "e" word, like a horse freezing at a jump that it knew was slightly too high to clear safely.

"Look. Raum has become a half-trillion-dollar company because it knows how to manipulate human beings. Its users, and its service providers; but also politicians, regulators, shareholders, and . . . guess what . . . reporters. We can only guard against being manipulated if we work as a team."

Lou barely registered the rest of Camp's too-close speech about risk-averse lawyers and there being rules for a reason, or his waffling about the boundless opportunities of youth and how this would likely be the best thing to ever happen to her. Over her boss's shiny shoulder, she'd caught sight of her own face, reflected and distorted in the doors of the elevator. At twenty-nine she already looked, and felt, middle-aged. Her mousy-blond hair was now hopelessly ratty, her green eyes bloodshot, and her complexion worthy of a faces-of-meth poster. How long had it been since she'd last bought a new shirt, or pair of shoes? Six months? A year? Surely all of her coworkers had realized by now that she owned only a single pair of frayed jeans and two white button-downs, which she washed along with gym shorts and underwear in the sink of the *Herald*'s omnisex bathroom. She cringed at the memory of Camp returning from a pee break with a stretched gray thong hanging from the end of his Bic.

Camp really thought he understood her; truly believed he knew all she had sacrificed, personally and professionally, just to tell the truth about Silicon Valley assholes. He knew maybe 20 percent of it. What would Camp say, for example, if he knew that for the past six months, Lou had been sleeping under her desk? That every night when Camp drove home to his weirdly attractive wife and their newly adopted Chinese daughter, his star reporter spent six freezing hours curled up, alone, under a pile of "Heralding San Francisco" promotional T-shirts, head resting on a stack of printer paper? That on weekends she scoured Craigslist for another miracle sublet—which couldn't possibly exist—before dragging her shirt-bed to the corner by the window, just so she could stare across the city skyline at Raum One, the towering glass obelisk where her apartment—and her life—used to be?

She'd given the *Herald* everything. Had forsaken comfort, safety, and savings—exploded friendships and torched relationships. And for what? Her reporting had occasionally moved stock prices, and forced minor boardroom reshuffles, but in the final analysis, most of the despicable assholes she'd written about—Alex Wu included—still had their jobs, or different jobs that paid even better. The stock always recovered, and the investors still made their billions. The rapists still stalked the streets, the sharing-economy workers still died sleeping in their cars, the trolls still stole elections and harassed reporters, and nobody gave a fuck.

Of all the companies in Silicon Valley, Raum was the best at turning rotten lemons into gold-infused lemonade. The same source who had given Lou the Wu lawsuit had previously tipped her off that a staggering percentage of vRaum's human drivers had failed to pass criminal background checks. Two days later, the company had used Lou's own reporting as an excuse to announce it was scrapping human drivers within a year and replacing the entire fleet with self-driving cars. Mass layoffs disguised as a public safety initiative. The tech and business press gobbled it up. Had her source really been playing her this whole time?

Stay away from Raum for a couple of months. That was the part of Camp's lecture that stung the worst: that her own editor thought she was an idiot. They both knew the statute of limitations for a defamation suit in California was a year. What was she going to write about in the meantime? Twitter? Uber? Dunk.ly? Grintech? Companies nobody had cared about for years? Twelve months without even a joint byline on Raum stories, cowering in Tommy's greasy, sycophantic shadow, might as well be a lifetime.

As Lou plodded back to her desk, head tilted to avoid eye contact with her office mates, it occurred to her that she couldn't remember how her conversation with Stephen Camp had ended. Was it possible she'd walked away with him still in midflow? No, she looked over and saw him back at his desk, tapping at his keyboard, presumably emailing Raum's general counsel to report that her fate had been accompli'd. On the bookcase behind him, his row of dusty journalism awards—Loebs and PENs and Lovejoys—teetered, as if waiting to jump. A few feet away, Tommy Paphitis lounged at his own workstation, phone wedged between bony shoulder and cheek, black hair spiked up in a series of painfully deliberate tufts. He seemed to be laughing at the world's funniest joke.

Lou slumped into her chair and struggled to open the small filing cabinet where she kept her crisis Diet Cokes. The drawer had become clogged with a tangle of shirts and socks and the famous gray thong. Exacerbating the jam was a free sample packet of Tide that had become wedged tight in the runners. After a few more seconds of tugging and rattling, she gave up the fight, slammed the drawer closed, and underscored the point with a kick.

This was bullshit.

The printout of the Alex Wu lawsuit was still clipped to the document holder on her monitor, phrases like "forcefully, and without consent" and "fully aware the plaintiff was intoxicated" picked out in yellow highlighter. What kind of scumsucker goes to work every day knowing his job is to fake documents and discredit journalists to protect billionaire sex offenders? How badly does your life have to have turned out for you to become a professional Rape Report Forger?

Lou gathered the pages of yellow legal paper scattered across her desk and arranged them in a neat pile. Then she removed the corona of Post-its from around her monitor and dropped them in a muddled clump on the top of the stack.

She couldn't bear the idea of walking back across the newsroom to deliver her notes to Tommy—not yet. Instead she fished her cell phone from her pocket and, after dismissing a string of missed calls from unknown numbers—most likely reporters at rival publications calling for comment on Raum's denial—swiped to her encrypted chat app. The software—fetishized by journalists, whistle-blowers, and White House interns—automatically deleted messages after six hours, but it still displayed the end of the last exchange she'd had with her source while writing the Alex Wu story.

LouM: I'm going to describe you as a source familiar with the details of the lawsuit. Accurate?

Raum101: LOL. Def accurate.

Raum101: Also, check out the Raum.com exec bio page. Notice anybody missing?

"Def accurate." Fuck you.

Lou minimized the chat app and flicked to a web browser. The mobile version of Raum's corporate home page was still open from the previous night, still with a yawning white space where once Alex Wu's name and bio had been. That had been the clincher: proof that Wu was being erased from Raum's website, and soon from the company entirely. Proof that the *Wall Street Journal* was about to break the story, and Raum was scrambling to do damage limitation. She took a screen grab of the page, tapped refresh, and watched as Wu's face shimmered, groomed and grinning, back into view. *Sons of assholes.*

Still, even if Wu's headshot was back in pride of place on the Raum website, his absence remained conspicuous elsewhere. The company had offered Camp a statement from their lawyer, an affidavit from the attorney named in the fake lawsuit, but not a word from Wu himself.

Now Lou tapped to the company's online NewsRaum. Since the date printed on the Jane Doe lawsuit, almost fifty press releases had come out of Raum's technology and applications division. A quick text search confirmed none of them included a quote from the head of that team, Alex Wu. A search of the *Herald*'s photo-agency database told the same story—a dozen recent press conferences, including a couple of significant product launches, and not a single sighting of Raum's number two executive in almost two months. Where the fuck was Alex Wu?

Lou looked more closely at the most recent picture of Wu in the Herald's digital photo library—the same photo she'd hastily added to her story. The photographer had caught Wu off guard, standing in the background at a Raum press conference about their self-driving cars. Had he always looked so gaunt? Had his eyes always been so bloodshot and sunken into his head? Didn't he used to have more hair?

"Hey? Lou?"

Lou looked up to find Tommy Paphitis looming over her, with the shifty look of a nervous high schooler about to ask a girl to prom. How long had he been standing there, watching her squint at Alex Wu's photo on her phone?

"Hey." Lou stood up, tucking the handset back into her pocket and commanding her face to smile, with mixed results.

"Those for me?" He nodded toward the messy stack of papers.

Lou scooped up the pile and handed it to him. "Figured they'd be helpful for your follow-up piece." She immediately regretted the attempt to save face. They both knew she was doing this under duress.

"Thanks," said Tommy. Then he frowned. "Look, I'm sorry about your story. For what it's worth, I read the lawsuit—it looked pretty legit to me."

"Yeah. I guess that was the point."

"I guess. . . ." Tommy's voice trailed off and his eyes shifted side to side.

"You don't think so?"

Tommy seemed even more flustered now. As if merely talking to Lou made him complicit in some horrible crime. He lowered his voice. "Look, I've spent a lot of time with the guys at Raum, and they all have like a gazillion stories about Wu and the women he . . . yunno."

Lou nodded. She did know.

"All off the record, obviously. But I don't get why they'd use him for a fake lawsuit instead of somebody who isn't . . . ah . . ."

"An actual rapist."

"I guess," repeated Tommy as he started to walk back toward his desk. "Just seems dumb, is all."

"You know—" Lou stopped him. If Tommy was going to take over her story, then he should at least have all the facts. "One angle you might want to consider in your follow-up is Raum's press page. Wu has been

AWOL from a bunch of recent events and product launches. Not a single sighting since the date on the lawsuit."

"Huh," said Tommy. "That's weird."

Lou pressed on. "If he's innocent and the lawsuit was bogus, why would he be in hiding? Have you ever known someone at Raum to voluntarily avoid the spotlight?"

Tommy laughed. "Nope."

"You'll let me know what you find?"

This question seemed to cause Tommy actual physical pain. "Ah . . . so . . . Stephen was pretty clear that I should just do a straight retraction. He doesn't want me to piss Raum off by doing any more reporting."

Because heaven fucking forbid that we do any reporting in the goddamned newsroom. Lou almost said that out loud, but what was the point? Tommy was already heading back to his desk, carrying with him Lou's notes and any chance that Alex Wu's victims might ever get justice.

Lou turned back to her phone and felt a chill as she saw the newest alert: *300 New Mentions.*

320.

380.

450.

So it began.

She tossed the handset onto her desk as if it were contagious. That many new notifications, that quickly, meant only one thing: Claude Pétain and his troll army had seen her story, and Raum's denial, and now they were tweeting for her blood. Again.

The #MLM creeps and their anonymous leader had a special fixation with Elmsley Chase—to the point where some people had even speculated that Chase might actually *be* Pétain. Chase and Raum had denied this, naturally—the great Elmsley Chase had far more important things to do than write ten-thousand-word daily Mailpile screeds or appear in endless Freestream videos, face digitally pixelated, railing about "fifth-wave feminists" and "transgender traitors." Whatever. Like clockwork, Pétain's trolls materialized any time a woman spoke out about a high-profile tech bro or, heaven help her, was careless enough to be assaulted while using Raum: they flooded dedicated right-wing social media platforms with threats of violence and vile Photoshopped "reenactments" of the crime, usually posted alongside the victim's name, home address, and dating history. Unable to go after the anonymous Jane Doe, they would now focus their rage on Lou and the "feminazi *Lügenpresse*," an epithet they used without irony.

Lou knew the drill, but also knew she was mostly protected. Her current home address was a pile of T-shirts under a desk, something that even Pétain's network of spies hadn't been able to figure out. They had mostly stayed away from her family too—a useful side effect of not having any, except her mom, whose former job in law enforcement kept her personal details off most public databases. Her pathetic dating life was another powerful weapon: Lou didn't trust apps, never sent nudes, and had deeply background-checked (right afterward, if not before) the handful of disappointing drunken hookups she'd had since starting at the *Herald*. Pétain's threats would fuck up her mentions for a few days, but once Tommy published his retraction, the trolls would move on to the next target.

Lou buried her head in her hands at the ridiculousness of her situation: her burning hunger for justice for a rape victim who—according to all available evidence—didn't exist.

Would you like to buy a machine gun on eBay and go on a killing spree, starting with Alex Wu and Elmsley Chase, whoever signed the order to evict your neighbors, the Raum staffer who fabricated this lawsuit . . .

Y/N

The thought was interrupted by a figure appearing in front of Lou's desk. She looked up with a sharp "Yes?" expecting to see either Camp or Tommy Paphitis, back to make her day even worse. Instead she met the eyes of a bored-looking bicycle courier who handed her a small white envelope and plodded off without a word.

"Thanks," shouted Lou, adding a quiet "sorry" toward the retreating figure. She considered the envelope: her name and the *Herald*'s address typed on a white label perfectly centered on the front. It looked official—a subpoena, perhaps—except for the word "urgent" scrawled in red pen, underlined twice, where normally there would be a postage stamp.

Later Lou would swear she knew what was inside the envelope even before she tore it open and saw the bright green skyline etched across the top of the thick white card. Some psychic warning from the universe: *Don't open it, Lou. The contents will bring nothing but pain and misery.*

ELMSLEY CHASE INVITES YOU

The letters were bold, and gold, and embossed deep into the card. Then, in a larger font . . ."

TO A VERY SPECIAL EVENT

CELEBRATING THE OPENING OF RAUM ONE

Lou stared at the invite, rubbing her fingertips against the glossy surface. Was this Raum's idea of a sick joke: sending a party invite to the reporter they just humiliated? A party being held in the place her apartment once stood. Was Elmsley Chase daring her to attend, or just gloating that she couldn't?

But then her fingers made contact with something stuck to the rear of the card: a small yellow Post-it note and more red ink . . .

Your story was good. Come tonight. Will explain everything. —Raum101

Lou stared at the note. Did this mean Camp was wrong? That her source was still out there, and ready to meet in person? She caught her own feeling of hope, and hated herself for it. This was what she did every time: believed that this story, this source, this hookup, this job offer, this fucking delicious sugar-free energy bar, would be the real deal. She'd gotten into journalism because she *knew* the world was full of frauds, so why did she spend her life trying to prove it wasn't? Obviously the invite was another trap, a lure to Raum One in defiance of Camp's order to stay away.

Lou's eyes flicked to the empty space below her desk. Maybe getting fired wouldn't be so bad. She pictured her childhood bedroom in Alpharetta, far away from Silicon Valley, and Raum, and Claude Pétain's toxic trolls. It was there whenever she needed it, her mom always reminded her. But the implication was clear: *I know you never will.* Bigshot journalist, fighting for truth in the big city.

You've made Raum into a personal crusade. It's made you easy to exploit. Camp's words still echoed.

"Fuck you," she whispered, and threw the invite card in the trash.

Two minutes later, she whispered the exact same thing as she took it out again.

10%

RAUM'S GLOBAL HEADQUARTERS had appeared on the San Francisco skyline like a toothache. Slowly at first—a few pangs of scaffolding and a dull, steady pulse of drilling and hammering, mostly hidden from view by large wooden billboards painted matte black. Then, overnight, the thing arrived in full force: a sharp, throbbing monstrosity of blue glass and searchlights, so ugly and aggressive that it was impossible to imagine a time without it.

The building was the most expensive construction project ever undertaken in Northern California. The tallest human-made structure west of the Mississippi. Home to the most valuable private company in Silicon Valley history. And the most transparent: Raum One had been constructed entirely from specially treated Maxiglass™, allowing an unobstructed view of the business being transacted within. For that billion-dollar gimmick, Raum had been awarded something called a "Corporate Accessibility Trophy" by the Digital Openness Group, a tech-freedom think tank funded by generous grants from Facebook, Palantir, and the US State Department. "Raum," the citation gushed, "truly is a company with nothing to hide." Nothing, that is, except for what might transpire on floors fifty-five through sixty-six, hidden from view by four giant LED screens—the world's brightest!—each display-ing a 3-D animated Raum logo.

Still. As the first of the tuxedoed guests arrived for the tower's Grand Opening Party—passing through glowing glass turnstiles that simul-taneously verified their invitations and sniffed for concealed weapons and contagious viruses—one could almost detect a frisson of anticlimax in the crowd. For all the Maxiglass and open space—maybe because of it—the sensation of standing in Raum One's soaring central-lobby atrium, six hundred feet wide and twelve hundred feet from floor to roof, was oddly and disappointingly like finding yourself trapped inside a giant crystal bowling trophy.

Had the architects been so pleased with their work on the exterior of the building that they'd plain forgotten to design any fixtures or fittings for the interior? Had the cost of obliterating three city blocks to accommodate the desks of fifty thousand Raum employees left no room in the $3.5 billion budget for even a modest waterfall or a discreet brace of Henry Moores?

Lou knew from her sources that the truth was even stranger. The sensation of yawning nothingness in Raum One's lobby—right down to the lack of a reception desk or any chairs or benches for waiting visitors—was something on which Elmsley Chase had personally insisted. This was the man who had built the most valuable private company in Silicon Valley history on a simple three-word promise: *Waiting. Is. Over.* Pursuant to that vision, anyone in America, and one day the world— anyone whose phone had the Raum app, or whose wrist bore a $200 Raum Band—could simply mutter a verbal command and summon a car, or a hotel room, a pizza, a sex worker, or a spouse . . . in an instant. Actually, Raum's core algorithm was now so good at predicting its users' desires that, increasingly, they didn't even need to ask. Lobby chairs and reception desks were artifacts of a world where waiting was tolerated— celebrated even. As such they had no place in Raum One.

The challenge of transforming such a cavernous greenhouse into an intimate venue would vex the most experienced party planner. Still, Raum's event staff had attacked the problem with well-compensated gusto. For one night only, the atrium's concrete floor danced with neon green- and-red Raum logos beamed from lasers hidden inside the building's four main support pillars. Long pennants bidding "Welcome to Raum One" swung heraldically from the lattice of elevated glass walkways that connected the upper floors. To further divert the eye, a menagerie of plastic creatures—a purple elephant, a yellow horse, a white beaver—had been scattered among the crowd. Each colorful beast paid tribute to the whimsical zoological code names Raum famously assigned to each new version of its core algorithm. The more plugged-in partygoers had already made that nerdy connection and were sharing it with their digital friends and followers with the officially sanctioned hashtag #waitingisover.

In the dead center of the atrium stood the slowly melting pièce de résistance. A thirty-foot-tall slab of ice, hand carved by an Instagram-famous chain saw sculptor into a jagged, impressionistic, and unabashedly phallic scale model of Raum One. The chain saw itself was still wedged in the base in lieu of the more traditional artist's signature. It was in the shadow of this sculpture that most of the partygoers were beginning to muster, snapping selfies, munching on gourmet hors d'oeuvres, and trying to hear themselves network over the pounding of early 2000s hip-hop.

They say you're alone / Ain't nobody but you / Always gotta watch your back / For someone tryin' to drag you down / You ain't invincible / One day justice will come . . .

The ice sculpture was also ground zero for the fourth estate. A local TV crew was hustling to reposition its single camera for the best shot of the revelers, while "content producers" from all the major web and print outlets bustled, hither and thither, soliciting quotes from anyone wearing a Raum T-shirt. In twenty minutes, Elmsley Chase would speak. Then there would be dancing and microdosing and HR violations till sunrise.

Away from the hustlers and bustlers and influencers, in a far corner of the huge atrium, next to a vast table laden with tiny Improbable™ meatless lamb burgers, Lou McCarthy of the *Bay Area Herald* stood staring up into the glass void. She was still just about holding her shit together, still just about remaining upright, and still just about keeping the anxious twitch that had begun in her hands from spreading across her whole body. She clenched her hands tighter, driving her fingernails even deeper into her damp palms. *Do not fucking cry, Lou, you asshole,* she told herself. *Do not pass out. Do not give these monsters the satisfaction.*

Lou tipped her head even farther back to take in more of the void and inhaled a lungful of dry, HEPA-filtered air. This was the exact spot, she was pretty sure, where the front door of her apartment building had stood. The base of the steep wooden stairwell that led thirteen flights up to her tiny sanctuary. The stairwell up which Mrs. Gee's children would bound, hooting and screaming at all hours, and down which old Mr. Cohen had once drunkenly slipped, breaking his leg and the banister in one fell swoop. The stairwell was now gone forever, along with Mrs. Gee and her children, and Mr. Cohen and his leg, and a hundred years of history.

As she'd watched Raum One taking shape from her office window, Lou had wondered what would fill the space once occupied by her apartment. An executive washroom? A snack bar or dry-cleaning service for coddled Raum workers? Now, as she looked up at the glass walkways surrounding the hollow central tower of Raum One, she had her answer. Her apartment had been obliterated and replaced with . . . nothing. Just empty fucking air. A single tear ran down her cheek, followed quickly by another. *Fuck. Asshole. Asshole. Asshole.*

She brought her fist up to her mouth and took a deep breath, in through her nose and out through her lips, then reached for a prosecco juice box—a condensated rectangle of millennial pink with a gold paper straw. Lou had a rule never to drink alcohol at work events, but she needed something to grip as she scanned the crowd for maybe the fiftieth time, looking for anyone who might possibly be the source she knew as Raum101.

It was weird that nobody from Raum had tried to stop her entering the building. The security barriers had recognized her face, or some tiny chip sandwiched inside her invite, and chirruped happily green to welcome her inside. The army of blond PR minders patrolling the party had spotted her immediately; urgent words had been exchanged through slim radio headsets and messages frantically tapped into wide cell phones. All of that she'd expected. But strangely, and unsettlingly, the minders had kept their distance. Perhaps Raum's PR machine had decided not to risk the "optics" of ejecting a reporter from the grand opening of the world's most transparent building. So long as she didn't try to get within a country mile of Elmsley Chase or any other senior Raum execs, maybe they'd decided to leave her be, satisfied that she had been completely defanged by their fake lawsuit and the threat of career ruin. Or perhaps it was a fucking trap.

Lou didn't care. She would give her source another ten minutes to show, get whatever smoking gun he or she did or didn't have, and get the hell out of this ridiculous, heartbreaking phallic greenhouse. So what if she was being set up? She literally had nothing to lose. She'd already been humiliated; seen her dreams of graduating from the *Herald* to the major leagues dashed. Not a single one of the other reporters—some of whom she'd once considered friends—had dared approach the buffet table while she was standing there; either afraid of somehow being humiliated by proximity or unwilling to risk upsetting the great Elmsley Chase.

And, speaking of the devil's asshole, there he was.

Elmsley Chase had appeared on the other side of the atrium, working the room, glad-handing the assembled dignitaries: the governor, the mayor, a Google founder or two, the rapper MC Hammer, and the CEOs of at least five major banks.

The hottest CEO in Silicon Valley looked much like he always did—a Hanna-Barbera Ryan Gosling in a tight black Raum T-shirt, paired with a charcoal-gray suit. He greeted reporters from the *Wall Street Journal*, Bloomberg, and MSNBC with fist bumps and hugs. The *Times*' business editor—a scrawny white dude wearing tortoiseshell glasses and a tweed waistcoat—was honored with an unfathomably complex series of hand-shakes and high fives that reminded Lou of a kung fu movie played in slow motion.

Brrrrrrrrrooooooh!

Pathetic. These were the great and the good of national business reporting. These were the hallowed ranks to which—six rejections and counting—Lou had repeatedly been denied entry. *Your work shows promise, but we'd need to see you break some bigger stories.* Or, failing that, graft on a penis.

Chase was flanked by his longtime girlfriend, a former Olympic swimmer or maybe gymnast who, according to the blogs, had raised $10 million for her disruptive puppy delivery startup, "WetNoze." The girl—who Lou thought might be a Maddison or a Meredith—had excellent cameradar, reflexively pursing her lips and lifting her chin whenever a lens swept close.

Completing the threesome was an older woman, although Lou couldn't tell exactly how old, as she stood constantly in shadow, doing her best to avoid being caught on film or phone. She wore a black jumpsuit and black heels, with a pair of Gucci sunglasses on top of her head, struggling to maintain discipline over a class of tumbling red hair. Lou noticed that whenever a reporter joined the group, the woman would excuse herself to take a phone call or study a concrete pillar.

Lou urged her brain for some spark of recognition. She had a flawless memory for faces, and for names, so was frustrated to be drawing a blank on both counts. She had refused on principle to install Raum's face-recognition app but had to admit this would be the perfect use case.

Her eyes flicked back to Chase's resting smug face. Did he know that Lou was at his party, thinking about stuffing free food into her backpack and trying desperately to save her career as he took a victory lap through his pulsating crystal fortress? Did he know they were standing in what used to be her home?

Lou considered again the ice sculpture with the chain saw still jutting out like an Instagram-ready Excalibur. How easy it would be to grab the hulking yellow-and-black machine and charge at Chase and his entourage. How many more of the overdressed sociopaths at the party—sipping bad, expensive wine as they compared notes on how many teenage suicides their apps had enabled, how many murders, how many elections they'd swayed, workers they'd crushed, and voters they'd suppressed—could she take down before being wrestled to the ground?

Lou felt a stream of cold liquid running slowly down her knuckles and realized she was squeezing the life out of her juice box. Obviously Elmsley Chase knew she was here. Face-recognition app or not, Raum knew everything about everyone.

Well, fuck him and fuck them. Raum101 had eight more minutes to show before Lou bailed. On Raum, and maybe even the whole of Silicon Valley.

It was at that moment that she noticed the familiar shape of Tim Palgrave, gangling toward her. More likely, Raum's chairman of the board was gangling toward the three-tiered platter of lamb burgers on the buffet table behind her—but the effect was much the same. Lou's eyes didn't stay on Palgrave for long, though, as they were drawn to the face of an angel in a shimmering green dress following a few paces behind him.

The woman was very *on trend*, certainly for Palgrave and, increasingly, for most other Silicon Valley superinvestors: Asian girlfriends were *so* last year. Today the must-have accessory for every top-rank venture capitalist was the Black girlfriend. Lou stared at the woman's perfect hair and supermodel features and felt a jolt of outrage that she was forced to spend time with so gross a man as Tim Palgrave. Like most on Sand Hill Road, Palgrave's dick was the only part of him that cared about either diversity or inclusion.

Her first instinct was to retreat behind a pillar. The last thing she needed was Raum's chairman confronting her about her Alex Wu story. But then she realized that not in a million years would he recognize her. Tim Palgrave was widely regarded as the dumbest venture capitalist in Silicon Valley, with stories of his idiocy traded like bubble gum cards. According to legend, Palgrave had lucked into his Raum investment after wandering into the wrong pitch meeting on his way back from the bathroom. After twenty minutes of *mmm*-ing and nodding, he'd written the company their first six-figure check fully believing he was funding a manufacturer of "smart" sweater vests.

As long as she kept her back to him, Lou could safely maintain her vantage point at the buffet table until Palgrave swallowed his shitty little burger and moved on.

For a second Lou allowed herself to wonder if Palgrave might actually be Raum101. His relationship with Elmsley Chase was famously antagonistic: Chase treated his earliest investor as little more than a glorified coffee boy in board meetings, while Palgrave often made dunderheaded statements to the press about Raum's house-of-cards business model. But, putting aside that he was far too stupid to be an anonymous anything, Tim Palgrave stood to make more than anybody, except Chase himself, from the company's successful IPO.

"Lou McCarthy?"

Lou turned and was surprised to find Palgrave's girlfriend towering over her. The woman was even more beautiful up close, with kind eyes that made Lou feel immediately bad for reducing her to the status of arm candy. "Sorry, I didn't mean to sneak up on you," the woman said, with a warm, embarrassed smile. "I just wanted to say I'm a huge fan of your work."

If Lou felt like an ass before, now she felt like an ass's ass. "My work?" she blurted, immediately realizing that the question sounded like a judgment. *Supermodels can read?* "I mean, thank you."

"I've read the *Herald* since college. Your reporting on Stanford's sexual-assault pipeline was so important. You should have won a Pulitzer."

Lou thought she might start crying again. The Stanford CS scandal had been one of her biggest scoops: a secret agreement between the college and a major Silicon Valley startup to guarantee jobs to male computer science students who'd been quietly expelled for sexual assault. It was also one of her biggest frustrations. Only one student was ever charged with a crime, and the judge agreed to a plea deal that would avoid ruining the young rapist's "otherwise promising academic career." The founder of the company that hired all the scumbag students—Tyrus Weber of Mushu Health—had also avoided responsibility, thanks to his terminal pancreatic-cancer diagnosis right before the story broke. A bitterly ironic end for the founder of a health app, and tragic enough that nobody wanted to follow up on Lou's story, leaving several dozen accused rapists and harassers free to continue their post-Stanford careers.

"It didn't change anything." Lou had tried to say something appropriately humble, but landed on bitter. This woman was probably the only person who still remembered the scandal. "History is written by the victors and all that BS."

"Actually," said the woman, "I'm pretty sure history is written by the writers." She seemed ready to expand on that thought, but stopped as they realized Palgrave had joined them. He was staring blankly at Lou from below gigantic white eyebrows and clutching a test tube of mashed potato. "Hello . . . ah . . . there," he said, finally.

"Lou," said Lou. "Lou McCarthy."

The clouds parted. "Ah, yes, from the *Herald*." His eyes stayed fixed on the name badge pinned to her boob.

"You must be very proud of Raum's new building," Lou said, aiming for the most vapid possible sentence and scoring a direct bull's-eye. Her source might show up any second. She needed to escape the conversation, and fast.

"Very proud!" Palgrave almost shouted this. "Raum is a fantastic company. Elmsley Chase is a world-class entrepreneur."

Lou nodded. Elmsley Chase could firebomb a wagonload of nuns, and investors like Tim Palgrave would still praise him.

Then Palgrave's date spoke again. "Lou published that Alex Wu story today. About the girl he attacked."

Goddammit. Palgrave was looking Lou in the eyes now, his mouth fixed in a rictus grin. How long might it take, Lou wondered, for a sexagenarian to grind his own teeth to dust? His date was staring too, but Lou noticed a smile creep across her lips. She was fucking with him. Amazing.

But now Palgrave blinked, as if someone had hit reset on his facial muscles, and the anger vanished. "Excuse me," he said. Then he lunged for a tiny duck-wing confit, shoved the whole gloopy appendage into his mouth, and gangled away.

"It was nice to meet you, Lou," said his girlfriend, who strode after him.

Lou watched her go, relieved they were both heading away from where Elmsley Chase and his entourage were still mingling. It would take only a word from Palgrave to have her ejected from the party. Still, it had been worth the close call: a tiny bright spot in an otherwise crappy day. Only later did Lou realize she had never asked the woman's name.

Lou felt a vibration against her leg. She had disabled alerts on her email and social accounts—the abuse from Claude Pétain's #MensLivesMatter trolls showed no signs of abating. The only app still set to vibrate was her encrypted chat app. A message from Raum101! Lou tugged the handset from her pocket and swiped to the conversation window.

No new messages.

She tapped refresh. Still nothing. The vibration was just a phantom. Frustrated, Lou jabbed at the on-screen keyboard.

LouM: *I'm in the main atrium, back right, next to the buffet table.*

A risky move. Raum would surely be monitoring digital traffic in and out of the building—this was a company built on the obliteration of privacy. How ironic that digital spying had become so efficient that it was safer to meet a source in the middle of a crowded party than to send an encrypted text message.

Lou scanned the crowd for the hundredth time. Everybody at the party was photographing, or tweeting, or texting.

LouM: *Where are you?*

As she stared at the phone, waiting for the three flashing dots that meant that a reply was forthcoming, she noticed a sudden flurry of activity in her peripheral vision. A gaggle of PR handlers had gathered by Chase's side, the tallest and blondest of whom was whispering something into his ear. Chase nodded and the women guided him through the crowd—a Secret Service detail in six-inch heels—toward the ice sculpture and the squat scaffolding platform from which he would give his grand speech.

Lou abandoned her juice box, retrieved her backpack from under the buffet table, and joined the crowd.

13

LOU MCCARTHY WASN'T the only person at Raum One who was running out of time. At that exact moment, nine hundred feet straight up, Joe Christian was slumped against the Maxiglass wall of Raum's east maintenance stairwell, head wedged between his knees, trying and failing to regain his breath. In his ultramarathon days, racing up fifty-five flights of stairs would have left him winded. In his current condition, even with his adrenaline levels off the charts, the hour-long ascent had brought Joe's lungs to the brink of surrender. He dabbed his mouth with a tissue and grimaced at the tiny drops of blood left behind on the paper. He had lost all sensation below his calves, but the sound of squelching assured him that his shoes must be filled with yet more blood.

It was a miracle that he'd made it so far, undetected by security. He'd been able to sneak in via Raum One's rear loading dock, a door to which had been left propped open, presumably by the party planners or caterers. From there he'd descended into the service tunnels running below the main atrium. It was in one of those tunnels that he'd found the building directory and learned, to his dismay, that the C-suite was located on the sixty-third floor. He couldn't risk taking the elevator, so he'd been forced to climb the maintenance stairs: in view of anyone who happened to glance at the lightly frosted glass column extending up the back wall. But either nobody had looked or no one had thought anything odd about the hunched wheezing figure struggling toward Raum's upper sanctum. It was as if Fate had wanted him to succeed.

As he sat panting and gasping, Joe thought back to the news story that had beeped onto his phone almost twelve hours earlier.

Alex Wu, finally brought to justice. More than a decade too late, and the wrong victim, but still, it couldn't possibly be a coincidence. And then this . . .

Tonight marks the opening of Raum One, the company's new $3.5 billion headquarters. As of press time, a company spokesperson had not confirmed whether Wu will still be in attendance.

If Joe had any doubt that Wu was another of Fate's victims—and why—that line had obliterated it. To be exposed as a predator was devastating at any time—Joe knew that well enough—but to have the bombshell drop on the night your multibillion-dollar IPO was due to be announced . . . the culmination of your life's work . . . well, only Fate could conceive such a bitter twist.

Fate was taunting Joe too: holding out the tantalizing prospect of an answer to the question of why he and Wu were being targeted. And, with that answer, perhaps the key to stopping his torment. Joe flashed back once again to the memory; the flicker of a past life that had lain dormant for more than ten years only to be awoken by the beep of a news alert. The night Joe first met Alex Wu—a night that would end in the men being bound together for life by a shared secret.

That had to be it. Fate wanted Joe to force Alex Wu to admit the truth, to the world.

Otherwise why send him the message? And to have Wu be secured inside the most heavily protected building in the city—wasn't that just perfectly, brilliantly cruel?

Come and get him, if you can! Clock's ticking!

But Joe Christian was determined: he would get to Alex Wu and demand he confess his crime. Tonight, with all the cameras looking on. Maybe then Fate would let Joe live.

Wishful thinking, perhaps, but also the only thinking Joe had left. If he didn't get to Alex Wu tonight and force him to confess, all would be lost, if it wasn't already.

Gripping the metal handrail with both hands, he pulled himself to his feet and prepared to attack the final ascent. Just eight more floors. He could do this.

14

BACK DOWN AT the party, the crowd had swelled to two, maybe three hundred. Two, maybe three hundred cameras were held aloft to capture history. Up on the platform, Elmsley Chase was a man transformed. A tiny cartoon douche no longer! Now he was the Duke of Disruption. The Chief Swagger Officer. A whinnying Pegasus in a field of mere unicorns.

The way he held the wireless microphone—tilted downward like he was chugging from it—and the way he spat the lines of his speech made him look more like a rapper than a CEO. Or so he seemed to think.

". . . Raum One is not just our global command center. It's our message to all the corrupt politicians and greedy lobbyists. To the haters . . ."

Yeeeeeaaaahhh . . .

Lou had to grudgingly admit: homeboy couldn't hold a microphone, but he sure as hell could hold a crowd.

"To the haters . . . and the *losers* . . ."

. . . aaaaahhhhhh . . .

"All the *fucking. Looo-sers* who hate the free market. Who want to tell you what you can do with your own property. With your own time. With your own money."

WOOOOOOO . . .

"It's a message even they can understand . . ."

. . . OOOOOHHHHH . . .

"Fuck you, you fucking motherfuckkkkkkkers."

YUUUUUUUUUUUUHHHHH!

The audience of Silicon Valley executives and investors and journalists was losing its collective mind. Screaming and whistling and wooooing and yeeeaaahhhing like they were being paid by the decibel; hands raised high, clapping against the sides of two, maybe three hundred smart-phones. Elmsley Chase was telling it like it is!

Lou was the only person in the atrium not applauding: a gesture of independence that suddenly made her feel extremely self-conscious. While every other reporter was packed into a roped-off press pen directly in front of Chase's platform, she had found her own nook, at the back of the crowd, next to a KPIX-5 news camera raised on a tall tripod. Lou had dragged a large orange cow alongside the camera, clambering on the creature's back to get a better view of the room. Its plastic legs buckled slightly under her weight, but maintained their integrity.

Chase raised his free hand for quiet. A few dudes competed to be the last "woo" but a woman from BusinessInsider.com gazumped them all: "We love you Elmsley!"

"I love you too." Another calming wave. "Listen up, I just wanna say one last thing. We have a phrase here at Raum. Some of you already know this. 'Stoked-ness.' Every day we ask how we can make our partners more stoked, and our users more stoked. Well, I gotta tell you, earlier tonight, before you guys got here, I took the elevator up to the top of Raum One—stood right on the roof, and looked down at the thousands of people in San Francisco . . ."

A man in a cowboy shirt embarrassed himself with an ill-timed "yuhhh."

"The billions of people around the world who are living their best lives with Raum. When I think of the millions of economic opportunities we've created for our partners, the trillions of awesome experiences we've curated for our users . . ."

Lou waited for the punch line, still scanning the crowd for her approaching source. Chase loved his surprise "one more thing" announce-ments—a cheap trick he'd stolen wholesale from his idol, and fellow prick, Steve Jobs.

There was no way he would squander all this media attention on the mere opening of the tallest building west of the Mississippi. The IPO announcement was definitely coming tonight—*waiting is over!*—and there was nothing she could do to stop it. In a few hours, paperwork would be filed with the SEC, and Raum would enter its mandated "quiet period," during which Raum executives would be legally barred from talking to journalists, even if they wanted to. After tonight, Elmsley Chase could refuse to answer any difficult question about Alex Wu and be applauded by Wall Street for his discretion.

But the punch line didn't come. Now Chase was standing in silence, staring out across the crowd, chewing his bottom lip in a pastiche of thoughtfulness.

"You know, before I get to the main event, there's something else I wanna address." Lou felt her skin chill. This was his caring, empathetic voice—the one he used on television when apologizing for the Raum-Service food order that had poisoned a toddler, or reminiscing about his younger brother, Ramsey, who'd died when they were growing up. In other words, any time he needed to sound like an actual human being.

"Earlier today the *Bay Area Herald* published a hit piece about one of my friends—a man who, as you guys know, is one of the most brilliant technical minds of our time." Chase gestured with his hand, allowing the spotlight to catch the gossamer-thin, platinum Raum Band encircling his right wrist.

The audience responded with a smattering of confused boos and applause as they tried to decide how to simultaneously praise Wu and condemn the *Herald*. Lou's heart was thumping. *This isn't good. This isn't good at all.* She began to slowly dismount the plastic cow.

Too late. Now Chase extended his arm toward her, palm upward as if offering her in sacrifice. "No, please, Miss McCarthy, don't try to hide." Chase's voice reverberated off the glass walls of the atrium. The audience turned as one and Lou suddenly found herself trapped in the glare of two, maybe three hundred camera lenses and twice that many eyeballs.

"Just before I came up here, my head of security told me that Miss McCarthy had gate-crashed our party." More boos. "I wish I could say I was shocked, but as you guys know, the *Herald* has been hating on us from the start." A slow, exaggerated headshake.

The room erupted. "Throw her out!" yelled a woman's voice, from somewhere close to the cluster of PR blonds. "Yeah, throw her out," came another shout, which soon transformed into a chant . . .

Throw her out!

Throw her out!

Lou could see two small platoons of security guards who, having somehow emerged from inside the glass walls, now jostled their way toward her in a pincer movement. Then she realized that all the TV cameras had now spun around to capture her humiliation.

Throw her out!

Throw her out!

Lou didn't know whether to run, and risk being chased by this red-faced, black-tied mob, or to stand her ground, knowing her humiliation was being broadcast live across the planet. Again, Elmsley Chase's voice cut through the noise. "Wait, wait, let's all cool down. I told my security team to let her stay because we have nothing to hide here at Raum. We're super transparent, even with haters from the press." He looked directly at Lou again. "Miss McCarthy, we're stoked to have you here . . ."

More boos and jeers.

". . . if . . ." He paused for emphasis. "If you are willing to apologize to Alex for publishing your fake story and trying to ruin the life of a great man."

Lou felt a microphone being pressed into her hand by one of the security guards. So Stephen Camp was right: Elmsley Chase *was* Raum101. He'd dragged her to the party for one final humiliation. A warning to any other journalist who might dare cross Raum. Lou felt sick, and embarrassed and . . .

Fucking furious. The anger she'd felt when Raum had evicted her from her apartment came flooding back, multiplied a thousandfold by the realization they were trying to evict her from the exact same space a second time, publicly and brutally. But it was so much more than that. She'd allowed herself to be conned, again, because she desperately wanted to believe her source was real. That she could actually get justice for Jane Doe. Elmsley Chase knew that, and had weaponized her hope.

Chase was still goading her from the platform. "Well? What do you say? Will you do the right thing and apologize?"

"Sure," Lou spat into the microphone.

The chanting stopped. Chase seemed genuinely shocked by her response. "You will? You'll . . . apologize? That's great news."

"Sure," Lou repeated. "If you bring Alex Wu out here right now, I'll apologize to him personally." Her voice echoed around the atrium. "Where is he?"

The crowd was already primed for chanting, and soon a new one began. "We want Alex! We want Alex!"

The guard was grabbing for Lou's microphone, but she held it tightly with both hands. "Where *is* Alex Wu, Elmsley? Why isn't he here?"

We want Alex!

We want Alex!

Up on the platform, Chase was slowly transforming back from badass to bobblehead, bobbling first toward the TV cameras, then down to someone in the front row, then across the rest of the crowd until he settled back on Lou, who had reclaimed her plastic cow.

We want Al-ex!

We want Al-ex!

The euphoria could be only fleeting. Lou was definitely fired now, and the terrified look on her face when Elmsley Chase had called her name would launch a million animated GIFs. But in that moment, listening to that crowd of investors and journalists and unapologetic fanboys calling for Alex Wu to show himself, she felt like queen of the world. No matter what happened next, Wu's absence from the IPO announcement party would be a talking point on a thousand tech-news sites and a hundred cable networks worldwide. Soon it would be ricocheting around the boardrooms of hedge funds and institutional investors. Quiet period or not, nobody from Raum would be able to appear on television or on Wall Street without being asked the question, "Where is Alex Wu?"

We want Al-ex!

We want Al-ex!

Except Lou was wrong. There *was* something that could knock the question off the front pages. And, at that moment, that thing happened.

At the top of Lou's peripheral vision, she registered a blur of black and yellow, followed almost immediately by a thundering crash and a sickening whooshing, squelching sound. At first she thought one of the "Welcome to Raum One" flags had broken free of its mooring and had crashed onto the ice sculpture. Elmsley Chase whipped around just in time to see a torrent of red gushing from the crumpled fabric that, Lou now realized, was tangled around the body of a man. A man who had apparently leapt from one of the upper floors of the atrium and impaled himself on the frozen peak of the ice sculpture.

The crash and the whooshing squelch were quickly followed by another remarkable sound: that of two, maybe three hundred men and women screaming at the top of their lungs. Lou tried to keep her balance, but was knocked from her cow by the rush of bodies now scrambling for the exit. As she regained her footing, she was briefly captivated by the sight of so many VIPs, fists held aloft, yelling commands into the cloud, hoping to hail an escape vRaum before so-called convenience pricing kicked in.

She shoved and elbowed her way through the tuxedoed mass, toward the ice sculpture. Steam was already rising from the corpse (no doubt now that it *was* a corpse), and the rapid thawing had made it sink even farther, displacing more blood and causing the banner to shake free. Lou stopped running, momentarily paralyzed as she registered the dead man's blistered face, his greased black hair—lank and missing in patches—and his trademark red corduroy pants, torn at the knees. The face that launched a thousand press releases, the face of the man who created the software algorithm that made Raum the most valuable private company on the planet. A face that, even in death, was still somehow capable of leering.

The ghastly, ugly, and very, very dead face of Alex Wu.

15%

JOE CHRISTIAN HAD watched him jump. He'd finally emerged onto the glass walkway of the sixty-third floor just as the chanting began. Using the very last of his strength, he'd heaved himself to the edge of the safety barrier and squinted down into the atrium. From that height, the heads of the partygoers below were like points on a scatter graph, and the small talk was diffused into a slow, pulsing roar. It took Joe a few seconds to decipher that the white stalagmite reaching toward him was the peak of an ice sculpture.

Then he'd peered across the expanse to the opposite walkway and seen the figure standing in the darkness, looking down over the rail. A flash of recognition as, across the atrium, the two men formed a perfect mirror: two victims of Fate both realizing their time was nearly up; two guilty men finally understanding the nature, and consequences, of their crime. Joe almost shouted out, but he didn't want to draw attention from below. He raised his hand as if to wave, then dropped it to his side.

It was too late.

Joe stood rooted in horror as Alex Wu leaned even farther over the barrier and then let himself fall gently into the void.

LOU RAN. AND ran and ran until ten minutes and almost a mile later, unable to take another step, she staggered into the boarded-up doorway of the O'Farrell Street adult theater.

Her legs and lungs were on fire, but as she slumped down to the greasy sidewalk, rough wooden boards scraping her spine through her thin shirt, she felt suddenly freezing. She gasped for air, but her nostrils filled with the acrid ammonia smell of urine.

She had made it to the Tenderloin: the poorest, most dangerous neighborhood in the city even before tech inflation had caused the homeless population to double and anger to quadruple. Now it was her sanctuary. Footage of Wu's suicide was trending on every social platform, alongside a hundred separately uploaded cell phone videos of Lou confronting Elmsley Chase.

Where is Alex Wu? she had demanded, and Wu himself had responded by leaping to his death on live television. Now Claude Pétain and his #MensLivesMatter army were coming for the woman they blamed for his suicide; demanding brutal, sexually depraved retribution for the death of one of their heroes. Pétain had already posted a response on Freestreem, issuing one of his infamous "red notices" against Lou—a declaration of all-out war that ordered his followers to action.

Lou curled up still tighter, grabbing her knees as she struggled to stay crouched above the carpet of needles and used condoms that littered the doorway. She had covered enough of Pétain's red notices to know how much danger she was in. The group had built a vast underground surveillance network—hacking publicly available facial-recognition tools, outdoor security cameras, cell towers, medical records—to seek and destroy their most high-value targets. Just one camera lens pointing in Lou's direction would be enough to summon an army. The only thing she could do was turn off her phone and focus on getting to safety: these few blocks where techies still feared to tread, that even the most desperate Raum drivers avoided for fear of having their cars hijacked or torched. Surely even Pétain's crazed followers wouldn't dare search for her in this war zone.

Now, though, as she slowly found her breath, Lou thought about her mom in Atlanta. In countless video tutorials, Pétain had reminded his troops that a red notice required no mercy—*Hit them where it hurts, go after their families, their lovers, their workmates. There are no civilians; there is no such thing as collateral damage.* Only a few weeks earlier, they'd posted the home address and Social Security number of the CIA director's daughter. The poor terrified woman was still in federal protective custody.

Lou had worked so hard to hide the reality of her job from her mom. The abuse, the threats, knowing that every date might be an alt-right setup or a PR pitch, the deep scars it had all left on her soul.

She forced her brain to think. Was today Wednesday? Yes. Wednesday was the night Lou's mom did dive-bar karaoke while her best friend, Carol, tried to pick up truckers. What if she arrived home, drunk and amped up on the Beastie Boys and Dolly Parton, and found the mob already waiting for her?

God help the mob if she did.

Lou retrieved her phone from her pants pocket and scrolled to her mom's number. The call went straight to voice mail—the default greeting of her cell phone provider. She hung up and tried Carol, but that went to an almost identical recording.

She tried her mom a second time and left a message. "Mom, it's me." Lou could barely get the words out. "Listen, I'm fine, but . . . well, something happened tonight—you'll see it on TV, I guess. Do me a favor and stay at Carol's tonight, OK?" She paused, waiting for confirmation, until she remembered that she was talking to a voice mail server. "I'll call you later. Go to Carol's, OK? I love you." She hung up and instantly regretted the instruction. Any mob showing up at Carol's house would find themselves on the wrong end of the .44 Magnum she kept in a lockbox above the front door. Which was about the worst possible way to respond to a mob of violent adolescents.

Lou held down the power button until her phone gave a long vibration and fell still. In the silence, she tried to piece together her new reality. Alex Wu, the man she'd outed as a rapist twelve hours earlier, was dead. Alex fucking Wu. Dead. He'd killed himself because of her story. Which meant it must have been true. Right?

She struggled to her feet. She couldn't go back to the *Herald* building. There was no coming back from a dead rapist on an ice sculpture. Also, her elevator swipe card was still in the backpack she'd lost in the chaos at Raum One. Not to mention her laptop, wallet, and cell phone charger.

She had to keep moving. She'd stick to the badlands—take a circuitous and terrifying route through the homeless encampments of South Van Ness until she reached the Mission police station. She had a source who worked the night shift—a veteran watch commander who hated arrogant, lawbreaking techies almost as much as she did. Maybe he couldn't give her any formal protection, but he might let her hunker down for a few hours while she figured out what the hell had just happened at Raum One.

She turned left, steeling herself for another jog, but had barely taken a single step out of the doorway when she collided with someone coming the other way. The man recoiled, just as startled to see her as she had been to see him. He was skinny and Asian and wearing a hoodie, bunched tightly around his face. "Excuse me," she said, trying to sidestep around him.

"It's all good," he muttered back. Two terrified strangers who had somehow blundered into the Tenderloin, and into each other.

Except, no. That wasn't what he'd said.

What he'd said was "It's all good, *Lou*."

In that split second of recognition, several things happened. First, Lou froze at the sound of her name. Then she turned to run, but found a second man standing behind her, blocking the sidewalk. This man was tall and sickly thin, with nappy blond hair jutting out from under a red baseball cap.

A third figure—stocky with a dark red beard—appeared at the curbside, blocking her only other means of escape. Lou reached for her phone to call for help, then remembered she'd switched it off. Not soon enough: the surveillance network had found her.

"How does it feel to be a murderer?" The baseball cap guy almost spat the words in Lou's face.

"Ethics in journalism, bitch," jeered Hoodie, who was holding up his phone, gleefully Freestreeming the ambush for Pétain's troll network. Now she saw the logo emblazoned on his sweatshirt: Jean-Claude the Pig, the obscure eighties comic strip character co-opted as an ironic shibboleth by Pétain's followers.

Fight, fly, fight, fly. Lou stared right ahead, eyes fixed on the phone lens as adrenaline stained the edges of her vision black; hoping beyond hope that a million witnesses would somehow keep her safe. Which they would not. Freestreem's offshore servers were packed with videos of women being beaten and assaulted by Pétain's followers, each accompanied by a waterfall of misspelled taunts and incitements from viewers at home. No matter how many of Pétain's acolytes were jailed for these on-screen attacks, the legal consequences always seemed to come as a genuine shock to these fucking idiots. She could scream, but who in the Tenderloin would care?

A fourth, larger shape had materialized in the gloom, towering behind Baseball Cap Guy. Lou couldn't make out the face of this latest arrival, only that he was a head taller than the other three men, and a foot wider. He was bald, or wearing a light-colored beanie, with a shiny black bomber jacket. The livestream was doing its job: Pétain's acolytes were descending.

Hoodie turned the lens toward his own face, seemingly oblivious to the new arrival. "What should we do with her?" he asked his at-home audience.

"Tell us in the side comments," brayed Red Beard, leaning over his friend's shoulder to read the on-screen responses.

For a moment, it seemed like the fourth man was also jostling to join the broadcast—wedging his body between Hoodie and Red Beard to get a better look at the screen. But then came a sudden flash of white—two giant hands reaching past the phone, thrusting toward Lou's face. She instinctively jerked backward, raising her hands and bracing for the slap, or punch. The back of her head slammed against something hard and metal protruding from the wooden boards. A jolt of pain shot through her skull.

That was all she felt. Because the slap, or punch, never came—just a sickening crunch that Lou would later identify as the sound of two skulls being cracked together with enough force to render their owners unconscious.

The crunch was followed by an equally nauseating thud as Hoodie and Red Beard collapsed to the sidewalk. Lou opened her eyes in time to see them both land at her feet, blood streaming from Hoodie's nose. Baseball Cap saw the same and turned to face the attacker, barely managing to blurt out a confused "duuude" before he, too, was silenced by a fist driven deeply into his nose. A fountain of red sprayed the front of Lou's shirt, and she screamed. The entire maneuver lasted maybe two seconds.

Lou screamed again as the big man grabbed her arm and pulled her out of the doorway, across the sidewalk, toward a black SUV idling at the curb a few feet away, its hazard lights blinking in the darkness. She fought against the man's grip, pounded her fist as hard as she could against his shoulders and torso, but she might as well have been punching an elephant.

"Quit it, you fucking crazy bitch." The man's voice was nasal, his vowel sounds pinched. Israeli? South African? He grabbed her arm tighter. "I'm the cavalry." *Kivilry.*

With that, and one last jolt, the man lifted Lou off her feet and tossed her into the back of the SUV.

17%

LOU MUST HAVE hit her head harder than she thought, or else her body was shutting down from exhaustion. Later, all she would remember of the abduction was lying on her back, sprawled across the leather rear seats of the SUV, staring up at the streetlights pulsing past the tinted window. Then after some amount of time—ten minutes? an hour?—the lights blinked out.

Eventually the vehicle slowed and then stopped, and all Lou could hear was the gentle purr of the engine. After that, she retained only a few still images of an elevator with mirrored walls and a low upholstered bench onto which she was being gently lowered. The bald man was beside her again—or had he been there the whole time?—the tang of bad cologne, a thick arm tightly around Lou's waist as they passed through a wooden doorway. The floor felt uneven below Lou's feet, and when she looked down, she was confused to see only a dusty foot where her shoe should be.

Blackness.

18%

LOU WOKE UP on a deep, plush couch. The back of her head was numb and she was shivering, despite the scratchy woolen blanket pulled up to her neck.

"Lou? Lou-ise McCarthy?" A woman's voice cooed gently through the mist. "Are we back in the land of the living?" Her accent twanged either British or Australian: Dame Judi Dench as played by Nicole Kidman.

"Ah, splendid, there you are."

Lou slowly opened her eyes and tried to locate the source of the voice. She could make out the blurry outline of a woman perched on the edge of a blue armchair, her head craned across the low glass-and-mahogany table that filled the space between them.

Lou planted an elbow into the edge of the couch and hoisted herself woozily upright. Her head was pounding, and as she swung her feet to the floor, bringing the blanket with her, she was sure she was about to throw up.

Further adding to the sensory overload, a trail of freezing goo ran down her neck. She glanced back at the couch cushion and saw that her head had been resting on a plastic ice pack.

The woman's face came into sharper focus: unhealthily thin, yet strangely unwrinkled, topped with red hair pulled back into a tight bun. It took Lou a moment to recognize the woman who'd been standing with Elmsley Chase's entourage at Raum One. She was still wearing her black couture jumpsuit but now with the addition of an expensive-looking cream denim jacket.

"What the fuck?" Lou's throat was scratchy and sore. "Where . . ."

"You're quite safe," said the woman. She pushed a tall glass of iced water across the coffee table. "Landon thinks you should be in hospital, but I

61

assumed you'd prefer to rest somewhere less . . . public." She tilted her head toward the doorway, and Lou felt a fresh spike of adrenaline as she saw the man who had bundled her into the SUV, now standing guard. The man shrugged, as if to confirm that he believed a medical facility to be the proper place for the victim of a serious head injury.

Lou tried to take in the rest of her surroundings. The room's furniture looked expensive, but insipid; the walls were covered with blandly corporate art: impressionist, yet perfectly calibrated not to leave an impression. Thick, beige drapes were drawn against the night, and the only illumination came from a collection of heavy brass table lamps. The unmistakable, inoffensive luxury of an upscale hotel suite. The St. Regis on Third Street, she guessed, or the Four Seasons on Market; Lou had attended conferences at both, and either was a short drive from Raum One. She looked in vain for something specific—a logo, or a key card—before turning back to the woman in the armchair. "I asked you a question. You can't just . . ."

"You are in my private apartment at the Four Seasons," the woman interrupted again, patiently but with an undercurrent of frustration, as if addressing a blind idiot. "And that"—the woman flicked a finger toward the couch—"is my chesterfield you're bleeding all over. Please, think absolutely nothing of it."

Lou glanced back down at the damp pink patch on the cushion where the condensation from the ice pack had mixed with her blood. An image flashed into view: a pair of red corduroy pants and a skinny chest, bloody and impaled on an ice sculpture. *Alex Wu is dead.*

"So, introductions!" The woman clapped her hands, instantly worsening Lou's headache. "My name is Helen. Helen Tyler."

"I know who you are," Lou bluffed, "and you can tell your boss not to worry. Elmsley Chase wanted me fired, and he got his wish. I'm done with his bullshit." Lou willed her legs to do their job and help her off the couch, but she was hit with another wave of nausea. It was all she could do not to fall back flat.

Even with a concussion, Lou could do basic math. She'd seen this woman talking to Elmsley Chase at Raum One. Now, having saved Lou from Claude Pétain's mob, she was playing Florence fucking Nightingale as her goon stood guard at the door. This person calling herself Helen Tyler was a member of Raum's fabled crisis-management team. A man was dead and still they were trying to do damage limitation—terrified maybe that Lou might sue Chase for encouraging Pétain's goons to attack her. There was no bottom for these monsters.

Tyler sniffed, with what might have been contempt or amusement. "Sadly, in my experience, Elmsley rarely worries about anything. Fortunately, I very emphatically do *not* work for him."

Tyler must have registered the look of incomprehension on Lou's face, because she smiled and quickly continued: "Off the record, please?" She paused for Lou to shrug her assent. "I am what you might call a hired gun."

Lou flinched at the phrase, and Tyler corrected herself. "Unfortunate choice of words. Sorry, it's been a difficult night for us all." She paused and lowered her voice. "Even if a painful death was the least Alex Wu deserved."

"Excuse me?" Had the woman from Raum really just wished death on the company's CTO? What new mind game was this?

"You disagree?" asked Tyler.

Lou still didn't respond. Whoever this woman really was, and whatever reaction she was hoping for, Lou meant what she'd said. She was done playing games. "I'll ask this one last time. Who are you and what do you want from me?"

Tyler sighed. "Again, *entre nous*, Raum's board has hired me to, shall we say, scrub the company up before going public. You might say that you and I have similar jobs—hunting for bad apples inside Raum One—only from different sides."

Lou heard herself laugh. "Your job is to *rehab* Raum before the IPO? Your rapist CTO just threw himself onto an ice sculpture, and your bro-ciopath CEO sent a mob of misogynist assholes after a female journalist. Five stars, would recommend."

Tyler gave a barely audible snort of amusement. "Succinctly put. Needless to say, if I'd known Elmsley was going to pull that stunt tonight, I would have put a stop to it. It was juvenile, pointless theater."

"I wouldn't call what Alex Wu did 'theater.'"

"We clearly attend different operas, dear." Tyler smiled. "Point being, Elmsley didn't have to humiliate you on national television and rile up Pétain and his ghastly social media mouth breathers. A red notice indeed." She pronounced the name the French way—*Pay-tahn*—not the Americanized *Pet-ain* used by Pétain himself and his fans. "It's bad enough you were duped by your source and imploded your own career." She shook her head in an approximation of sympathy.

Lou finally managed to struggle to her feet and pulled her cell phone from her pants pocket. The mention of the red notice reminded her she still hadn't heard from her mom.

Whoever this woman was—and she didn't talk like any crisis manager Lou had ever met—they both knew that Raum was anything but disgusted by Claude Pétain's trolls. She pressed the on button with her thumb, but the screen remained resolutely black.

"I have to go."

She tried again to resuscitate her phone, still to no effect.

Tyler seemed briefly puzzled. Then she reached into her pocket and removed a slim silver cell phone and handed it to Lou. "Please, call anyone you need."

Lou knew better than to give a Raum crisis manager her mom's number, but she also had no other choice. It took her until the fifth or sixth ring to realize she was wasting her time. Even assuming Pétain's crazies hadn't found her already, her mom never picked up unknown numbers, and Lou had left her a voice mail warning her to expect calls from crazy people. She hit cancel and tapped out a short text. *This is Lou. My phone is dead. Pick up!* Then she dialed again, saying a silent prayer as she did so. This time her mom answered on the first ring.

"Lou! What the fuck?"

"Hey, Mom. Did you get my message?"

"Yes, but the assholes were already at the house when I got back from karaoke."

"Are you OK?"

"I'm fine. Carol struck out, so she gave me a ride home."

Lou laughed. She couldn't help it. "Oh dear."

"Fuck right, oh dear," said her mom. "Maced one of the little shits, and the other got a slugger to the nuts." Lou remembered the aluminum bat Carol always carried in the rear footwell of her car, along with the Taser and pepper spray in her glove box. Could have been worse. Twenty years as a federal prison officer and fifty as a single woman in Georgia had taught Carol plenty of ways to incapacitate a man, many of them permanent.

"Where are you now?"

"We're back at Carol's. Local cops came by and told us we should go somewhere safe, because I guess they think we're total dumbasses. You want to know what they sprayed on the garage door?"

Lou was confused. "The cops?"

"No, Louise, your psycho fans. Apparently my daughter is a . . . you want to write this down for your next article? A slut cunt!" She paused. "All one word. Slutcunt. So that's something for the neighbors."

"Jesus, Mom, this isn't funny."

"It's called gallows humor, Louise. The cops said you were on TV. Which techie did you piss off this time? Not the electric-car dickhead again?"

"No, different dickhead. I'm really sorry they came to the house. Hey . . . will you do me a favor? Turn your cell phone off for the night?" Lou tried to make it sound more like a request than an order.

"Don't worry about us. We're watching *Murder, She Wrote* with Carol's friends Smith & Wesson. Nobody's getting in here tonight. I'll leave my phone on in case you need anything."

Lou wondered if Helen Tyler could hear her mom's side of the call, and what she must be making of it. "Mom, just do it for me, OK? They can use your cell phone to track you." She stopped, anticipating her mom's response.

"I need my phone for work. It's important."

More important than your daughter? Lou didn't take the bait. "I know, I know. It's just . . . for one night, please?"

Silence.

"Please?"

A sigh. "Fine. But if I don't hear from you tomorrow, Carol says she's getting on a plane to take care of those tech nerds herself." Lou started to tell her mother that Carol should not, under any circumstances, get on a plane to San Francisco, but she had hung up. Almost thirty years and Lou had never heard the woman say good-bye.

Lou handed the phone back to Helen Tyler. "Thank you."

"You're quite welcome. If you'll allow me, I'd like to take care of the cost of any damage to her home?"

Lou shook her head, firmly. "It's fine."

Tyler nodded, but said nothing, perhaps trying to decide whether to press the issue. Then: "A *slugger* to the *nuts?*" The phrase sounded even more ridiculous in a British accent.

"My mom's friend's a trip." Lou was done talking about her family. "I still need to go."

"I understand. I'll have Landon order you a vRaum . . ." Tyler paused and gave an indulgent smile. "A *taxi.* To take you anywhere you want to go." She turned toward the door as if to issue the order, but the giant man was gone. Another smile. "Ah. I'm sure he'll return presently. Actually, before you leave, I did want to ask for your help with something."

Lou shook her head in disgust, or maybe pity. Of course the phone had been a quid pro quo. "Honestly, fuck you. I'm not interested in your damage limitation. I'm not going to sue Elmsley Chase or Raum. You won, OK?" She moved toward the door.

Tyler's eyebrows shot upward. "Who said anything about suing? I've already told you, I don't work for Elmsley." She paused. "I just wanted to ask you how you got into the party tonight. Nothing more."

Lou stopped and turned back toward Tyler, still sitting in her armchair. "You know who invited me. Elmsley Chase wanted to humiliate me, and it worked."

"Ah," said Tyler. "You mean the mysterious Raum101. How very awkward."

So there it was. "You're Raum101." Lou felt her fingers curl into fists. What was she going to do? Punch this woman, who must be about her mom's age? Maybe.

Tyler pursed her lips. "A sordid little ruse, but you left me very little choice. I couldn't have you scooping me by reporting on our CTO's . . . *proclivities* before the board had a chance to line up his replacement. Try as I might, you wouldn't bloody quit. Tracking down the Stanford girlfriend was the final straw."

"Sophie," said Lou. "Sophie Aker. The *Stanford girlfriend* has a name."

"Indeed she does, along with a sprawling new condominium in Woodside."

Tyler seemed to catch herself, but Lou jumped on the confession. "So you admit Raum paid off Wu's victims?"

Tyler took a breath before responding, carefully. "I'm saying—off the record—that we're not all the ogres you think we are."

"No, you're a fucking saint, who paid off a victim of assault, forced her to sign an NDA, and publicly destroyed my career because I dared to report the truth."

A flash of anger appeared on Tyler's face and then dissolved instantly, as if imprinted on memory foam. "I did nothing of the sort, and it's important you understand that. I created an easily discredited lawsuit, and gave you the gentlest nudge toward publishing it." She put her hands together in prayer. "*Mea culpa.* But only one of us hit that publish button. Only one of us chose to hang her entire reputation on the word of a single unverified source. Only one of us destroyed her career by allowing her hatred of Raum and Elmsley Chase to weaken her judgment."

Lou felt her outrage deflate. She knew Tyler was right: She had been so desperate to believe her source was real that she'd marched straight into Chase's trap. Then she'd lashed out at her tormentor, which had done nothing except bring the whole fucking world crashing down—on herself but now on her mom too. She braced against the sickening echo from her childhood—an image of her dad standing in the kitchen, goading her . . . the weight of the gun . . . no. Lou forced the memory back down. This woman knew nothing about her. "And Miquela Rio at the *Journal*? I know you sent the story to her too."

Tyler nodded. "Though you'll note Miss Rio didn't publish it. After what happened to Alex tonight, I understand her editors have encouraged her to take a more cautious approach to covering Raum executives. All's well that ends . . . well . . ."

Lou shook her head. Maybe this Helen Tyler woman was right and everything was her own fault, but that still left a mountain of unanswered questions. Starting with . . .

"Why did you ask how I got into the party? You sent me an invitation." Lou suddenly remembered her backpack, containing the invitation card, was still somewhere at Raum One, lost in the chaos.

Tyler blinked slowly. "You have my solemn word: I didn't have an inkling you were at Raum One tonight. Not until you messaged me—that is, Raum101—with the unwelcome news that you were standing by the buffet table. I thought you'd snuck in with the caterers." She gestured toward Lou's bloodied white shirt. "Until I checked the security footage."

Snuck in with the caterers? Was Tyler seriously admitting to being her fake source, to setting her up, to destroying her career . . . but denying it was she who sent the invite? And why the weird syntax when she mentioned Wu's death? Suicide doesn't "happen *to*" someone . . .

Before Lou could ask more, Tyler reached beneath her chair and retrieved a slim manila folder from which she slid a stack of large black-and-white photographs. "Please," she said, gesturing toward the sofa. Lou sat.

"Thank you. Now, I won't insult you by asking you to keep this part of our conversation off the record. Not least because this conversation never happened, and these"—Tyler pushed the photographs across the coffee table—"do not exist."

As Lou picked up the stack, Tyler stood and padded across the room. Lou assumed she was going to shut the door; instead she gently slid aside a section of wood paneling on the adjacent wall, revealing the entrance to a modern-looking kitchen. Tyler stepped through and Lou heard the sound of running water.

She peered down at the first image, a grainy close-up of what seemed to be a man leaning over a glass balcony. She twitched in her seat as she read the time stamp printed on the bottom right corner—*63fl walkway east: 8:23 p.m.*—and recognized the blurry face of Alex Wu. *Oh God.* The image must have been captured seconds before Wu jumped. She was looking at a still from a snuff video.

Hands shaking, Lou flipped to the second photograph, which seemed to show the same scene from a different angle. Except the man in this shot was at least a foot taller than Wu and looked to be missing most of his hair. Also, the time stamp was slightly different: *63fl walkway south: 8:23 p.m.* She exhaled another quiet curse. The second image must have been captured on the opposite walkway from Alex Wu. Tyler returned from her culinary Narnia, carrying two more glasses of water, one of which she placed in front of Lou.

"Who—" Lou started to speak, but Tyler cut her off with a twirled finger, indicating that she should continue flipping through the photographs.

The third image also showed the second man, but in much sharper focus, like it had been cleaned up or digitally enhanced.

"Oh God." Lou held a fist to her mouth as she recognized the face staring back at her.

"Indeed."

Throughout her career, Lou had written maybe five hundred stories about tech founders behaving badly. A handful of the men had been fired, and some had been forced to issue groveling public apologies, but only two could honestly be said to have had their lives ruined by something she'd written. The second was Alex Wu. The first, almost two years earlier, was the sleazy CEO of a small micropayments company who, Lou reported, had been screwing a nineteen-year-old intern. His name was Joe Christian, and, so far as Lou knew, he had absolutely zero connection with Raum or Alex Wu. But there he was, clear as Maxiglass, standing opposite Wu on the sixty-third floor of Raum One, watching him jump.

"What . . . why are you showing me this?" Lou's mouth was running on autopilot, and the pain in the back of her head was now throbbing right through to her eyeballs.

"You recognize our mutual friend, obviously," said Tyler, pointing at the photo of Alex Wu. "But our cameras also captured this other fellow. His face rings a bell?"

"Is that Joe Christian? From Grintech?"

Tyler nodded slowly.

"I thought he was dead." Lou clarified, quickly: "Not dead but, you know, gone. After the intern scandal." This had been one of Lou's few semi-triumphs: helping to expose Joe Christian as a sexual harasser just as his company was rumored to be in acquisition talks with a major bank. He had been ousted with a multimillion-dollar golden parachute, but at least he hadn't become a billionaire. Unlike most of his disgraced peers, he'd also failed to rehabilitate himself back into tech society. No weed-delivery startup, no cryptocurrency podcast, no speaking tour.

Tyler shook her head. "It would seem he's . . . well, perhaps not *very much* alive but at least not dead . . ." She was staring intently at the images spread across the table. "Our supposedly omniscient face recognition lost track of him after he left Raum One. We have no idea where he went, or how he got into the building in the first place. More critically, there seems to be no meaningful connection between him and Alex Wu or Raum except . . ." Another twirl of Tyler's finger indicated Lou should flip to the last photograph in the stack. But it wasn't a photograph at all—rather a printed list of names, divided into two columns.

"This is from the invite list for tonight's party, pulled from our intranet a half hour ago. The left column is the name of each invited guest. On the right is the name of who authorized their invitation."

Lou ran her finger down the left column until she found her own name: McCarthy, Louise, annotated with the printed letters *[VIP]*. That explained Tyler's question about how she'd gotten into the party, and why Raum's PR minders had been so hesitant to throw her out. She dragged her finger slowly from the left column to the right until it landed on . . . *Guest of . . .*

"What the fuck?"

. . . Joseph Christian [VIP].

"*He* invited me?"

"As you might imagine," said Tyler, "our security team is struggling to explain how an industry pariah like Mr. Christian not only added himself to our guest list but was also apparently able to hack our military-grade intranet to issue VIP invitations to bloody journalists. No offense intended."

This was too much. Lou had tumbled down a rabbit hole where nothing could possibly be real. "You expect me to believe that Joe fucking Christian returned from exile and somehow hacked your guest list just so he could invite me to Raum One and we could both . . . what? Eat canapés and watch Alex Wu hurl himself onto an ice sculpture?"

Tyler shrugged. "I'm not expecting you to believe anything, Lou. What I'm showing you is the very definition of unbelievable. All I can tell you is what the security footage and guest list tell me, which—I agree—makes no sense to man nor beast. Nor does it answer the more baffling question of why the hell Alex Wu would throw himself off that walkway."

"He killed himself because I had just outed him as a rapist." Lou caught the hopeful inflection in her own voice. This was the second time Helen Tyler had hinted that Wu's suicide might not be, well, a suicide.

"Death by investigative journalism?" Tyler actually rolled her eyes at this. "Tell me honestly, did Alex Wu seem like a man capable of shame to you? Your story was discredited—*mea maxima culpa*—and in a few weeks, Raum's IPO would make him richer than almost anyone on the planet except for Elmsley Chase. Hardly a recipe for terminal despair."

"Maybe he was depressed about something else . . . Who the hell knows what other shit he was into?"

Tyler slapped her palms against the coffee table, then rolled back in her armchair. "That's exactly my point, Lou. *I* know. Alex Wu was the key to Raum's successful IPO, which means it was my job to know precisely what *shit* he was *into*. The drugs, the booze, the women . . . well, you of all people don't need me to spell out the full ugly range of his depravity.

Just believe me when I tell you I knew it all, and then some." She paused. "But there's the rub: I've spent my career tracking powerful men and their self-inflicted downfalls. I know the pattern, and I know when something doesn't fit. And this . . ." She jabbed a manicured fingernail on the photo of Alex Wu. "Does. Not. Fit. You think a few bags of Bolivian marching powder and a brace of venereal diseases do *that* to a man?" Another jab. "You think a broken ankle and a nasty bout of food poisoning can bring someone like Alex Wu so far beyond the brink that he'd rather die tonight than wait a few weeks to become a multibillionaire? And while we're on the subject, do you really believe a horny little *prat* like Joe Christian has the chops to hack the most sophisticated building security system on the planet, even if he wanted to? And why would he want to?" She paused. "No. I'm certain whoever invited you to Raum One tonight, it wasn't Joe Christian." Another pause, longer this time. "Perhaps it was Alex."

Lou reached for her water and took a shaky sip. She had been about to make the same obvious suggestion. "So why do *you* think he jumped? And why invite me and Joe Christian to watch?"

Tyler turned her palms to the ceiling. "I haven't the foggiest idea. I hoped you might be able to shed a glimmer of light, which is why I sent Landon to find you." She nodded toward the bloodstained couch cushion. "And thank goodness I did."

"Maybe if . . ." Lou stopped as she registered something Tyler had said. "Wu had a broken ankle?"

Tyler smirked. "I thought that would please you. Yes, this past Thursday. Alex was run over by one of our self-driving cars, while he was inspecting the new fleet."

Lou smirked too. Couldn't help it.

"Wonderful, right?" said Tyler. "And here's the really funny part. Two hours earlier, our safety team had sent him a report about a problem with the car's collision-detection system. It seems our facial-recognition technology has a problem recognizing people with dark skin. Alex told them to ignore the findings and go ahead with the rollout."

"Wow," said Lou. "Sounds a lot like karma."

"Doesn't it just," said Tyler. "Same with the food poisoning. You'll recall Raum's recent *contretemps* with the department of food safety?"

Lou did recall. She'd broken the story herself: The city had threatened to shut down RaumService after a spate of E. coli poisonings, all linked to its San Francisco kitchen and distribution center. Alex Wu himself went to city hall to argue that RaumService was a mere *technology platform* and so should be exempt from food-service regulations. "The technology-platform bullshit?"

"Exactly so," said Tyler. "Two days after the hearing, Alex came down with a particularly violent bout of E. coli. A dodgy shrimp in his RaumService biryani. I could give you a fistful of other examples, but suffice to say karma seems to have taken an unusual interest in Alex Wu recently."

"So you don't think he jumped?"

Lou felt another involuntary, barely suppressed note of hope, but Tyler snatched it away. "There's the other rub. I *know* he jumped. Footage shows it clear as day. Nobody, including Joe Christian, was standing within ten feet of him when he went over that ledge." Tyler leaned back in her chair. "I investigated the E. coli incident myself, and our tech team tore the self-driving car apart looking for sabotage. Both were exactly as they appeared: unfortunate, deeply ironic accidents." She paused. "Unless . . ."

"Unless what?"

Tyler's eyes flicked back toward the doorway. Then, satisfied they were still alone: "Based on the facts, there are two possible explanations for what happened tonight. The first is that—as you say—karma finally caught up with Alex Wu and he decided to kill himself. That theory falls at the first hurdle. We both know karma doesn't exist—especially not for men like Alex Wu. Recent history has told us that."

Lou nodded. In the years since Silicon Valley's supposed "Me Too moment," she'd watched with frustration, but zero surprise, as almost every single predator had wormed his way back into power and influence. This was an industry built on the promise of limitless memory, by people who couldn't remember what happened last week.

Tyler continued: "Which leaves explanation two: that somebody very,

very clever worked very, very hard to ruin Alex Wu's life, to the point where suicide was his only option. And they did it in a way that looked—to the casual observer—like karma."

"Which is impossible."

Tyler shook her head. "Please. We've both worked in this town long enough to know that 'impossible problems' are just problems that rich men don't want to solve. Equality in the workplace; how to refrain from fucking the interns; banning Nazis from social media . . . these are all"—she raised her fingers as air quotes—"'impossible problems.' Ruining someone's life and making the world think it was their own silly fault . . . well, that's Silicon Valley's bread and butter, isn't it?"

Lou's eyes widened. Tyler might as well be quoting from one of Lou's own articles. *Is she quoting from one of my own articles?*

Tyler continued. "What I'm describing is improbable and expensive and complex, but certainly not impossible. Especially given sufficient financial motivations."

Lou understood her implication. "You think someone did all this to sabotage Raum's IPO?" There were endless companies, or countries, with the resources to sabotage America's flagship tech startup.

"That was my first thought. Bumping off the CTO right in the middle of Elmsley's big announcement is a little *gauche*, but there's no denying the result. But if the goal is to derail Raum's public offering in a way that looks like a common suicide, why involve a journalist and a disgraced intern fucker? And why do it in a way that simply honks 'expensive conspiracy'?" She didn't wait for Lou to answer. "Then we hit upon the second problem: the who. Our culprit must have almost unfettered access to Raum One. Except . . ."

"Everyone inside Raum One stands to make bank during the IPO." Lou reached back to grab the ice pack, and pressed it to the back of her neck. "You claim to know everything about Alex Wu, so you tell me: who wanted him dead?"

"I have absolutely no idea." The look on Tyler's face was pure exasperation, as if Lou hadn't been listening to a word she'd said. "All I know is he *is* dead. And until we know why, and what our killer's ultimate aim is, we can't be sure there won't be any more arseholes sent tumbling off balconies. That's why Landon is currently searching high and low for Joe Christian. Clearly he's been dragged into this for a reason."

"You think the same person is setting Joe Christian up to die too?" Lou felt the nausea returning.

Tyler gave the pile of photographs another tap. "I admit I'm not overly optimistic for his long-term health."

Tyler was right. The Joe Christian in the photograph was a shadow of the man Lou had written about two years earlier. Gaunt, hunched, almost bald, and with what seemed to be scabs or scars covering his face. But he wasn't the only one who'd been dragged to Raum One. "Sucks to be Joe Christian. But right now I'm more worried that Pétain's psychos are trying to pin all of this on my reporting. They're threatening my family."

Tyler was already scrolling through her phone. "Let me see what I can do. Mob management is one of my specialties." Moments later, Tyler had reached Anabelle Slate, the head of Raum's comms department, and was slowly dictating a press release:

"I was shocked and saddened by the sudden death of our colleague Alex Wu. I was equally troubled to read reports concerning Alex's private life, which, sadly, seem to be accurate. I would like to personally thank Lou McCarthy of the *Bay Area Herald* for her diligent and fearless reporting . . ."

After dictating a few more short paragraphs, Tyler hung up. "There," she said, turning in her seat to face Lou, "it'll be on the home page in a few minutes, then sent to every newsroom from here to Timbuktu."

"That's it?" Lou slapped the ice pack down on the couch beside her. "They came to my mom's house. They sprayed a bunch of disgusting shit across her garage door. You think a press release from Anabelle Slate will stop those psychopaths?"

"No. I think a press release signed personally by *Elmsley Chase* will stop those psychopaths. Pétain's freaks worship Elmsley. Once they know you and he are on the same team, I feel certain they won't go anywhere near you or your family. If you like, I can also—"

But before Tyler could finish her sentence, three shrill beeps shattered the tension. She retrieved her cell phone and Lou saw her jaw muscles tighten as she read the new text message.

"It seems our fears about Mr. Christian were well founded." Tyler leaned across the table and rotated the screen toward Lou. "This is from a friend at SFPD. Half an hour ago Joe Christian walked into the Pacific Medical Center's Tenderloin campus and plunged a six-inch kitchen knife into his own neck. My friend says he probably won't survive the night."

THE BLACK SUV sped its way along Market Street, then swung a right on Taylor, narrowly avoiding an old man pushing a shopping cart laden with trash bags.

The CPMC's Tenderloin campus—open less than twelve months, and entirely paid for by tech billionaires to assuage their guilt for destroying the universe—was barely eight blocks from Raum One. They could have walked from the Four Seasons, but Landon insisted it was safer to drive.

In the back seat, Lou felt anything but safe as she gripped the plastic handle above the window, convinced at any moment the door would fly open, flinging her onto the street. In the front passenger seat, Tyler stared out of the window, her face fixed in concentration, or consternation.

The car screeched up to the hospital entrance, and Tyler, who hadn't been wearing a seat belt, bounded out into the path of an oncoming ambulance, which missed her by inches. She seemed not to notice. Lou struggled with her own seat belt and then followed Tyler toward the set of glass doors marked EMERGENCIES. Two baby-faced SFPD cops stood guard, and the youngest of them opened his mouth as if to say something but closed it again as Tyler rushed past. By the time Lou made it inside, Tyler had already found her contact: a bull-necked giant in an Oakland A's T-shirt, a brass shield looped around his neck. He was talking to a nurse, who seemed to have been crying.

"Stanley!" Tyler's voice bounced off the walls of the otherwise empty waiting room.

"Ah shit." The detective blanched as he saw Tyler barreling toward him. "The words 'stay away' mean nothing to you, do they?"

"Everything you say means the world to me, Stanley," said Tyler airily. "So what do we know?"

Lou was surprised to see the detective's face soften into a smile. "Thank you, ma'am," he said to the shell-shocked nurse, "we'll be done here as soon as we can." Then he guided Tyler—Lou still trailing behind—to the far corner of the room.

"It's like I said in my text," said the cop, speaking only to Tyler as if Lou were entirely invisible. "You asked me to BOLO for this Joe Christian guy, and ten minutes later he shows up here, ranting and screaming and waving a fucking blade." He seemed to register Lou's presence for the first time— "Pardon my French"—then turned back to Tyler: "A dozen witnesses, and one woman got it on video." He removed a plastic evidence bag from the back pocket of his jeans and turned the contents—a rose-gold iPhone— toward Tyler and Lou. He tried to activate the screen through the bag, but when that didn't work, he ripped open the seal and slid out the device. On the iPhone's cracked screen, Joe Christian was waving what seemed to be a carving knife. "I am Joe Christian," he was yelling, so loudly the audio was distorted. "I am still Joe Christian. I am still Joe Christian." *Still?*

The voice on the video grew even louder and more frantic. Now he was screaming another name. "Amelia. Amelia. Listen to me. She did this."

"Amelia's the ex-wife, we think." With his free hand, the cop tugged a second evidence bag from his pocket and turned it to reveal a crumpled and bloodied passport-sized photo showing Joe Christian and a younger and significantly more attractive blond woman, faces smooshed together, beaming toward the camera. "Bad divorce, maybe?"

Lou gave a slight nod, as if she didn't know every last ugly detail of Joe and Amelia Christian's breakup.

"Wait, wait . . ." Tyler raised a finger, her eyes still fixed on the phone. "What did he say? There."

The cop returned the photo to his pocket and dragged his finger back across the phone screen, rewinding the video a few seconds. Joe Christian started yelling again. Another drag. And again.

"It sounds like he's saying 'it's the . . . cherry'? It's her cherry?" Tyler pursed her lips. To Lou's ear it sounded more like "cherry tree," but she forced herself to stay silent.

The cop shrugged and let the video play again. Lou turned away—she'd seen enough blood for a lifetime—but there was no escape: the corner of the waiting room was a pool of deep red, with bright tendrils reaching in all directions. A cleaner was hovering boredly alongside, ready with his mop and yellow wheely bucket, waiting for the OK to clear up the mess. Lou heard tinny screams coming from the phone's speaker, and then silence.

"Any theories on why he came here?" Tyler was talking again.

"You see the state he was in? If I was that fu—messed up, I'd probably come to the emergency room too."

Tyler exhaled a dismissive burst of air through her nose. "And plunge a knife into your throat? Seems rather counterproductive, no?"

The cop sighed. "Crazy fucking people do crazy fucking things. San Francisco news flash! Speaking of which, what's your connection with this guy? Something to do with the jumper at Raum One tonight?"

"We're not sure," Lou heard Tyler lie. "Facial recognition caught him lurking around the building, probably just a trespasser, but tonight's a big night for Raum. Wanted to make sure he was on your radar."

The cop grunted in acknowledgment, as if acting as Raum's detective for hire was his regular side hustle.

It was jarring how casually Tyler asked her questions, like she hadn't seen the footage of Joe Christian at Raum One. Hadn't expected him to die next. Was this just a normal Wednesday night for her? Or was it just easier to be so fucking casual when you weren't the one personally invited to witness a suicide?

Lou took a slow breath. She needed to stay present, to think like a reporter. Something about the location of the pool of Joe Christian's blood bothered her. As if he'd chosen the absolutely ideal, most central spot for his very public suicide: visible from the plastic waiting room seats but also in perfect view of at least two security cameras. Now she spotted the knife, still lying in the pool of blood. Even with the bloodstains, it seemed shiny and new as if it had been purchased specifically for this gruesome performance. Come to think of it, everything about the scene felt staged for some imaginary audience.

Now her eyes fell on the wall behind the pool of blood, or more specifically on a column of direction arrows pointing visitors to various areas of the hospital: the Zuckerberg Pulmonology Center, the Musk Trichology Wing, the Chase Childhood Cancer Unit . . . But when Lou saw the uppermost sign—which must have been almost exactly at Joe Christian's eye level when he stood under the cameras—she had to grit her teeth to avoid letting out a gasp. The sign directed visitors to the Amelia Christian Women's Trauma Center.

Lou remembered the press release, sent to Tommy but not to her: Joe Christian's ex-wife had used her divorce settlement to fund a nonprofit rape-crisis foundation, with a particular focus on young victims of sexual assault. Given Joe Christian's intern was barely out of her teens, it was widely interpreted as an attempt to distance herself from her husband's behavior. Could that be what he was saying in the video? "It's her *charity?*" *Amelia's charity?* Shit, it had to be.

Lou turned back to Tyler and the cop. Her instinct was to keep the discovery to herself until she had more time to process it. But what was the point of hiding something that the cop would surely see for himself before long? He might know more than he'd already told them.

But then she made eye contact with Tyler, who gave an almost imperceptible shake of her head. *I saw it too. Don't say a bloody word.*

Lou didn't know if the detective had noticed the glance, but suddenly he stopped talking and turned to Lou. "Sorry, and you are?"

"Oh, where *are* my manners?" Tyler was using her Judi Dench voice again. "Detective Stanley Martinez, meet my new research assistant, Louise. First day on the job, but I'm anticipating good things."

Martinez looked her up and down, and Lou realized her shirt was still covered in dust and blood. Before the cop could say anything, though, Tyler put her hand on Lou's shoulder. "Actually, dear, I could murder a cup of coffee. Would you mind terribly?"

"Not at all." Lou smiled. "I think there's a vending machine . . ." She paused, looking around for the correct answer. "Down that way." She nodded in the vague direction of the elevators.

"You're a sweetie," beamed Tyler.

"Hell of a first day," the cop called as Lou walked away.

"Tell me about it," said Lou, without turning back.

Lou emerged from the elevator on the eleventh floor, which, according to the label next to the button, was the location of the "Eric Schmidt Intensive Care Unit." She had already taken a quick detour via the Amelia Christian Trauma Center but found only a locked door and a dog-eared paper sign, dated three months earlier, saying the center was temporarily closed. Hopefully her next stop would be less frustrating.

She expected the ICU floor to be swarming with uniforms, but realized her mistake when she saw only a bored-looking receptionist and a single security guard. To them, Joe Christian was just another mentally ill homeless person who'd reached the end of the road.

Lou approached the huge, curved desk while trying to affect the look of someone who knew exactly what she was doing, and where she was going, and that, really, there was no need to pay her much attention at all. "Joseph Christian?" she called airily.

The receptionist, who barely looked up from her monitor, tapped at her keyboard. For a moment Lou thought she might just get away with it.

"You family?"

Lou instantly switched her expression from airy to concerned. "My brother." She knew Helen could distract the cop for only so long. It helped that Lou's filthy shirt and blood-crusted hair and collar made her look the part of a junkie's sister, and that security in San Francisco hospitals was so laughably bad. There on a gigantic whiteboard for all to see were the words "Christian, J." and the room number, "8." The receptionist raised a single drawn-on eyebrow, gave another couple of taps on her keyboard just for show, and then shook her head. "No visitors. You can try tomorrow."

Lou considered histrionics—crying, pleading, *You heartless monster, my poor Joseph* . . . all that crap—but realized that was only likely to draw the attention of the security guard still slowly pacing the reception area. She murmured a quiet "OK" and then turned crestfallen toward the elevator.

After taking a few paces, she swiveled back to face the receptionist, wiping away an invisible tear. "Where's your restroom?"

The receptionist didn't look up. "Third door on the right. Code is three eight three eight."

Lou thanked her and headed off down the hallway.

The ICU was silent, except for the *squeak-squeak-squeak* of the slightly too-small Prada tennis shoes she'd borrowed from Helen Tyler. Room seventeen, nineteen, twenty . . . dammit, the numbers started in double digits and were going up—but then she rounded a corner and found room three, then four until . . .

The door to room eight was closed, but through a narrow glass panel, Lou could see Joe Christian lying in a bed, a nest of tubes and wires spreading in all directions. A nurse wearing light-blue scrubs was examining the screen of a heart rate monitor, scribbling the details on her translucent plastic clipboard.

Lou walked a little farther, then bent down to untie and then retie her shoelace. She reprised this performance a few more times until she heard the click of the door followed by the rubber *slap-slap-slap* of the nurse's clogs disappearing into the distance.

Lou retraced her steps back to room eight and gripped the door handle, listening carefully for any more approaching medical staff. She stepped inside and let the door swoosh gently closed behind her.

Joe Christian lay motionless, a waxwork of the man Lou had watched screaming and ranting on the video. The only sounds in the room were the slow *blip, blip* of an electronic heartbeat and the soft pant of a breathing tube. The air reeked of disinfectant, mixed with a faint floral perfume left behind by the nurse.

Lou stepped a little closer to the bed and tried to take in what little she could see of Joe Christian's face. His neck was wrapped in a thick gauze, and his mouth was hidden behind a translucent green oxygen mask. Even besides the medical paraphernalia, Christian looked worse than he had in the black-and-white security footage from Raum One. His skin was deep yellow, and his forehead, his scalp, and even his gently fluttering eyelids were covered in angry red blotches. Something very weird had happened to his eyebrows. His posture was odd too—arms splayed by his sides, palms down as if bracing himself against the bed.

It was impossible to reconcile this pathetic, dying creature with the Joe Christian who had once strode the stage at Davos and the TED Conference, explaining Grintech's plan to distribute billions of dollars in "microloans" to poor people in the developing world. Or the one who six months later appeared on CNN to apologize for how many of those borrowers had been driven to suicide, unable to afford Grintech's sky-high interest payments. The list of people who might want Joe Christian dead would stretch from here to Bangladesh. Same for those with reason to hate Alex Wu. But still. Two accused sexual predators, both who'd ruined countless lives in the pursuit of personal profit—both choosing to end their lives on the same night . . .

Lou stared for a moment longer and thought about the text from Helen's pet detective. *He probably won't last the night.* Listening to the wheeze of the ventilator, Lou wasn't sure he'd last the hour.

She stepped closer to the bed and gagged, struck by a smell that over-powered even the disinfectant: putrid and necrotic, like rotting meat, only sweeter. She raised her hand to cover her nose and mouth as she real-ized the smell was emanating from the red and purple pustules covering almost every visible inch of Joe Christian's body. She clamped her fingers tighter over her nostrils and leaned closer. For all the stench, Lou wanted to shake him. To pull off his oxygen mask and demand answers. *Why were you at Raum One? How did you know Alex Wu was going to jump? And why did I need to see it?*

But she knew these were answers Joe Christian couldn't give; likely would never give. Because she'd been here before—a different state and a lifetime ago, but the same tubes and masks and smells, the same realiza-tion that it was all far, far too late. Back then the man was her dad, coma-tose from alcoholic cardiomyopathy and cirrhosis of the liver; skin yellow, body so wasted it was as if his bones had shrunk. Lou remembered the texture of the soft rubber mask she'd pulled away from his wispy beard, and whispering the only question she'd cared to hear him answer: *Are you sorry? Are you fucking sorry now?* Until a nurse dragged her away, still screaming and cursing the asshole's name. With Joe Christian, she knew better than to try.

Lou stepped away from the bed. Across the room was a small table with a gray pitcher of water, a single paper cup, and a tray containing what must have been Joe Christian's only worldly possessions. Lou walked over to examine the tray's contents in the half-light. An orange ballpoint pen, maybe fifty cents in change, a small glass bottle with some kind of Chinese instructions typed on the label. There was a jacket too, slung over the back of a chair. It was made from thin cotton and had once been green. Now it was brown with filth, and stank of bodily odor, which mixed with the smell rising from its owner.

Lou glanced back at the closed door. The hallway was still empty, the world still oblivious. She patted the jacket with the back of her hand, turning her head away from the stench. Where exactly was the line between an efficacious lie and a felony, between trespassing and theft? She frowned as she realized. She had snuck into an ICU room, after posing as a near-dead man's sister and lying to a cop working an active crime scene. Whatever legal line she had to worry about was at least a hundred miles behind her.

There seemed to be nothing in any of the pockets—nothing to indicate why Joe Christian had chosen to end his life in this particular hospital, or what the connection could be between his ugly appearance and his ex-wife's foundation.

Her eyes fell again on the supine and barely alive body. Specifically, she considered Joe Christian's hands, and the curious, unnatural way they were positioned. When she'd first walked into the room, Lou had noticed the prominent blue veins on the back of his right hand. But now, standing on the other side of the bed, she realized that what she'd thought was veins was actually blue ink.

She crouched to look more closely. Through the sores, she could just about make out a row of numbers: 65021035 . . . The last two digits overlapped a pustule and Lou had to squint to decypher them. A phone number, with a Palo Alto area code, maybe scribbled as a reminder. But why then was it written on the *back* of his hand, not the palm?

Lou instinctively felt for her phone to take a photo, then whispered a quiet *fuck* when she remembered the device was still bricked. Instead she plucked the ballpoint pen from among Christian's possessions and copied the numbers onto her own palm, even duplicating the slashed lines he had drawn through the zeros: the hallmark of a software engineer. It might be nothing, but at least it was something.

Lou had just copied the last digit when she was startled by voices—a man and a woman—outside in the hallway, getting closer. Lou dropped from her crouch to lie flat on the floor, her cheek pressed against the cold vinyl. The smell of disinfectant was stronger than ever, but almost refreshing by comparison with the stink of Joe Christian. She watched under the bed toward the door, waiting for it to crash open and security or the cops to charge in. Her heart thumped, jarringly out of sync with the slow beat of Joe Christian's electronic pulse. The voices were close enough now to be almost intelligible: Lou caught the word *security*, while the breathless male voice was telling the woman to go ahead; he'd catch up. Lou closed her eyes and begged the universe that they were heading to some other emergency, some different crime in progress.

They weren't. The door clicked open and a pair of feet appeared, clad in a nurse's rubber Crocs. The feet paused briefly—long enough for Lou to take in a pair of thin, light brown ankles peeking from the bottom of a slightly too short pair of scrub pants. The Crocs were joined by a second pair of shoes—shiny and black. "Well, she's not here now," said a woman's voice.

"You're sure she wasn't from culinary?" came the still-panting male response.

There was a pause, before the nurse asked incredulously: "You think this guy ordered a pizza?" They both laughed, the sound echoing off the walls of the room, despite the dying man in front of them. A rustling of paper, the click of a pen, and . . . the two sets of shoes were gone, the door gently closing behind.

Lou opened her eyes and exhaled slowly. The panic over, her eyes shifted focus, away from the base of the door and onto another object lying under the bed. It was black and rectangular, and at first Lou thought it was some piece of medical equipment embedded in the floor. She reached out and with her fingertips was able to retrieve what proved to be a slim black notebook; the pointlessly expensive type popular with journalists and Silicon Valley entrepreneurs.

It might have been dropped by a doctor, or a previous occupant of the room. But now, as she extracted the notebook from under the bed, Lou saw the yellow Post-it note affixed to the cover. On it was written a single word, in the same blue ink as the number on Joe Christian's hand. The word was "Amelia."

A HALF HOUR later, Lou McCarthy and Helen Tyler were back at the Four Seasons. They sat in Helen's kitchen, perched on high white leather stools, on opposite sides of a thin marble counter, watching footage of Joe Christian's suicide playing on an antiquated iPad.

Helen set a patterned china cup of tea in front of Lou and jabbed at the screen of the device. Joe Christian froze, his face a mask of panic and desperation, the silver blur of the knife gripped in his right hand just coming into shot. "I promised Stanley we'd delete the video before morning. It's evidence for the medical examiner now."

That grim update, and the video attachment, had arrived moments after they'd left the hospital. Joe Christian had suffered a massive seizure and died without ever regaining consciousness. The news was shocking but, given what Lou had seen in the ICU, not surprising.

She looked down at the legal pad where she'd been scribbling notes. Doodling, really, still too shaken up to have any coherent thoughts—*It's her. It's a charity? It's her charity*—above the phone number she'd copied from Joe Christian's hand. On the drive back to the Four Seasons, they'd tried dialing the number but had got only a "not in service" tone. Helen had forwarded the number to her "research chappy" who, she assured Lou, had a "gift" for tracing numbers and other hard-to-track personal information. She didn't say whether the "chappy" in question worked at Raum or was another freelancer like Helen. Another co-opted cop?

"It can't be a coincidence, can it? Screaming about his wife's nonprofit?"

". . . standing next to a bloody great sign pointing to that exact same charity?" Helen completed Lou's thought. "I'd say that stretches the boundaries of coincidence. Especially in light of this . . ." Helen picked up the black notebook, still with its "Amelia" Post-it, and began to flick through the pages. Lou had already examined the book in the elevator right after she'd fled Joe Christian's hospital room. It was some kind of handwritten journal—listing in date order (complete with Christian's telltale slashed zeros) the many escalating tragedies that had befallen him since his forced departure from Grintech. There were pages early in the book focused on his divorce; then came an entire section documenting the series of failed investments—everything from cryptocurrencies to recreational-weed startups—that had first decimated, then obliterated his Grintech payoff. Each turn of the page described a fresh spread of tragedies: every health crisis, personal betrayal, eviction, drug experiment, sexual misadventure, and resulting STD logged in excruciating detail. The last entry was the most cryptic of all. The one-word question "Eyebrows?" crossed through with a single shaky line.

Helen stopped flipping pages and set the book back on the countertop, rotating it so Lou could see. Spanning the center spread was a neatly and intricately drawn flowchart: a series of boxes, circles, and triangles, each with an apparently significant word or phrase in the center—"Pills," "Diner," "Tahoe," "Doctor." Some of the shapes contained only initials . . . "BA," "EC" . . . and each connected to one or more other shapes by a web of carefully straight lines. There were also street addresses, email aliases, and phone numbers, none of which matched the number on Joe Christian's hand. In the center of the diagram was a rectangular box, larger than all the others, with a single four-letter word in block capitals.

"'FATE,'" Helen read out loud, tapping her fingernail on the word. "Do we think this is what he blames for what happened to him? As in karma? Some kind of cosmic justice?"

"Or a name," said Lou. "A nickname for whoever he thought was doing this to him. Although if he was trying to blame his wife, surely he'd just write 'Amelia.'"

"And probably wouldn't leave the journal under his bed, addressed to her," Helen added.

Lou took a sip of her tea. She was uncomfortable at how quickly she and Helen had fallen into this collegial back-and-forth. It was partly a survival instinct: the apartment was safe and warm, and Lou had no intention of spending the night in a Tenderloin doorway. Mostly it was good to feel validated, to meet someone else who understood the twisted depravity of Silicon Valley as she did, albeit from the other side. Lou didn't have to like Helen Tyler to feel vindicated by her existence. "Maybe Fate is someone involved with the charity? Or one of his victims. Isn't that what Amelia Christian's foundation does? Helps file police reports against abusers?"

Helen seemed to weigh up the possibility, rolling out a slow, "Maaaaybe. But if the Amelia Christian Foundation was digging into Alex, I'd know about it. I'd definitely know if law enforcement was involved."

Of course you would. Lou thought back to the cop in the emergency room and the familiarity between him and Helen. "It also doesn't explain the connection between him and Alex Wu."

Helen flicked inexpertly at her chunky iPad, and the video of Joe Christian was replaced by the home page of the Amelia Christian Foundation—a single page of HTML with a mission statement about helping victims of abuse, a couple of local police department logos, and a black-and-white portrait of a smiling Amelia Christian—her blond hair cut into a professional bob. The combination of hairstyle and grayscale photo added a decade to her real age, like a twenty-five-year-old in a 1940s movie. There was an email address for inquiries, and a phone number. Lou reached over and tapped a link at the bottom of the page, labeled "Financial disclosures."

Two more taps and they were looking at a single-page PDF document showing the totality of the Amelia Christian Foundation's income and expenditures for the past eighteen months. Lou processed the numbers quickly; she had read a million documents like this while hunting in vain for Raum's secret slush fund. The only significant sum in the income column was a payment of $10 million—the famous divorce settlement—followed by a trickle of smaller amounts from other local foundations that Lou vaguely recognized. More recently, though, the cash—both in and out—had dried up. In the current financial year, the charity had raised less than $20,000, and spent the same.

"That's weird at least," said Lou. "You think twenty k is enough to fund a rape-crisis center?" She remembered the locked door she'd found at the hospital.

Helen gave a look that almost passed for approval. "In this country? I'm not sure twenty thousand dollars is enough to pay for an aspirin."

"So perhaps the foundation is involved in some financial scandal?" Lou was grabbing at straws.

Helen glanced back down at the iPad. "Or they might just be broke. Neither possibility explains why Joe Christian or Alex Wu needed to die."

Lou took a sip from her teacup and caught a glimpse of the phone number still written on her palm. An image flashed deep inside her brain.

"Can you play the video again?"

Helen swiped back to the media player app, Joe Christian's tortured face once again almost filling the screen, the knife still gripped, about to slash . . .

She dragged a finger across the image, rewinding the video to the start. The hideous performance began again. Lou watched as the camera settled on Joe Christian, already ranting—so it seemed—about his wife and her charitable foundation. The onlookers screamed as the blade appeared, swinging in and out of shot . . .

Lou touched the screen to pause the video. Then she dragged her finger back, just a fraction, to rewind a few seconds. The knife began to swing again. Another touch of the screen, another swipe. Lou stared even more closely at the video this time.

Pause. Rewind. Swing.

Pause. Rewind. Swi— Pause.

There. Lou felt a chill as her suspicion was confirmed. The image on the screen was blurry—Lou had paused it just at the second Joe Christian's right hand came into shot, clutching the knife—but there was no doubt.

"What have you seen?" Helen squinted at the iPad.

"Nothing," Lou replied. She hit play again. "I mean, that's the point. There's nothing written on the back of his hand. Or at least I don't think there is. No phone number."

Helen peered closer, nose almost touching the screen. "You're right. And the number was definitely on the back of his *right* hand when you saw him? It couldn't have been his left?"

"Yes," said Lou. She tried to orientate Joe Christian in his hospital bed. "At least I'm almost certain it was."

"Which would mean . . . what? Someone else wrote the phone number on his hand after he was already unconscious?"

Lou slammed down her pen. "Maybe I'm wrong. It would help if we knew who the damn number belonged to." She was too exhausted to be sure of anything.

Helen raised a calming hand. "Don't stress about it. My researcher will figure out if the number is significant. He's terribly good."

Lou reached to touch the growing lump on the back of her head. She had washed away the last of the blood in Helen Tyler's bathroom sink and refused her offer of another ice pack, but the cut still stung like a motherfucker. "You really don't think any of this is connected to Raum or the IPO? I mean, Joe Christian aside, you can't deny Alex Wu being dead has royally fucked Elmsley Chase's plans." That was still the simplest explanation, wasn't it? That someone wanted to fuck with Raum's IPO? And that Joe Christian had somehow gotten tangled up in the plan.

Helen stared over Lou's shoulder toward the window. Then, after several seconds of silence, she suddenly met Lou's gaze. "Honestly?"

Lou let out an involuntary splutter of laughter. A Raum crisis handler promising honesty! "Sure. Why not?"

"Honestly, I would like nothing more than to believe this has something to do with Raum's IPO. I would give my eyeteeth, and whatever's left of my career, for this to have something to do with Raum's fucking IPO."

Helen set her teacup down and began pacing behind the countertop. "I'll go further than that. You and I should be on our knees praying that this has something to do with Raum's IPO. Because then at least we have the option to simply walk away. To finish our chamomile and go to bed, then wake up tomorrow and get as far away from Raum as possible."

Lou was shocked by the sudden crack in Helen's studied British reserve. "What are you saying?"

"I'm saying killing Alex Wu makes a kind of ghastly sense if you want to stop the IPO. Jump. Splat. Mission accomplished. But killing Joe Christian as well, and going to all that trouble to make sure we're there to witness it, and now this notebook, and the screaming about Amelia Christian's foundation . . . it's all too weird and all too messy. Too public. Too loud."

Lou picked up her pen again, and underlined the words *It's her charity* on the legal pad. "The charity thing feels like a red herring. Nothing about tonight feels financial or domestic or small . . . It feels somehow . . ."

"Medieval." Helen perfectly filled in the blank. "A mob informer left swinging from a bridge, or a head stuck on a pike."

"Exactly. It's like someone is sending a message. But a message to who?" Even as she asked the question, Lou could feel her throat tighten. The thought had been building over several hours, despite her best efforts to suppress it. Two scumbags whom Lou had exposed as creeps had both apparently killed themselves on the same night. Whoever was responsible had made sure that she was there to witness both deaths. Helen Tyler was silent again, her expression impassive, but surely she'd made the same connection: whatever message the killer was trying to send, he was sending it to Lou.

Eventually Helen spoke. "There is *one* connection between both of the dead men, beyond the fact that the world is better off without them."

Lou didn't need to hear it out loud. "I know. I get it. The obvious connection between everything that happened tonight . . . is me."

Helen didn't reply. She took Lou's empty cup and deposited it in the sink along with her own, then turned on the faucet and squirted dish soap onto a small yellow sponge. Lou thought back to Stephen Camp's daily rants about how nobody in the *Herald* newsroom knew how to clean a goddamned cup. "I mean," Lou continued, "everyone already thinks Alex Wu jumped because of me. When they hear about Joe Christian, they'll think that was my fault too . . ."

Helen turned from the sink, her eyebrows raised. "And why would our killer want people to think that?"

"I don't know. He's trying to show me the consequences of my reporting? Like, he's some anti-media psychopath?" He wouldn't be the first. "Or maybe the opposite. Someone with a grudge against big tech, using my stories like a hit list. Finishing the job I started."

Helen waggled her head from side to side as if weighing up the logic of Lou's argument. "Except it wasn't you who ruined their lives." She said this without emotion in her voice, as if simply stating a fact, then turned back to the sink.

"No, it . . ." Lou hesitated as she processed Helen's words. Obviously it wasn't her fault that Joe Christian had an affair with a teenage intern, or that Alex Wu was a serial sexual predator. She hadn't created the scandals that brought them down, just reported on them. But something in Helen's tone suggested a different meaning. "Then who did?"

Helen walked back to the kitchen sink, slid open a drawer, and took out what looked like a pile of playing cards. Only when she tossed them onto the countertop did Lou recognize their true purpose: a half-dozen RFID swipe cards, the kind issued to employees to gain access to their office buildings. Each bore a different logo: Raum, Sleapster, Uber, Twiddle, Dunk.ly . . . and Grintech. It was like a who's who of once-hot Silicon Valley companies.

Lou stared at the logos as their significance slowly dawned on her. "You worked at Grintech? And all these other companies?"

"And yet you've never heard of me?" Helen smiled. "That's rather the point. I told you, I'm a gun for hire. My specialty is getting rid of bad apples from inside highly valuable organizations, in the hope of making them more palatable to the public markets. If I do my job well, nobody knows I was ever there."

"Did you do your job well at Dunk.ly, or Uber?" Lou hadn't meant to sound like quite such a dick—but it was true that of all the companies represented in Helen Tyler's drawer of key cards, only Raum was still riding high. The others were either dead, sold for parts, or trading for a fraction of their IPO price. All those venture capital dollars spent trying to silence critics, cover up scandals, battle lawmakers, and for what? The founders and a few early investors might have gotten rich from their pre-IPO stock, but a rotten company is still a rotten company.

If Helen was irked by Lou's dig at her professional abilities, she didn't show it. "My job was to get them to IPO. What happens next is someone else's responsibility. The point is, Raum was not my first—as you Americans love to say—rodeo. I've ousted more CEOs than you've had hot dinners."

"Including Joe Christian?"

Helen shrugged. "After the scandal broke, the board of Grintech hoped Mr. Christian would do the noble thing and resign. Unfortunately he became obsessed with the idea he was being set up, and refused to go. You don't need me to tell you how delusional and paranoid these masters of the cyber universe can be. In any case, I was asked to produce a report for the board showing how his continued role as CEO would be ruinous to Grintech's future prospects. Your article formed a small part of that report, but if anyone could truly be described as Joe Christian's executioner, it is I. Just as, ultimately, I would have done for Alex Wu, once his successor had been appointed."

"You think someone killed Alex Wu and Joe Christian to send a message to *you*?" Just for a moment, Lou felt a weight lift.

Helen removed the cups from the sink and placed them upside down on a metal drainer. "A macabre prospect, isn't it? But an unlikely one. For one thing, it's not a very good message if neither of us can agree who it's for or what it means."

Lou gave a half smile as she took Helen's point.

Helen continued: "Much as I'd like to believe you or I are so important that someone would go to so much trouble to bring us together, I feel sure we are little more than pawns." She paused, seemingly reconsidering the metaphor. "Or perhaps a pawn and a bishop . . . or a bishop and a rook." She shook her head. "It doesn't matter. What matters is we're neither the queen nor the king."

Lou did not feel reassured by this. "It's a long time since I played chess, but don't bishops and rooks usually get taken out before the end?"

Helen nodded. "Frequently, yes. Unless they stick together."

"Which is what you think we should do? Work together to figure out who's doing this?" That's why Helen was so reluctant to let her leave.

"Safety in numbers. Two heads are better than one. Choose your preferred cliché. But, yes, I do think our interests are best served by collaboration, and full transparency, despite our natural professional distrust of one another. Call it a temporary cessation of hostilities, if you prefer. A game of football in no-man's-land."

"Transparency?" The woman who had admitted to creating a fake lawsuit to destroy Lou's career was now asking *her* to be more honest. That was . . . interesting. Still, Lou didn't have the stomach for a fight, and Helen was right about one thing—they were more likely to figure out what the hell was going on if they worked together. "OK, you start. You said your specialty is ousting CEOs. Does that mean Raum's board hired you to get rid of Elmsley Chase?" She knew the question was ridiculous—there was no way Raum's board would risk ousting such a popular CEO right before their IPO—but if she was going to trust Helen, she needed to know exactly what her deal at Raum was.

Helen didn't seem shocked at the question, though. She perched herself on the stool opposite Lou's and spoke quietly, as if she might be overheard in her own kitchen. "Officially my assignment is exactly as I told you: to help Raum clean up its act before going public."

"And unofficially?"

"Unofficially . . ." Helen paused. "There are powerful forces inside Wall Street pushing for a change of leadership at Raum before the IPO."

Lou started to interrupt—*oh, come on!*—but Helen silenced her with the slightest wave of her hand. "You asked for candor." Helen's voice dipped still lower. "For all of Raum's apparent success, the bankers know—as you do—that there are just too many scandals bubbling under the surface, too many bad apples packed into this particular grossly unprofitable and overvalued barrel. Elmsley's fanboys might excuse Raum's scandals, but the public markets are less forgiving. The bankers are terrified of the barrel bursting, the stock tanking right after the IPO. They have made these *concerns* known to the board." Helen's emphasis made clear those "concerns" were in fact holy writs from the banking gods.

"So they're going to make Elmsley a scapegoat for all the company's sins." Lou was almost impressed. She'd always thought of Tim Palgrave and the rest of Raum's board as a gaggle of spineless enablers, unwilling to stand up to Elmsley Chase. She even felt a twinge of sympathy for Chase: He was a dick, but unlike other executives at the company, he hadn't been personally implicated in any scandals. Firing him was like repainting the barrel but keeping all the rotten fruit inside.

Helen pointed to a paper calendar hanging on the kitchen wall, showing a vista of London at night. "This coming Monday, the board meets for its quarterly meeting where they're expecting me to present my findings—a report which will recommend that Elmsley be replaced with someone less *problematic*. A fresh start."

Lou shook her head. "And he has no idea the board wants him gone?"

"He thinks he *is* Raum. Can't imagine anyone would want rid of him. Or at least I thought he couldn't, until twenty-four hours ago when he surprised us all by suddenly inviting the world and his dog to Raum One to announce the IPO a month early. I suspect somebody tipped him off, and he figured it would be much harder to get rid of him if the announcement had already been made, with his face plastered all over it."

"Tipped him off? Who?"

Helen raised a finger, like a teacher congratulating a pupil who suddenly understood a math problem. "The five-hundred-billion-dollar question. As you know, there are only two people remaining on Raum's board, apart from Elmsley himself. Of the two, the most likely explanation is that Tim Palgrave was dumb enough to let something slip to Elmsley. But when I grilled him about it last night at the party, he swore his lips had remained sealed. Which only leaves an even more unlikely possibility . . ."

"Charlie Brusk?" Lou knew there was no way Brusk would have tipped Elmsley Chase off. As head of XXCubator, Silicon Valley's largest "startup incubator," Brusk had a stake in almost every successful tech startup in the past ten years. His pitch was simple: XXCubator would provide seed investment, free office space, legal advice, beer kegs, and everything else young entrepreneurs needed to get started. In return Brusk—aka the Bro Whisperer—got a big chunk of early stock and a board seat. XXCubator had invested in Raum later than normal—after the company was already operating—but still early enough to grab a hefty ownership stake for just a few hundred thousand dollars. Charlie Brusk had a lot to gain from a successful IPO, and the most to risk from Elmsley Chase fucking it up. In fact, Lou was pretty sure that when Helen said "the board" wanted rid of Chase, what she really meant was Charlie Brusk wanted him gone and had bullied Palgrave into agreeing. Unlike the dumbly loyal Palgrave, Brusk regularly ousted pre-IPO founders who he thought were doing a crappy job.

There was another reason to assume Brusk was involved in the board-room coup: his close ties with Raum's Saudi investors, in particular Prince Bansar, oldest son of King Faisal Al Saud. Until six months ear-lier, the crown prince had been Raum's fourth board member, until his father's latest human rights outrage—the public execution of two Ameri-can journalists who had written a book critical of the kingdom—had forced Raum to make a big show of firing him. Nonetheless the prince's Royal Wealth Fund remained Raum's fourth-largest shareholder, with Brusk, himself a former oil lobbyist, representing the prince's interests on the board along with his own. (Another persistent rumor was that the Saudi royal family had provided most of the capital for Brusk to establish XXCubator and fund its investments.) If Brusk wanted Elmsley gone, that meant so did the Saudis, and vice versa.

"Charlie bloody Brusk," echoed Helen. "The bane of my existence since time immemorial and, as you have surely surmised, the ringleader in this little coup. With the support of his Arab friends, obviously."

Obviously, thought Lou, while also wondering if Helen's comment was perhaps incredibly racist. And then: "What do you mean 'since time immemorial'?"

"More candor." Helen gave an awkward smile. "Charlie and I were at business school together in London, a million years ago. We . . . knew each other quite well. A tangled web." The look in Helen's eyes left no doubt about the type of relationship she was talking about.

As Lou battled her gag reflex, Helen Tyler continued unspooling her history of Charlie Brusk. "He was a shit then, and he's most definitely a shit now, so you can imagine my delight when, quite out of the blue, he telephoned me on behalf of Raum's board to ask if I was available for hire. My reputation had apparently gotten around." She tipped her head toward the pile of swipe cards, still scattered across the countertop.

"Wait." Lou kicked the base of the kitchen island in frustration that she'd been so slow. "XXCubator invested in Grintech too. Both Alex Wu and Joe Christian were involved with companies that took investment from Charlie Brusk."

Helen shrugged this off. "XXCubator invests in literally everything. Also, nothing about tonight is good news for Charlie. He hired me to get rid of Elmsley to save the IPO. Wu's death ruins all of that."

Lou gave the island another kick, harder this time. There had to be *some* connection between Wu and Christian, something ugly enough to explain the timing and brutality of their deaths. It was out there somewhere, if they just knew where to look.. . .

An idea limped its way into Lou's tired brain. "You said Brusk and the rest of the board are expecting you to deliver your report about Elmsley on Monday, right?"

Helen nodded.

"So you still have access to Raum One for at least the next five . . ." Lou looked at the digital clock on the oven, which had just blinked past midnight. ". . . four days?" It was often said that Raum's servers contained more information about the movements and habits of its users than all the combined data gathered by every other corporation and every government in all of recorded history. That was how the company's algorithm could predict with near 100 percent accuracy when you'd next be hungry, and for exactly what flavor pizza. Stephen Camp once joked that Raum was even smart enough to know not just the person you'd marry but also the person your wife would one day run off with. (Camp had been married three times.) If Helen Tyler had access to Raum's database, then surely they could find out whom Joe Christian and Alex Wu had interacted with in the weeks running up to their deaths. Somewhere in all that data must be the identity of the mysterious "Fate" and the connection, if any, with Amelia Christian's charity.

Helen gave a wry smile. "I have free run of the place. Including admin-level access to Raum's user database, which—I *suppose*—might prove useful as we try to understand what happened tonight, and I try to salvage the IPO and my job."

"Good." Lou didn't care about saving the IPO or Helen Tyler's job, but was fine with whatever justification Helen needed to use to grant them both access to Raum's data. At the *Herald*, most of her best sources had their own selfish motives for helping her. "And then I'll go see Amelia Christian to see if I can figure out the charity connection."

"Good," Helen echoed. "Might be worth taking a quick nose around in her Raum data too."

"And if we can't find a connection?"

Helen leaned toward Lou conspiratorially and then answered almost in a whisper, "Then we're both buggered, aren't we?" She threw her head back and let forth an explosion of laughter. To Lou's own surprise, she found herself laughing too, at the ridiculousness of her situation but also, somehow, from relief that she was no longer alone in the madness.

The moment of crazed camaraderie quickly passed, and Helen nodded toward the iPad. "Speaking of unpleasant business. I trust the crazies have calmed down?"

"Seems like it." Lou knew better than to use a Raum iPad to check her emails, but she'd braved a glance at her social media feeds while Helen was brewing the tea. There were still a few terrifying tweets, a death threat or three; but the contrast from just a few hours earlier was dramatic. The moment Elmsley Chase's press release defending Lou had hit the wires, Pétain's red notice had been revoked, exactly as Helen had predicted.

A nod of satisfaction. "His master's voice. And your mother?"

Lou didn't return Helen's smile. Just because the Twitter chatter had calmed down didn't mean she—or her mom—was safe: it still only took one crazy, one prank call to SWAT . . .

"Would you like to call her again? Just to check in?" Helen extended her phone toward Lou, like some eerie British mind reader.

Lou shook her head. "She'll be asleep now. I'll call her tomorrow."

Helen pocketed the handset. "Of course. We should all try to get some rest." She gestured toward the open door leading to the living room, where she'd arranged a small pile of blankets and pillows on the couch. "I'm just down the hallway if you need anything." Then, without saying good night, she was gone.

Lou sat at the kitchen counter, staring down at her notes. She was way too wired to sleep. How could she possibly rest with an invisible killer on the loose—and the whole world blaming her for the deaths? She had to figure out the connection between Wu and Christian and prove that none of this was her fault. But what more could she do tonight, bloodied, beaten, and so exhausted that her writing shimmered and danced across the page?

She moved into the living room, closing the sliding pocket door behind her, and tried to arrange the pillows and blankets into something resembling a bed. She held one of the pillows up to her cheek. Compared with a pile of T-shirts under her desk at the *Herald*, a chesterfield couch was "The Princess and the Pea"-level luxury. Somewhere down the hallway, she could hear Helen Tyler, talking loudly on the phone—although thanks to the thick oak doors of the Four Seasons, she couldn't make out any actual words.

She forced herself to turn off the table lamp and lie down. But the very instant she closed her eyes, the room was suddenly filled again with light, jolting her back upright.

"Well!"

Lou turned to see Helen Tyler standing in the doorway, wearing a Four Seasons bathrobe and a lime-green face mask, and holding her phone aloft as if its very existence were a revelation.

"That was my computer whiz," she said, sounding more like a

technophobic British grandmother than an employee of the most advanced startup on earth.

Lou nodded, still dazzled by the explosion of light. "And?"

"He was able to trace the number on Joe Christian's hand—we were right that it was a burner."

Lou hauled herself upright. "Does he know whose?"

Helen continued into the room and took her place in the armchair opposite Lou.

"The owner bought it from a drugstore in East Palo Alto, paid with cash, but my chap was able to trace it based on . . . actually I have no idea based on what. IMEI numbers or some other gobbledygook."

She slid a Four Seasons notepad across the table, and Lou saw, scribbled in pencil, the same digits she had found on Joe Christian's hand, and below them a name, double underlined and capped with an exclamation mark.

Lou's eyes widened. "Seriously?"

"Apparently so. The number belongs to your friend and mine: Charlie. Fucking. Brusk."

Well! was right.

Helen continued: "My man is still trying to get a list of calls, but he says there's no doubt the number is Charlie's. Or *was* Charlie's. It was disconnected earlier this evening."

Lou picked up the notepad and held it alongside the number still written on her palm. "So Joe Christian goes to the emergency room, stabs himself, and before he dies, he—or someone else—writes Charlie Brusk's burner phone number on the back of his hand?" A thought occurred to her as she said this. "Do you think that could be what he was saying on the video? 'Charlie'? Not 'charity'?"

Helen grimaced, then repeated the words: "Charity—Charlie—Charity—Charlie. Hardly a homonym. Also, he said 'it's her charity.' Wrong pronoun if he was saying 'it's her, Charlie.'"

Helen fetched the iPad from the kitchen and they played the video a couple more times. Whatever Joe Christian was saying, it didn't sound like "Charlie," but neither was Lou so convinced now that it was "charity."

"Can we call Brusk and ask him about it?" It was way past midnight, but Lou wasn't going to sit on anything that could be a lead.

"We can do better than that," said Helen, rising from her chair. "Tomorrow, before we see Amelia Christian, you and I will pay a visit to XXCubator and interrogate Charlie in person. Much easier to tell when someone's lying face-to-face, don't you find?"

Lou stared back at her. She hadn't actually invited Helen to come with her to Amelia Christian's. But she was also so exhausted and overwhelmed that it was possible she was already asleep and dreaming. "Sure," she managed to say. "Fine."

Helen gave a smile of what Lou could have sworn looked like excitement. "Bright and early, then," she said, and then shuffled back off toward bed.

THE PRIUS HAD been parked outside the Four Seasons for more than an hour, since tailing Lou and Helen back from the Pacific Medical Center. In all that time, nobody had given the car a second glance. Why should they? It was just one of a billion such Priuses with a vRaum sticker affixed to the front windshield trundling around San Francisco that night. There was a reason drug dealers and burglars traded vRaum placards like they were crack—the simple application of one to a vehicle allowed a driver to park anywhere, in any neighborhood, without drawing suspicion.

This particular driver was not a drug dealer, though, nor a burglar. It was safe to say that a license plate search of any local or national police database would draw a complete, and deliberate, blank.

Fate.

The driver had been amused to learn the nickname Joe Christian had given to the person who had been torturing him into a slow grave. *Fate!* That was good. A little Dan Brown, perhaps—the kind of name an author of airport thrillers might give to the clichéd Jolt-swilling super nerd that always seemed to crop up in those types of stories. A spoiled, white, trust fund brat, aggrieved at his inability to get girls and furious at his parents for cutting his allowance. Sticking it to Dad by hacking the Pentagon and starting World War III.

Fate glanced up at the rearview mirror and laughed out loud at the thought. *Yeah, not even close.*

Up in Helen Tyler's apartment, the last three rectangles of yellow light—the living room windows, Fate knew from the floor plan—clicked out for the second time that night. A few seconds later, Helen's bedroom also fell into darkness. Fate would stick around for a few more minutes, watching the front door of the building just to make sure Lou McCarthy didn't slip out to pay a late-night call to Charlie Brusk. But even if she did, Fate knew she wouldn't stray far from the Four Seasons. Not now that she'd met Helen Tyler.

For the first time in almost twenty-four hours, Fate felt completely in control again. The drama at Raum One, the run-in with Claude Pétain's dipshits on the street, the dramatic rescue—all had gone exactly to plan. Joe Christian had performed his own role in the drama with aplomb, drawing Lou McCarthy and Helen Tyler irresistibly to the Pacific Medical Center and the tantalizing clue Fate had left for them to find. Watching Lou arrive at the PMC and make her way to Christian's hospital room was deeply satisfying, but also frustrating not to know exactly what had happened next. The important thing was that Lou had found the number written on Joe Christian's hand and, with a little help, now knew to whom it belonged.

Tomorrow she and Helen would set off to grill poor old Charlie Brusk about why his secret burner number was written on a dead man's hand—and then it'd be on to the next phase.

Fate's mind lingered for just a moment on the unplanned glitch that had triggered such a frantic rush to get everything back on track: Joe Christian's performance in front of the security camera. An egotist to the last.

No use dwelling on it. Even if Lou McCarthy had figured out what he was yelling, she couldn't possibly know its significance, at least not until it was already far too late. Especially not while so distracted with worry about her mom. Fate didn't like having to drag Lou's family into this, but sometimes an emotional button had to be pushed *pour profiter les autres*.

Fate stared back up at the blackened windows. Not a creature was stirring, not even a mouse. Which meant it was time for Fate to rest too. Tomorrow was going to be a busy and dangerous day.

The thought of a comfortable bed was interrupted by the chirp of a cell phone. Fate retrieved the cheap burner handset from the Prius's glove box and read the new message. *G'day.*

Fate frowned at the absence of the customary exclamation point or smiley emoji and felt a pang of guilt. Some deceptions were harder than the others, and this one was particularly agonizing. A mark who didn't deserve to be a mark; whose entire life had already fallen apart once, and soon would again.

G'day, Fate tapped in reply. *How's your night going?*

Not good. Pretty traumatic, actually, came the response.

Shit babe I'm so sorry. Fate tapped out the words mechanically, channeling the assumed persona like a seasoned method actor. *Wanna talk about it?*

A row of dots flashed on the screen, indicating that the mark was taking his time over the reply. Fate looked once again out of the window at the dark sky, and the even darker clouds gathered around Raum One. Still the dots blinked, until finally . . .

Maybe later.

Later, thought Fate, lips tight with sadness. *If only you knew how little time we have left.*

Fate replaced the handset in the glove box, clicked the Prius into gear, and felt a slight jolt as the engine sparked noiselessly into life.

Never, never let your gun
Pointed be at anyone
Calm and steady always be
Never shoot where you can't see

LOU WAS SLAPPED awake from a nightmare by a shaft of sunlight crashing through one of Helen Tyler's floor-to-ceiling windows. In her dream, she and her mom's friend Carol were crouched in the hallway of her childhood home as Claude Pétain's mob pounded on the windows and walls. Carol had her assault rifle, taking potshots through a boarded-up window. Lou was holding a shotgun, open and unloaded, as she tried desperately to reach her mom on the phone. But every time the line connected, it was her dad's voice, not her mom's, that she heard, telling her to stay strong, that everything would be OK. Lou begged for him to help, but he just kept repeating the same words—lines from the poem that had haunted her dreams since childhood.

Never, never let your gun / Pointed be at anyone . . .

Do you hear me, Loubear? Say it back to me . . .

For those first waking seconds, Lou had no idea where she was, or on whose couch she was lying, under a woolen blanket, fully clothed except for her shoes. Gradually, the memory of the previous evening came back to her—the two dead men, the attack in the Tenderloin, the hospital visit, Joe Christian's journal, and then the phone call from Helen's technical expert, revealing that Christian had died with Charlie Brusk's number written on his hand.

Lou closed her eyes again, as if by refusing to shift from the couch, she could avoid setting foot in this terrifying new world. Her confusion and fear were soon joined by a much heavier emotion: a crushing sadness that came from knowing her life, as she knew it, was over. She would never again taste the *Herald*'s terrible newsroom coffee, or roll her eyes at another of Tommy's pun-ridden headline suggestions. There would be no more of Stephen Camp's BART commuter stories, or gym socks washed in the sink. That stupid fun-sized box of Tide—the one she'd swiped from her ex, Darya's laundry room in a fit of petulance the morning after their third, and final, date. *I need a job, Lou, and Mushu needs designers. I thought you'd be happy for me.*

Another realization. She was homeless. She'd always wondered how that happened, and now she knew. Everything she owned was still locked in a drawer under her desk.

Lou listened for signs of life inside the apartment. There were none, just the distant hum of an air-conditioning unit and the clanging and clanking of cable cars making their way up Powell Street toward Union Square.

The sunlight continued its assault. Lou was certain she had closed the curtains before going to sleep, which meant that Helen Tyler must have opened them already. She pushed herself upright and looked around the room. Helen's dossier of security-camera photographs had disappeared from the coffee table, replaced with a stack of gym clothes and a note scribbled on a small rectangle of blue notepaper.

Had to go to Raum One. Elmsley called an emergency all-hands meeting. Back before lunch, then we can visit AC and CB. Apologies! —HT

And then a rushed PS, crammed at the end of the note, along with Helen's phone number:

Hope these clothes fit, if not help yourself from the wardrobe. Have left some money on the hall table. Buy shoes.

Lou felt the note crumple between her fingers. Helen had promised to wake her so they could go to see Amelia Christian and Charlie Brusk together. Was this "emergency meeting" really a delaying tactic so Helen could do some digging of her own before confronting her old friend? Or worse, had she already set off to see Amelia Christian without her?

Lou had fallen asleep cycling through the many things about Helen that didn't add up, starting with her purported job description. If Helen really was a hotshot scandal-squasher, with a trophy drawer filled with key cards from companies she'd helped, why were all of those same companies, except for Raum, now dead or on life support? Companies died all the time in Silicon Valley, but that was an impressively bad mortality rate. A man might be allowed to fail upward so dramatically, but not a woman. And why, despite years covering Silicon Valley scandals, had Lou never even heard the name Helen Tyler before last night?

At about two a.m., she'd snuck back to the kitchen to retrieve Helen's iPad so she could stalk her on Hopsearch's people-finder tool. A search that, despite Hopsearch's millions of data sources, had revealed almost zip. No social media, no profiles on business-networking sites, no recent news stories or property records. The only hits came from an archive of British newspaper articles from the pre-Hopsearch—pre-Google, even!—era: a flurry of political stories from the mid-to-late nineties bylined to a young reporter, and later politics editor, named Helen Tyler. A profile of Britain's new transport minister; a scandal involving a parliamentary researcher; countless reports about Prime Minister Tony Blair and his relationship with George W. Bush. Each of these long-forgotten scoops was accompanied by a photo of one or more old white men in ill-fitting suits. Frustratingly, there were no photographs of the journalist herself. It made sense that Helen might have once been a reporter in London, but staying off the grid for nearly two decades was suspiciously impressive. Was it even possible?

Lou's head was starting to throb again. She didn't have to trust Helen, or know her background. Nor did she need permission from Raum's crisis manager to go see Amelia Christian or Charlie Brusk.

Lou took off her disgusting, bloodstained clothes—leaving them in a neat pile next to the couch. Then she wrestled herself into the sweatpants and sweatshirt that Helen had left on the table. They fit almost perfectly, surprisingly, given Helen was at least three inches shorter than Lou. Finally, she wedged Helen's Prada tennis shoes back on her feet and set off toward the front door, stopping only to pick up the stack of crisp new twenty-dollar bills from the hallway table.

A little over an hour later, Lou arrived in Palo Alto, and found herself standing in front of a modest, two-story house with peeling yellow paint and a terra-cotta tiled roof stained with patches of black. On her feet were a brand-new pair of slip-on sandals, bought from the Shoebasement discount store across from the Caltrain station. She had stuffed Helen Tyler's $300 sneakers into the bright orange carrier bag that, thanks to the city's plastic-bag tax, had cost her only slightly less than the bright orange sandals themselves.

Finding Amelia Christian's address had been easy enough. A couple of years earlier, right around the time Lou was reporting her story about Joe Christian's infidelity, Amelia Christian had given an interview to *Palo Alto* magazine about the family's charming new home. Lou and Tommy Paphitis had spent an entire lunch break mocking the breathless prose, which they agreed represented perfectly the kind of access journalism neither of them ever wanted to do. Lou could still remember practically every word.

Located in the fancy Crescent Park neighborhood of Palo Alto, the property is a master class in tasteful restraint—its soft yellow exterior and neocolonial fixtures, with a rickety iron gate and a gravel pathway leading up to a front door with peeling paint. The property stands in stark contrast to the rest of the small cul-de-sac, which is boldly modernist: glass walls, sharp metal edges, and smooth beech security gates, all packed tightly together as if a single unit. "Come in," Amelia Christian beams as she welcomes me into the home she

*shares with her husband, famed tech founder Joe Christian, and
their two children.*

*And that's when the trick is revealed—as Amelia Christian waltzes
me into her vast, open reception room and I see the long hallways snaking off in all directions. The modest tumbledown house is just a front.
"We own the whole street," Amelia laughs. And it's true. The Christians
have bought the entire cul-de-sac; a half-dozen houses hollowed out and
interconnected to form one palatial whole. "It was Joe's idea," Amelia
Christian says, still beaming . . .*

And so on for ten thousand more beaming, waltzing, nauseating words.

During the forty-five-minute Caltrain ride down the peninsula, Lou
had activated her new Walgreens pay-as-you-go smartphone, paid for
with the bulk of Helen's shoe money. She had tried to call her mom, but
the call went straight to voice mail. That wasn't great. *Please, God, let her
be at work and not on a plane to SFO.*

As the train neared Palo Alto, she'd texted Helen Tyler her new number,
with a quick message:

*Heading to see Amelia C as agreed, call me when your meeting is done
and we'll meet at XXCubator!*

When Helen called, she would feign a misunderstanding over the note
on the coffee table, share any relevant discoveries from Amelia Christian;
then they could go together to see Charlie Brusk. No harm, no foul!

Next, Lou had used Hopsearch maps to locate the only cul-de-sac in
Crescent Park that matched the description of Amelia Christian's house
from the article. A real-estate portal confirmed that the property had
been neither bought nor sold in the past six years. If Amelia Christian
owned this house two years ago, she still owned it now.

And yet.

As Lou stood outside the front gate, she realized that the street didn't
quite match the description she had committed to memory from the

article. The tumbledown house was still there, still with its little iron gate and *aww shucks* charm. In any other city in America, it could have been described as "modest"—in Palo Alto, this kind of modesty starts at around $10 million, assuming you can find anyone willing to sell it. The adjacent modern homes were still there too—the ones Joe and Amelia Christian had bought and gutted to store their art collection, and as a garage for Joe's menagerie of high-performance cars. But where the article had described those other houses as identical, Lou saw that each of them was now slightly different: some had well-manicured lawns, others paved driveways filled with BMWs and Teslas. Most had mailboxes abutting the front curb.

As Lou was still taking this all in, a young woman emerged from one of the modernist houses, cradling a crying baby in a fabric sling. She gave Lou a polite smile as she strapped the baby into a car seat in her white gull-wing Tesla and drove away. That confirmed it. All these properties that had once formed part of Joe and Amelia Christian's sprawling estate had been resold as separate homes.

Lou was not looking forward to seeing Amelia Christian. She thought about the last (and only) time they'd spoken, outside the San Francisco courthouse where Amelia's divorce petition was being heard. Or rather Amelia Christian had spoken: a quiet *bitch* hissed in Lou's direction before she disappeared into a black vRaum.

Hakuna matata. Lou removed Joe Christian's black notebook from her pocket and reaffixed the "Amelia" Post-it note to the cover. Her game plan was a simple quid pro quo: give the book to Amelia Christian, and hope in return she'd at least answer a few questions about her husband and her charity. *Hi, Amelia, remember me? Any idea why your husband killed himself while screaming about your foundation? Oh, here's a loony notebook.* How could it possibly fail?

Lou gave the front gate a push, and it responded with a piercing squeak. Next came equally loud crunching as she trudged her way down the gravel pathway in her new plastic shoes. This was not a house you could sneak up on. The doorbell was an old-fashioned wrought iron pull chain, which gave far more resistance than Lou had expected, so she ended up ringing it twice; once with a feeble *ting*, and the second time with a *clang* loud enough to summon monks to prayer. Then she waited, listening for the sound of footsteps and wondering if Amelia Christian had already watched her approach on the security camera she now spotted above the door.

There were no footsteps. Instead, Lou was startled by the sudden click of a latch and the wooden door swinging open to reveal Amelia Christian, dressed in spandex workout pants and a baggy blue sweatshirt, which— Lou was pretty sure—was the exact same brand as the one Helen had loaned her. Her blond hair—longer than in the headshot on her foundation's website—was held back from her (noticeably more lined) face with a pink-and-yellow floral headband.

"You have thirty seconds to get off my property." Lou waited for the "or," but Amelia Christian just stood silent and staring, beaming pure hatred from her piercing green eyes. Eyes that, Lou now saw, had recently been crying.

So what now? Apologize for their encounter at the courthouse (but not for exposing the woman's husband as a predator)? Wasn't Amelia as much of a victim as anyone else tied up in her husband's bullshit? Maybe, but Lou had nothing to be sorry for. She extended her hand, holding out Joe Christian's notebook. "I came to give you this."

She saw Amelia Christian glance at the Post-it bearing her name, and waited for a reaction—perhaps even a flicker of recognition that might suggest she had seen the book before. But all Lou saw in her green eyes was blank incomprehension—a look that only deepened as Amelia flipped open the book and began to leaf through the pages. Once she reached the final page, and still holding the notebook, she slammed the door.

Well played, Lou.

A few seconds later, the door swung open again. "Where did you get this?"

"I'm sorry," said Lou, still not quite sure what she was apologizing for. "Your ex-husband left it, at the hospital—"

Amelia Christian didn't let her finish. "You were with Joe last night?"

Lou apologized again. It was fast becoming a verbal tic. "I got a tip saying someone had shown up at the emergency room, waving a knife." That was mostly true, although Lou heard how callous the words sounded as she said them.

Fortunately, Amelia seemed more interested in the book than how Lou came to obtain it. "And you brought it to me, why?"

Because your name is written on a Post-it note on the cover?

No.

Because I need you to let me into your house so I can ask you about your charitable foundation, and your dead husband?

No.

Because I already photographed the contents using my shitty new camera phone, so I don't need it anymore?

Definitely not.

Because I need someone to tell me I'm not going fucking crazy. Because I need you to explain why your sleazeball ex-husband dragged me into this mess?

"I'm not—"

"I know why," Amelia interrupted again. "Because you're chasing a story. Because that's all my family has ever been to you. A story. A headline. A tip. A few meaningless clicks and never mind who you hurt, or who ends up dead, or ruined. You think if you bring me Joe's notebook, I'll give you a quote about his suicide. It's not enough that my sons' father is dead—you just have to keep hounding us until we have nothing left."

Nothing left? Lou glanced over Amelia Christian's shoulder at the cantilevered ceiling and the priceless art hanging on the walls of the entrance lobby. The quickest possible flick of her eyes, but still not quick enough . . .

"Oh don't you dare judge me," Amelia Christian snapped. "Yes, the children and I got to keep *part* of our home, and a small amount of their trust fund. Which is lucky because it barely pays for half of the cost of their private tutor. And before you judge them for that too, do you want to know why they have a private tutor?"

Lou decided it was best to remain silent.

"Because," Amelia Christian continued, "after you published your *article*, and Joe was fired, the bullying—the taunting, the name-calling—it all became so bad that our seven-year-old son started wetting the bed." She dropped her voice on those last three words and Lou wondered if the son might be home right now. "Seven years old," Amelia repeated.

"I'm . . ." Lou was about to apologize yet again, but stopped herself. She wasn't sorry for doing her job, but neither could she find the nuance to express her genuine sympathy for a seven-year-old child being so traumatized by the news that his father was a cheating scumbag that he lost control of his bladder. She *was* sorry for that. Sorry too that Amelia Christian had borne the brunt of being a single parent, while Joe Christian—selfish asshole till the end—had just up and abandoned all his responsibilities as he spiraled toward a slow death. Ah, there it was. The words she was looking for:

"I truly am sorry for what you've been through," she said. "For what it's worth, my dad left when I was a kid. He moved to South Carolina with my elementary school teacher. The whole town still blamed my mom for the divorce."

"Where is he now?"

"My dad? Westview Cemetery in Atlanta."

"I'm sorry. That must have been tough on your mother."

Lou shrugged. "She's better off without him." The words almost stuck in her throat. She didn't mean to sound so callous to someone whose own shitty husband had just killed himself. She remembered how her mom had still grieved her dad, even after all those years.

Amelia, who had seemed to be listening, had now turned her back and was walking into the house's open-plan living room. Was this her way of telling Lou the conversation was over? She didn't seem the kind of woman to be indirect or passive-aggressive. So Lou took a chance and stepped through the doorway, across the hall, and down two small steps that led to the living room. The room was empty, and Lou was briefly baffled, until she noticed the set of patio doors leading out to the backyard.

Lou found Amelia sitting on an L-shaped lawn couch, which looked like plastic but Lou suspected was probably some kind of rare fiber, custom made by one of those hideously expensive stores with a name like Design Within Reach or Luxury for the People. The rest of the yard was huge and overgrown, and dominated by an empty swimming pool partly covered with a blue tarp. Amelia sat with her legs pulled under her, still flipping through the notebook. As Lou approached, she looked up, shielding her eyes from the sun. "Do you understand what this is?"

Lou confirmed she did not.

"He called me—Joe did—for months after we divorced. Every night, sometimes more than fifty times. If I answered, he'd go on these crazy rants. Insane stuff about fate and justice and how he was the victim of some grand conspiracy. The affair. Him never showing up to therapy. The drugs. Losing all his other houses, and the cars. For months he was convinced I'd plotted the whole thing with Bella—that was the girl he . . ." She glanced back toward the house, then lowered her voice. "You know who Bella is."

"Plotted? You mean with your foundation?" Lou seized the opening to ask about the charity, and test her theory that "Fate" might be someone Joe had harassed, or worse.

But Amelia seemed confused by the question. "We gave support and counseling to victims of sexual assault. Bella didn't need that kind of help." She glanced down again at the notebook. "Joe thought Grintech's investors had paid her to put all the blame for their affair on him so they could fire him."

"Did he say which investor?" The yard was bathed in midmorning warmth, but still Lou felt herself getting goose bumps. If Joe Christian blamed Charlie Brusk for his downfall, then maybe that was the relevance of the phone number? It didn't explain the charity connection—but it was something.

Amelia Christian shook her head. "Joe said a lot of crazy things. I had to change my cell phone number, disable my voice mail, tell the kids not to open any packages, but still he always managed to find me. My therapist said it was classic narcissistic personality disorder; told me he was having a breakdown, and that the best thing I could do for him was cut off all contact."

She flipped more pages of the book, tears now flowing down her cheeks. "It made sense. The last few times he called, he sounded more unhinged than ever. Said he finally understood I had nothing to do with his downfall. That's when he moved on to the theory that someone—or something—was sabotaging his entire life, trying to destroy him. Some days it was karma or the universe . . ."

Fate.

". . . but other times it was some person, or a group of people. Said they knew his every move, and how to hurt him while making it look like an accident. He begged me to help him. I told him if he kept harassing us, I'd call the cops. Finally one night I threw my cell phone in the trash compactor."

She slapped the notebook closed and gripped it with both hands, the light glinting off her gold plastic Raum Band. "But it's all here, isn't it? Everything he told me but I didn't believe. This journal is his way of proving that he was telling the truth, about the whole conspiracy."

"Proving it how?" Just because Joe Christian had written his crazy paranoid fantasies in a journal didn't make them any more true. Was Amelia Christian so desperate to believe that her shit of a husband was really a victim?

"This was Joe's specialty—his gift." Amelia held up the book again, opening it to a random spread of pages, covered in her husband's handwriting. "I saw him make lists like this before—of cause and effect, knowing how to identify bad actors no matter how well hidden they are. He could see patterns where no one else could. That's how he made Grintech's payment platform so good at detecting fraud." She paused, seemingly lost in a memory of the man she fell in love with. "That's what this is . . . This is his proof . . . But I didn't believe him, and now . . ." She collapsed into deep, horrible sobs.

Lou was still looming over Amelia, or so she felt: her shadow spreading across the chair and onto the wooden fence behind. She perched herself down on the other end of the L-shaped chair, and felt its plastic legs sink slightly into the grass.

"I'm so sorry," said Lou, and meant it. Joe Christian was a cheating sociopath, but for whatever reason, this woman had loved him, just as Lou's mom had loved her dad no matter how cruelly he'd treated her. But Amelia didn't seem to hear her, just kept sobbing and sobbing.

Suddenly she spoke again. "How old were you?" It took Lou a moment to connect the question to her story about her mom.

"Ten."

"Do you wish they'd stayed together?"

"You mean, do I wish my mom had never found out, or that she'd stayed with someone she knew was cheating on her?"

"Either, I suppose," said Amelia.

"It was me who told her."

"Jesus," said Amelia, shaking her head, and almost smiling. "A born journalist. The truth no matter what the cost."

"A born something," Lou said, with a frown. And, for a fleeting second, she considered telling Amelia the rest of the story. Her ten-year-old hands struggling to hold her father's shotgun, screaming at him to get out while her mom begged her to stop. And all the lies she'd told afterward: how she'd done it to protect her mom, because she was scared of what he might do to them, how she didn't even know how to fire a gun. A born journalist? A born fucking liar. But then from across the lawn came a child's cry—a long pained *Mommm!*—and Lou turned to see a young boy of maybe seven or eight bounding through the patio doors, pursued by a harried-looking Asian woman in T-shirt and jeans. "Linus!" the woman called after the fleeing child.

Amelia was already on her feet. She raced across the lawn to meet her son and scooped him into her arms. He was tall—at least half his mom's size—but Amelia showed no strain in lifting him as he wrapped his arms around her shoulders and squeezed as tightly as he could. "It's OK," she said, first to the child, and then over his shoulder to the young woman still in pursuit. "It's OK."

"I couldn't find you," Linus sobbed, face nuzzled deep into his mother's blond hair. "You weren't where you said."

"I'm right here," said Amelia. "I'm just talking to my friend until you finish your class." She kissed the side of his head. "I'm not going anywhere, I promise. I'll always be here." She said it so sincerely that Linus stopped crying and allowed himself to be lowered back to the ground.

The other woman—a nanny? a home-school teacher?—had made it across the yard and took his hand. "I'll come see you when we're done," Amelia said as Linus was led, still gently sniffling, back toward the house.

Amelia Christian watched them go, then turned back to Lou. "It's hard," she said.

Lou nodded. "He's lucky to have you."

Amelia didn't respond to this and for a second or two, they sat in silence, except for the distant bark of a neighborhood dog. There was no easy way to segue back to their conversation.

"How is your foundation going, by the way?" Lou tried to make the question sound like small talk. "You mentioned it in the past tense before."

"Why do you keep asking about that?" Amelia narrowed her eyes again, this time not against the sun. Lou was back to playing ghoulish journalist, looking for scandal inside an anti-rape charity.

Lou feigned shock. "At the hospital, Joe was yelling about it. I assumed someone had told you." Another lie—so far as Lou knew, only she and Helen had connected Joe Christian's dying rant with the Amelia Christian Foundation.

Amelia bowed her head and Lou thought she might break down again. Instead she let out a loud, bitter laugh. "He was furious when he heard that's how I'd spent the divorce settlement. Like I'd done it just to spite him; how dare I use a rich man's money to help vulnerable women? He and his friends made sure we could never raise another dime."

Lou felt the goose bumps return. "His friends at Grintech? You mean investors, the board?" Lou stopped herself from saying Brusk's name.

But Amelia Christian still wouldn't bite. "I don't mean any one person. It's all a giant boys' club. They silenced me, just like they silenced Bella, just like they silence everyone. I mean, you don't need me to tell you that . . ."

Lou's cheeks flushed. Like the rest of the world, Amelia Christian must have seen Lou's televised humiliation at Raum One the previous night.

"When you say they silenced Bella, you mean they paid her off?" Lou thought back to her long-held theory that Raum had a slush fund for paying off victims. Maybe Grintech had one too.

Amelia dismissed the idea. "Nobody paid that girl a dime. I know because it was me who pleaded with the board to give her something. She was nineteen years old and Joe was forty-two. He destroyed her life. But they refused. I'm telling you: they hate women."

Lou didn't know how to process this. If Brusk and the rest of the Grintech board didn't buy Bella's silence, then why wouldn't she talk to the press? Or sue? She could have made a fortune. Lou was so puzzled by this that she almost didn't register what Amelia said next.

"I guess I should be grateful that they at least pay half of Nikola and Linus's tuition." She nodded toward the house.

Lou raised her palm. "Wait, Grintech still pays for your sons' home-school tutor?" The same people who sabotaged her charitable foundation and refused compensation to her husband's victim were still helping pay her bills?

"You can't tell anyone, OK?" Amelia looked briefly terrified until Lou nodded her assent. Was there anyone in this town who *hadn't* signed an NDA? "The payments started after Joe was fired, wired every month from some offshore account."

"Like a Swiss bank?"

Amelia shrugged. "Mauritius, I think. Honestly I don't care if Joe arranged it, or if it's meant as hush money, so long as it keeps arriving. I work at a wedding-dress shop in Redwood City. I get paid eighteen dollars an hour, which is almost enough to put food on the table. The monthly payments and the kids' trust fund covers everything else." She anticipated Lou's next question. "Joe cashed in his life insurance policy a long time ago, so that's all we'll ever get now."

Lou heard another shout from inside the house, either a whoop of joy or a yelp of pain. It was time to leave Amelia with her grief, her sons, and her husband's notebook. She had more than enough other leads to follow up, not least this mysterious offshore bank account. But as she stood, she realized she still hadn't mentioned Joe Christian's weird gate-crash of the Raum party right before he died.

"Can I ask you about one more thing? Before Joe went to the hospital, he went to Raum One. I think to see Alex Wu . . ."

Amelia gave a loud gasp. "Alex Wu committed suicide, didn't he? You don't think Joe had anything to do with it?"

Lou regretted the clumsy way she'd delivered this bombshell. "No, no, I've seen the security footage and nobody was close to Wu when he jumped . . . I just thought, given what you told me about the notebook, maybe he could have been targeted by the same person who was victimizing your ex-husband. Maybe Joe was trying to warn him?" She perched herself back on the edge of the lawn seat.

"Warn him?" Amelia's eyes were wide. "Christ, if Joe found out someone was trying to kill Alex Wu, he'd have probably offered to help." She clamped her hand over her mouth. "God, that sounds terrible, doesn't it? I just mean . . . the truth is my ex-husband *hated* Alex Wu. Despised him." She paused. "You ever see that *Wired* cover with Wu on it?"

Lou nodded and rolled her eyes in a single fluid movement. The image was iconic in its awfulness—Alex Wu splayed out like da Vinci's Vitruvian Man, surrounded by bullshit fake computer code and the tagline "Wu Dares, Wins."

"Exactly. When Joe saw that, he tore the cover off and threw it in the fire pit." She tilted her thumb toward an upturned metal bowl on the other side of the yard, half-covered by a hedge.

"Wow. Why did he hate him so much?" There were twenty thousand reasons to hate a man like Alex Wu, but he tended to enjoy unwavering support from the kind of spoiled white tech bros who subscribed to *Wired* and had fire pits on which to throw copies of it.

"No clue. I just know it went back years to when they were both in college."

Lou did a mental double take. "Your ex-husband and Alex Wu were at college together?"

That definitely wasn't right. Lou made it her business to know where tech founders had gone to school—there's no better way to understand Silicon Valley than to trace the path from feeder schools like Stanford through incubators like XXCubator, all the way to the Nasdaq. Alex Wu's Stanford days were part of Silicon Valley legend: how Alex and his roommate, Tenrick Wheeler, had built what became the Raum algorithm as part of a student hackathon contest, the main judge of which happened to be a third-tier startup founder named Elmsley Chase, whose struggling "lifesharing" company, then called Lebensraum, was famous only for its jaw-droppingly tone-deaf name and its founder's earth-shattering self-regard. Two months later, Chase acquired Wu and Wheeler's algorithm for $5 million—basically every penny the company had left—appointed Wu as CTO, and rebranded his company as Raum, and the rest was . . . well, the biggest and most successful private company in Silicon Valley history. Without Alex Wu, Ten Wheeler, and that startup contest, there would be no Raum.

Joe Christian, on the other hand, graduated from MIT, all the way across the country in Boston. A capable student, but not particularly remarkable until he was suddenly invited by Charlie Brusk to take part in XXCubator's yearlong "entrepreneurial boot camp." It was during that year that Christian conceived the idea for a company that would bring "financial independence" to poor people halfway across the world. Alex Wu and Joe Christian may have crossed paths at XXCubator, but they were definitely not at college together.

"I might be wrong about all this." Amelia seemed suddenly unsure of herself. "I just know Joe hated Alex Wu for a very long time."

"So you've no idea why he went to Raum One last night?"

Amelia shrugged. "Maybe he wanted to fix whatever beef he had with Alex Wu. Some people do that, don't they? At the end?"

Before Lou could respond, a series of shrill beeps filled the air. They jumped in unison and Lou muttered an apology as she pulled out her new pay-and-go phone to silence it. She glanced at the screen and froze as she saw the phone number above the new-text alert. The same number she had found on the back of Joe Christian's hand. The apparently disconnected number belonging to Charlie Brusk.

She clicked on the alert and the full message appeared: five words, all equally terrifying and entitled.

Come to XXCubator HQ asap—CB

Lou tucked the phone back into her pocket and turned back to Amelia. "I'm sorry—it's my mom. She's worried about me."

Amelia gave a sympathetic smile. "I'd be worried too. Elmsley Chase is such an asshole."

Lou stood up from the chair. "I'm so sorry again for your loss."

Amelia stood too. She extended her hand, holding out her ex-husband's journal. "Here, take this."

Lou shook her head. "He wanted you to have it."

Amelia Christian held the book out even farther toward Lou. "Joe wanted lots of things. You were able to figure out his secrets before—now I need you to do it again. My children deserve to know the whole truth about their father."

Lou flashed back to the video of Joe Christian screaming about his wife's foundation before thrusting a knife into his own neck. She knew as well as anyone that there were plenty of things kids didn't need to know about their dads.

As Lou set off back down the cul-de-sac toward the main road, she dropped the journal into the plastic bag containing Helen's shoes. Then she looked again at the bizarre text from Charlie Brusk. No doubt it was his number, although she had no idea how and why Brusk might be using it to summon her to XXCubator.

Unless. The only person who had Lou's new number was Helen. She must have called Brusk, told him what they'd found on Joe Christian's hand, and warned him to expect a visit. This was Brusk's, and Helen's, way of retaking control of the situation.

Lou scrolled to the address book and clicked on the sole entry, which she'd labeled *Helen T.* She held the phone to her ear and waited for the ringtone.

Silence.

She went through the irritating phone-book process for a second time, impressed at how terrible the user experience of a sixty-dollar phone could be. Again the call disconnected without ringing even once.

She swore loudly at the device and tossed it into the bag along with the notebook and shoes. XXCubator was only twenty minutes away on foot, and hopefully Helen would be waiting for her when she arrived.

Lou's fight with technology kept her distracted enough that she didn't pay any attention to the dark-colored car idling directly across from Amelia Christian's house. It had arrived about a half hour before Lou, so had been parked there for almost two hours. Yet not a single neighbor spotted it, nor thought it suspicious. Lou barely registered its existence, nor did she recognize a familiar face sitting behind the wheel, watching her go.

Fate watched as Lou reached the end of the cul-de-sac and paused, just for a moment; a moment that stretched into a lifetime as she seemed to debate whether to turn left toward the Caltrain or right toward downtown Palo Alto.

What should have been the simplest part of the plan—to get Lou McCarthy, Helen Tyler, and Charlie Brusk in the same room—was becoming an epic pain in the ass. The burner number written on Joe Christian's hand was supposed to have sent Lou and Helen running straight to XXCubator. That was all Fate needed to set in motion the next phase, without either of them getting anywhere close to Amelia fucking Christian.

Instead Fate had watched in frustration that morning as Helen set off for a meeting with Elmsley Chase at Raum One, leaving Lou to head in a far more dangerous direction. How much did Amelia Christian know about that night, so long ago, when her ex-husband made the unforgivable decision that a decade later would lead to his suicide? Fate had had to work fast, allowing for the two possible outcomes: that Amelia Christian would tell Lou nothing useful, and that she would tell her everything. Fate wouldn't know which option was playing out until Lou arrived at XXCubator.

And now there was this new development. The small black notebook that Lou had handed to Amelia Christian and which seemed to grant her instant access to the house? What the fuck was that?

There was only one logical answer: the book belonged to Joe Christian, and Lou had found it in his hospital room when she went snooping. This was beyond a worst-case scenario. Given Joe's love of data and logs and flowcharts, Fate had worried about the existence of a journal and had searched the hospital room and Christian's SRO thoroughly. There had been no notebook. And yet there it was: an atom bomb possibly capable of destroying years of work, dropped casually into an orange plastic carrier bag.

I have to get that bag.

Fate stared into the rearview mirror, where she could see Lou still hesitating at the end of the road. The text message from Charlie Brusk had been a risk, but surely it was worth it. Women, Fate thought with some satisfaction, were infinitely harder to predict or manipulate than men. Which was the whole point.

40%

ANY UNSUSPECTING TOURIST visiting downtown Palo Alto would be forgiven for mistaking the imposing, art deco building capping the south end of University Avenue for a crumbling old hotel. Not least because 102 University Avenue *was* a crumbling art deco hotel: the formerly resplendent Royale Court, built in 1924 and once the jewel of the South Bay.

But if that tourist were more eagle-eyed, they might notice the tall neon signage jutting from the building no longer advertised the Royale Court, but had been refashioned to blink first the letters xx, and then CUBATOR, in lurid red neon. At which point, our tourist might be forgiven for mistaking Silicon Valley's biggest startup incubator for a multistory strip club.

Lou stared up at the sign, then scanned her eyes across the upper-floor windows: at the strings of drying T-shirts and hoodies, and the faded "Feel the Bern" and "Musk/Rogan 2024" campaign stickers affixed by the hundred or so young entrepreneurs and early-stage employees living rent-free inside, packed ten to a room. She hated this building, and everything it represented: a factory farm for privileged white adolescents, churning out "disruptive" startups by the score, including both Freestreem and Mailpile, the "free speech" platforms Claude Pétain used to spread his hate.

Lou had walked the perimeter of the building and found no sign of Helen Tyler, leaving her with a dilemma of whether to wait or to gamble that Helen was already inside. She decided to wait another five minutes as she mentally rehearsed what she'd say to Brusk. She would start by asking him about the burner phone, making clear that she didn't care about his private business affairs, or any other kind of affairs. She was interested only in why the number was written on Joe Christian's hand when he died. Depending on how he responded to that, she'd try to find a segue into mentioning Amelia Christian, her foundation, and the secret payments she received from an offshore account each month. If Lou could find some link between Brusk, the payments, and Amelia Christian's charity, surely that would also have to point toward the identity of the mysterious Fate.

As she made her way back to the front of the building, Lou thought about Stephen Camp's favorite rule of confronting a hostile source. Never ask a question you don't already know the answer to. Here she was about to confront Charlie Brusk—a man who regularly sued reporters who crossed him, and bragged that he'd invested in Mailpile and Freestreem to combat "the dishonest media"—and not only did she not know the answers to any of her questions; she barely knew the questions. What would Camp say if he were here? "You're fired," probably.

Tough shit, Stephen, you can't fire me twice.

Her palms suddenly clammy, Lou stepped through a set of revolving doors into the tin-ceilinged, marble-floored lobby.

"Not a hotel!" Behind the polished mahogany reception desk of the otherwise empty lobby, a teenager in a gray XXCubator T-shirt eyed Lou with studied disdain. For all the data proving that female founders outperformed (and outreturned) their male peers, women were still viewed with suspicion inside startup incubators, especially women who didn't appear to be cleaners, lawyers, RaumService delivery workers, or trophy girlfriends. Lou was clutching neither a mop, a briefcase, a pizza, nor a tiny dog.

"There's a hostel two blocks further down," the teen added, confirming he'd pegged Lou for a backpacker, despite her lack of backpack. Then again, Lou detected something slightly performative—practiced, almost—about the way he said it.

Lou smiled a tight, patient smile; the type of smile she imagined Helen Tyler would give in this situation. "Lou McCarthy. Here to see Charlie Brusk." God, was she actually doing the accent?

"Charlie's not available." The teen shook his head, while still avoiding eye contact.

Lou maintained her smile as she marched up to the desk, waving her phone in the air. "I think Helen Tyler might be joining us too?"

The teen cut her off. "You need to use the contact form on our website." He slid a shiny white postcard across the desk, bearing the nonsensical URL XXCubator.ly.

Lou held his gaze and slid it back again. "Please tell Charlie I got his text and I'm here to talk to him about the death of Joe Christian." *The death of Joe Christian.* Spoken out loud, the words sounded strangely formal, like the title of a Russian play, or a Netflix original.

The teen gave no outward signs of recognizing Joe Christian's name but, perhaps unsettled by the confidence with which Lou said it, sullenly picked up his iPhone and tapped out a message. A few seconds later, he received a reply that, judging by the way his eyebrows spiked upward, surprised him as much as it did Lou.

"Elevator two, sixth floor, end of the hallway, glass door," he stammered. "You can go right in." As Lou walked toward the elevator, she heard him mutter a quiet "Shit."

"I don't know what else to tell you. I have no idea why you're here or what you're talking about."

Whatever Lou had expected Charlie Brusk to say, she hadn't expected that.

Brusk sat with his fat white sneakers resting on his large wooden desk, which had been constructed from a thick oak door balanced on two roughly sanded trestles.

His blond hair flopped louchely over his tanned forehead. As he reached up to brush it away from his eyes, Lou noticed he wore a chunky gold watch that likely cost more than a sports car. On the same wrist he had a variety of colored bracelets and VIP passes for music festivals and sporting events. Even in his early fifties, Brusk retained a boyishness that—were it not for the tiny Medusa logo on his otherwise unremarkable black T-shirt and that watch and those $1,000 shoes on his feet—might almost allow him to pass for one of his own portfolio founders. Aside from the sneakers, the only items on the desk were an iPhone and two industrial-sized bottles of hand sanitizer. Brusk was famously germophobic, since long before it was fashionable.

Lou sat six feet away, on a beanbag, still wearing her borrowed clothes and plastic shoes. A study in income inequality. She held up her new phone, the screen pointed toward Brusk. "You're saying you didn't text me? This isn't your number?"

Brusk gave an exaggerated sigh, his palms raised skyward as if in despair at Lou's relentless idiocy. "Should I try speaking a different language?"

Lou knew she had no choice but to brazen out the conversation. "And you also don't know why this same number was written on Joe Christian's hand last night when he died?" She read out the digits directly from the scrap of Four Seasons notepaper she pulled from her pocket. "You don't deny that you knew Joe Christian?"

This at least did get a reaction, though not the one Lou was hoping for. Brusk's eyes widened in a caricature of bemusement. "Why would I deny it? He was one of our portfolio founders. Look. I really can't help you. I agreed to see you because my front-desk associate said you had some news about Joe's tragic death. For all of his problems, Joe was still a member of the XXCubator family. I'd like to help, but . . ." Brusk shifted in his seat as if he was about to stand, but didn't actually get up.

Lou was suddenly aware she was grinding her back teeth. Not because Brusk was lying, but because he was doing it so badly. Even if the phone number really didn't belong to him, and the text—signed *CB*—came from someone else, there was *still* no way he'd have invited her up just because she wandered into the lobby and mentioned Joe Christian's name. So why all this gaslighting bullshit? It was like he was goading her—waiting for her to give the secret password that would unlock whatever it was he wanted to tell her.

She leaned forward in her beanbag, doing her own impression of someone about to leave. "You know what? I'm sorry to have wasted your time. It's just . . . Joe Christian indicated you might know why someone wanted him dead, so I figured I should ask you before I pass the information on to the cops. I'm meeting with them this afternoon, as a witness." *Now,* that *is how you tell a lie, you smug prick.*

"Wait, whoa, hold on now!" Brusk pulled his feet off the desk and planted them firmly on the floor. Then he leaned across the desk toward Lou, his eyes wide: "Joe told you *I* knew someone wanted him dead? I thought he killed himself?" His facial expression flickered as he realized the obvious follow-up question. "Also, why are *you* a witness?"

Lou raised a hand. She'd waaay overreached, but at least Brusk was talking. "He wasn't making much sense at the end. I arrived after it had all happened. All I know is that he wrote your phone number on his hand in a way that made sure it would be seen." She paused, but Brusk remained silent, staring. "Also, he went to Raum One—was he looking for you?"

Brusk's face contorted into a frown. "At Raum One? . . . You mean when Alex . . ." He massaged his forehead with the tips of his fingers. "Christ."

"You didn't see him?" Lou hadn't seen Brusk at the party—which wasn't surprising given the man's reputation as a virtual recluse.

"No," said Brusk firmly. "I wasn't at the party. I always try to support Elmsley and Raum, but . . . well . . . since you ask, at the time hell was breaking loose at Raum One, I was stuck in traffic on the 280 thanks to my Tesla's piece-of-shit GPS."

"Seriously?" Lou hadn't meant to say that out loud—but it was an oddly specific detail for Brusk to have shared. He didn't owe her an explanation for his absence at the party, and yet seemed very keen to offer one. That was something else she knew from the *Herald*: the more specific, irrelevant details a source includes in his story, the more likely it's all bullshit.

"Look." Brusk put his palms on his desk, again telegraphing he was ready to end the meeting. "I'm sorry I can't be more help. I understand as a journalist you want there to be a scandal—I'm sure two of our alumni dying on the same night will be great for the conspiracy freaks. But the fact is more than eleven thousand founders have passed through our doors, so two suicides isn't statistically significant. You can look up the data yourself." He paused. "I'm sure you think that sounds callous. It's just I prefer to feel emotions, but speak in facts."

Lou felt her pulse quicken. "Feel emotions, but speak in facts" was an almost-verbatim quote from one of Claude Pétain's awful self-published how-to-be-a-sociopath e-books. A book that Lou had forced herself to read as research for a story about online hate.

"This is all very distressing for us all—Alex had a lot of friends at XXCubator. Joe . . . less so, by the end."

"He had kids, and an ex-wife." Lou studied Charlie Brusk's face carefully as she added, "Amelia?" If she was about to get thrown out of Brusk's office, she needed to see if he reacted to the name.

He did not.

Brusk sighed deeply, his face slowly transforming into a perfect facsimile of genuine grief. "So very distressing. Emotionally speaking."

Lou was tired of playing around with this asshole. Joe Christian had died ranting about his wife's charity, with Brusk's burner number on his hand, for a reason. Almost certainly the same reason she'd been attacked on the street and her mom had been forced into hiding. "Do you know anything about Amelia Christian's charity and their work with sexual-assault victims?"

Brusk froze, then slumped back in his chair. "Why do you ask about that?"

Bull's-eye!

"Something else Joe Christian said before he died. Right before he wrote your number on his hand, he was yelling about the Amelia Christian Foundation."

Brusk was trying to recover his composure, and failing badly. His right hand had gone straight to his forehead, while the fingertips of his left were drumming on the desk. "Have you asked his wife about it?"

Lou held his gaze. "Ex-wife. And I'm asking you."

Brusk stayed silent for an uncomfortably long time, but then did something that Lou hadn't expected. He slapped the desk so hard the entire room shook, and then burst into booming, angry laughter. "You want to know what I think? My deep fucking insight? What I think is that Joe Christian is—sorry, was—a certifiable fucking nutjob. A nutjob who has been calling me nonstop for the past two weeks. On my cell—my *actual* cell—in my office, even at my homes. BIANCA!"

That last word was screamed over Lou's shoulder. Almost immediately the office door clicked open, and a tall, auburn-haired assistant appeared, dressed head to toe in purple pastel and holding a matching lavender iPhone. It was a lot of look, but she pulled it off.

"Bianca," Brusk continued, "how many messages has Joe Christian left for me this week?"

Bianca tapped at the screen of her phone. "Eighty-four. Sixty-three voice mails, and twenty-one emails before you told me to block his number."

"And what did he say in all of them?"

For this, Bianca apparently didn't need to check her phone. "He said someone was trying to destroy you. But that he could help, if you agreed to meet him. He sent calendar invites."

"Anything else?"

Bianca thought for a moment. "He said XXCubator was part of a Silicon Valley death cult, and that you were in league with the NSA, Digital Openness Group, Amnesty International, and . . . I don't remember the others, but I wrote them down when he called."

"Did he mention the Amelia Christian Foundation?" Lou asked the question more out of completeness than in the hope of getting a useful answer.

"I'm pretty sure. I can fetch the list?" Bianca directed this question to her boss, but Brusk waved her away.

"No, thank you, Bianca." So Bianca was gone.

Brusk was on his feet too, marching toward the door, which he held open to make clear the meeting was definitely over now. "Again, I'm sorry I couldn't be more help, to you or to Joe. Please let Bianca know if there's anything more you need." He reached out and gripped Lou's hand with both of his, and pulled her so close she could smell his disgusting cologne. He was still waffling about how sad he was about Alex Wu's death, and the tragic lack of mental health resources available to people like Joe Christian.

But Lou couldn't concentrate on the words coming out of Brusk's mouth. Instead she was staring a few inches higher, at his forehead, which she was now able to see up close for the first time. *Oh my God.* She snatched her hand from Brusk's grip as she registered the faint red blotches running across his hairline. The rash wasn't anywhere near as severe as the one she'd seen covering Joe Christian's body, but there was no mistaking the same mottled bumps, which Brusk had tried to hide by letting his hair fall down over his forehead. Lou managed to blurt a few words of thanks as she fled toward the elevators. For all of Brusk's bluster and denial, the rash told the real story: that whoever or whatever had targeted Alex Wu and Joe Christian had also set its sights on Charlie Brusk. *That* was the connection between the three men. They were all victims of Fate.

"Hey!" She turned to see Brusk still standing in his office doorway. "You don't think Joe was serious about all that fate stuff?" Brusk had lowered his voice, and for the first time—perhaps in his entire life—sounded genuinely nervous.

Lou took a deep breath as she considered her response. Should she ask Brusk directly about the rash? Or pretend she hadn't noticed, at least until she had more answers? In that split second, she auditioned at least ten possible responses, but before she could settle on the right one, Bianca reappeared, gesturing with her iPhone. "Your two p.m. is still waiting in the conference room."

Brusk gave Lou an overly cheery wave down the hallway, "Let me know how I can be helpful!" and then allowed himself to be led away to his meeting.

Only as she descended in the elevator did Lou realize the most alarming thing of all about her encounter with Charlie Brusk. The only reason she'd been able to see the blotches and bumps on his head in the first place. Charlie Brusk—Silicon Valley's most famous journalist-hating germophobe—had made a point of shaking her hand.

42

THE ELEVATOR DOORS opened onto the lobby, but Lou made it only a few hurried paces toward the exit when she was called back yet again, this time by the same teenage receptionist who had confused her for a backpacker. "Miss McCarthy?" His voice was polite, almost deferential.

Lou swung around in time to see him replacing a landline handset on its receiver. "What?"

The question was answered by another *bing* of the elevator and the appearance of Brusk's assistant, Bianca, out of breath and flustered. "Oh good," she panted, "I was hoping I'd catch you before you left. Thank you, Danny." The teenager blushed.

Bianca was clutching a sheet of paper, which she waved in Lou's direction while staying rooted in the elevator door, preventing it from closing.

"I just wanted to make sure you had the list of organizations you asked about," she trilled as Lou trudged back toward her. Bianca's smile and tone remained that of a helpful assistant doing her boss's bidding. Lou took the paper and glanced at it. At first it seemed to be exactly as Bianca was describing: a long memo she had prepared for Charlie Brusk, logging each of the bizarre calls Joe Christian had made to XXCubator. Included was a neat bullet-pointed list of the organizations Amelia's ex-husband apparently believed were out to get him. The CIA, the NSA, Mossad, followed by various women's rights charities and rape-crisis organizations. Sure enough, the Amelia Christian Foundation was on the list, sandwiched between the Vatican and a local Lutheran church that offered sanctuary to homeless teenagers.

Lou gave a half smile and muttered her thanks. She appreciated Bianca's conscientiousness but was also frustrated—she didn't care about the memo, and wanted to get back to the city to find Helen Tyler and tell her about the rash on Brusk's forehead.

Bianca smiled back, and lowered her voice. "I hope you don't mind, but I printed it on the back of some old notes. Charlie is big on saving trees." She accompanied this last statement with a stare that could burn through concrete. Lou took the hint, flipping the paper over and then immediately flipping it back when she saw a tightly spaced list of times, names, and numbers: a phone log of some kind. Bianca's stare told Lou everything she needed to know about its significance and the fact that her boss must never know Lou had it.

"Thank you," said Lou, with a conspiratorial nod.

Bianca switched back to her regular volume. "If you need anything else at all, don't hesitate to get in touch." Then she stepped back into the elevator, allowing the door to close in front of her, leaving Lou alone in the lobby.

Lou strode two blocks from XXCubator before stopping in the doorway of a Starbucks to examine the printout Bianca had given her. It was exactly as she'd suspected: a detailed call log from the burner number that Brusk had just sworn didn't belong to him. Specifically, it showed a flurry of maybe a dozen calls made between "Brusk, C (Cell)" and "Wu, A (Cell)" in the hours before Wu killed himself. Some of the calls lasted just a few seconds, while others went on for three or four minutes. Lou's hand began to shake as she saw the time stamp of the final outgoing call to Wu, lasting just thirty seconds: 8:20 p.m. Only a couple of minutes before he leapt to his death. Wu must literally have hung up with Brusk and walked straight out onto the balcony.

This was proof that not only had Brusk been in contact with Wu right before he died, but they'd used the secret burner number for their conversations. The number she'd found written on Joe Christian's hand.

Lou's whole arm was trembling now, and she had to set down her bag to clutch the sheet with both hands. A picture was starting to form in her mind—of Charlie Brusk using his XXCubator investment fund to secretly pay off dozens of women assaulted or otherwise harmed by powerful men like Wu and Christian inside his portfolio companies. And now this mysterious person—Fate—was targeting them all. Out of revenge? Blackmail? Destroying their lives, just as they had destroyed the lives of others. Lou exhaled slowly. Finally she had a theory that actually held water. It still didn't explain why this "Fate" character had dragged her into it, or *how* exactly he—or she—had driven two men to suicide . . . but it was a start. If she could get back to Raum One and use Helen's access to the company's user database . . . map out all the connections between Wu and Christian and Brusk . . . see if there was anyone else they were all in contact with . . .

Oh. Shit. Lou's eyes landed on another pair of calls that Brusk had made. One a few minutes before his last call to Wu, and the other right after. Both were to the same person.

Tyler, H (Cell).

Lou stared at Helen Tyler's name in its basic Courier font. She thought back to the very first time she'd seen Helen—at the Raum One party, disappearing into the shadows to take a phone call. Helen, who had sworn she had no idea why Lou was at the party, hadn't recognized Brusk's burner number . . .

And that's when it happened. Still distracted by the phone log, and trying to process a thousand possible explosive implications of seeing Helen's number, Lou didn't notice something brushing past her leg. She looked up to see the back of a navy blue hoodie—hood up, completely covering the wearer's head—diving into the back of a dark gray vRaum. Only as the door slammed shut and the vehicle sped away did she register with horror what the passenger had clutched in his or her hand. Lou's orange carrier bag, containing Helen Tyler's shoes – and Joe Christian's journal.

43

AN HOUR LATER Lou arrived back in the city, still shaken by the loss of the notebook. She'd been deliberately targeted, she knew that. No opportunist thief would ignore all those people working on expensive laptops outside the Palo Alto Starbucks to steal a plastic bag from Shoebasement Discount Shoes. Also, what kind of mugger used a vRaum as a getaway car? That was one silver lining: once Lou met back up with Helen, they could easily check Raum's database for the name of the passenger and where he or she was dropped off.

Lou stepped out of the Caltrain station and began the long walk up Fourth Street toward Raum One. She'd barely made it a block when her phone suddenly sprang back to life, delivering a voice mail left twenty minutes earlier.

"Lou? I'm terribly sorry—quick change of plans. Could you . . . well . . .please don't go to Raum One. I'm outside the Ferry Building on the Embarcadero. I'll . . . Sorry . . . I'll explain when you get here. Sorry sorry."

Lou hung up, frustrated. She wanted to go to Raum One, but instead Helen Tyler was dragging her to a tourist trap a mile from anywhere useful. Lou shoved the phone back into her pocket and quickened her pace.

It took almost half an hour to reach the goddamned Ferry Building, where Lou found Helen sitting on a green metal bench, facing out toward the bay, watching the ferries bob slowly in and out of the terminal. The Embarcadero was packed with the usual mobs of tourists and cyclists and joggers, but Helen sat alone, unmoved by the chaos. She must have sensed Lou's arrival, because now she turned and gave a small, almost regal wave.

As Lou reached the bench, she saw Helen's cheeks were red, chapped by the raw wind coming off the water. "I thought we agreed you wouldn't visit Charlie without me." Helen's greeting sounded more puzzled than angry.

Lou wasn't in the mood to be scolded. "I thought you were meeting me at XXCubator. Brusk texted me and ordered me to come running."

Helen appeared even more confused. "That's not what Charlie says. He just phoned me, incandescent with rage. Denied texting you, or even having any idea who you were until you—quote—barged into his office. I only just got out of my meeting and called you right away."

Lou didn't back down. "I didn't barge anywhere. He invited me up. Also how did he get my number if you didn't give it to him?"

It was a damn good question, but Helen didn't answer it. Instead she shuffled a few inches farther down the bench and gestured for Lou to join her. "I'm sorry. It's been an . . . eventful few hours." Helen reached into her purse and produced an organic salmon sandwich, wrapped in plastic. Slowly and deliberately, she removed the packaging and set one half on her knee; the other she held out in offering.

Lou shook her head. She was starving but had no appetite for food, or olive branches. "Probably not as eventful as mine," said Lou. She told Helen what had happened outside the Starbucks.

"Good God. Are you OK? Did you get a look at the mugger?" Helen seemed genuinely concerned for Lou's well-being. Or was this just more acting?

Lou shrugged off her concern. "I wasn't really mugged. I only saw the back of their hoodie."

"A man? A woman?"

"I couldn't tell. They got your shoes too . . . sorry."

Helen waved away the apology. "I have more than one pair, and your safety is considerably more important." Now she took out her phone and tapped a number from her address book. From the brief conversation that followed, Lou surmised Helen was speaking to someone high up in Raum's customer service department. Helen gave him the details of the mugger's vRaum getaway car.

"Uh-huh," she said. "Would you be good enough to check again?"

"No dice," said Helen as she hung up. "Or rather no vRaum. Nothing in the database within ten minutes or three blocks. Either your mugger faked their own vRaum or they've somehow hacked our database. Either way, I don't think we're going to see that notebook again."

Lou frowned. "I took pictures of it," she said, "of the journal entries."

Helen gave a quiet chuckle. "How funny. I took the liberty of doing the same this morning while you were still asleep. Just in case you felt obliged to leave the original with the ex–Mrs. Christian."

Lou was tired of having her behavior so smugly predicted. "So why did you drag me out here?"

Helen gave her half sandwich a cautious sniff and then took a large bite. "Forgive the cloak-and-dagger. I assume you have places you come when you don't want to be overheard? To meet sources and suchlike?"

Lou nodded. She always took her contacts to the Pinecrest Diner on Geary Street.

"This bench is mine," said Helen. "You see, things have got a little more . . . complicated . . . back at Raum One."

"Complicated how?" What could possibly be more complicated than a dead CTO and a possible mass murderer roaming the halls?

Helen looked around, but the only people paying them any attention were two Japanese children and a homeless woman in a stained rabbit onesie. "First, what did you learn from Amelia Christian?"

"Pretty much nothing." Lou wasn't ready to share her theory about the secret slush fund just yet. "She confirmed her foundation is basically broke. Insists nobody there was investigating her husband, and denied any connection with his death."

"You believe her?"

"I think so. Honestly, I think she pitied him by the end. Seems convinced the journal proves he was being set up—but she didn't know why, or by who." Lou raised a finger as she remembered another interesting detail. "She did say Christian hated Alex Wu since they were both in college. Except I know for a fact they weren't in college together."

"Interesting," said Helen, nodding slowly. "And Charlie?"

The moment of truth. Lou took the folded call log from her pocket and handed it to Helen, watching her face carefully. She didn't have to wait long for the reaction. Helen reached the bottom of the page and her eyebrows arched upward.

"Well," she said. "That explains that."

"Explains what?"

"Why Charlie sounded so desperate when he called me. I could barely hear him over the noise of the party—he was whining about being stuck on the freeway in his car and wanted to know if I was already at Raum One and who else was there."

"He called you from his burner phone?"

"Absolutely no idea," said Helen. "The call came from a withheld number. I almost didn't answer it, but I was concerned it might be some VIP unable to get past door security, so I picked up." Again Helen sounded totally convincing.

"Did he mention Alex Wu?"

Helen squinted out across the bay, as if summoning a painful memory. "I don't think so—although I could only make out every other word. I told him I wasn't going to read the guest list down the phone, and then hung up. I assumed he was trying to decide if there was anyone important enough in attendance to warrant him making an appearance. But this"—she gestured at the calls to Wu—"would seem to indicate he was checking on Alex specifically." A pause. "Charlie gave you this?"

Lou shook her head. "A source." Adding quickly, before Helen had time to press her for a name: "And this second call?"

Helen peered down again at the list. "If he tried to call me back, I didn't get it. But things were a little *chaotic* by that stage."

Lou glanced down at the paper that was still in Helen's hand. Sure enough, the second call—made right after Wu's fatal leap—showed no duration.

Helen Tyler handed the list back to Lou, then carefully folded up her sandwich container and tucked it back into her purse. "Did Charlie explain his conversations with Joe Christian?"

Lou felt her stomach rumble and wished now she'd taken the half sandwich. She hadn't eaten anything since the party. "He acted like he hadn't talked to Joe in months. Maybe if you'd been there, we could have pushed him harder."

"Don't worry," said Helen, ignoring Lou's not-so-subtle rebuke. "We'll get another crack at him."

"There was one other thing," Lou continued. "When I left Brusk's office, he made a point of shaking my hand, and—"

Helen interrupted, her eyes wide. "I'm sorry. Charlie Brusk—Charlie 'strangers are a disease vortex' Brusk—shook your hand?" She practically yelled this, and at least one tourist turned to stare at the noisy Brit.

"Exactly," said Lou, lowering her own voice to compensate. "And when I got close, I swear he had the same rash on his forehead that Joe Christian had on his whole body. Not as bad, but the same. It's almost like he wanted me to see it."

Helen gazed out across the bay. "I'm going to tell you something quite revolting, Lou, and I don't expect you to repeat it to another living soul."

Lou agreed, because what else was she supposed to do?

"I told you I knew Charlie when we were both at the London School of Economics. These were the nineties, and as I've said, he was a different man. But also physically different. Younger, more vibrant, jawbone sharp enough to clean crumbs from a restaurant table." Helen gave a wistful sigh. "Still a complete arsehole, of course. Anyway. The first time Charlie and I had sex"—she said this like it was the most banal anecdote in the world—"he insisted we do it in his dorm room shower under scalding, soapy water. The second time too. And every other time."

Lou's face twisted itself into a mask of horror and amusement. "You're not serious?"

"It gets worse. He even carried a special medicated body wash clipped to his rucksack, formulated for use in biological and chemical attacks. He applied as frequently as people today slather on Purell—and not just to his hands." She paused to allow this image to embed itself in Lou's brain. And it did, forever. "My point is that if Charlie Brusk voluntarily shook your hand—allowed a stranger that close—then there is absolutely no doubt that he wanted you to see something of life-and-death importance."

Lou glanced down at her own hand. Was it her imagination or were her knuckles redder than usual, her skin visibly more dry?

Helen caught her looking. "Oh dear, now you're worrying about killer rashes?" She waved the idea away with a manicured hand. "I'm fairly sure that whatever caused Alex Wu and Joe Christian—and now apparently Charlie—to look so plague-ridden was at worst a nasty symptom, not the root cause. I simply meant that Charlie must have needed you to see that rash so badly that it overrode decades of germophobia."

"A cry for help, you mean?"

"Perhaps. Except if he was that desperate, why wouldn't he just call and ask me?"

Lou considered this. "Are you guys still friends? Would he tell you if he was in trouble?" Until now she'd assumed that Helen Tyler and Charlie Brusk's present-day relationship was purely business.

Helen bit her lip, as if trying to stop an emotion from escaping. "It's been a long time, but one hopes . . ." Then she abruptly changed the subject. "Why don't you ask me how the all-hands meeting went?"

Lou could think of a dozen more important topics, but did as she was told. "How did the all-hands meeting go?"

Helen gave another long sigh, followed by a half smile. "I thought you'd never ask." She stood up, and turned to face down the waterfront, away from Raum One. "Shall we walk and talk?"

45

AND SO THEY walked, farther along the Embarcadero, away from Raum One, weaving slowly through gaggles of tourists, some of whom moved to let them pass but most of whom did not. "The meeting itself was exactly as you might expect," said Helen. "Lots of pablum from Elmsley about how when a family suffers a loss, we all pull together . . . trained counselors available on the fourth floor for anyone who wants to put a permanent psychological red flag on their HR file . . ."

"But?" There was definitely a but.

Helen moved closer to Lou so they were practically shoulder to shoulder. "But after the meeting, Elmsley took me aside and told me—*informed* me—that he has already found Alex Wu's replacement."

"Already? Who?" Lou was astonished. Whom could Elmsley Chase possibly have found so fast who was both capable of getting Raum ready for IPO in a matter of weeks and willing to fill a dead rapist's shoes? Whoever it was had to be desperate, and with zero moral scruples. Jack the Ripper, perhaps? The Unabomber?

Helen Tyler ducked her head and spoke the name directly into Lou's ear.

Lou was so shocked she stopped in her tracks, almost causing a tourist to slam into her rear. Helen kept her forward momentum, though, and now Lou had to jog to catch up. "Martina Allen? From Hopsearch? That can't be true."

Martina Allen was, by any metric, the best engineer in Silicon Valley. Not the best *female* engineer, as most men felt the need to qualify before complimenting her skills, but the best engineer. Allen had built Hopsearch from the ground up, and in the process, the company had achieved the impossible: unseating Google as the world's most popular search engine. In return, she was paid hundreds of millions of dollars a year in salary and bonuses with maybe a billion or two more in stock, half of which she had pledged to donate to end world hunger. Oh, and she also happened to be married to Thomas Milton Calder, the legendary hedge fund manager turned Arctic explorer turned—all but certainly—the next governor of California.

"Completely true, I'm afraid. Elmsley said he made the offer last night and she accepted—six billion in cash and stock, assuming the IPO prices as expected."

"Six *billion?*"

"Six, and then another nine zeros, yes. Everyone has her price, it turns out."

"Unbelievable." Lou felt personally betrayed. She had never met Martina Allen but had allowed herself to believe the hype. Martina Allen, the anti-bro. Martina Allen, the role model for any woman who dreamed of making it to the top in Silicon Valley without compromising her values . . . Lou mentally dragged and dropped Allen into her recycle bin of letdowns. "So the IPO is saved. Elmsley must be thrilled."

"Smug as a goose. Elmsley Chase finally gets his Sheryl. Wall Street will do somersaults."

Lou got the reference. Ever since, years earlier, Sheryl Sandberg had been hired by Facebook to curb Mark Zuckerberg's most reckless impulses, every Silicon Valley investor had pressured their portfolio companies to find "a Sheryl." That is, an adult woman hired to keep their immature male founders in check—and to reassure investors that there's a grown-up in the room (then ultimately to take the blame when this babysitting failed). Elmsley Chase had always resisted demands that he find a Sheryl—ostensibly because he found the notion "offensively sexist," but really because he didn't want anyone telling him what to do. Especially a woman.

But now Alex Wu was dead, and Elmsley Chase knew exactly how to change the narrative: by paying Martina Allen billions of dollars in cash and stock to be his Sheryl. No wonder Helen wanted to meet away from prying ears. This was huge. Huge for Raum. Huge for the IPO. Huge for

Silicon Valley. Huge for everyone except the shareholders of Hopsearch, who were about to see that company's stock take a serious nosedive, and for . . . ah . . . now Lou realized why Helen Tyler was delivering the news like her puppy had just been hit by a car.

"Shit," said Lou. "I guess that fucks up your hired-gunning. Elmsley's not going anywhere now."

Helen had said it herself: Raum's board had offered her a fat check to get rid of Elmsley Chase. With this incredible hiring coup, Chase had simultaneously salvaged the IPO, saved his own skin, and made Helen's task impossible. He had won again, and the cost was one woman's dignity and another's paycheck. "I'm sorry," said Lou. And, to her own surprise, she actually meant it.

Helen went silent for so long that they were halfway to Fisherman's Wharf by the time she spoke again. "You have it backward," she said eventually. "As soon as Martina Allen is announced as CTO, there's really no reason to keep Elmsley around. They can still use whatever findings I present on Monday to sack him, ask Martina to take over as CEO, and sit back as the market rejoices at the brand-new, scandal-free Raum. Job done, well played, Helen."

Now Lou was really bewildered. "And yet you don't seem very happy."

Helen ducked into the gated archway of Pier 19, and Lou followed behind.

"Happy that Elmsley is made a scapegoat while Raum gets a reputational reset while remaining institutionally rotten? Or do you mean happy at the prospect of all the workers who will continue to be exploited, women who will be attacked, pedestrians mown down by self-driving cars . . . ? Or perhaps you think I should be glad that even Martina Allen isn't immune to the siren call of dirty money?"

"Excuse me?" Lou had the sudden feeling she and Helen Tyler had switched bodies. "I'm pretty sure I'm the one who is supposed to care about Raum's exploitation of users, and getting away with murder. You're the one who's hired to help them get away with it. To give them their scapegoat."

But as she said that, and saw this new fury in Helen Tyler's eyes, another possibility began to assemble itself. A possibility that had been nagging at her—at least subconsciously—since she'd seen the drawer filled with key cards from Helen's former clients. Sleapster, Uber, Twiddle, Dunk.ly . . . the boards of all these companies, according to Helen, had paid her obscenely well to oust their founders or CEOs to fix their toxic culture. Helen, by her own telling, was very good at her job, and yet every company she helped "save" was now dead, or irrelevant, or trading for pennies on the dollar. "Oh my God," Lou whispered. "Do you actually *want* Raum's IPO to fail?"

Helen gave a mischievous smile, with a tilt of her head that said she knew Lou would get there in the end. "Not at all. I assure you I want Raum's IPO to succeed. To be an enormous success. The biggest ever." She paused for effect. "And *then* I want to watch it all burn to the fucking ground."

46

FATE REACHED THE last page of the black notebook and allowed a long, slow sigh of relief to escape her lips. She had to hand it to Joe Christian. For such a pathetic and broken shell of a man, he'd done a pretty good job of following all the threads, right up until the end. It was all there in black and blue: from the first recruitment ad that had sent eighteen-year-old intern Bella Marcos to Grintech, the carefully orchestrated late-night meetings, to Amelia Christian's early arrival back from Tahoe to catch them on the living room floor. The rogue prescriptions, the spiral into addiction and sexual desperation, and ultimate physical and psychological collapse. Every dangerous and destructive choice that he had made, entirely of his own free will, all precisely documented and diagrammed. Objective, method, results.

All that was missing was the conclusion. The identity of his tormentor.

Fate really hadn't meant it to be a puzzle. She'd assumed that Joe Christian and the other men would quickly make what addicts called a moral inventory; to consider the long list of people they'd wronged, and draw up a short list of those who might want to see them suffer. From that list, perhaps two or three names would stand out clearly from the rest. To a man capable of feeling shame or guilt, that list would have been a starting point: to repent, to make amends. But Joe Christian's journal contained no such moral inventory, just a list of humiliations and grievances, each recast to make himself the innocent victim.

Had his victim complex really been so total that he couldn't imagine he might *deserve* what was happening? That it might actually be justice?

Had he really needed a news alert about Alex Wu—a photo of the man covered in the same scabs and scars—to awaken the distant memory of that night ten years ago? The night Fate began.

Even after he finally figured it out, his first instinct—even before updating this sad little misery memoir—had been to rush to Raum One to see Wu. To warn him? To commiserate? Fate tried to imagine Joe Christian's logic in the final moments of his life. Had he seen the sign with his ex-wife's name on it and been unable to resist one last egotistical performance for the cameras? A final I-told-you-so?

Not for the first time, but definitely for the last, Fate had handed Joe Christian two paths and he'd taken the wrong one.

Fucking dumbass.

Fate wasn't going to call herself a genius—her victims, her guinea pigs, could testify to the dangers of that kind of hubris—but she was pleased with how quickly she'd reacted to Joe Christian's little on-camera show, spinning an alternative narrative so convincing that even his ex-wife had accepted it without question. And that curveball with Charlie Brusk and the burner phone—inspired!

The moment of self-congratulation was interrupted by the buzz of a cell phone: one of four phones assembled in a neat row on Fate's desk. She glanced at the screen and greeted the single-word incoming message—"Crikey!"—with a smile, followed by another long sigh. *I hate that you're part of this. I love that you're part of this.*

She reached for the device, unlocked it, and scrolled through the long, and troubling, update from her inside man at Raum.

Martina Allen?

"Crikey!" didn't really cut it.

Fate jumped up from her chair and headed to the bathroom to get dressed. She would have to work fast.

47

"SO WHAT ARE you telling me? You're some kind of corporate black widow spider? You pretend to help companies while killing them from the inside?"

Lou and Helen were walking again. They'd made it as far as the Marina and were now headed along the other side of the Embarcadero, back toward Raum One.

"Not the sobriquet I'd use," said Helen. "Let's say I know where a lot of Silicon Valley's bodies are buried, because I'm the one they paid to bury them. After the IPO, I just drop an anonymous tip to a friendly journalist, or an SEC investigator, pointing them where to dig."

"But why?" Lou still couldn't tell if she was being made a fool of, or somehow being entrapped, or if Helen Tyler really was making the most incredible confession she'd heard in a decade of journalism.

Helen allowed a man in a blue pinstripe suit to walk by. "Why does anyone do anything? Money. Before I send my anonymous tip, I short the stock. Bucketloads of it, through various proxies and foreign accounts. The companies' losses are quite literally my gain."

Lou stopped dead. "Bullshit." She had known Helen Tyler for less than twenty-four hours, but she had seen enough to know that, with her brains, connections, and accent, she didn't need to commit securities fraud to get rich in Silicon Valley. "I thought we were being honest with each other."

Helen stopped a few paces ahead, turned, and waited for Lou to catch up. "Honest? I just told you I've been"—she lowered her voice to a whisper—"insider trading for close to a decade."

Lou nodded slowly. "And I asked you why."

"Why would I want to take down the companies who are destroying the world?" Helen gave a wistful laugh. "Only in a town as fucked-up as this would you need to ask that question. Perhaps you should ask it this way. Why would someone who has spent her entire working life surrounded by the most powerful sociopaths on the planet—watching incompetent pathetic little men get the jobs I've always been more qualified for, while I'm hired to cover up their crimes—decide that maybe it was time for some payback? Why would I be furious that arseholes like Charlie Brusk get to decide which apps get built, or who gets funded—despite the fact that those same apps are overwhelmingly used by women?" She ran her hand through her nest of red hair. "Or perhaps you mean why would a girl who, barely seven years old, was adopted—sold, more accurately, by her impoverished biological parents to a pair of stockbrokers who liked the idea of parenting but without the messiness of childbirth and babies . . . why would that girl possibly grow up to resent an industry that brought us the sharing economy—the most efficient marketplace for human life since the Ottoman slave market in Constantinople?" Helen took a breath and Lou heard a crack in her voice: the first honest hint of weakness from a woman who up until then had seemed indestructible. "Therein lies the greatest irony. Only in this town would I be able to get away with it, time and time again. Would it not occur to a single one of these monsters that a woman could be smarter than them, might be conning them just as they themselves con the rest of the world? That's our advantage, Lou. They underestimate us every time."

Lou's moral compass was spinning like a top. Helen must have made millions from leaking dirt on some of Silicon Valley's worst companies after shorting their stock; robbing from the rich to give to . . . herself. The end result, though, was something Lou had never been able to achieve. She thought again about all the dead companies in that kitchen drawer, and about all the men who had underestimated her. The CEOs who told her too much because they expected a puff piece, Mr. Brady in high school who laughed when she wrote "journalist" on her career counseling form, her dad's dumb smirk when he saw her in the kitchen doorway, right before he noticed the gun. "Well . . . fuck."

Helen guided her into the doorway of a shuttered Walgreens, as the shoppers and tourists continued to flow past. "And the collapse of Raum was to be my last and greatest achievement. The very worst example of human commoditization, a glass house filled with rapists and sociopaths—" She jabbed a finger toward Raum One. "I was going to watch Elmsley Chase ring that Nasdaq opening bell on television and then make the phone call that brought it all down before he even left the stage. Then I intended to enjoy a very comfortable retirement on an island in the Indian Ocean. I even had a little plot of land picked out, a cottage right on the beach."

"If that's true, then what's changed?" Surely Helen must have enough dirt on Elmsley and his crew by now. "You can still bring them down after the IPO?"

Helen slowly shook her head. "I could, yes. But now that would mean bringing down Martina Allen. Believe it or not, Lou, I absolutely *refuse* to do that to a woman whose only crime will be taking the CEO title that has been unfairly denied her at Hopsearch or elsewhere, in favor of—"

"Incompetent, pathetic little men."

"Precisely."

"Charlie Brusk must have noticed that his companies keep failing when you're done with them?"

Helen let out a loud snort of laughter. "Speaking of incompetent, pathetic little men? I've wondered the same myself. Maybe he doesn't care. The IPO is his liquidity event. So long as it goes out at the right price, he makes his killing and he's on to the next startup."

"What if he's doing the same as you? Shorting the stock? That'd be a pretty good reason to hire you."

Helen shook her head. "I can get away with it because barely anybody knows I exist, and those who do think I'm on their side. A lot of people pay attention to what Charlie does with his money, and none of them trust him. King Faisal would cut his balls off if he was double-dealing like that."

It was a valid point. Assuming the Saudi royal family really were the secret funders behind XXCubator, they wouldn't take kindly to Brusk double-dipping. "Aren't you worried the king might do that to you?"

"I don't have any balls."

Lou disagreed. "So why are you telling me this? We don't owe each other anything."

Helen didn't reply. Instead she reached into her coat pocket and, looking around to make sure they still weren't being watched, retrieved a flat rectangle of cardboard and handed it to Lou. It was the green-etched invitation Lou had received to the Raum One party. Still stuck to the back was the yellow Post-it and the message scribbled in red ink: *Your story was good. Come tonight. Will explain everything.* "Building security found your bag under a buffet table at Raum One."

"And you looked through it?"

Helen rolled her eyes. "*Mea culpa.*" And then: "You think this note was written by Fate?"

"Assuming you didn't send it, yes."

"I did not. And nor did I send this." Helen dipped back into her pocket, this time producing a folded sheet of cream-colored paper, which she unfolded and handed to Lou.

The notepaper felt expensive. At the top was the name and gold logo of the Redwood Hotel on Sand Hill Road. On the paper, someone had handwritten a set of numbers in thick black Sharpie. The numbers—God, Lou was sick of numbers—meant nothing to her, but she recognized the handwriting immediately: the same bold strokes from the Post-it. This time, the chill Lou felt definitely had nothing to do with the fog.

"I received this eight weeks ago, delivered by courier."

"Eight weeks?"

Helen nodded. "My very first day at Raum."

Lou examined the paper again. "What are these numbers?"

"It took me a while to figure that out. They're map references. Latitude and longitude. A certain beach on a certain island in the middle of the Indian Ocean."

"Your secret retirement plan."

"I thought someone was trying to blackmail me—maybe some bitter CEO had figured out my role in their downfall." She held the letter next to the invite card. "Of course now we know better."

"You didn't go to the Redwood?" Lou pointed at the letterhead. "To see what they wanted?"

"I thought about it but . . . no. I was hardly going to do a blackmailer's job for him. Also, it'd be a waste of everyone's time. I assure you, the contents of my bank account would be terribly disappointing to any self-respecting blackmailer."

Lou was puzzled by that comment. "You've been insider trading for ten years. You must have made millions." Lou imagined a Swiss bank account vault, piled high with cash and gold bars.

Helen's gaze strayed over Lou's shoulder. "It's all gone."

"Gone? All of it?" The piles of cash evaporated.

"Every penny."

That wasn't possible. A retirement cottage on the beach couldn't be *that* costly, even with Helen's expensive tastes. But now, the image of the bank vault was joined by another thought that came washing back to Lou, as if on the tide. *Robbing from the rich to give to . . .* Lou raised her hands to her cheeks. "Which island?"

Helen tilted her head. "What?"

"Your retirement plan. You said you had chosen an island in the Indian Ocean. Which one?"

"Oh," said Helen. "Mauritius."

Lou's whole body electrified. The same tingle she always felt when she uncovered a huge story, only a thousand times more intense. "All those payoffs to Wu's victims. It was *your* money, not Raum or Grintech or Charlie Brusk." She could barely gasp out the words. Amelia Christian's tuition payments, paid from a secret bank account in Mauritius . . . "*You*'re the secret slush fund."

Helen stared deep into Lou's eyes. "When you asked about Sophie Aker and her condo, I told you I wasn't a monster. I meant it. I'm paid generously for my day job—I'll make enough from Raum to last a lifetime—everything else I distribute to those who deserve it. Call it my modest attempt to make things right, though buying a house, or paying off student debts, or medical bills, only goes so far."

Lou was awestruck. This woman who, twenty-four hours ago, represented everything that was evil about Raum was now claiming to have spent a decade committing epic financial fraud and using the proceeds to compensate the victims of the companies that employed her. "That's . . ." Lou struggled for the right word, just as she was still struggling to unpack the full implications of what Helen Tyler had confessed. "That's fucked-up."

And it was.

"*You're* the reason none of those women would go on the record? You're the one who made them sign NDAs?"

Helen took a step backward. Had she seriously expected Lou to be impressed? To understand? Apparently so, because her next words came out as barely a stammer: "Fucked-up? I've paid compensation to hundreds of victims, not just at Raum but at Grintech, Dunk.ly—"

Lou raised a palm. "Oh, I get it. You bought their silence—prevented them from speaking out, so their attackers and abusers could target more and more victims. You could have ended it, but instead . . ." Lou watched a small fleck of saliva leap from her mouth and land on Helen Tyler's shirt. "Or am I supposed to believe you didn't make them sign NDAs?"

Helen stood openmouthed. "I needed them to believe the money came from the companies. I couldn't have them running around boasting about payments that Raum and the others knew they hadn't made." She took a breath, and in that moment her entire posture transformed from defensive back to offensive—a half step closer to Lou, shoulders pulled back, neck extended. "Let's be clear of the moral calculus here: the choice isn't between me paying them compensation with an NDA or compensation without an NDA." She paused again, Lou assumed, to swallow her urge to shout. "The choice is between compensation with an NDA or the boards of those companies doing every goddamned thing they could to smear, slander, and destroy their lives." Another half step closer. "It's very important that you understand that."

Lou opened her mouth to respond, then slammed her lips shut. Because, for all that she detested Helen Tyler's version of reality, she knew it *was* reality. She'd seen it herself, countless times. One way or another, with or without her, Silicon Valley's victims would always be silenced. Helen was only trying to sweeten that pill.

"Do you think that's why Fate contacted us?" Lou grasped for common ground, to salvage their conversation. For good or ill, Helen Tyler was her only hope of finding Fate and understanding how and why any of this was happening. "She's killing off tech assholes, I'm exposing them in print, and you're stealing their money and paying it back to their victims? She wanted us all to work together?" Lou felt her stomach tighten as she said this. Finding a killer was one thing—joining forces with that killer was a whole other level of terrifying.

Helen raised an eyebrow. "It would hardly be the weirdest strategic partnership in Silicon Valley."

Lou rubbed her cheeks with both hands and felt them burning in the cold air. "I mean, Fate has to be a woman, right?"

Helen smiled, their entire fight already water under the bridge. "Given the elegant brutality of her methods and the crimes of her victims, I'd say that's a virtual certainty. Also, if your theory about her trying to hire us is correct . . . well, how many men do you know in this town who would try to recruit two women?"

Lou laughed, involuntarily, at Helen's flawless logic. "She seems to be doing fine without our help."

Helen was suddenly moving again, as if they'd both agreed it was time to resume their trek to Raum One. "That's the frightening question, isn't it? If she's capable of driving three men to suicide without assistance, then what must she be planning next that requires reinforcements?" Helen took back the folded hotel notepaper and tucked it back into her pocket, leaving Lou holding the invitation. "And why would she be so sure we'd do it?"

That, at least, was something Lou could answer. "Because she knows we hate them as much as she does."

50%

A BEEP ON one of Fate's phones indicated the arrival of a new photo message. She plucked the device from her purse and waited for it to recognize her face, a process that always took half a second longer when she was made up for work.

It was a photograph, taken from across a busy street by one of her contacts, showing Lou McCarthy and Helen Tyler standing in the doorway of a shuttered store—a Walgreens or maybe a CVS.

Fate pinched and expanded the photo so Lou's face and torso filled the entire screen. In her left hand she was holding a white invite card, and in her right, a larger sheet of darker-colored paper. She was examining both intently.

Fate tossed the phone back into her purse, then clapped her hands once in satisfaction. She was looking forward to seeing Lou McCarthy again.

51%

HOURS LATER, LOU and Helen still hadn't made it to Raum One. Instead, Helen had summoned Landon to bring Lou's backpack to the Four Seasons along with a collection of office supplies and the ingredients Helen required to make a surprisingly delicious pad thai.

While Helen cooked, Lou had sat on the couch poring over the photos she'd taken of Joe Christian's journal. Any person or place that seemed significant, she'd transcribed on a blue neon Post-it note and stuck it to one of Helen's living room windows in the hope it might spark a revelation. She wasn't going to just sit around and wait for Fate to make contact again—she was determined to find her first.

At around eight o'clock, Lou's mom had finally answered her damn phone, apologizing airily for going AWOL and explaining that she and Carol had spent the morning cleaning the profanity off her garage door before heading off to work. That figured—Lou knew her mom had no cell reception at the domestic-violence shelter where she worked as a case manager—but something in her voice suggested there was more to the story than she was letting on, as was usually the case when Carol was involved. Still, at least she was alive and well, the mob hadn't returned, and her garage door was now apparently slutcunt-free.

By ten o'clock Lou and Helen had opened their third bottle of wine, but were still no closer to identifying Fate. For all the Post-its, the only things directly connecting all three of her confirmed targets—Wu, Christian, and Brusk—were XXCubator and the Redwood Hotel. Wu and Christian were both involved in companies backed by Brusk. Joe Christian had mentioned the Redwood three times in his journal (he was apparently banned from the hotel after this third visit), it was the source of the letter sent to Helen, and—according to a story by Tommy in the *Herald*—it had been the venue for the launch party of the Amelia Christian Foundation. None of which helped a damn. The Redwood was *the* social hub for Sand Hill Road, meaning everyone important in the Valley passed through it at some point. They might as well try to find a link between everyone who visited both Union Square and San Francisco Airport.

"So what do we think?" Helen returned from her latest trip to the window and took a long swig from her fishbowl-sized glass of Pinot Noir. "A trip to the Redwood tomorrow? Or back to the hospital to see if anyone noticed Fate writing a phone number on Joe Christian's hand?"

Lou slammed her laptop closed in frustration. A fishing expedition or a shot in the dark. "If she wants our help, why doesn't she just fucking ask? Why send invitations and letters and burner phone numbers and spoofed text messages, like it's all a big game?"

Helen sighed. "This is the worst part, isn't it? When you know there's a huge story there. You have all the puzzle pieces: little pieces of sky, a dog's nose, what seems to be a foot. But there's a deadline looming, and you just can't find all the bloody edges." She took another sip of wine. "Except this time we're not worried about being scooped, just that another arsehole might leap off a balcony and make the world a better place. So for once, maybe it's better that we do nothing and let Fate do whatever she's trying to do?"

Lou caught the obvious pang of nostalgia in Helen's voice. "How long were you a journalist?"

Helen gave a wistful smile, betraying no surprise that Lou knew her career history. "Fifteen years. A brief but glorious career. I helped bring down governments, expose child abusers—I even stopped a genocide once, from a pay phone in a Fleet Street pub."

"Impressive," said Lou, sincerely.

"Yes, I'm the reason we have no more genocides," Helen said, deadpan.

"How did you wind up in Silicon Valley?" Lou kicked her feet up onto the arm of Helen's expensive sofa and scooped up her own wineglass. A depressing number of PR people and crisis managers were recovering journalists who'd gotten sick of the thanklessness and shitty salary. Although most of them just wanted better pay and health care, not to become some kind of morally tortured corporate black widow—using their investigative skills to bring down the billionaire patriarchy from within.

Helen turned to either stare out of the window or reexamine the Post-it notes. "Via Downing Street." She sighed. "Another naïve attempt to make a difference. I was an advisor to Tony Blair when that was still a job for idealists. I lasted almost three years, until Tony found God and George W. Bush, and I was kicked out on my ear."

"You were fired because of George W. Bush?"

"Technically for attacking Rupert Murdoch with a rubber hose." Helen paused. "Long story. He deserved it."

Lou laughed as Helen continued. "Cue a misguided relationship with an old colleague, followed by miscarriage and very ugly breakup. Tired of London and of life, as Johnson put it. Spent the next half decade bouncing around various industries, crafting after-dinner speeches for retired politicians and has-been cricketers, occasionally advising companies on how to avoid scandals, generally feeling sorry for myself. Then one day—this would be late 2008—I get a phone call from a friend in Mountain View who needs a spot of crisis PR for a couple of his portfolio companies. I was aware of Silicon Valley, naturally, and had a general sense that it was run by sociopathic infants."

"So you decided to bring them down?"

"On the contrary. I wanted to help them! I was still an idealist, just about, and really thought all they needed was schooling in old-fashioned ethics. Most of the truly wealthy and successful people I'd encountered in British media and politics were obsessed with the notion of being thought of as *decent*. It took me—well—maybe three meetings to realize that the new tech emperors literally don't think in terms of good or bad, decent or indecent. All that matters is . . ."

"Money," said Lou.

"Data," Helen corrected her. "That's what drives every decision. They leave money to the venture capitalists."

Lou snorted. "You made it through three whole meetings at tech companies before you figured out they were immoral."

"Well, the first two were mostly HR orientation things. The third was with the founder of a dating app that wanted me to silence the mother of a fourteen-year-old girl who'd been killed by a convicted child molester she'd met on their platform."

"Jesus."

Helen poured herself some more wine and set the empty bottle on the coffee table next to Lou. "That's what broke me. Dropped the scales from my eyes. There wasn't even the facade of wanting to do the right thing. She was just a cell in a spreadsheet to be deleted. So I drove out to see this poor woman. I mean literally dirt-poor. She was living in an illegal sublet in Victorville in just the most appalling poverty you've ever seen, or at least that I'd ever seen. But you could tell her daughter—Maria was her name, I'll never forget—was just her whole world. School photographs, awards for dancing and drama and academics—every surface was like a shrine to this girl. The poor mother was just sobbing and sobbing. It soon became obvious she had no intention of suing the company—couldn't have afforded a lawyer if she wanted one. Knew no journalist would care about her daughter—even the local paper didn't give a toss. I could have given her a warm hug and driven away and everything would be fine. But the company didn't care. Either I came back with a signed NDA— essentially blaming her daughter for her own assault—or they'd hire a private investigator to burn her life to the ground, *just to cover all the bases.* That was literally how the CEO put it to me."

Lou knew she should feel revolted by that. But the truth was, she'd heard tech founders say far worse, publicly, and without shame. Surely Helen had too. "Who was the CEO?"

Helen shook her head. "It doesn't matter, he's dead now."

Lou's eyes widened, but Helen clarified that this one couldn't be pinned on Fate. "Snowboarding accident. Lots of witnesses. Point is, we both know he could have been any Valley CEO. And this was 2008, long before things got truly ugly."

Lou nodded. She was still in high school in 2008—one of the last of her friends to sign up for a Facebook account. Back then, if she ever thought about Silicon Valley, it was as a magical utopia filled with nineteen-year-old nerds, slaying dinosaur industries and making music free. Had that ever been true? "So what did you do?"

"My job. I got the mother's signature on the NDA. Then the next morning I left my entire payment for the job in a duffel bag on the mother's doorstep with a note telling her it was from a friend at her church. I have no idea if she kept it. All I know is two months later I drove back to Victorville, and she was gone."

"You didn't try to find her?"

Helen shrugged. "I'd already decided how I was going to spend the rest of my career. That's the good thing about being adopted by bankers: one picks up the basics of short selling and money laundering. They would be so proud of me."

"That's insane."

Helen dismissed the compliment. "You'd have done the same."

Lou took a slug of wine as she considered this. Would she have done the same? Her mom loved to tell people that her daughter had moved to Silicon Valley to "comfort the afflicted, and afflict the comfortable"—something she'd heard a guy say once on TV. Maybe that was half-true. Lou loved watching those comfortable fuckers squirm, but how many afflicted people were truly better off after she hit publish? Why did it always strike a nerve when a turd like Brusk accused her of pursuing a vendetta against success, or an anonymous troll sneered about her daddy issues?

"Fuck your parents." Lou's head was fuzzy from all the wine, and she heard herself say the words before she had consciously thought them. "*You* should be proud of you."

Helen slammed down her glass, so hard that Lou thought either it or the table might shatter. "Not to sound like a revolutionary, Lou, but we need to dismantle the structures." She lifted the glass, but only to slam it down again. "That's why taking down Raum after the IPO was to be my pièce de résistance. Millions of dollars for the victims, yes, but more importantly I want to teach Tim Palgrave, Charlie Brusk, and his Saudi friends a lesson. To make other investors see that you can't build a house of cards without an ethical foundation." A pause. "A total, irreversible shift in thinking."

Lou looked again at the Post-it notes. She was suddenly reminded of Carol's favorite joke: *What do you call a hundred lawyers at the bottom of the ocean? A good start.* "You think that's what Fate's trying to do? Bring it all crashing down, one predator at a time?"

Helen stood and began collecting the empty bottles and glasses. "I think I'm a little drunk and a lot tired and we've exhausted every line of inquiry for tonight. Don't forget we have to be up early to watch Elmsley triumphantly announce the hiring of Martina Allen. I assume you'd like to join me to witness that in person?"

Lou nodded. She had not forgotten, nor could she stay away. "Unless Fate has other plans."

Helen didn't answer. Instead she set the empties in the kitchen, then returned for her papers and phone. "Let's get some sleep and see what fresh hell tomorrow brings."

AT EXACTLY SEVEN o'clock the next morning, Lou's alarm woke her with a jolt, albeit a very comfortable one. For the first time in months, she was lying in an honest-to-God bed, underneath an honest-to-God duvet, her head resting on a pair of honest-to-God pillows. The comfort of Helen's spare room was almost enough to compensate for the mild hangover she had from the five glasses of wine.

The feeling of well-being lasted for at least twenty-five seconds as Lou stretched, silenced her phone, and remembered that she and Helen were due at Raum One in an hour, to watch Elmsley Chase crown Raum's new CTO.

As Lou stood under the too-powerful shower in Helen's cavernous marble bathroom, she wondered what Martina Allen must be telling herself to justify taking the job. That going to work for Elmsley Chase—as his "Sheryl"—might somehow fix Raum's toxic culture? That, really, the astronomical paycheck was irrelevant? This was about changing the world! She'd seen her husband make similar compromises—he was running for office as a Democrat, but almost all his campaign funds had come from his old one-percenter Wall Street buddies. The greater good was a powerful justification for cozying up with awful people. Martina Allen could dress it up however she wanted, but in less than an hour, she would stand next to Elmsley Chase and—unless Fate pulled another of her stunts—announce to the world that she had decided to take a job as Raum's new CTO. Chase would smile his smug smile and Wall Street would immediately forget that there had ever been a rapist named Alex Wu.

Lou couldn't stop thinking about Helen's self-described loss of idealism after coming to Silicon Valley, and how similar it had been to her own. They'd both started out as journalists (Lou, for a time, had also flirted with the idea of covering politics) who came to make a difference and ended up angry and disillusioned. Helen had reacted by trying to bring the system down from within, but Lou hadn't lost faith that a headline or leaked document could still change the world.

Or at least that's what she'd told herself. Now, as the water pounded her scalp, she was ready to accept the truth. She *had* lost faith, a long time ago. The only reason she'd kept banging her head against her computer screen for so long, trying to get someone—anyone—to care about her stories was that she hadn't been able to come up with a better way to take down these assholes. Now there were two women—Helen, and whoever Fate was—who had found better ways. She felt strangely—what was the feeling? flattered? grateful? relieved? exhilarated?—that they seemed to want her along for the ride.

Lou stepped out of the shower and wrapped herself in a fat, warm towel. Moving to the double sink, she brushed her teeth with the toothbrush Helen had left out for her.

If nothing else, Martina Allen's arrival at Raum One would knock Alex Wu's grisly death off the front pages. For an egotist like Wu, that must surely be the ultimate humiliation: to die so publicly and yet be denied the months of news coverage that would normally follow. The same had happened to Joe Christian, hadn't it? His public suicide denied its news cycle by Wu's own death.

Lou spat the toothpaste into the sink and watched it describe a slow frothy spiral toward the plughole. If Fate really was so good at manipulating human behavior, was it so far-fetched that she could also persuade Elmsley Chase to hire Martina Allen to bump both deaths off the front page? So that journalists wouldn't dig too deep?

Lou switched on the hair dryer and pointed it toward her too-long hair. As she did so, she examined her scalp and was relieved to find no traces of blotching, or anything else to indicate that Joe Christian's rash might have been contagious. She pulled on her shirt, freshly pressed by some unseen Four Seasons worker, and walked into the kitchen to find Helen munching a triangle of toast. "There's cereal in one of these cupboards, I expect," she added, waving her hands to demonstrate that she herself was above such infantile breakfasts.

Lou declined the offer, pouring herself a cup of black coffee.

"So, what's your plan B?"

"Plan B?"

"Assuming Fate doesn't sabotage Martina Allen's new job? I know you're not going to sit in the audience and clap politely as she saves Raum's long-term future and nukes your retirement plans."

Helen dabbed her lips with a starched napkin. "I told you. Martina Allen is off-limits, for me at least. I won't deny her the promotion she deserves."

Lou took a slice of toast from the counter and bit into it, mostly to avoid vocalizing something that still really bothered her about Helen Tyler. Helen had drawn a line in the sand when it came to Martina Allen, but in her day job, she constantly covered for men who victimized far less privileged women—justifying it by secretly paying them compensation or buying them houses or paying their therapy bills. Maybe some of those women would have preferred not to have been assaulted or harassed in the first place?

"So we just sit back and let Elmsley save his IPO. Never mind all that shit about smashing the structures. Can't upset the rich white lady."

A flash of annoyance crossed Helen's face, and for a second Lou thought they were about to get into another fight. Instead Helen lowered her voice, almost as if she thought there might be a listening device hidden in the coffeemaker. "Absent some intervention from our mysterious mutual friend, there's nothing either of us can do to stop today's hiring announcement. *But* I was thinking perhaps Ms. Allen might be persuaded to put off her start date for a few weeks if she had to deal with some kind of family crisis. Give her some time to consider whether Raum really is the right next step for her."

"A family crisis?" Lou knew Martina Allen didn't have any children. "You mean her husband?" Thomas Milton Calder—a hedge fund manager turned politician—probably had a closet full of skeletons. Lou remembered Helen's boast about Alex Wu—that it was her job to know what *shit* powerful men were *into*.

Helen finished chewing another morsel of toast. "I would have to figure out a few details to avoid humiliating his wife. But yes; I thought, after the press conference, while you start sifting through the Raum database for clues about Fate, I might do a little digging into future governor Calder. What do you say?"

Lou said that sounded like an excellent idea.

"Splendid." Helen glanced at her watch. "Shall we go?"

They made the short walk to Raum One, and Helen's security pass whisked them through the glass entrance gates and into the lobby that, two nights earlier, had been the site of Lou's career implosion. Gone were the cocktail tables and neon lights; gone, too, were the colorful plastic animals and the stage from which Elmsley Chase had watched his IPO hopes come crashing down. The only echo of the party was the stub of a mostly melted ice sculpture, cordoned off with blue-and-white SFPD tape and guarded by a single uniformed police officer.

Otherwise, life at Raum One seemed to have returned entirely to normal. Raum employees in black T-shirts and jeans rushed to and from the elevator banks. A few gave her sideways glances as they passed: Lou McCarthy—hater of all things Raum—back at the scene of her recent professional humiliation.

"Feeling OK?" Helen sounded genuinely concerned—was Lou's discomfort that obvious? "Perhaps we should have taken the side entrance."

"I'm fine," Lou murmured, resisting the impulse to add, *There's a fucking side entrance?*

They took the elevator to the second floor, where a glass-walled conference room, bigger than the entire *Herald* newsroom, was already half-filled with reporters from all the national and local media, plus at least a dozen friendly tech bloggers all tapping away on identical Mac laptops. Lou stayed in Helen's wake, hoping her cloak of invisibility would extend to cover them both.

"Shit." Lou spotted Tommy Paphitis among the bloggers. She whispered it again when, at that same moment, Tommy glanced up and they made eye contact. His brow furrowed in confusion, but then his expression changed to something like delight at seeing his old workmate. He gave a wave and, to Lou's horror, began making his way toward them.

Shit, shit, and a million more shits. How could Lou possibly explain why she was back at Raum One, palling around with one of the company's crisis managers? The last thing she needed was for Tommy to tell everyone at the *Herald* that she was now working at Raum.

Then relief—Tommy had taken no more than a couple of steps when a T-shirt-clad security guard with a neck like a festive ham blocked his path. Lou watched Tommy gesture plaintively in her direction as the guard emphatically shook his head. Crestfallen, Tommy returned to his seat.

"Sequester us a spot in the corner?" Helen gestured toward a row of transparent plastic chairs that had been cordoned off on the back row. "I should try to find Elmsley, and make sure his speech is in the prompter. Help him tie his shoelaces, pull up his socks."

Lou nodded and set off toward the farthest, darkest corner, scanning the room as she walked. Was one of these people Fate? The only women she could see in attendance were Miquela Rio from the *Journal*, a tech blogger from *Forbes*, and a brace of Raum communications staffers whom Lou recognized from the party two nights earlier. One of these PR flacks gave her a confused smile, which Lou returned at least 20 percent more sarcastically than she had intended. Did Elmsley Chase know that Lou was in the building? It was one thing sending out a bullshit press release praising her reporting on Alex Wu, but how would he react when he saw her sitting with the woman hired to save his precious IPO? Lou found an empty seat tucked into the corner, placing her cell phone on the one adjacent to reserve it for Helen. This proved prescient, as when Helen finally returned twenty minutes later, the conference room was filled to bursting. The throng of journalists had been joined by a couple dozen Raum employees, and a smattering of the kind of besuited, phone-pecking hangers-on that always filled out important corporate events. Last to arrive was Tim Palgrave, who sat at the far end of the front row, gnawing on a dry bagel. Lou wondered where he had gotten it from.

Notable, but not really, by his absence was Charlie Brusk. Apparently even the hiring of the most famous woman in Silicon Valley didn't justify leaving his neon-and-ivory tower in Palo Alto.

Helen's reappearance—so discreet that it was as if she'd simply materialized in the chair next to Lou—still somehow signaled to the audience that the main event was about to occur. The gaggle of journalists fell quiet, and only the light tapping of a dozen MacBooks punctuated the silence. Moments later a glass side door swung open and Elmsley Chase bounded through, beaming like the cat who had just taken delivery of an oil tanker filled with cream. He was wearing a dark suit and a deep red tie, and Lou could swear he'd dyed his hair gray around the temples. Two nights earlier Chase had appeared youthful, carefree, arrogant—today he was artfully transformed into a pastiche of a grown-up CEO. The Raum staffers burst into sycophantic applause. To their eternal shame, the press corps joined in the ovation as Chase prepared to make the big, belated announcement that would mark the great selling out of Martina Allen. Lou scanned the room again. What was she expecting? Fate to storm in with a machine gun? A sudden power cut to derail the press conference? Neither happened.

Chase walked, alone, onto the stage. There was no sign of Allen herself. Evidently her entrance was to be a complete surprise—a dramatic *holy shit* moment for the press corps.

"Still doing OK?" Helen leaned close and whispered in her ear.

"Top of the world," said Lou. "Excited to have a gallery seat at the sell-out of the century." She tried and failed to make that sound like a joke.

"Better to be on the inside of the Big Top, pissing out," said Helen.

Elmsley Chase took his place behind the podium, nodding in appreciation at the applause. His eyes fell on the back row and he did a brief double take when he saw Lou. He quickly looked away, the merest trace of a smug smile playing across his lips. Helen had warned him.

"Ladies and gentlemen," he read from the prompter, slowly, his face now a mask of seriousness. "Thank you all for coming." He paused and took an artfully choreographed breath. "These past twenty-four hours have been very difficult for all of us at Raum, and I'd like to take a moment to remember my friend Alex Wu, who—as you know—passed away two nights ago."

Passed away. Had ever that euphemism been so stretched past its breaking point? *He passed away peacefully, covered in pustules, impaled on a thirty-foot-tall ice dick.*

A noise erupted from the center of the room, causing Lou to jump almost out of her shoes. But it was only more fucking applause. The Raum staffers and journalists were now clapping for the memory of Alex Wu. An ovation for a serial rapist. Where was Fate with that machine gun?

Chase waited for this latest ovation to subside before continuing his heartfelt speech. "It's in moments like these that we must take pause. Pause as human beings, pause as friends, and—yes—pause as leaders. It's moments like this that force us to reflect on our contribution, and our responsibility, to the universe." Chase reached a knuckle to his eye and wiped away a nonexistent tear. "To that end, I have realized that it's time for Raum to enter a new phase. Time to recognize that a public company needs a leadership team that reflects the rich diversity of our users and our employees. And so that is why, I . . ."

Another pause, to build up yet more anticipation for his bombshell Martina Allen announcement. The room gladly obliged—even the tapping of the journalists' keyboards fell silent, waiting for him to reveal how he planned to save Raum's IPO. Five seconds passed, then ten. The longer the silence lasted, the lower Lou felt her body temperature drop. Elmsley Chase's face, once rosy with arrogance, was now white with what seemed to be shock, or fear? Chase was still standing at the podium, his mouth still open, but he was frozen. Mute. This wasn't a dramatic pause; it was . . . something else. Something bad.

Lou instinctively looked upward, but all she saw was the low ceiling of the conference room. She glanced toward Helen and realized she had done the exact same thing, as if anticipating another Raum executive would come tumbling from the rafters. Still in perfect sync, they turned to look along the back wall of the room, but saw only a wall of cameras blinking back at Chase, alone and silent on the stage, staring into space.

Not into space. Lou realized now that Chase was staring into the teleprompter, his eyes flicking back and forth across the screen.

"Uhhh." Chase turned back to the crowd, and the cameras. "I'm sorry, excuse me." He shook his head as if mentally rewinding his speech. "And that is why, I . . ." But this sentence stalled too. A murmur spread through the crowd. *And that is why you what?* Was Elmsley Chase having a stroke?

With great effort, Chase seemed to finally regain control of his faculties. "And that is why, in the coming days I will be announcing Alex Wu's replacement . . . very soon. Thank you." And with that tautology, and one last puzzled look toward the prompter, he walked quickly off the stage, leaving the entire room in stunned silence.

"What the fuck just happened?" Lou whispered to Helen.

"I have absolutely no fucking idea," Helen whispered back. Then, grabbing her purse with one hand and Lou's forearm with the other, she took off after the retreating CEO.

55

"THREE ARMENIAN CALL girls and a king-sized Toblerone? You can't be serious."

In an underground meeting room, two floors below the lobby of Raum One, Helen Tyler was pacing around a conference table, waving her arms in a pantomime of despair.

But Elmsley Chase, he assured them, was as serious as dick cancer. "*Politico* has photographs. And video. They've made a fucking slideshow." Chase slammed his palms on the table, making the frosted glass walls shake. "I thought you vetted her."

Helen stopped her pacing and wheeled toward him. "Oh ho ho, no, you most certainly did not think that. What happened, *Elmsley*, is that I suggested that perhaps it might be a good idea to vet your new stunt hire before agreeing to pay her six billion dollars to save your IPO." A pause. "And you said . . . I quote . . . 'There's no need to vet Martina fucking Allen.'"

Chase opened his mouth to respond, but Helen wasn't done. "And then what did I say after that?" It was a rhetorical question. "I said, 'She might be little Miss Whiter-than-White Feminist Poster Child, but her husband is. A. Fucking. Politician. We don't need . . .' and I quote"—she raised her voice to a yell—"'SOME HIGH-PRICED ESCORT COMING OUT OF THE WOODWORK AND GIVING US YET ANOTHER SEX SCANDAL TO DEAL WITH.'"

Another attempt by Chase to respond was met with another onslaught. "THREE ARMENIAN CALL GIRLS AND A FUCKING KING-SIZED TOBLERONE."

Lou sat at the other end of the table, in stunned silence. Of course Helen had spent the time right before Chase's speech trying to sow doubt about Allen's vetting. That way when she and Lou found some dirt on

Calder, she could remind him that she'd been the one to warn him. They didn't expect the warning to be so immediately relevant.

It had to be Fate's doing. She'd sabotaged Martina Allen's new job by targeting her cheating husband—almost exactly as Lou and Helen had proposed back at the Four Seasons. *Had Fate been listening to their conversation and decided to take matters into her own hands?*

Lou was suddenly aware that Elmsley Chase was jabbing his finger toward her end of the table. "Remind me why the fuck we have a journalist in the room?"

Helen took a deep, slow breath and forced her lips into a smile, intoning as if to a child, "Elmsley. As I explained, Lou is no longer employed with the *Herald*. She has kindly agreed to help us—that is, help you—figure out what prompted Alex Wu to jump off a balcony two nights ago. I assumed you'd welcome her assistance?"

"She's signed an NDA?"

"Would she be in here if she hadn't?"

Chase scowled and turned to Lou. "So can *you* tell me how a copy of *Politico*'s front page—complete with photos of Thomas Milton Calder and three Armenian whores—ended up on my teleprompter screen?"

Lou was saved from having to answer the most batshit insane question she'd ever been asked by the sound of the door crashing open, and a large man—in both height and girth—barreling through it. He was bald except for a black goatee and was draped in a baggy T-shirt and sagging jeans. He had a bulky black laptop in one hand, a gigantic can of Rockstar energy drink in the other, and was panting and sweating like he had just run an ultramarathon.

"They're not on *Politico*, boss."

He addressed this not to Chase but to Helen. Lou stifled a gasp of recognition, because surely the man who had just burst in was the legendary Tenrick Wheeler. Alex Wu's roommate turned business partner—and the co-creator of the Raum algorithm. Helen Tyler's "research chappy" was *Ten fucking Wheeler*? Lou knew that Wheeler had taken a job at Raum after the acquisition, but assumed he was either long gone or locked away inside a lab, developing new and innovative ways to track Raum users and obliterate what was left of their privacy. One of the smartest engineers in the world was working on Helen Tyler's smear squad? Was there anything this company couldn't ruin?

"Glad you could join us, Ten." Helen spoke to Wheeler with a tone that was familiar, bordering on maternal. "Now, what in the name of fuck are you talking about?"

"The gross photos. The sex tape. They're not on *Politico*. The page that showed up on Elmsley's prompter—it wasn't real. Or at least it was real—by which I mean it physically exists—but it didn't come from *Politico*."

Elmsley Chase held up his phone, which showed a column of pixelated Thomas Milton Calder porn. Lou winced at what, even in thumbnail form, was unmistakably a half-unwrapped bar of Swiss chocolate. "I'm looking at it right now."

"You are, but nobody else is," said Ten emphatically. "The page is spoofed, only visible on devices with Raum One IP addresses. When I accessed Politico.com through a VPN, it showed this." Wheeler opened the lid of his hulking laptop and turned it to show an entirely different front page, topped with a story about corn subsidies. "Someone hacked our local DNS and redirected the domain to a fake page, hosted somewhere in Ukraine. I assume the same person who hacked your prompter and, judging by the IP address, also the same person who messed with the guest list to the party two nights ago."

"Thank fuck," said Elmsley Chase, his head lolling back in relief. "There's no sex tape?"

"Oh, there's definitely a sex tape," said Wheeler, clearly delighted. "That's Calder with the escorts, no doubt about it. I checked the metadata on the photos and also Calder's Raum Band data. He was positively in room 681 at the Redwood Hotel in Palo Alto last night, and so were . . ." He paused and clicked open a new tab on his laptop. ". . . Martika, Milena, and Becky."

"Becky?" said Elmsley.

Ten shrugged. "Armenia has Beckys too."

Lou didn't give a shit about Becky. She was far more interested in the first part of what Ten had said. "This happened at the Redwood?" She looked at Helen, whose wide eyes confirmed that she was just as excited by that revelation. No question where they were both heading as soon as the meeting was over.

Ten paused and looked at Helen, evidently confused.

"This is Lou McCarthy," said Helen. "She's working with me."

At this, Wheeler's face brightened. "Lou McCarthy! I just didn't . . . yunno . . . in context. Shit. I'm a huge fan." In the stark light of the conference room, he appeared to be blushing. "Your takedown of Tyrus Weber was epic . . . What a prick." How was she supposed to respond to that? *Thanks! Sorry my more recent story made your pal Alex Wu jump off a ledge.*

Wheeler's enthusiasm did little to improve Elmsley's mood. "So nobody has the story. This is just another attempt to sabotage my fucking IPO?"

It was impressive how quickly Elmsley had cast himself—not Calder or Allen—as the primary victim in all of this. He hadn't asked Lou for her opinion, but she gave it anyway. "If someone wanted to embarrass you, they could have let you finish the announcement and left you standing on an empty stage. Or waited a few hours and leaked the photos for real. Martina Allen would have had to resign—there's no way she could handle such a high-profile job while her marriage was being torn apart in the tabloids. Whoever did this didn't want it to become public." Lou turned to Tenrick. "I assume Martina Allen was sent the fake website too?"

He nodded. "Based on how quickly she left the building, yeah. They spoofed the cell phone towers around Raum One too, so she'd have seen the same thing we did." His face lit up as he realized: "Shit, imagine when she starts freaking out at hubby and neither of them can find the article?"

Now Helen spoke. "It doesn't matter. They'll both know it's real. The wife always knows."

"No way he runs for governor now," Lou added. "Nobody will know how or why Calder went from master of the universe to world's biggest loser, overnight."

Again Chase slammed his palms onto the glass table. "Awesome, so Calder gets to skulk away, his wife stays at Hopsearch, and meantime I still don't have a fucking CTO, which means we're still fucking fucked." He redirected his rage toward Tenrick Wheeler. "I want to know who is doing this. And I want to know yesterday."

Wheeler nodded and puffed back toward the door, pausing to smile at Lou. "Really nice to meet you," he said. Then he turned and added the words that would take Lou's week from the bizarre to the full-blown insane: "Oh, and tell your mom she's a badass too. Those assholes deserved it."

He was gone before Lou was able to ask him what the hell he was talking about.

Lou raced after Tenrick Wheeler, just in time to see him disappear through a door at the end of the hall. She followed him and immediately felt like she'd passed to another dimension, or at least the storage room of a small electronics retailer. Computers littered every available surface, each in a different stage of autopsy. Piles of books and magazines formed a stumpy labyrinth on the floor, leading to a reproduction of the phone booth used in the *Bill and Ted* movies. On the wall was a crooked framed photo of Wheeler, standing arm in arm with Steve Wozniak. Lou was impressed at how much lived-in chaos he had managed to establish in a building that had been completed only a month earlier.

"Hey? Tenrick . . ."

Wheeler turned to face her, clearly alarmed that someone had invaded his personal sanctum.

"Oh, uh . . . hey."

"What did you mean back there, about my mom being a badass?"

Wheeler furrowed his brow. "Oh shit, you haven't seen the video?"

Forty-five seconds later, Lou had seen the video. Tenrick had plugged his laptop into one of three monitors on his desk (after first clearing aside a collection of empty Rockstar cans and a stuffed kangaroo) and pulled up the shaky camera-phone video of a pale young man—a boy really—clutching a stiff wire brush, sobbing as he frantically scrubbed a patch of red graffiti from a dusty white garage door. Lou felt sick as she recognized the door and, below the bristles and bleach, saw the scrawled letters *UTCUN*. The camera zoomed out to reveal two more figures: the first was unmistakably Lou's mom, shouting directions at the petrified adolescent, and the second was her best friend, Carol, a few feet away, brandishing a shotgun. This couldn't be happening.

The headline above the video—which had originally been posted on Reddit but had since spread across social media—read *Badass lesbian vigilantes kidnap graffiti kid, make him clean their door.*

Things got even worse when Ten scrolled down to the comments. As Lou read them, all thoughts of Martina Allen and Fate vanished so completely that they might as well have never existed. Left behind was a feeling of pure panic and the absolute certainty that whatever the cost, and whatever the consequences, she had to get to Atlanta.

56

THE COMMENTS WERE bad. Each time Fate scrolled, another fifty appeared, an infinite feed of bloody vengeance sworn against two women who had given one of Pétain's trolls a taste of his own misery. Ugly, violent, threatening, but, above all, tedious.

> *Let's see how brave those fucking dykes are when the real men show up.*
> *Their shotgun vs my AK = no contest.*
> *These bitches need to die.*
> *Fuck yeah, bro. Count me in for some of that action.*

What they lacked in creativity they made up for in efficiency. Pétain had filed his latest red notice just an hour earlier, and it had taken his supporters less than twenty minutes to find Kerri-Ann McCarthy's address, then only another ten to find the location of the domestic-violence shelter where she worked. Soon after, a Russian kid had found a copy of Carol Brook's Federal Bureau of Prisons ID, identifying her as a senior correctional officer at Atlanta's federal penitentiary.

Fate scrolled deeper. Twenty more comments. Fifty. They were already inside Kerri-Ann's bank accounts, her tax returns, her medical records—ransacking her life, excavating her past. It wouldn't be long till they found her divorce petition, still officially sealed by the court and packed with her ex-husband's lies. Then the mob would be back outside Kerri-Ann's house, this time armed with weapons far more deadly than paint.

Fate whispered a quiet *shiiit*. This had not been her plan. Lou's mother was never supposed to be more than a bit player in the drama—some quick and easy leverage to convince her loving, protective daughter to stay in San Francisco with Helen Tyler.

Helen's press release had worked exactly as expected; the mob had moved on from Lou and her family, with the only casualty a vandalized garage door. All Kerri-Ann McCarthy had had to do was clean her own damn door, go back to work; continue with her life. All Lou McCarthy had had to do was stay in San Francisco, and everything would have been fine.

But Carol Brook was a loose cannon. She'd leveraged—brilliantly, Fate had to admit—her access to law enforcement databases to track down one of the dumb kids who had called her friend's only daughter a slutcunt. The two women had shown up at his work—a Best Buy in Decatur— ordered him into their truck, then forced him at gunpoint to perform this very public penance. Because of *course* she fucking had. In hindsight, everything Fate knew about Carol and her relationship with Kerri-Ann and Lou should have indicated this outcome.

At the far end of her desk, one of Fate's phones chirped a familiar, private chirp heralding the arrival of a chat message: *You seen this?* She knew what *this* was without even clicking on the link. The whole world was forwarding this damn video of Kerri-Ann and Carol.

She started to type a response, but then stopped herself. She needed to take a breath. To regroup. Recalculate. She had made too many knee-jerk decisions in too-fast succession, and now things were starting to seriously unravel.

Inviting Lou McCarthy to the party at Raum One had been rash, but the gamble had paid off. Sabotaging Martina Allen's new job at Raum had involved an insane amount of personal risk, way too close to home for comfort—but that gambit had worked too, and Fate had told herself that she was still in control. But it had taken her eye off the ball—and that loss of focus had now put two innocent women's lives in danger. Probably more than two, unless she repaired the damage fast.

Fate leaned back in her Aeron office chair, inhaled deeply, and closed her eyes. When she opened them again, she was looking up at the row of photographs tacked above her monitor, three of which already had small nicks torn in the top right corner.

She had spent years studying these assholes, following their careers, learning their habits, not just their Achilles' heels but their Achilles' knees and elbows and ears and most of all their Achilles' cocks. Each disgusting domino had been positioned perfectly to fall at the time of her choosing. And fall they had.

The irony was as stark as it was bitter. The men had behaved exactly as predicted, but it was the women—the background players about whom Fate had barely given a second thought—who had proved themselves endlessly complex, and boundlessly frustrating.

Fate focused back on her computer screen. This was nobody's fault but her own.

It was she who had taken Kerri-Ann McCarthy and Carol Brook for granted, denied them agency, and—the greatest irony of all—underestimated them, just as Fate herself had been underestimated by every man she'd ever met.

As if to underscore the point, an alert box blinked onto Fate's monitor. A ping from Helen Tyler's credit card company, reporting that her Amex had just been used to book a seat for Louise Bryce McCarthy on the 3:45 p.m. flight from SFO to Atlanta Hartsfield-Jackson. Fate exhaled slowly at news of yet another unintended consequence. A mouse click brought up a city map with a blinking dot of confirmation: Lou was already in a taxicab headed for the airport. ETA, thirty-five minutes.

Fuck.

So what should she do now? Ground the flight? Call in a bomb threat? Cancel the ticket, and Helen's credit card? She did her best to mentally game out these and a dozen other possible responses. Al Capone had gotten himself nailed on tax fraud charges—Fate sure as shit wasn't going to jeopardize all she'd worked for by calling in a bomb hoax to SFO.

She drummed her fingertips on the mouse. Wasn't that exactly what she had already done? Risked a decade of work, and her chance to rip a hole in the fabric of the universe, because she nudged a gang of angry little boys to spray-paint a fucking garage door without properly gaming out the consequences?

Fate watched the dot blink, blink, blinking its way through Potrero toward I-280. How the hell do you stop a daughter from flying across the country to save her mother, and the woman who helped raise her?

When the glaringly obvious answer came to her—a full two minutes later, as Lou's blinking dot was already zipping along the freeway—she laughed out loud. When you're as smart as Fate, sometimes it's good to be reminded that you're a fucking idiot.

57

"LOU, CAN YOU hear me?"

Her mother's voice on the other end of the phone sounded breathless, which wasn't surprising in the circumstances.

"Jesus, I've been trying to call you. What the hell were the two of you thinking?" She hadn't meant to shout. This was almost certainly Carol's fault, not her mom's. Also, she needed her mom to stay calm, and not to do anything else crazy.

There was silence on the line, although Lou could still hear breathing, and what sounded like a car engine, until: "You're not seriously blaming us for this?"

Lou looked out of the cab window at the names of the airlines above the terminal doors creeping past. Their slow progress was mostly due to the clusters of vRaums illegally double-parked every few feet. Better to risk a fine from airport police than a disastrous 4.5-star review by forcing passengers to walk an extra few paces to their terminal.

"None of this is your fault, Mom . . . " *Who takes a shotgun to a Best Buy and kidnaps a teenager?* "I'm just glad to hear your voice. Where are you?" They could have the fight in Atlanta.

"We're on our way to the airport."

The connection was breaking up, as it always did close to SFO, thanks to the anti-drone jammers, and Lou assumed she'd misheard. She was the one who was on her way to the airport. "Say that again, Mom? Where are you guys?"

"I told Carol we shouldn't come, but she said it's not every day a billionaire flies you first-class. We didn't even have time to pack."

Lou's cab finally made it to the curb, and the driver started fussing with the meter. Lou leaned forward between the seats. "Wait . . . keep that running, please." She ignored the driver's sigh. "Mom, I don't understand what you're saying. Pack for what? Who is flying you where?"

"We were going to surprise you, but I figured you'd had enough of surprises. Your pal Elmsley sent two tickets to San Fran, arriving tonight. A bullshit kind of apology, but I suppose he doesn't want the blame if we get ourselves killed."

Lou ignored the cabdriver's continuing grumbling. "Elmsley sent you plane tickets to San Francisco? When? How do you know they were from him?" Lou had seen Pétain's followers use scams like this before—sending their victims to airports or federal buildings, then calling in fake terrorist threats in their name. People had been arrested, and worse.

"I'm not an idiot, Lou. He had his assistant video-call us—Helga . . ." She paused and Lou heard Carol shouting in the background. "Helen. Right. Australian woman, redhead, weirdly smooth forehead. She's booked us rooms at the Four Seasons and gave us her personal number if there was anything else we needed."

"Helen video-called you?" She had left Helen in a hurry back at Raum One, but surely she'd been clear? Her mom was in trouble and she needed to go to Atlanta. If Helen could pay for the flights, then she'd pay her back. Had Helen misunderstood? Was this a ploy to keep Lou in town so they could keep investigating Fate? Either was better than the alternative: that Pétain had created a deepfake video of Helen to trick her mom and Carol into getting on a plane.

Her mom was still talking—yakking about flight times and instructions that Helen had supposedly given to her and Carol. "She told us some guy named Landon would meet us at arrivals."

Lou considered her options. She had tried so hard to shield her mom from the epic shitpile that was her life and career, and all it had done was make things worse. If only she'd been honest about how dangerous these monsters were, then no way they'd have grabbed that little punk from Best Buy. More lies, more consequences. At least if they came to San Francisco, they'd have Landon to protect them. And Lou could keep searching for Fate.

"Sounds good, Mom. Text me when you're boarding, OK?" She ended the call, then leaned forward again and told the exasperated driver to turn the car around and head back to the city.

Fate watched Lou's dot blink slowly outside the terminal entrance—then felt a wave of relief as it began moving again, returning toward the freeway. Her panicked Hail Mary had worked. If she wanted to stop Mohammed from flying to the mountain, then she needed to fly the mountain to Mohammed. QED.

There would still be consequences—thousands of new variables, starting when Lou got back to Raum One and Helen Tyler confirmed the video call was a fake. But those were nothing compared with the curveball that Lou would now be babysitting two middle-aged women, one of whom worked in law enforcement and never went anywhere without a firearm and a metal baseball bat. A radical new reality, with just four days to go until zero hour.

Four days that had just gotten much longer.

She tried to consider the positives. Martina Allen was out of the equation, for now at least. And with her mom in town, and still in danger, Lou McCarthy would be even more motivated to help Helen Tyler identify the person working so hard to control their movements. She would be desperate. Maybe even recklessly so.

Fate allowed herself a smile as her screen displayed the first of its recalculations. So far, so good. And Lou's cab was almost back at Raum One.

This is good. Everything is good.

She was back in the driving seat. Now it was time to accelerate for the finish line.

58

"**LOU! HELEN TOLD** me you were in Atlanta!"

Lou had barely set foot back in Raum One when she was intercepted in the hallway by a very animated Ten Wheeler, still clutching his oversized laptop.

Lou considered explaining everything that had just happened in the cab, then realized she couldn't. "My mom and her friend are coming here instead," she summarized.

Ten didn't ask any follow-up questions. "You need to see this," he announced instead, turning his laptop so she could see the blurry image filling the entire screen.

It was a video still of a very toned, very tanned butt.

"Jesus, Ten." Lou most certainly did not need to see that.

Ten angled the laptop back toward himself and clicked twice on the trackpad. "Sorry, I mean this. In the mirror." He showed the screen again, this time with the butt shrunk to half size, revealing another part of the image: a flat-screen TV reflected in a mirrored headboard. Lou could just about make out a reversed Redwood Hotel logo and some block-capital text—the standard welcome message displayed on the TV to new guests.

"What am I meant to be looking at?" She didn't have time for guessing games.

"OK," Ten said, incapable of brevity. "We know Calder met the escorts in the bar of the Redwood, right? Then took them upstairs."

Lou nodded. "I assume."

"His Raum Band data shows he didn't spend the night, which makes sense given his wife is in town. But here's what I couldn't figure. If he wasn't staying at the hotel, then why was he there in the first place? A man like Calder isn't likely to go somewhere so public just to pick up random chicks."

Ten's enthusiasm for the puzzle was obvious, and now Lou was interested too. "Someone must have invited him—for a business meeting or something—and then introduced him to the girls?"

"That's Helen's theory too." Ten raised a finger. "So I checked the security footage from the bar, elevator, and hallways, and it had all been erased." He paused for effect. "Also, the sex tape was shot from multiple angles. Whoever did this must have spent some serious time rigging the joint. They knew he was coming."

They. Fate.

"Do you know who paid for the suite?"

Ten was beaming now, and Lou realized this was the punch line he'd been building up to. He angled the laptop back toward himself and began performing another magic trick with the keyboard. "You ready for this?"

Lou was two days past ready. "For fuck's sake Ten, just tell me. Whose room was it?"

With the widest grin yet, Ten slowly rotated the screen back. The TV image was perfectly sharp now and Lou instantly understood the reason for Ten's excitement.

"Holy fucking shit."

There it was, reversed in the mirror but crystal clear, the name of the person who had set up Thomas Calder:

Welcome to the Redwood, Palo Alto. Ms. Louise McCarthy.

Lou was lost for words. "I didn't . . . it wasn't me who set him up."

Ten rolled his eyes. "A suite at the Redwood costs two grand a night, and you just used Helen's Amex to book a coach seat on Frontier. *Obviously* you didn't book the room. That's what makes it so cool."

"Cool? My name is on Thomas Calder's sex tape." This was the literal definition of not cool.

"Technically impressive, then," said Ten. "Whoever set Calder up somehow knew Raum was about to hire Martina Allen and was able to lure her husband to the Redwood and get him to fuck three escorts, on camera. That's some next-level social engineering on its own. But then they took screen captures from the tape, and created the whole fake *Politico* page and uploaded it to an air-gapped teleprompter to nuke Elmsley's press conference. Which you have to agree is insane. But then—*then!*—this person knows you and Helen will try to figure out who paid for the room . . . so they put your name on the fucking TV screen, just to mess with you. Come on. That's just Olympian-grade trolling."

Lou didn't find it Olympian; she found it terrifying. The invite to Raum One, the nudge toward the emergency room and Amelia Christian's house, the fake text message from Brusk, her mom's plane ticket, and now this. This wasn't trolling. Fate was showing off—demonstrating that Lou was nothing more than a chess piece she could move at will.

Well, fine. It was time to settle this once and for all. To meet this Fate person, hear her out, then either agree to help or tell her to leave her, and her mom, the fuck alone.

"Where's Helen?" She was already halfway to the elevator as she called back to Ten.

"Meeting upstairs with Elmsley," Ten called after her. "Big 'do not disturb' energy."

That was fine too.

For all of Helen's theorizing that Fate was trying to send them both a message, there was only one name on that TV screen. Fate had sent this invitation to Lou alone—so now Lou was going to accept it, alone.

59%

A LITTLE OVER an hour later, after a pit stop at the Four Seasons to shower and change, Lou arrived at the Redwood Hotel. She passed through the ornate arched entrance and into the needlessly sprawling lobby. She was immediately hit by a blast of air mixed with the scent of synthesized roses.

The Redwood was situated in the dead center of Sand Hill Road, but architecturally it was better suited to the Las Vegas Strip: faux-Grecian pillars, shimmering gold ceilings, and curved marble staircases with thick red carpets that stopped deliberately short of the edges. The centerpiece of the lobby was an enormous crystal chandelier, suspended over a trickling fountain set inside a shallow bronze bowl. The combined effect was of disgusting opulence, as if all the excess money overflowing from the venture capital firms on Sand Hill had poured downhill and pooled right here in the hotel, with nowhere to go but into the fixtures.

Lou walked purposefully across the Carrara marbled floor, although it was more like a teeter than a walk, thanks to the four-inch heels on her feet, held in place with just a thin strap of suede and a tiny gold buckle.

She passed the mirrored front desk and caught sight of her own reflection. The shoes, the makeup, and the emerald-green DVF wrap dress—the sole garment she had found in Helen's closet that even came close to fitting—made her look like a child playing dress-up.

This was the irony of the Redwood Hotel. Only by dressing to stand out could Lou hope to disappear into the background. Her only plan was to head straight to the lobby bar and order a drink. Fate had done everything she could to point a big neon arrow at the hotel, so presumably it wouldn't be long before she made an appearance.

Lou's heart was pounding in her chest as she took one last look at her reflection, this time up in the glittering entranceway to the bar. Even her own mother wouldn't recognize her.

The thought of her mom made her walk even faster. She was running out of time. God only knew how she was going to explain any of this to her mom or Carol. After some cajoling, the desk clerk at the Four Seasons had confirmed that someone had booked a room for the two women on the floor directly below Helen's own apartment. More Olympian trolling by Fate.

Lou had canceled the reservation and asked Landon to make alternative arrangements, all in cash, then to deliver Kerri-Ann and Carol safely from the airport.

Lou opened the velvet clutch purse she'd found on Helen's dresser and unfolded the photos showing Becky's and Milena's faces, which she'd asked Ten to print from the video stills. She'd wanted a picture of Martika too, but the only still that showed her face was . . . well . . . unsuitable to be carried around in such a classy purse. As she went to close the purse, she noticed it wasn't empty. Tucked in the bottom with a lip balm and a folded tissue was a gym membership card and a Platinum American Express bound together with a hair tie. How many Amexes did this woman own? And who takes a purse like this to the gym? Pausing behind a pillar, Lou deftly retrieved her own Chase debit card and driver's license from her bra and dropped them both into the bag.

Now she took a seat at the far end of the bar, positioning herself to take in the entire human zoo that was the Redwood on a Friday evening: khakied venture capitalists, hoodied founders, and the occasional expensive suit paired with neon sneakers—the standard uniform of the thirty-year-old public-company CEO. It was telling that the only really well-dressed people in the bar were those who couldn't afford to be slovenly: the waiters, the wives, and the working girls.

It was barely six thirty, but already the escorts had started to gather, making discreet eye contact with prospective clients, setting out their stall for the evening. Lou had once heard an amazing rumor about how prostitution worked at the Redwood. According to a former receptionist, even the billionaire masters of the universe blanched at openly charging sex to their credit cards and so had created an elaborate system where they paid girls with expensive jewelry from the hotel's high-end gift shop. The next day, the women returned all the jewelry and pocketed the cash, minus the hotel's cut. There was a certain $10,000 tennis bracelet that had featured on every Centurion Amex card from Woodside to Menlo Park. Lou had no idea if the story was true, but dearly hoped it was.

The bartender poured Lou's still water into a highball glass with lemon, and smiled with studied politeness as Lou retrieved her battered Chase debit card and scribbled a two-dollar tip on her six-dollar check. She had considered using Helen's Amex but decided she didn't need to risk getting tossed out of the hotel for credit card fraud. The charge was approved, thank God.

"How you doing tonight?" The bartender was making small talk. Did he think she was an escort? So what if he did? Lou took a slow sip of her water, her cheeks tightening at the kick of lemon as she tried to imitate a desperate housewife of Silicon Valley nursing her third vodka tonic of the evening. She couldn't know if anyone was watching her, watching them.

"I'm good," Lou replied. "I'm supposed to be meeting someone." Absent a photo of Fate, she slid the photo of Becky toward the bartender, who barely glanced at it as he slipped a coaster under Lou's glass.

"Blind date?"

"A friend."

"Well, your friend is very attractive."

Lou smiled. She hadn't asked for his approval. "You haven't seen her?"

The bartender shrugged, again not really looking at the photo. "We get a lot of beautiful women in here."

A lie? Professional courtesy? Lou wondered how many wives came to the Redwood seeking vengeance against their husband's mistress. How many undercover cops hoping to bust a prostitution ring? What was she expecting him to say? *Sure! Everyone knows Becky! She works here every Monday, Wednesday, and Friday! One of our house escorts!*

Lou glanced toward the other end of the bar, where a second bartender was straightening a row of martini glasses ahead of the evening rush.

Maybe she'd have more luck with him. But before she could switch stools, she was startled by a soft, familiar voice whispering conspiratorially in her ear.

"Busted!"

Lou turned to see an angel in a brown silk dress. An angel with dark, piercing eyes and black hair stacked on top of her head in an elaborate twisted bun. "Oh hey . . ." she practically shouted.

"Mindy," said the woman, completing the thought. "We met at Raum One. I'm your stalker fan!"

As if Lou could forget. "Of course. Tim Palgrave's . . ." She swallowed the next word. *What the fuck is wrong with you?*

Mindy smiled, a big warm smile. "Friend with health care benefits."

Lou laughed. "Really? How generous of him." She could smell Mindy's perfume now—the same floral scent she'd been wearing at Raum One.

"Dental too." She tapped her teeth with her dark green fingernails. Mindy looked Lou up and down. "I love that dress! You here on a date?"

"God no," Lou answered way too quickly. "Just waiting for a friend."

"Trust me, honey, you're leaving money on the table looking like that. Lots of guys in here who'd buy you jewelry, if you know what I mean."

Lou smiled at the . . . was it a compliment? "The tennis bracelet thing? That's really true?"

Mindy grabbed her arm and pulled her close like they were old friends. God, she smelled good. "Oh, you have to go see it on your way out. In the gift shop of the lobby. It's the ugliest ass piece of crap you've ever seen!" At this she gave a loud laugh, before catching herself when the bartender stared back.

"I'll definitely check it out," said Lou. "I actually have to leave soon. I don't think my friend is going to show." She would happily have spent hours longer talking with Mindy, but she also knew there was zero chance Fate would make an approach unless Lou was alone.

Lou noticed Mindy looking at the photos she had left unfolded on the bar. "That's her?" she asked. "Your friend?"

Lou nodded.

Mindy picked up the photo and examined it carefully. "Eastern European?"

"Armenian," said Lou.

"Damn, I'm good. This is for a story?"

"I'm not sure yet," Lou replied, wondering if Mindy was more or less
likely to help her if she said it was. "She was here a couple of nights ago,
I think with the husband of a tech exec." Lou decided not to mention
either Calder's or Allen's name.

Mindy shook her head as she handed the photo back to Lou. "Not working, she wasn't. If she was, I'd know her. Everyone who works here is a
regular—the managers kick out the freelancers. Standards to maintain."
She glanced over Lou's shoulder and swore quietly. "Oh shit . . . ten o'clock."

Lou looked at her watch, but Mindy shook her head again. "*Your*
ten o'clock, schlubby sack of shit who just walked in. Khakis with a
button-down. Know who that is?"

Lou looked at the man reflected in the mirrored wall of the bar. "I
don't think so?"

"Brett Palgrave. The dumbass son of his dumbass father. Pro tip: if he
buys you a drink, don't even pick it up."

"Seriously?"

"Some things I never kid about. Every girl in this bar knows Brett
Palgrave. Now, *that's* a story you should write." She got up from her stool
and gave Lou a tight hug. "So good to see you. Good luck finding your
Eastern European. And make sure you swing by the gift shop. Tell them
Mindy sent you!" Then she swept away, as fast as she could, in the oppos-
ite direction from Brett Palgrave.

A half hour later, Lou was still at the bar, sipping her third water on the
rocks. Mindy was right about Tim Palgrave's son: there were now at least
twenty escorts working the room, but every one of them was giving Brett
Palgrave a conspicuously wide berth. How had Lou never heard those
rumors? She had been vaguely aware that Palgrave had a son from his
first marriage, and that maybe he did something in banking or Bitcoin.

Probably Bitcoin judging by his dress sense. But a skeezy predator too? Someone had to write that story. Maybe she should send a tip to Miquela Rio at the *Journal*. Later. Her mom's flight landed in half an hour and she was still no closer to finding Fate.

She decided to check in with Helen, to make sure Landon would be there to meet her at the airport. She retrieved her clunky drugstore cell phone from the clutch purse and started toward the lobby.

She paused in front of the famous Redwood gift shop, or "Guest Boutique," according to the calligraphy above the door. There in the window, exactly as Mindy had described, was the ugliest ass silver tennis bracelet she had ever seen. The bracelet itself was fine—silver and studded with small diamonds dazzling in the display lights. The problem was, the designer had decided the piece also needed a half-dozen silver charms dangling from it—a small silver tennis racket, a ball, what seemed to be a frog wearing a crown, an owl riding a toucan. These accoutrements transformed a $10,000 piece of jewelry into something that belonged in a dumpster behind the Westfield Mall.

Lou squinted more closely at the frog. Maybe the charms meant something—a code between the johns and the escorts. Did each one represent some gross sex act? In which case, what the hell was an owl riding a toucan? She made a mental note to ask Mindy if she ever saw her again. At the very least, Mindy would make a gold mine of a source. Lou could only imagine the amazing stories she had about the great and gross of Silicon Valley. From Raum One to the Redwood—there couldn't be many people in this town with that kind of intel. And, based on their conversations here and at Raum One, she and Mindy obviously had the same deep distaste for toxic tech bros. It was amazing how similar they were.

Lou gasped as the thought hit her; stared at her own stupidity reflected back to her in the glass window of the gift shop. Mouth hanging open, hand rubbing her forehead as the realization slowly made its way through from her subconscious to her conscious.

No.

It wasn't possible.

Mindy?

Fucking *Mindy*.

Moments later, Lou was back in the bar, Helen's annoying strappy shoes now clasped in her hand. She had thought it herself, hadn't she? *Dressing like this will make me invisible.* Even Lou hadn't noticed Mindy until she came and whispered right into her ear. Just like at Raum One on the night Alex Wu died, Mindy was just another escort hanging off Tim Palgrave's arm. All that shit about how she was a fan of Lou's writing about awful Silicon Valley men—she might as well have screamed it out loud.

And her perfume. The sweet floral perfume Mindy was wearing at the bar. Now Lou knew where she'd smelled it before—not at Raum One but later that night. Lou had noticed it the moment she walked into Christian's ICU room. Since when did ICU nurses wear perfume?

Jesus Shitting Christ on a Toucan.

Lou stood in the middle of the bar, frustrated, shoes in hand, looking for all the world like a drunk bridesmaid adrift from a wedding. Brett Palgrave was still slouched in his seat, arguing with a man in a black suit who was telling him he wasn't allowed to vape indoors. But Mindy was nowhere in sight.

Lou scanned the bar again. It was like finding a hooker in a haystack. Her mom's plane would be landing any minute. *Come on, Lou. Think!*

The answer came faster this time, and she sprinted back toward the lobby. Mindy had practically spoon-fed her the instructions: *Tell them Mindy sent you!*

"*Bonsoir*, good evening," beamed the pale, thin man behind the glass counter of the boutique. Then, in the same high school French accent: "Please let me know if there's anything I can help you find."

Lou smiled and tried to regain control of her breathing as she made a show of carefully examining the items in the glass case below the counter before finally . . .

"I'm looking for some jewelry. For a new friend."

Was that right? Had she emphasized the word "new" in a way that telegraphed her real objective? She glanced up and caught a brief flash of confusion in the man's eyes. A good sign.

"Your friend, she is staying at the hotel?" he asked tentatively.

"Yes," said Lou. "Although I don't know her room number. I hoped you could help with that."

"*Bien sûr, mademoiselle.* Perhaps if you could tell me the lady's name?"

"Mindy."

That did it. The faux-Frenchman's eyebrows shot up, then immediately returned to their previous, professional location. He gestured to a tall glass case to the right of the counter: "I'm sure that any of these pieces would be appropriate for your friend."

Lou was in so much trouble. Nine thousand fucking dollars. She stood in the elevator, clutching the small brown jewelry case, watching the floor numbers slowly tick upward, and considering the full magnitude of what she'd just done. She'd put almost ten grand on Helen Tyler's Amex in exchange for the ugliest diamond bracelet the world had ever seen. The man in the store hadn't even asked to see her ID. Rich people!

Now Lou was heading to suite 521—the number he'd carefully written on a hotel gift card and attached to the case with a brown ribbon. "Please have a wonderful evening!"

What was she going to say when she got to the room? What was Mindy going to think? Lou felt sick. Literally the best-case scenario was that she had just committed felony credit card fraud so she could falsely accuse an innocent woman of driving two men to suicide. Worst case, she was a credit card fraudster who was about to confront a double murderer in a hotel bedroom.

Lou emerged on the fifth floor and tried to decipher the wall signs. Rooms 500–530 to the left. Rooms 520, 525 to the right. She turned left. Thirty seconds later, she retraced her steps, and this time turned right.

The door to room 521, when she finally found it, had a second brass plaque indicating that it was better known as the Hopper Suite. Lou

remembered now. All the suites at the Redwood were named after famous technologists—the Noyce Suite, the Musk Suite, the Jobs Suite—but it seemed fitting that Mindy would have chosen the only one named after a woman. Also, who wants to have sex in the Musk Suite?

A velvet rope was slung around the door handle, an upscale interpretation of a Do Not Disturb sign—the billionaire equivalent of a sock on a dorm room door. Lou looked up and down the hallway—none of the other handles had velvet ropes.

Lou slid the brown ribbon from the jewelry box and flipped open the lid. Away from the flattering lighting of the boutique, the ugliness of her purchase—the frog, the dog, and the toucan—was even more profound. She could feel the blood in her thumbs pulsing against the plastic box; her throat tightening. Again, she prayed that she was wrong, imagined how, after the initial shock and embarrassment, she and Mindy would laugh about it. The very idea that Mindy—delightful, beautiful, fangirl Mindy, keeper of tantalizing Silicon Valley sex secrets—might be the devious, invisible killer that Joe Christian called Fate!

Then they'd go together to the Guest Boutique to return the bracelet and perhaps even let Pierre, or Chad, or whatever gift shop guy's name was, in on the big joke. Maybe Helen wouldn't even notice the temporary charge on her Amex.

The fantasy was shattered by the sound of a door opening behind her. She swung around and saw a familiar figure standing in the doorway opposite room 520, dressed in a white flannel robe, a towel bunched up on her head.

Mindy glanced down at the box in Lou's hand. The look on her face making clear there had been no mistake.

"For me?"

THE BEDROOM HARDLY looked like a bedroom at all. For starters, there was no bed. Also, no lamps, no soft furnishings, no minibar. Not even a television; just a trio of AV cables—red, green, blue—jutting from a hole in a bare wall stripped of its wallpaper. The drapes were closed tight, and the only illumination came from two cheap Ikea floor lamps in the far corners of the room.

The sole significant piece of furniture was a single trestle table running the full length of the wall to the right of the window, even blocking the doorway that presumably led to the bathroom.

The table sagged alarmingly in the middle under the weight of the computer equipment it held: three monitors, and two open-fronted flight cases packed with what looked to be hard drives, a pair of keyboards, and a graphics tablet. Below the table, Lou could see a router winking with green and red lights, gray Ethernet cables snaking in all directions. A black Aeron office chair sat angled toward the door as if Mindy had only just stood up from it. Leaning against the wall next to the doorway was a second chair: a folding plastic one, also from Ikea.

"Sorry for the mess," said Mindy, as Lou followed her farther into the bedroom. "I don't get many guests."

Lou retrieved the Ikea chair, unfolded it, and set it in the center of the room. She didn't wait for an invitation to sit. She was too stunned to stand.

Mindy, meanwhile, had reached behind one of the flight cases and produced first a bottle of champagne, then two glasses. The bottle glistened with condensation. Lou continued to examine the room—she spotted a hole drilled in the ceiling with yet more cables snaking down into the back of one of Mindy's flight cases. Did they stretch all the way to the cameras hidden in the room in which she'd set up Thomas Calder?

How many other powerful men had she caught on tape from this secret control center? Lou thought about the symbiotic relationship between the working girls and the hotel management—the bar, the gift shop, the bedrooms, the escorts that lured in the wealthiest men in the Valley every night without fail. The hotel profited at every level. In the tech industry this was what was known as owning the full stack. Would they really care what Mindy got up to behind these expensive doors? So long as the money kept flowing, she could probably do whatever she liked, no questions asked.

Mindy opened the champagne with a muffled pop and poured the first of two glasses, handing it to Lou. "You probably have some questions," she said with an apologetic smile. Then Mindy sat down in her swivel chair and turned to face her.

Lou took the glass, trying unsuccessfully to appear relaxed and unfazed—or at least to keep her hand from trembling. Now she watched as Mindy reached behind a monitor and produced a can of Monster Energy, which she cracked open and poured, fizzy and neon orange, into her own glass. She tilted her hand back expertly just in time to stop the bubbles overflowing the rim. "I never drink alcohol when I'm working," Mindy explained. "This shit keeps me awake."

Lou nodded—every software engineer she knew was addicted to energy drinks, the more luminous and supersized, the better. Ten Wheeler had cans of the same stuff strewn around his office. So did that mean Mindy—or Fate, or whatever the hell she wanted to be called—was an engineer?

"So it was you who . . ." Lou hesitated, not quite sure how to phrase the question. She'd faced down dangerous people before, but nothing like this. A woman who could kill without leaving a trace. "You made Alex Wu and Joe Christian kill themselves?"

"Amongst others," said Mindy, with a shrug. "But I didn't make them do anything they didn't want to."

Amongst others? Mindy must have noticed Lou's eyes narrow in confusion: "I pretty much confessed to one of them when we met at Raum One."

Lou tried desperately to recall her first conversation with the woman she'd dismissed as Palgrave's by-the-hour girlfriend. Mindy had complimented Lou's reporting of the Stanford pipeline scandal—where a scumbag startup founder named Tyrus Weber had conspired with the university's computer science school to guarantee a job to anyone quietly expelled for sexual assault. There had been plenty of shitty men involved in that story, but so far as Lou knew, none of them was dead. Except . . .

"Tyrus Weber? He had cancer."

"So his wife told the world. So tragic. So young. So sudden. So fortunate nobody thought to actually check with the medical examiner, or the cops, or his housekeeper, who found him surrounded by all those empty pill bottles . . . You were the only reporter who thought to investigate his relationship with Stanford, but even you didn't think to question how he really died. Why would you?"

Lou pinched her brow and squeezed as hard as she could. Stephen Camp had told her to call the coroner for the death certificate, but she was so pissed that Weber had escaped justice that she'd blown him off. "How do you make them do it? Men like that don't just kill themselves."

"Thank you!" Mindy slapped her hand hard against her thigh, still covered by her robe. "You're exactly right. When a man like Joe Christian destroys his marriage and gets himself fired, he doesn't end up living in an SRO, hooked on pills and covered in syphilis sores. He gets a press conference, an apology tour, a TED Talk." Mindy swiveled back and forth in her chair as she spoke. "When a man like Alex Wu gets accused of multiple, brutal rapes, he doesn't end up in handcuffs, or even fired. He gets protected, promoted. It's crazy that Weber would actually face consequences for what he did. Consequences are for women. Minorities. Poor folks. If you or I jumped in front of a train tomorrow, the world would shrug." She paused. "You can give me that disbelieving look, but it's true. Definitely for me, but probably for you too. A truck driver fucks a teenager, then winds up dead in an emergency room. A Mexican dude ends up in an SRO addicted to pain meds, scribbling crazy shit in a notebook about Fate, and—well—who gives a fuck? A female reporter humiliates herself on TV and gets fired. A Black woman is forced to drop out of Stanford . . . You think anyone's hiring an investigative reporter to solve *that* mystery? But Alexander Xavier Wu . . ." She said his name with mock grandiosity and then, adopting a pastiche of a redneck accent: "Well, it just doesn't make sense that he'd want to die. He had so much to live for."

Lou registered Mindy's reference to Stanford—her second in as many minutes—and filed it away. If Mindy was a Stanford graduate, that could explain her technical abilities, even as it raised a million other questions. "That's what all this is?" She gestured toward the bank of computer equipment and the trail of cables. "You figured out how to make men like Alex Wu face the consequences of their actions? You hacked into their lives somehow?"

Mindy swiveled to face one of the monitors sitting on the trestle table. "A hack only gets you the raw data—it's what you do with that information that changes lives." She rapped her knuckles against the computer mouse, and one of the screens burst to life—revealing an explosion of colorful charts and graphs that appeared to be updating in real time. "Take a random guy. Successful company founder, with a preference for interns." It was obvious she was talking about Joe Christian. "We know from his dating profile that he's cheating on his wife every time she's out of town. He's not even trying that hard to hide what he's doing—he knows he'll get away with it, because he always does. And yet." Mindy clicked an icon and Lou saw the graphs morph themselves to reflect some shift in reality. "All it takes is a quick tweak to the wife's travel plans—maybe her hotel gets a power cut, or their kid's school calls, or Hopsearch Maps says there's gonna be heavy traffic the next day. Boom. The wife comes home early, and our guy is suddenly facing a hundred-million-dollar divorce. Then his friends start hearing rumors—maybe he has a thing for even younger girls, or a problem with Black people—so they unfollow him, stop inviting him to their parties. Then"—Mindy clicked another icon and again the screen transformed—"he runs into a guy who can sell him some pills to dull the pain. By the time he starts to realize his privilege isn't working anymore, and shit is actually falling apart in a way it never has before, it's too late. Nobody's taking his calls. Nobody remembers his name. Soon he starts yelling about how someone must be doing this to him. Even gives this person a name . . ."

"Fate."

"Exactly." Mindy slapped both hands on the arms of her chair. "So much hubris, for a man who lived his last days covered in his own puke in the Tenderloin. It couldn't just be that when you do shitty things, there are consequences. You know what they say about people who are accustomed to privilege?"

Lou recited the quote: "To the privileged, equality feels like oppression." The phrase had become a rallying cry for feminists and social-justice activists online. What most people didn't know was that it had actually been coined by a man, railing against the "privilege" enjoyed by women.

"Don't it just," said Mindy. "To men in Silicon Valley, equality feels like an existential threat. A death sentence. The technical challenge is figuring out how to deliver that equality: processing all the data, knowing exactly what to tweak to make things happen the same for a guy like Joe Christian as they do for the rest of us. For that, you need an algorithm. Something to game out the variables and consider all the possible outcomes."

"And you built an algorithm that can do that?" Lou left the next part unsaid. *You—a Redwood escort—seriously built an algorithm to take down some of the richest men on the planet?*

But Mindy raised an eyebrow. "Why don't you ask Joe Christian or Alex Wu what I can do?"

Lou had heard some crazy pitches in her life, but there was something about the way Mindy spoke—the certainty, the *I don't give a shit if you believe me* tone—that made it all sound true. Not just true: obvious. Lou's eyes flicked around the room again, taking in all the computer equipment, as she tried to comprehend the magnitude of what Mindy had built. An algorithm that could make powerful men face the consequences of their behavior.

Mindy caught her looking. "Don't be fooled by all this shit." She pointed to a blinking box on the floor. "The algorithm is all on that one machine, though really it could fit on a USB stick. Plug and play. The hard part is gathering enough data." She reached again for the mouse, and after a few clicks, the screen was covered with black windows and scrolling white text.

The flow of words and numbers was mesmerizing. Human lives reduced to a stream of user IDs; free will to mathematical probability; life-and-death consequences to raw, unfeeling code. "That's why you work out of the Redwood. Everyone and everything flows through here."

Mindy shook her head. "I work here because I like their cheeseburgers." A pause as she straightened the towel still wrapped around her hair. "And so everyone will make the same crappy assumption about me that you did, and Tim Palgrave did when I showed up as his hired date for the Raum party." She let Lou stew in her guilt for a moment longer before adding, "I pay the ladies downstairs twenty percent for investment tips. VCs love to brag about their huge throbbing deal flow, and those loose lips pay for my two data centers in Reykjavík plus whatever else I need to keep my operation running."

"Reykjavík . . . Iceland?"

"Feminism and geothermal cooling, baby." Mindy gestured back toward the flickering data stream. "I'm serious, though. You can't do this shit with a few overheard rumors and a hacked cell phone. It takes petabytes of data just to figure out what kind of pizza a guy will order tomorrow, or what he'll buy his sidepiece for Hanukkah."

Lou set down her glass of champagne on the floor beside her chair. "Why those men in particular? Alex Wu? Joe Christian?" She remembered what Helen had said about how Wu's and Christian's deaths seemed *almost medieval . . . like a mob informer left swinging from a bridge, or a head stuck on a pike.* "What did they do that was worse than a thousand other scumbags?"

"Nothing," said Mindy. "They were no better or worse than most successful men in this town. One day I'll have enough processor power to make every tech guy on the planet face the consequences of their behavior—and not just the tech guys. But first I needed beta testers to train the algorithm, and Wu and Christian and Weber happened to stumble across my radar." She looked away as she said this, and Lou knew she wasn't telling anything close to the whole truth. A bullshitter knows a bullshitter, as her mom liked to say.

"And Charlie Brusk?"

"What about him? XXCubator is everything wrong with this industry—churning out the next generation of white privileged man-child CEOs."

Lou sat forward in her chair. "Joe Christian went to see Alex Wu the night he died. Christian had Charlie Brusk's number written on his hand. I know it was you who stole Joe Christian's notebook from me in Palo Alto—" She waited for any flicker of disagreement on Mindy's face, and saw none. "Clearly he thought there was a connection. Something about his wife's charity?"

This time Mindy did react. The faintest flicker of a smile played across the gloss of her lips.

"Exactly," said Lou. "So how about you stop fucking around and tell me why I'm here."

Mindy took a deep breath and held it for what seemed to Lou to be an unhealthily long time. When she finally exhaled, something had changed in her face. She was no longer Mindy the escort, pretending to be a fan of Lou's work. Nor was she Fate, the avenging angel who'd just confessed to building an algorithm that could somehow eradicate male privilege. She was someone new.

"What do you know about the creation of the Raum algorithm?"

Was she serious? Lou knew *everything* about it. She rattled off a summary: how college kids Alex Wu and Ten Wheeler had created their magical code, capable of predicting users' deepest desires, then presented it at the Stanford startup contest where Elmsley Chase swooped in and bought it—and them—for five million bucks, simultaneously transforming Raum from struggling startup to sharing-economy powerhouse.

Mindy listened, nodding slowly. "And, just to be clear, which one of those guys—Ten or Alex—actually *invented* the algorithm? Like whose *idea* was it?"

Now Mindy was definitely fucking with her. "I assume Ten." That part was Silicon Valley gospel: Ten was the tech genius, while Alex was the product and marketing savant. But now as the word "assume" escaped her lips, Lou was suddenly filled with doubt.

Another slow nod from Mindy. "A reasonable assumption. Because of pattern recognition. Steve and Woz, Larry and Sergey, Bill and Paul, Jack and Ev. Alex and Tenrick. You knew the story before it even happened, right? What was it you said at Raum One? 'History is written by the victors'?" She added what sounded like a non sequitur. "The startup contest wasn't at Stanford. It was the Stanford–MIT intramural hackathon. The year they won, it was hosted at MIT."

Lou's first impulse was to defend herself. So, fine, the contest was at MIT, not Stanford. What difference did it make? Then she saw Mindy's expression, beneath the perfect makeup. It was one she'd seen many times in the mirror. Not anger, or frustration, or disappointment—just exhaustion.

"If Ten didn't create the algorithm, then who did?" Lou already knew the answer, even as her brain was racing to piece it all together. She'd remembered something else: the persistent rumor that Alex Wu had raped a classmate who had been forced to leave Stanford and abandon her brilliant academic career. And then the last piece . . . Amelia Christian's insistence that Wu and her husband had hated each other since college even though one went to Stanford and the other MIT. And those last words, screamed in a hospital waiting room. *It's her charity.*

It's her, Charity.

"You're Charity," said Lou, her voice barely a whisper.

65%

Boston

Eleven years earlier

CHARITY JONES REACHED back to pull the flaps of the green paper robe tighter across her spine. She'd been sitting, waiting, freezing in this tiny cubicle for almost two hours, her legs dangling pathetically over the side of the long, plastic-covered examination chair. For the first hour, a nurse had appeared every few minutes to reassure her that a doctor would see her soon; Friday nights were crazy at Mass General; she was really sorry. Now the nurse had disappeared—hadn't been back to check on Charity for at least a half hour. Occasionally a different medical professional would peer through the curtains and pull a face that seemed to her to be one of disappointment at finding a crying, near-naked Black woman occupying valuable hospital real estate.

Charity wiped her eyes, her face raw from the tears. Then she looked again at her hunched, pathetic form in the long mirror opposite the chair. The red finger marks above both elbows were already starting to darken into bruises, and the cut on her lip, made by Alex Wu's signet ring as he'd held his hand over her mouth to stop her screaming, had hardened into an ugly scab.

The nurse—Amelia, according to her name badge—had given Charity a glass of water and ordered the two police officers to wait outside in the hall. They'd made some bullshit protest about chain of evidence, but Nurse Amelia had given her head one firm shake. Sexual-assault examinations were done in private; there was nothing Charity could do in an empty room to tamper with evidence of her assault. Still, the cops had stood resolutely, and obnoxiously, outside the curtain while the doctor stuffed Charity's torn, bloody underwear into a plastic evidence bag and handed it out to them. They were still out there in the hallway, pacing and grumbling about how they had better things to do on a Friday night than wait for . . . they stopped short of completing the sentence, but she knew.

Was everyone hoping she'd get tired of waiting and leave? Was that how this worked? Even now, Charity—by a mile the best comp-sci student in her class—couldn't help but think of her situation in algorithmic terms. Was there a certain type of treatment—kindness followed by isolation followed by despair—that made women more likely to decide not to make a complaint after all? Were the cops deliberately allowing her to overhear their grumbling? Was that all part of the tried-and-tested system? What *was* the data on initial rape reports versus those women who successfully completed the process? She thought about the other students in her class. At enrollment, 50 percent of them were women. Now—less than a year in—it was 40 percent. Soon, if the data held, it would be less than 20 percent. Stanford had perfected its own algorithm—the perfect system to drive women out, through assault, harassment, and ignoring their complaints about threats and violence. Just enough to keep women out of engineering careers, to force them into "softer" majors like English and history, but not quite enough to reduce female comp-sci graduates to zero, which would draw too much attention to the crisis.

Another tear burned a hole through Charity's paper smock. Had *she* been part of the algorithm? All her friends at Stanford were men. Her partners in the hackathon—Ten Wheeler and Alex Wu—were men. She hung around with the boys at the computer lab, laughed at their unfunny jokes, and disdained the on-campus women's groups as exclusionary or irrelevant. She knew that to succeed in Silicon Valley, she'd have to be one of the boys. Would have to rely on those same boys to open doors for her and talk her up to interview panels. That need was what kept women like her from speaking out, even when she heard female classmates describe being assaulted at parties, or harassed by male professors. *I don't go to parties, and I don't flirt with professors. It won't happen to me. I won't be a statistic.*

And now she was.

She wouldn't leave. Even if this freezing, dehumanizing process took all night and she had to go straight from the hospital back to the contest venue at the Marriott—even if she had to pitch her algorithm still wearing this tear-splatted paper robe—she wouldn't leave before putting on record what Alex Wu had done to her. He wasn't going to get away with it. She and Tenrick were going to win the startup contest with their algorithm, and Alex was going to jail.

Charity looked up at the wall—her phone was back at the hotel, so the analog plastic clock was her only tether to reality. Almost three a.m. Even if she left now, she'd be lucky to get two hours' sleep before her wake-up call for day two of the hackathon. Not that she could sleep. Her body felt heavy and battered and exhausted, but her mind was still racing.

Had Alex already been arrested? When she'd left the hotel, bracketed by her own police escort ("normally we'd send female officers, but it's a Friday night . . ."), he was sitting, slumped on her bed, red-faced and outraged, as a pair of cops transcribed his declaration of innocence into their notebooks. Was he now waiting in a police cell just as she was waiting in this medical cell, their fates both contingent on the slow bureaucracy of this hospital and the outcome of the rape examination kit? Had the cops already seized the security camera footage from the hotel? And what about the other men from the bar—the short, intense guy with the slick hair and the tall jock with the too-big teeth—contest finalists from other schools whom Wu and Ten were hanging out with when she told them she was heading up to her room, to get an early night? Joseph Christian, Tyrus Weber—she forced herself to remember the names of the MIT students written on their contest lanyards. Would they be called as witnesses to support what Ten Wheeler had already told the cops: how Alex had bragged about how much she wanted him? How they'd all watched him follow her out of the bar.

She had no idea how any of this worked, but now she wanted to know. To understand every detail of the process she was about to commit herself to. To understand the data and what elements made the difference between a man like Alex Wu spending decades in jail and him being released to prey on other women. Yet another algorithm. Charity was really, really good at algorithms.

She had worked for months nurturing her idea—an algorithm that could predict what users really wanted, even before they knew it themselves, and then figure out the quickest course of action to make their deepest wishes come true. It was an insanely ambitious idea, but even if she and Tenrick could only solve the first part, then the implications—for food delivery, for dating sites, for Wall Street—were epic. Her professors had seen it—that's why they'd chosen her, and Ten, and Alex, to fly across the country to compete at the hackathon. The judges would surely see it too.

But now she wondered whether Wu's absence would affect their chances in the finals. She hated thinking it, but wasn't that the whole point of Alex? To slip on a suit and wrap their code in bro-pleasing bullshit about "disruption" or "user delight"?

Fuck Alex.

Charity hadn't wanted him on their team in the first place, presenting her work, but Tenrick was convinced Alex was some kind of marketing and presentational genius; that his ability to spin their code as a magical God 2.0 (his phrase) algorithm would wow the judges and guarantee them victory.

Fuck "God 2.0." Charity and Tenrick's code would speak for itself. Even without sleep, even without her mind being entirely present, and especially without Alex Wu, she and Tenrick would win because they were the best.

Charity's ears pricked up at the sound of heavy footsteps, and then a familiar voice. The two cops were back in the hallway, talking loudly again. Talking about her.

"Total fucking waste of time," one was saying. The bigger of the two, she thought—the Neanderthal with the blond buzz cut and the gun strapped to his thigh like some kind of SWAT role-player. He was louder and dumber than his partner, and hadn't thought twice about cursing in front of her, even while asking her to describe what had happened after Alex had forced his way into her room, wasted drunk. *If you want us to nail this fucking guy, you gotta tell us everything you remember.*

The other cop was shorter and skinnier, barely filling out his blue Boston PD uniform, his belt hanging slack around his waist. He'd been more patient, had taken down her statement carefully, and she'd believed him when he told her to take her time, that there was no rush. Meanwhile, the larger cop had paced the room, a caged animal waiting for his chance to escape.

"I hear you, man," said the second voice; quieter, noncommittal.

"What did she expect? Girl like her, hanging around with a bunch of horny nerds. I mean, Jesus . . ."

Charity hoped the second cop would protest. Maybe even remind his partner that rape was never the victim's fucking fault. But she knew she'd be disappointed. White men in blue uniforms were never going to take her side, especially not against other white men in blue uniforms.

"Happens every year at that geek event," Charity heard him say. "The boys all think they need some eye candy to impress the judges, and someone gets overexcited."

Charity's flesh froze. *Happens every year?* Did he mean a woman was attacked at the hackathon every year? Surely that couldn't be true. Also, Alex Wu didn't get *overexcited*—he wasn't a child who ate too many Skittles and knocked over a vase. He raped her. He was a premeditating, violent rapist. Charity could feel the muscles in her arms and legs tighten, flexing the bruises on her arms and sending a pulse of pain through her whole body.

Her chill had turned to anger. *Eye candy? The boys?* There were thirty-three women in this year's contest—she had counted them on the attendee list. It was her fucking algorithm—not Tenrick's clean code and ability to churn it out for days without sleep, and definitely not Alex Wu's shiny fucking Brooks Brothers suit—that had taken them to Boston. If anyone was *eye* candy, it was Alex "God 2.0" Wu.

Charity took a deep breath, in through her nose, out through her mouth. This feeling, at least, was familiar territory. Ever since she'd first announced her love of *Star Trek*, aged five, or joined her high school's Dungeons & Dragons team, aged fourteen, she'd had to breathe her way through the bullshit assumptions. To bury her rage at being told that she wasn't supposed to like the stuff she liked. And the questions. *How do you cope with all those boys? Wouldn't you rather be playing outside in the sun?* The unstated implication: that girls were supposed to be seen and not heard. That either she had failed her gender, or she was only hanging with the boys to score dates. Because where better to pick up hot guys than a high school D&D game?

The attitude, and the judgments, had continued even at Stanford. No, *particularly* at Stanford, where every stratum of the Computer Science Department shared the same bullshit prejudice: that men were the brains and the women were there to be tolerated, or harassed. Barely worth the sum of their body parts. She'd felt it every day—every time she'd set foot in the lab. The sudden silence. The raised eyebrows that said *What are you doing here?* More than once, she'd been mistaken for the cleaner and handed an empty paper cup or an apple core.

But she'd kept her head down, pushed herself ever harder, and gotten herself ever smarter. Convinced that there was some magical point in the distance—some IQ number or hours toiled—at which she'd earn the respect of her dumber, lazier peers. Wasn't that the promise? That for a woman to attain a man's level of success, she had to work twice as hard and be twice as smart? She'd passed that milestone long ago, and all she'd attracted was more harassment, more scorn. And now . . . She watched herself sobbing in the mirror, felt the fresh bruise on her cheek.

How had she been so dumb? It didn't matter if she made it back to the Marriott in time, or whether the rape kit was processed, or if she testified in court. Didn't matter if she won the contest, standing alone on the stage. The boys' club would find a way to beat her, just like they always did. Somehow she'd be written out of her algorithm's creation story; somehow Alex Wu would avoid jail—*he's a good kid, a promising student, such a shame to send him to prison! Boys will be boys!*

The witnesses—slick-haired Joe Christian, toothy Tyrus Weber . . . and you too, Tenrick?—would all be struck down with amnesia. Bros before hos.

The boys would continue their journeys to Silicon Valley to make their billions, while, like a thousand female engineering cofounders before her, Charity Jones would be written out of the story before it even got started.

"I'd like to install my hard drive into her software."

And there it was. The cops outside the curtain had forgotten she was there, or they didn't care. At least at Stanford the gross innuendo was technically accurate. These were the cops—the dedicated public servants, sworn to protect and serve—who she was supposed to believe were going to send Alex Wu to jail. From the sound of them, there was more chance they'd give him a high five.

"Bro, you can have her. I'm having breakfast with Carlotta."

"The DUI chick?" The second cop laughed. "You gotta be careful, brother."

"It's all good. Told the wife I'm pulling a double shift."

The conversation tailed off as the cops walked away again. Charity had heard enough. She wiped her eyes, then reached for her clothes, still folded neatly on the chair in the corner along with her shirt and shoes. It took her only a few seconds to get dressed, although the act of pulling on her jeans revealed more bruises. Her shirt, she saw, was smeared with blood. She crumpled the paper robe and tossed it into the medical-waste bin.

Another deep, slow breath. She knew if she stepped through the curtain and out of the hospital, Alex Wu would definitely get away with what he'd done to her. But she also knew this: even if she stayed in this tiny cubicle all night and all the next day, the outcome wouldn't be different.

She could take her notes, her code, get back on a plane to her parents' house in Burlingame, and finish building her own version of the algorithm. It'd take her much longer without Ten's lightning-fast coding skills, but the result would be better without Alex's constant bullshit. Then maybe she could take her chances on Sand Hill Road, pitching it directly to the venture capitalists there. Love it or hate it, they couldn't give the credit to her male cofounder if there was no male cofounder.

The cops were right; the hackathon was no place for someone like her. She would quietly join the invisible army of female Stanford computer science undergraduates who dropped out before completing their studies. The silenced majority of female students who reported being assaulted or harassed on campus.

Nobody on campus would care, or remember her. Which was fine. She didn't want to be remembered as a victim, or as the eye candy hired to support Alex Wu's and Ten Wheeler's brilliance.

She slipped on her shoes and listened for the sound of voices in the hallway. Silence. The cops had probably gone for another cup of coffee, a simple courtesy that nobody had thought to extend to her. She pulled down the back of her shirt and stepped out through the curtain. *Shit.* The taller, uglier of the two cops was still leaning against the wall, tapping into his cell phone.

Fuck fuck fuck.

She really didn't want a confrontation with this asshole. She took a step farther down the hallway, trying to find a balance between creeping and nonchalance. Maybe he wouldn't see her. Then she caught herself; what the fuck was she doing? Why was she acting like she had something to hide, something to fear? Charity adjusted her posture, straightened her shoulders, stood a little taller in her sneakers, and set her gaze dead ahead. If the cop looked up, if he tried to talk to her, she wouldn't react. She kept walking. And the cop didn't look up. Just kept *tap tap tapping* on his cell phone, presumably confirming his hot date while his wife waited at home. Unbelievable. Men like him deserved to have their dicks cut off and stuffed in their mouths. Charity had watched a National Geographic show once about how the Mafia did that to adulterers, or some shit. She kept walking and the cop kept *tap tapping.*

"Hey."

Charity was already a couple of paces past him when he called after her. *Just keep walking,* she told herself. *Don't even hesitate.*

"HEY," he was yelling now. A cop yelling at her in the hallway of a hospital.

She turned around, and stared, silently. He was still leaning against the wall, his phone still extended, midtext.

"You getting outta here?"

What did that even mean? *You getting outta here?* Like she was bailing out of a party, or walking out for a smoke.

"Yeah." She forced herself to be as curt as possible.

"OK," said the cop. He said it as if this was what he'd been expecting all along; as if it had been only a matter of time before Charity changed her mind about pressing charges against Alex Wu. As if this was what always happened. What girls like her always did.

And then: "You need a ride?"

"No," she said, and kept walking. Then she stopped. Because in that moment, in that hallway, she saw the whole picture. Saw herself as this cop saw her: as barely more than a common streetwalker—a piece of meat without any possible value or utility in the world. She turned back to face him. "But thank you." She forced herself to smile.

He smiled back. "No problem. Hey, I'm really sorry about what happened to you tonight—if it were up to me, all the guys who did stuff like this would be strung up by their balls—pardon my French—but . . ." He shrugged. "The courts and the DA. Your friend would probably walk anyway, and you don't want to put yourself through something like that—testifying in court, I mean. Classy girl like you, why would you want to . . . you know?" He was babbling. Men did that, sometimes, and that's when she knew she had him.

"So." She hesitated, doing her best to pantomime both innocence and guile. "If I change my mind, should I . . . call you?"

Asshole could hardly hide the smirk playing across his lips. He'd been right about the kind of girl Charity was. "Sure. I'll give you my number."

Charity shook her head. "My phone is still at the hotel." Then, acting like she was coming up with an idea right there on the spot: "I'll put my number in yours." She reached out her hand.

"Sure." His fingers danced across the password screen and then swiped and scrolled, presumably closing out the conversation with "the DUI chick." Then he handed his phone to this total stranger.

And that's all it took. In the twenty seconds it took Charity to pretend she didn't understand how a phone or an address book worked—to pretend she wasn't top of her class in the best computer science school on the planet—that's all the time she needed to export his address book and send it to her email. To delete the sent message and then, for good measure, to screenshot his conversation with Carlotta. In a half hour, back at the hotel, she'd text the cop's wife—helpfully stored as his In Case of Emergency number—and tell her he'd gotten off work early, and did she want to meet him for breakfast? If only she could see his face when both women arrived at the same time and he realized what she'd done.

Except he'd never realize. She'd already deleted the message thread, and there was no way in hell he'd think that a woman—a *girl* like her—could possibly have the ability to blow up the life of a big, powerful cop like him. He'd likely blame bad luck, or karma, or his partner. Chances were, what with his marriage about to implode, he wouldn't even remember her or go looking for the phone number he'd never find in his address book.

Likewise—Charity's mind was whirling now, as she walked out into the freezing Boston morning—when his email accounts were compromised and his texts all made public . . . And what about the other cops in his department? That level of corruption must be institutional, mustn't it? . . . God, the damage Charity could inflict, after just thirty seconds with a shitty cop's phone.

She thought again about her algorithm, and suddenly she no longer felt the cold, nor the throbbing of her bruises. She'd designed it to give users what they *wanted*, even if they didn't yet realize it. But now she gasped as another thought occurred to her—what if she could rebuild it to give men what they *deserved*?

69%

"I'M SO SORRY." Lou heard how trite the words sounded, but what else could she say? To watch your rapist steal everything you'd worked for. To see those magazine covers, and rich lists, and fanboys praising his brilliance. She glanced over Charity's shoulder at the banks of computer equipment. And then to do all of *this*, to use your talent—and your invisibility—to so perfectly dismantle the perpetrators and the underlying structures that enabled them. Suddenly every trauma Lou had felt in her entire life—everything with her dad, the attack in the Tenderloin, the threats against her mom—fell into sharp perspective. Every article she'd written was just a pathetic, impotent joke compared with what Charity had built inside this hotel room.

Charity popped another can of energy drink but set it down on the desk without taking a sip. "You don't have to believe me, but I really didn't plan for them to die. I just wanted them to see what a world looked like with all their unearned privilege taken away."

"And Charlie Brusk?" While Charity was telling her story, Lou had been waiting for Brusk's role to be explained. Wu, Christian, and Weber had all joined startups that raised investment capital from XXCubator, but so had thousands of other MIT and Stanford graduates. There must be another reason she had targeted Brusk.

At the sound of his name, Charity dug her nails into her palm. "Raum was XXCubator's first big investment." She rocked back and forth in her chair, feet tapping on the floor as she spoke. "After Elmsley Chase announced he was buying Alex and Ten's algorithm—*my* algorithm—Brusk became obsessed with the idea of owning a stake in the company. He hired a bunch of due diligence lawyers to examine the deal, and it took them about two days to find out what happened at the hackathon.

As Raum's newest investor and board member, Brusk had a choice. Try to find me and make things right—financially, legally, morally—or bury the evidence to protect his investment."

"And he chose the latter."

"He got the Boston PD files sealed, convinced Stanford and MIT to drop their investigations, even tracked down Christian and Weber and offered them funding from XXCubator in exchange for their silence. Problem was their startup ideas were so bad that Brusk had to create Mushu Health and Grintech for them. That's why ten years later he hired your friend Helen Tyler to oust them before their companies went public and the markets realized they were a pair of dumbasses."

Lou was both stunned and entirely unsurprised. "All that effort and money just so Brusk could avoid doing the right thing."

"I haven't told you the best part. After everything was over, Charlie sent Joe Christian to Mass General to clean up any loose ends: to make sure I hadn't mentioned Alex's name, or anything that could lead back to those assholes. The first person he found was my nurse."

Another puzzle piece snapped into place. "Nurse Amelia was Amelia Christian."

"That's her married name obviously, but yeah. Their first date was just a ploy so Joe could figure out what she knew." Charity slapped her palms on the arms of her Aeron chair. "There is literally nothing they won't do. Nobody they won't use. They'll never stop. Not unless . . ." Charity swept her hand toward the blinking lights and snaking cables.

"Unless we burn it all to the ground." Lou heard herself echoing the words Helen had used the previous day. Their theory was right: Fate wanted to bring down the entire misogynist pig pile, starting with the occupants of Raum One.

Charity picked up her Monster can and raised it in a mock *cheers*.

"What can I do? I'm not a journalist anymore."

"Fuck journalism," said Charity with a dismissive wave of her hand, still clutching the can. "Nobody cares. If you want to change the world, you have to do it yourself." She lowered her voice and shuffled her swivel chair closer to Lou's plastic one. "Let me ask you something: why is Raum so desperate to IPO?"

Was that a trick question? "They need capital. They're burning about a billion dollars a month."

Charity nodded. "Closer to two billion, in fact. But that's OK, because as we all know, Wall Street believes that growth is more important than profitability. As long as Raum is still growing like a weed—faster than any company in the history of capitalism—then their ultimate payday is guaranteed." She paused. "Except what if it isn't?"

"Isn't guaranteed?"

Charity shook her head. "Isn't growing. What if the numbers are bullshit? What if, thanks to all the scandals and Elmsley's horrible leadership, Raum's active user base is actually shrinking, dramatically? Elmsley Chase and Charlie Brusk have been deliberately lying to investors, to Wall Street, to the world, about Raum's growth ahead of the IPO."

Lou shuffled her own chair closer. "Are you joking? Raum is burning twenty billion dollars a year for zero growth?"

Charity corrected her. "For *negative* growth. And Chase and Brusk have been lying about it for months. The crown prince too. They're all trying desperately to get to the IPO before the truth comes out. Raum is fucked."

"That's insane." It really was. If Raum had lied on its SEC filings, Chase and the rest of the board would go to jail. You can hire predators, threaten journalists, and kill your customers with self-driving cars, but the first commandment of corporate America is that you don't ever fuck with Wall Street. "And you have internal documents to prove all this?" Of course she did. Charity had already proved she could hack into Raum's secure intranet.

Charity smiled and reached into the pocket of her robe and produced a silver USB stick, which she tossed across the room onto Lou's lap. Lou picked it up and examined it, as if she could somehow read the contents just by staring. Her hand was shaking. The contents of that USB stick, if they were leaked to investors, were enough to reduce Raum One to rubble. And worse. Lou felt sick as she imagined King Faisal's reaction to hearing that his least favorite son had brought yet another scandal on the family, and set fire to billions of dollars of the kingdom's money in the process. That was the second commandment: don't fuck with the Saudi royal family, even if you're a member of it.

"Nobody knows who I am," Charity continued, her voice now a conspiratorial whisper, "but if the former journalist hired to investigate the death of Raum's CTO"—she gestured theatrically toward Lou with an open hand—"discovered that Alex Wu had been about to blow the whistle on the whole conspiracy, right before his shocking and bloody suicide . . . what would Wall Street think? What would the world think?"

Lou was suddenly confused. "But that's not what happened. Alex Wu killed himself because you . . ." She could feel herself deflate in her chair—her excitement atrophying into nausea. "It's not true, is it? The stuff about the user data? Raum isn't really failing."

Charity shook her head. "What is truth? If the contents of that USB stick somehow ended up on Raum's server, overwriting the real data and sprinkling in a few suggestive emails that indicated the conspiracy I've just described . . . well, wouldn't that be true *enough*? By the time anyone figures out what is *true*, Raum will be out of money and out of business. And the assholes who run it . . ."

Lou felt hollow. "You want me to help you hack into Raum's server and plant fake data to sabotage the IPO?"

Charity raised both palms and patted the air. "No, no. I'll take care of planting the files. I just need you to stumble across them and pass the discovery along to certain interested parties: banks, investors, private-equity journalists. You'll have total plausible deniability."

In a previous life Lou would have walked out of the hotel room and never looked back. But here she was, still sitting, listening, thinking. Men like Elmsley Chase lied all the time; they'd say or do anything just to make the next billion. Was Charity really asking Lou to do anything worse? To undo all the bullshit and empty promises that had made Raum so valuable, despite all the losses, and harm. "And you think these interested parties will believe me? That I just happened to stumble across this insane fraud?"

Charity gestured again toward her bank of computers. "I do think that, yes. But more importantly so does my algorithm. I didn't choose you by accident, Lou. I chose you because, based on every piece of available data, you are the only person who can do this."

Lou let a puff of air escape from her lips. She knew that wasn't true. "You mean the only person apart from Helen Tyler?" Lou remembered the letter Helen said she'd received, on Redwood letterhead, all those months ago.

Charity didn't deny it. "I wrote to her when she took the job at Raum, but she ignored my invitation."

"Because she thought you were trying to blackmail her."

Charity tipped her head back and gave a quiet snort of laughter. "She didn't mention that Elmsley Chase had promised her a hundred million dollars if she defies the board and helps him keep his job until after the IPO?"

"A hundred . . . million? Just to keep him in his job for a few more weeks?" Somehow the idea of Elmsley Chase paying someone like Martina Allen $6 billion to save his ass was easier to comprehend than Helen—*a real person*—making an obscene fraction of that. She remembered Helen's boast that she'd make enough money from her job at Raum to last a lifetime.

Charity drained her can of Monster Energy. "What's the price of one man's ego? Point is, you're the only one with the credibility to do this. I brought you together with Helen Tyler to help her investigate Alex Wu's death, knowing she'd convince Elmsley Chase to issue a press release confirming that every word you published about Wu is true. He vouched for your credibility and apologized for doubting you."

Lou saw it all clearly now—how Charity had played every string perfectly to take Raum's biggest critic and give her the credibility of an insider. But she also knew the plan couldn't possibly work. "Elmsley will just say the data is fake. He'll bring in an auditor to prove Raum really is growing."

Charity nodded. "I'm sure he'll try, but the whole world watched Alex Wu jump off that balcony. What would you believe, if you were an investor?"

"Good God, that's . . ."

"Horrible? Macabre?"

Lou gave a loud laugh. For the first time, Charity had completely misread her. "I was going to say that's brilliant."

"It really is, isn't it?" Charity reached out a perfectly manicured hand. "So, partners?"

Charity stared deep into Lou McCarthy's eyes, watching as the young woman in the borrowed green dress processed everything she'd just been told. She knew that the next words out of Lou's mouth would tell her if she'd been right to put this impulsive journalist at the center of her plan. Right to tell her what she'd told her, and trust her not to go running straight to Helen Tyler, or Elmsley Chase, or the cops.

Because that much was true. Charity's plan was almost complete. In just a few days the era of powerful men using their money and privilege and technology to oppress the rest of humanity would be over. When the dust settled, she hoped Lou would understand why she hadn't been able to tell her the whole truth. Hoped she would forgive her.

Yes, Charity told herself, one day Lou would forgive her.

Until then she had to do everything she could to keep Lou out of danger and also to make sure she couldn't—by accident or design—jam a wrench in her plan before it was time. Something else that was definitely true: Charlie Brusk, Elmsley Chase, and their Saudi royal backers needed this IPO to happen and would do almost anything to make sure it did. The danger was very real, and Charity didn't want Lou to get hurt.

She kept staring at Lou, who kept staring back. Until . . .

Lou took a deep breath, took Charity's hand in her own, and uttered the word that Fate was hoping to hear.

"Partners."

71

AN HOUR LATER, Lou let herself into Helen Tyler's apartment at the Four Seasons. Judging from the noise coming from the living room, not only had her mom and Carol arrived, but they were quickly making themselves at home. She hesitated in the hallway as she heard Carol's famously loud "arguing voice." "C'mon, lady, we're not fucking idiots. We land into a tsunami of bullshit about our hotel reservation being screwed up. Then you bring us here and there's no sign of our girl."

Then came the sound of a heavy glass clonking down on the coffee table as her mom took up the theme. "I told her—I *told* you—that Elmsley Chase would never pay for our flights. That guy only cares about two things: himself, and himself."

Lou took a half step toward the living room door, torn between wanting to hug her mom and to creep straight to the guest bedroom to avoid Helen's questions about what she had found at the Redwood. She set her borrowed purse down quietly on the hall table. At least she didn't have to worry about Helen freaking out at the huge charge on her Amex—before leaving the Redwood, Lou had returned the bracelet to the gift shop, and Charity had promised to digitally erase any evidence of the transaction from the cloud, plus any security footage from the gift shop and the hallway.

"Ah, Lou!" Helen had looked up and noticed her standing in the hall. "These ladies were starting to think you'd been kidnapped." Her tone suggested she considered the whole notion a gas.

Lou smiled as broadly as she was able, before bounding into the living room and giving her mom a tight hug. "I'm so sorry, I had to finish up some work. Helen told me your hotel booking got screwed up."

Lou released her grip on her mom and shifted it to Carol. As they embraced, Lou smelled the alcohol on Carol's breath and saw over her shoulder that Helen had opened a fresh bottle of Basil Hayden's whiskey. *There's no angry way to say bourbon,* Lou's dad always used to say. Never mind that he usually said it right before blasting a shotgun round through the empty bottle.

Lou's mom waved her glass toward Helen. "Is it true my daughter is working for Raum now? Or is that more bullshit?"

Lou pulled away from Carol. She could hear the disappointment in her mom's voice, but before she could explain herself, Helen jumped in. "It's OK, Lou, you can tell the truth. You're helping me investigate Alex Wu's suicide in the hope of uncovering a scandal inside Raum." She turned to Lou's mom. "Sadly, your daughter usually knows more about what's happening inside our company than I do."

Lou headed to the side table and poured a splash of whiskey into the last unused tumbler. A few moments later, Helen walked over to refresh her own glass and asked quietly, "Any joy?"

Lou added a second splash. "Another dead end." If Helen really was being paid $100 million to save Elmsley Chase's job, Lou definitely wasn't going to tell her about Charity Jones and her plan to frame him as the greatest con artist since Bernie Madoff. She ignored Helen's disbelieving eyebrow raise as she took a swig from her glass and felt the burn of the whiskey as it hit the back of her throat. Then she reached again for the bottle.

72

BY THE TIME Lou woke up the next morning and reached groggily for her phone, it was already past ten. She had stayed up with her mom and Carol until almost three a.m., when Landon arrived to take them to their hotel. Helen had slipped away sometime after one a.m., promising to wake Lou in time to head to Raum One in the morning. Another broken promise.

Lou forced herself out of bed and immediately felt the full force of her hangover. She'd drunk two full glasses of water before bed—a third sat half-empty on the bedside table—but her stomach still felt as though it were filled with burning sand.

Hangovers always made Lou feel more emotional, more raw—but just thinking about Charity's story was enough to choke her up with tears. It was an almost perfect metaphor for how Silicon Valley treated women—stole their ideas, abused their bodies, marginalized and brutalized them.

Lou gulped down the rest of her water and pulled on a Four Seasons bathrobe. Then she staggered to the bathroom and spent a full five minutes with her forehead just resting against the mirror above the sink.

She thought about what Charity had promised. That at some point in the next twenty-four hours she'd hack into Raum One's most secure server and plant a trove of documents—emails? spreadsheets? financial statements?—to implicate Elmsley Chase in a massive corporate fraud that she had invented from whole cloth. Fabricated documents that would prove beyond doubt that Chase and the board had dramatically inflated Raum's real user numbers to con their way to the biggest IPO in history. Once the fake evidence was planted, Charity would tell Lou how to "find" it so she could leak it to Wall Street. No more IPO, no more Raum, and—by Charity's telling—the start of a reckoning for all of Silicon Valley's bro-fueled bullshit.

Was Lou really going to do this?

Fuck yes, she was.

When Lou made it to the kitchen, she was surprised to find her mom and Carol waiting for her. Even more surprising was the third person sitting at the counter: Stanley Martinez, Helen's pet detective. She froze. This couldn't be good.

"Mornin', sleepyhead," said her mom. "We were just talking about Claude Pétain. Helen's friend Detective Martinez is interested in him too."

Lou felt a rush of relief. She took in the scene in the kitchen. Every available surface was covered in paper: case files, black notebooks, and, in the center of it all, a stack of fat black binders. Three of the binders were open on the counter in front of the two women, while Martinez was peering at a chunky police-issue laptop.

"Interested how?" She addressed the question directly to Martinez.

Carol looked up from a binder. "Stanley thinks Pétain is operating inside his jurisdiction—that he runs a tech company in the city."

"Or at least somewhere in the Bay Area or Silicon Valley," Martinez clarified. "But my captain won't let me investigate unless someone makes a criminal complaint . . ."

Carol finished the sentence for him: "Which they won't, because everyone is terrified of the bastard. I told Stanley we don't scare easily." She put an arm around Martinez, who didn't seem the least bit uncomfortable with the physical contact. Lou glanced at Martinez's hand—no ring. *Quick work, Carol!*

Lou decided to appeal to the saner of the two women, which admittedly was a moving target. "Mom, you came here to get away from danger. Please don't go marching back into it." What she wanted to add, but couldn't, was that the last thing Lou needed was Pétain's mob setting their sights back on her, right as she was preparing to bring Raum crumbling down.

"Oh, you're a fine one to talk about walking into danger, Louise Bryce McCarthy. We know that psychopath booked our flights and pretended to be your friend Helen. I'm guessing we're already in plenty of danger. How about you let us pick our own battles?"

Lou had no answer to that. She could hardly explain that they had the whole thing backward. That it was Charity, not Claude Pétain, who had booked the flights. And she'd done it to keep them safe from Pétain's mob. Or at least that's why Lou assumed she'd done it—frustratingly, she'd forgotten to ask her about Pétain. Surely with all that technology, she must know his identity?

Lou sighed and ambled over to the freezer to retrieve a bag of coffee beans. She poured the beans into the grinder and braced her hungover brain as she pushed the ON button.

"Why do you think Pétain runs a tech company?" she asked. The first dark drips began to gather in the glass pot.

"It's just my working theory," said Martinez. He leaned back in his stool, hands planted on the countertop. "We know our guy is technically sophisticated, right? Probably has a computing background, or at least studied computer science at a good school. The guys in tech ops tell me the equipment he uses—video tools, voice distortion, all that shit—is all top grade, maybe even military. None of that comes cheap. But he spends hours making these videos, so either he can afford not to work or he's so important that he can sit online all day harassing women and still take home a paycheck. Also, the fact that even the FBI can't get a bead on him tells me we're looking for someone well funded, well connected."

Lou considered this. "A foreign agent?" As she heard herself ask the question, Lou instinctively put her arm around her mom's shoulder. The only thing more terrifying than Claude Pétain the troll was Claude Pétain the cutout for the Saudi intelligence services, protecting the king's investment in Raum.

"I don't buy it," said Stanley, taking a sip of coffee from one of Helen's porcelain cups, which looked ridiculously small in his giant hands. "My gut says our guy is American. He talks like a punk—an angry kid with a grudge.

That's what got me interested in the first place—he's always screaming about pigs, the fascists running the prison system, all that bullcrap."

Lou bit back her urge to note that the need for prison reform might be the only issue on which she and Pétain agreed, as Martinez continued: "Normally guys like this, they talk a good game about being antiestablishment, but deep down they love authority."

Again Lou stopped herself pointing out that plenty of cops loved Pétain right back.

Martinez scratched the back of his neck. "Pétain is different. He hates us almost as much as he hates women. So I figure we're looking for someone who's been through the system. Maybe done time."

Lou felt her nausea subside slightly. Martinez made a good point. "Have you searched SFPD records? There can't be many people who match that profile."

Stanley grimaced. "This ain't like the movies. Without a name, I can't just go on a fishing expedition. Fortunately that's where your mom was able to deliver the goods." He gestured toward the piles of black binders.

Lou looked at her mom and raised an eyebrow. Whatever the goods were, no good could come from her mom delivering them.

Kerri-Ann McCarthy pointed to the binder open in front of her. "The shit list. Every city has one. Totally unofficial, and privately circulated in all the shelters and refuges. The names, photos, work and home info, and criminal history of all the men who are violent against women, so we know who to look out for."

Lou considered the giant, bulging file, which her mom had somehow managed to obtain sometime between leaving the apartment at three a.m. and arriving back before Lou woke up. Had she just waltzed into one of the city's domestic-violence shelters, explaining that she worked in a refuge in Atlanta, and they'd handed over copies of their files? "This is the list for San Francisco?"

Her mom shook her head. "Just the Tenderloin. Figured we should start in Raum's backyard and work out from there. You wanna look through it? Maybe recognize someone?"

Lou wanted to help. She really did, not least because she knew that unmasking Pétain was the best—maybe only—chance to get the angry mob off their trail for good. But she'd wasted enough time trying to act normal in front of Martinez. She had to get to work.

Lou walked to Raum One as fast as her stomach would allow, and headed straight for Ten Wheeler's office. In her semidrunken state last night, she'd emailed Ten, asking him to dig into Tyrus Weber's cause of death. She hadn't given him a reason, except a vague hint that it had something to do with her investigation into Alex Wu.

Before she got herself any deeper, she needed to know for sure that Charity's story was true, and the Weber part was easiest to verify. She also wanted to understand Ten Wheeler's role in everything. Charity said he'd called the cops on Alex Wu that night at the hackathon, but then he'd sat back quietly as Wu had gotten away with rape and sold their algorithm to Raum? So why hadn't she chosen him as a target too? Lou had a theory: What if they were still in contact? What if Ten was Charity's mole inside Raum One? That would explain why a world-class software engineer— whose contract with Raum let him do whatever the hell he wanted—had agreed to take a lowly gig as Helen's researcher.

Lou tapped on Ten's door and waited for a response. The last time she'd seen Ten, she was about to head to the Redwood to investigate Thomas Calder's sex tape in the hope of unmasking the mysterious "Fate." She tried to get herself back into the character of baffled/deter-mined reporter.

A few seconds later, she knocked again but louder. Still nothing. After a third attempt, she carefully pushed the door. It swung open and Lou saw Ten sitting at his desk, back to the doorway, wearing a pair of com-ically large red headphones. On the computer screen, partly visible over his shoulder, was a photograph of a young woman, blond, wearing a bikini, and standing on a white sandy beach. Lou bit her lip, embarrassed at whatever private moment she had stumbled into. She started to back out of the room but was stopped dead by a sickeningly loud crunch as her foot made contact with something solid on the floor. She looked down to see a plastic drone, which now lay in a hundred pieces below her shoe. Ten swiveled around in his chair, then fumbled for his mouse, minimizing the photograph of the girl and replacing it with a page of white-on-black computer code.

"Shit, sorry," said Lou, "I knocked, but . . ."

Ten stood and rushed over to retrieve the pieces of his splintered drone. His pants were still buttoned, thank God. "You were right about Weber," Ten said matter-of-factly as he gathered up the shards of plastic, transferring them carefully to his desk before apparently realizing it was a hopeless cause and scraping them into the trash can on the floor. "Dude definitely didn't have cancer. But he had done some serious damage to his liver."

"Damage how?" Lou asked the question as a reflex—Ten had already told her enough to make her stomach flip. The founder of Mushu Health hadn't died of cancer.

"Pills. Booze. Mostly booze. He was taking Disulfiram, a drug that makes you puke if you drink. I guess it didn't work."

"You got this from the autopsy report?"

Ten dropped back into his chair. "We have a data-share partnership with Mushu Health. I just queried the API to pull Weber's medical records." Did Ten appreciate the dark irony of using Mushu's data to investigate the death of the company's own CEO? "Should I send the data to Helen too? Does she think Tyrus and Alex's deaths are connected?" Ten looked suddenly terrified. Did he remember Weber from the bar in Boston all those years ago? Was this the terror of a man who thought he might be next, or of a mole about to be exposed?

Lou shrugged, as casually as she was able. "I'll tell her myself. It was really just a hunch. How did you two end up working together?" She tried to make the question sound like more small talk.

Ten blushed again. "You really want to know?"

"She can't recruit everyone on her team by sending Landon to scrape them off a Tenderloin sidewalk, right?"

Ten exploded in laughter, tipping his head back in delight. "My recruitment story is way more embarrassing. She gave me dating advice."

This was about the last thing Lou had expected Ten to say.

"It was her first day at Raum, I guess," Ten continued. "The company was still officially based in the old South of Market building—most of us hadn't moved to Raum One yet, but the engineering team had been sent to supervise the installation of the new staging servers. I came down here and hijacked an empty office when I needed to focus. You know?"

Lou did know. "I did all my best thinking late at night at the *Herald* office after everyone had gone home."

Ten rocked in his chair, evidently feeling acute embarrassment at the story he was telling—but telling it nonetheless. "So I'm hunkered down here one night, thinking I'm the only one on the entire floor, and I'm talking to this girl I'm dating. Like, over IRC." Lou nodded. *Internet Relay Chat.* It was not a natural image—Ten with a girlfriend—but she could tell from the way his eyes had lit up that he really liked this particular woman.

"Holly—my girlfriend—is telling me about her surfer ex-boyfriend and I'm about to type a reply . . . calling the guy an asshole, or making a joke about the Beach Boys or whatever, when suddenly this weird Mary Poppins woman appears behind me—poof! Like magic. She has her hands on my shoulder, and is coaching me. 'She's testing you. She wants to know if you're the jealous type.'" Now Ten adopted a cartoonish British accent: "'I strohngly suhhjest that you do not take the bait!'"

Lou laughed at Ten's impression of Helen, although she couldn't shake the creeping suspicion that she knew the real significance of the story.

"Holly lives like seven thousand miles away—there's literally no way Helen can know her, or anything about her. But now I find myself typing everything she's telling me. Like how this asshole surfer sounds like a really great guy, and how I'd love to meet him. And Holly is responding with smiley faces, telling me that I'm a much nicer guy than he is and how she wishes she could fly and see me right then. Then . . . here's the mind-blowing part . . . The next day she pings me . . . boom! Wants to make it official. Like, boyfriend and girlfriend. I'm telling you, Helen

Tyler might look like a tight-ass, but she is some kind of relationship genius."

"That's an amazing story," said Lou. "But . . . wait . . . you said Holly lives seven thousand miles away. You've never met?"

Ten nodded. "Sydney. Australia." He reached across his desk and retrieved a tiny stuffed kangaroo, a novelty key chain, onto which Ten had attached a cluster of USB security keys, memory sticks, and—so far as she could see—no actual keys. "She sent me this."

Lou was now totally convinced of her theory. "Holly" was really Charity, and she'd catfished Ten into acting as her spy inside Raum. She thought about the photo of the surfer chick that Ten had been staring at when she walked in. Was that what Charity meant by how easy it was to manipulate men? And the kangaroo key chain: a cute gift to prove her love? Or might it be some kind of bugging device? That must be how she'd found out about Helen's $100 million deal with Elmsley.

Jesus, Lou, careful with the hungover paranoia. Then again, was it possible to be too paranoid when it came to Charity Jones?

"So you offered to help Helen with research. As a thank-you."

Ten shook his head. "That was later. She called to say she'd been hired to clean house at Raum One . . . She knew it was mostly me, not Alex, who built the earliest version of the algorithm, and wanted me to help her understand Raum's data so she could figure out the nasty shit he was doing."

Lou registered the way Ten had casually omitted Charity's name from his personal history of Raum and felt a pang of outrage on her behalf. But she let him continue.

"After the IPO, she was going to tell Elmsley to give Alex the boot. She offered to recommend me for the CTO gig if I helped her." Ten looked disgusted by the idea. "I told her I wasn't interested in Alex's job. Not then, not now, not ever."

So there it was. *After the IPO, she was going to tell Elmsley to give Alex the boot.* Confirmation from Helen's own lips—albeit via Ten Wheeler— that she expected Elmsley Chase to still be in charge of Raum after the IPO.

"Why shouldn't you be CTO? You built the algorithm that ended up powering the whole of Raum, didn't you? You deserve the credit." Lou felt gross echoing this false narrative back at Ten, but she wanted to hear him say it.

Ten's shoulders dropped into a sad shrug, and for a moment Lou thought he might be about to confess to the existence of Charity. "Do you know what Alex did all day?" He paused. "I don't mean the weird stuff—I mean for his job. He went to meetings, he appeared on TV, then he went to more meetings. I don't think he'd touched a line of code in over a year. He was an *executive*"—Ten said the word like an expletive—"and he was really good at that shit."

"So it never bothered you that he ended up taking the credit for someone else's work?"

Lou's anger was getting the better of her. She didn't want to tip Ten off to what she knew, but also couldn't bear to hear Charity erased from history yet again. But before Ten could answer, the door to the office flew open to reveal a very irritated-looking Helen Tyler. "Good news," she bellowed, looking for all the world like she was about to deliver the exact opposite. "You'll have another chance to wear that DVF dress. Elmsley is hosting a party tonight, and we're both invited. He has another foolproof plan to save the IPO."

74

A HALF HOUR later, Lou arrived back at the Four Seasons to find her mom and Carol still at Helen's kitchen counter. Martinez had gone, but he'd left his SFPD laptop, into which Carol was furiously two-finger typing. Lou almost kept walking. With everything she was dealing with, she didn't have the energy for another fight about the danger they were putting themselves in. For now, they were safe inside the Four Seasons rather than roaming the streets looking for that psychopath Pétain. That was enough.

"Hey, honey," Lou's mom called from the kitchen with surprising, almost exaggerated cheeriness. "Want some lunch?" She gestured toward a cold, half-eaten Hawaiian pizza next to the sink.

"Sure," said Lou, taking a slice and joining the two women at the counter. Just for five minutes; she had to eat. "How's your day going? You guys making any progress?"

"We're fine," Lou's mom replied, a little too quickly and a little too loudly. Lou knew that tone, and it was never good. She should have kept walking.

Carol filled in the gap. "If by 'fine' you mean there's a mob of angry virgins armed with flaming torches heading right for us, then yeah, we're peachy."

Lou let her pizza slice drop back onto the plate. "What are you talking about? Mom?"

Her mom rotated the laptop and Lou saw a familiar silhouette staring back at her, backlit in red. She reached over and tapped the space bar.

"Bonjour à tous!" Claude Pétain's synthesized voice boomed his trademark introduction from the laptop's tinny speakers. *"Some people just don't know when to quit. Sources tell me that Kerri-Ann McCarthy and*

Carol Brook—the crazed bitches who tried to take on our army in Atlanta—have brought their fight to San Francisco. They are working with the city's pig police to try to bring me to justice. Unless we find them first. The hunt is on, mes amis . . ."

Here Pétain burst into maniacal robotic laughter as a gaggle of cartoon Jean-Claude the Pigs holding machine guns and, for some inexplicable reason, wearing yellow Stars of David came running across the screen.

Lou slapped the laptop closed. "How does he even know you're in San Francisco?"

Her mom seemed confused by the question. "He paid for our plane tickets."

"Right," said Lou, remembering they still didn't know about Charity. She took a bite of pizza and immediately felt her blood sugar spike from the pineapple. It couldn't be a coincidence that just as Lou was getting ready to help Charity bring down Raum, suddenly Claude Pétain ordered his mob to threaten her mom again. More proof that he was in cahoots with Raum's Saudi investors.

Lou put her hand on her mom's shoulder. "We need to call Landon right now. He can get you somewhere safe."

"We're fine," Carol interrupted. "We don't need men to protect us. Not when we have you, Terminator."

Lou felt a slap of déjà vu. Carol's nickname for Lou hadn't been funny when she was ten, and it definitely wasn't funny now.

Her mom shrugged Lou's hand away. "We're going to figure out who this guy is, and Martinez will sling his ass in jail. Then we'll see who the real bitch is, the first time he takes a shower."

"Mom!"

"Careful, Kerri-Ann," said Carol. "We're in California now, where jokes and plastic bags are outlawed."

"Right, sorry. I mean Martinez will sling his ass in jail, where he'll be given the benefit of due legal process and have all his needs respectfully met."

"Like the need for some jailhouse dick up his ass," muttered Carol.

Lou raised her hands. *Enough.* She knew there was no point in trying to argue with her mom when she was like this, feeding off Carol's energy. "I have to go out for a few hours to a Raum thing. I'll be back later, though—then I swear I'll help you look. In the meantime, please, please stay inside. OK?"

She left them still joking about the man who'd threatened to kill them.

Just after four thirty, showered and changed, Lou arrived breathless back at Raum One, where she found Helen already waiting outside, tapping her slim gold watch impatiently. Helen was dressed in a black silk jumpsuit, similar to but not quite the same as the one she'd worn a few nights earlier at the party. Did she keep a stock of evening wear in her office? Lou had forgone the DVF number and opted instead for her own freshly laundered white shirt and jeans. This was partly an act of independence—she wasn't in the mood to play dress-up for Elmsley Chase—but also of practicality, as her jeans had pockets big enough for her notebook and pen. Charity might call her at any moment with instructions on how to find the fake data planted on Raum's server, and she wanted to be prepared.

"All's well?" asked Helen, looking Lou up and down before they climbed into the waiting vRaum.

"Great," said Lou. At some point she'd have to confront Helen about her side deal with Elmsley. She needed to know if Helen could be trusted to help if anything went wrong with Charity's plan. Until then she'd act as if everything was normal and she was still hunting for Fate. "Still nothing from . . ." Lou mouthed the word *Fate*. "I'm still working on possible connections with the Redwood." She fastened her seat belt. "So what's Elmsley's big plan to save the IPO?"

Helen smiled in response. "And spoil the surprise?" She raised her eyes and gave a slight nod toward the driver's seat—a reminder that the walls had ears.

They sat mostly in silence as the vRaum crept through downtown San Francisco. Helen spent the entire journey tapping at her phone, speaking only once to instruct the driver to stop trying to make conversation and focus on driving. Lou stared out of the window, trying to imagine what possible plan Elmsley Chase and Helen might have cooked up to save the IPO and Elmsley's job. And hoping Charity already had a plan to stop it.

75

THE VRAUM PULLED up outside Elmsley Chase's town house in Pacific Heights. Since the earliest days of the city, the area—nicknamed "Specific Whites" by locals—had been home to the wealthiest San Franciscans. At this particular juncture of the twenty-first century, this meant tech billionaires, bankers, and the author Danielle Steel.

Elmsley Chase's home lay at the end of a treelined cul-de-sac. As the vRaum approached, a guard wearing the gray uniform and cartoon sheriff's badge of a private security company stepped out of a tall white tent and gestured for them to stop. He scrutinized Lou's and Helen's faces through the window and compared them with something on the screen of a gray iPad. Lou felt the same way she did when passing through airport security: nervous and guilty, even though she hadn't done anything wrong. Yet.

The guard was not alone in his tent. Peering over his shoulder at the iPad screen was a man in a much more expensive-looking, dark gray suit. After a few moments longer, when he was satisfied that Lou was Lou and Helen was Helen, the man in the expensive suit nodded that they could proceed.

Almost immediately they were stopped again by another man in an identical gray suit. He, too, made a performance of walking slowly around the car before opening the rear passenger door and inviting—ordering, really—the two women to step out and walk the rest of the way to the house. Lou knew Elmsley would have private security, but still something about the behavior of the guards felt very off. The men in suits seemed more like Secret Service than the standard rent-a-cops, and every one of them—Lou suddenly realized—looked Middle Eastern.

Casa Elmsley was a gigantic sandstone town house with a pair of concrete lions standing guard on either side of an enormous oak front door. Lou and Helen scaled the five stone steps leading up to the entrance, Helen's heels clip-clopping as they went. At the summit, Helen yanked on a ridiculously Gothic doorbell chain, which responded with equally comic silence. Everything about the house had been styled to evoke some strange cross between a medieval fortress and a seventeenth-century French château, though judging by the pair of Roman numerals etched obnoxiously in the stonework—a pair of intertwined *M*s—the house had been constructed as recently as the year 2000, probably for some lucky beneficiary of the first dot-com boom.

Helen looked at Lou and raised an eyebrow at the absurdity of the door, the doorbell, the Roman numerals, and the lions. Lou responded with a tight smile. Why was Helen suddenly being so cagey? Did she know Lou had lied about what she'd found at the Redwood?

Seconds later, the wooden front doors swung open—powered by some unseen mechanism—to reveal a grand, oak-paneled entryway, dominated by a wide staircase built entirely from frosted glass. Less French château than medieval Apple Store. A gaggle of expensively dressed guests was already climbing the stairs. This *was* a party, then.

At the top of the stairs, Lou found herself in a large living room, though it looked more like an art gallery: a yawning space, with stark white walls, onto which someone had hung some of the most obnoxious artwork Lou had ever seen. One side of the room was plastered with enormous graffitied canvases, all themed around wealth or greed: huge neon dollar signs, sprayed next to caricatures of hundred-dollar bills— on each bill the face of Benjamin Franklin had been replaced by that of Elmsley Chase. Evidently, Raum's CEO wasn't just a lover of terrible art, but also its patron.

Lou took in the other guests. She recognized the immaculately dressed British consul general whom she'd once interviewed for a story about European startups relocating to the Bay Area. He was deep in conversation with an equally dapper Chinese man. A delegation of Russians— easily identifiable by their suits—stood alone, talking to nobody at all.

Lou stifled a gasp. Across the room, a cluster of men in flowing white robes were talking to the CEO of Samsung and his entourage. The presence of a Saudi delegation must mean that the crown prince wasn't far away.

"This is as far as I go," Lou whispered to Helen as they stood at the threshold. "Until you tell me why we're here."

Helen gave a nod and leaned close to Lou's ear. "We're here to witness a deal with the devil." Then she strode into the crowd, making directly for the Saudis, leaving Lou with the choice to either follow behind or go home. Which was no choice at all.

Now Lou spotted another familiar figure: Tim Palgrave, standing hand in hand with a Black woman who was very definitely not Charity. She thought about how effortlessly Charity had manipulated her way into Palgrave's life—and the party at Raum One—by posing as the person he expected her to be: an escort sent by his usual agency. She wondered if Palgrave was also her ticket back inside the building, to plant the files that would allow her to bring Raum crashing down. Maybe she was there right now.

Lou stepped into the throng with renewed purpose, still scanning for familiar faces and any clue as to why they were all here. Of the very few women in the room, the only two Lou recognized were Miquela Rio from the *Wall Street Journal* and Elmsley's girlfriend, whose name Lou still couldn't recall. Madeline? Maude?

Definitely Not Maude was dressed in a skintight black dress with matching patent leather heels, and a red limited-edition Tiffany Raum Band (retail: $30,000, or three tennis bracelets). She was flitting from group to group, smiling, *cheers*ing and generally playing the model host. Elmsley Chase was nowhere to be seen—always the master of the dramatic entrance.

Lou plucked a glass from a table of orange juices. She took a sip and braced for the spike of vodka, but remarkably for a Raum event, it really was just juice.

Lou watched Melanie? Monica? slowly take another lap of the room before arriving front and center, where she traded her glass for a wireless microphone. "Good evening, everyone," she said, amplified over the chatter. In most rooms, the former Olympic gymnast's mere presence would be enough to stun men into silence, but not so in this one.

Lou was startled by the sound of Helen Tyler, now standing right behind her, tapping a spoon against the lip of her own glass. Helen bellowed a curt, "Quiet. Please," also far too close to Lou's ear.

The chatter ceased, all except that of the Russians, who continued to mutter and joke among themselves until Helen silenced them with a shouted *"Molchaniye!"*

"Thank you," said Chase's girlfriend to Helen as much as the room. "My name is Meredith Maitland—and Elmsley and I are delighted to welcome you all to our home for what I know will be a historic night."

These were the words coming out of Meredith's mouth, vocal fry and all. But the look on her face told a different story—the broad smile battling with the narrowed eyes, the universal sign of a woman doing her duty while secretly wanting to murder everyone in sight. It was a look Lou had never been able to pull off. As Meredith spoke, a projection screen slowly descended from a slit in the ceiling behind her. When it reached its full extension, a projector that had emerged from a similar compartment in the center of the room burst into life, tattooing her dress with a spinning Raum logo. Squinting against the beam, Meredith stepped aside and announced with another unconvincing smile: "It's showtime!"

The ceiling lights faded. Lou took a small step back so she was next to Helen, and the two watched as the Raum logo on-screen dissolved into a 3-D spinning Raum Band. Over a thumping bass soundtrack, the band was magically transported onto the wrist of an attractive young woman hailing a cab at the end of a night out, from where it leapt again to a man ordering pizza, a homeowner arming his security system, a college student paying for a pile of textbooks, a nurse checking her patient's vital signs . . . the same inbuilt blood-monitoring technology that Alex Wu had weaponized to find his victims. Another visual effect and all these characters shared the same screen, each one in a small box. The boxes and faces multiplied and remultiplied as the camera zoomed out to reveal hundreds, thousands, millions of these boxes covering a map of the United States . . .

Abruptly, the music stopped and the screen turned to black, with the first half of Raum's tagline picked out in simple white text. *Waiting . . .*

Now a second spotlight picked out Elmsley Chase, who had taken his place alongside Meredith, his black jeans and T-shirt helping him to remain invisible until the spotlight hit him. ". . . is over!"

An ovation from the room: booming laughter and clapping from the Russians, polite applause from the Chinese, and eye rolling from the Brits.

Chase tamped down the applause. "Let's cut the bullshit. Everything you just saw . . ." He paused to allow the room to fall silent again before resuming his shtick. ". . . you already know. You know that we have forty-two million Raum Band users in the United States. You know that the Raum Band has transformed the way Americans live, work, play . . . and . . . well, do a whole bunch of other things that the marketing team wouldn't let me include in the video."

More laughter, more applause. The Brits—famous connoisseurs of smutty innuendo—seemed especially delighted. "You also already know we've barely scratched the surface. Raum has more than a billion active users across the globe—all of them desperate to get hold of a Raum Band so they can unlock the full potential of our platform."

Lou's eyes were still fixed on the screen, but her mind had jumped back to Charity. God, she couldn't wait to leak the "proof" that Raum's numbers were bullshit. To wipe the smug smile off this asshole's face.

Another pause from Elmsley, a sweep of his arm. "Gentlemen . . . ladies, Your Royal Highness, Mr. Ambassador, Mr. Consul General . . . I didn't bring you here just to get you drunk and tell you things you already know. I brought you here because tonight, with your help, we're going to do something most tech companies only pretend they want to do. Tonight we're going to change the world."

The room exploded into yet another ovation, even though, so far as Lou could tell, none of them had the first idea what he was talking about. Out of the corner of her eye, Lou noticed that Helen was enthusiastically clapping too. Then Lou looked down and realized, to her horror, that she was doing the same. Maybe it was just a reflex, a survival instinct to make sure nobody suspected a traitor in their midst. But there was also no denying that Elmsley Chase at his best was a hell of a showman. Across the room Miquela Rio of the *Wall Street Journal* was the only one not applauding. She was bookended by two Raum PR flacks as she transcribed Elmsley's words into her notebook. That's why the party had started so early in the evening: East Coast print deadlines.

"I know a lot of you have been waiting for us to roll the Raum Band out to users outside the US. And tonight I'm super stoked to say . . ."

The on-screen image zoomed out again, and now the tiny faces covered the entire world.

". . . the waiting is over."

Lou stood rooted to the spot. For months Raum had hinted it might roll out an international version of the Raum Band, but it had always been foiled by the enormous technical cost of pushing the voice-activated band—complete with its medical sensors, secure payments technology, and the rest—to millions of potential new users. Even at $200 a band, plus thousands more for the premium versions, the device was a huge loss leader. Just as Charity said, processing all that data required eye-watering infrastructure. It also needed an endless supply of human labor: to deliver the pizzas, build the vRaums, handle customer service. Had Raum really overcome the logistical challenges of a global rollout? Even if they had, would the promise of a few million international sales really be enough to get the IPO back on track? Elmsley Chase obviously thought so.

Lou glanced across the room and felt the corners of her mouth twitch into a smile. *This is fine.* Miquela Rio could write her puff piece in the *Journal*, but in a few hours Raum would be the subject of a much bigger story: that for all Elmsley Chase's promise of a global rollout, hardly anyone actually wanted to buy his overpriced wristband or download his magical app. He'd been lying about Raum's user numbers the whole time. The whole company was a mirage. *What is truth?*

The applause died down again, and Elmsley stood in silence—for so long that Lou looked around to see if Charity had decided to pull another of her stunts. All she saw was more grinning men, and she realized—they were waiting for the real punch line. Elmsley Chase always had "one more thing."

Her smile faded as she waited to hear the real reason they were all here.

Elmsley raised the microphone back to his lips. "With one simple product"—he tapped the band on his own wrist—"anyone in the world can access information, food, transportation, health information, shelter, even love. We hope one day it'll also be used for voting, for diagnosing and curing disease, but . . ." A much longer pause. ". . . we can only achieve that dream if the benefits are available to all, regardless of location, or income level."

Lou caught the emphasis in his voice. *Regardless of income level?* Was he about to announce some kind of cheaper, entry-level Raum Band? A Raum credit card to put it on? These were all things other hardware manufacturers had tried. Yawn, yawn, yawn.

But now Lou noticed a very slight shift in Elmsley's facial expression. A very specific look—wide-eyed, smirking, but somehow projecting an aura of calm control—that she'd seen only twice before: when Elmsley and Alex had first launched Raum's algorithm, and when they'd later stood onstage to reveal the Raum Band. She felt her heart beating harder.

"The Raum Band is expensive. Too expensive when half the planet still lives on less than two dollars a day. So, we're going to fix that."

Oh my fucking God. Lou knew how Elmsley Chase would save his IPO.

". . . three months from today, the price of the Raum Band will drop . . . *to zero.* Through thousands of partnerships with governments and private foundations around the globe, every man, woman, and child on the planet will be able to access the power of the Raum Band without paying a dime. We're calling it Raum For Everyone."

The crowd literally gasped in wonder, followed by instantaneous and deafening applause. On the projector screen, a stylized "R4E" logo appeared alongside a photo of a woman in a hijab, holding up her fist in a gesture of power and independence. On her wrist was a green plastic Raum Band.

Lou's heartbeat thumped in her ears, accompanied by a high-pitched whistling. What Chase was promising—free Raum Bands for the entire world—was impossible. Not Silicon Valley impossible, but actually, literally impossible. The amount of bandwidth and data storage and employees needed to power eight *billion* Raum Bands, with zero revenue . . . The logistics of distributing that many devices . . .

But as she looked at the awed faces of the assembled diplomats, all tapping frantically into their phones, and then to Miquela Rio scribbling in her notebook, she realized that economic reality didn't matter. All that mattered was that Wall Street believed "Raum For Everyone" was happening. That's why Elmsley had claimed the rollout would start in three months—at least a month after the IPO. He was proudly and openly doing exactly what Lou and Charity were about to falsely accuse him of: exaggerating Raum's user numbers to save his IPO.

After tonight, Lou could leak whatever fake numbers she liked, and nobody would give a shit. Who cared if he was lying before? Who even remembered what the old numbers were? *An industry built on the promise of limitless memory, by people who can't remember what happened last week.*

Lou turned to Helen. "You knew about this?"

But in lieu of an answer, Helen grabbed Lou's arm and squeezed it. "It gets more disgusting, I promise you."

Still standing at the front of the room, Chase gestured toward a man Lou recognized from Raum's shareholder capitalization table and a dozen *Fortune* magazine covers.

"I'm privileged to welcome my friend Crown Prince Bansar bin Faisal. As representative of his father's sovereign investment fund, His Royal Highness has been Raum's single biggest investor and one of the biggest champions of democracy in the Middle East. As of tonight, I'm proud to say he is the first world leader to sign up to help bring Raum For Everyone to his citizens."

On command, Prince Bansar strode into view, joining Chase at the front of the room. "Thank you, Elmsley." His accent sounded almost British, as well it might, given his Oxford education. "And thank you, Meredith, for welcoming us into your magnificent home."

Lou felt herself tumbling further down the rabbit hole. Just months ago, Raum had quietly ousted the prince from the board after his father had crossed one line too many: bone saws and tech unicorns make unseemly bedfellows. But all that seemed to have been forgotten. Here was Elmsley standing side by side with a murderer's son, sharing the adulation of the crowd. This was Helen's deal with the devil—the Saudi government had promised to become the first customer for Raum For Everyone, the essential first proof point for Wall Street, in exchange for the prince's rehabilitation back into American corporate high society.

"When my dear friend Charlie Brusk told me about Raum For Everyone, I knew it was the initiative that—as you like to say, Elmsley—we had been waiting for. My country has already made great strides in ensuring everyone has access to the latest technologies—including women and other minority groups."

"Women are not a minority, you piece of shit," whispered Lou to nobody at all. She hadn't noticed Brusk until now, but there he was, nodding and grinning in the corner of the room.

"I am therefore proud to announce that we have placed an initial order for thirty-five million Raum Bands—for every man and woman over the age of eighteen in our kingdom. They will be made available without reference to gender, ethnicity, or sexual orientation."

Here Elmsley quickly interjected: "That's something I made very clear. Raum For Everyone will not support discrimination of any kind." There was a reason the king had appointed his son as emissary to Silicon Valley: a young, photogenic modernizer paid homage to diversity and inclusion while back home the proceeds from his investments funded bigger and better jails for LGBTQ campaigners and armies of police to blockade polling booths against women voters.

The pitch continued, with Chase and the crown prince doing everything short of tap-dancing to sell the idea of Raum For Everyone to the assembled representatives of every major democracy on earth, and a couple of dictatorships. When finally the presentation ended and the dignitaries clamored to glad-hand Chase and the prince, Lou took Helen's arm and urged her toward a distant corner of the room, next to an oil painting of what was supposed to be either a fat Ron Paul or a thin Penn Jillette.

"Fucking assholes. Fucking evil assholes."

Helen broke free of Lou's grip. "Probably best to keep your voice down." She nodded toward the prince's entourage.

"I don't care," said Lou. Did Helen really expect her to believe Elmsley Chase and the prince just so happened to come up with the perfect IPO-saving plan on the eve of the board meeting, without any help? A plan that would make them both incredibly rich, sure, but would also guarantee Helen her $100 million payday. "We both know . . . you know who . . . will figure out a way to stop this." She pictured Charity hearing the news about "Raum For Everyone" and quickly reconfiguring her algorithm to stop it. Elmsley and Prince Bansar had no idea what they were up against. It was going to be OK, she told herself. They'd come this far.

Helen gave another pained *inside voices* frown. "I'd be more sure of that if we knew who she was and what she wanted."

Lou hesitated. Was Helen saying that she knew about Charity, and giving Lou a chance to come clean?

"Tyler!"

Lou clenched her teeth at the sound of Charlie Brusk's voice. Helen, however, had long ago perfected the art of gracefully welcoming an asshole. She turned to greet him.

"Charlie! Sometimes a pleasure, rarely a chore."

Tonight, Brusk had traded his trademark T-shirt and designer jeans for a jet-black suit and white shirt. "Did Helen tell you?" Brusk addressed his question to Lou but didn't wait for an answer. "How she convinced Elmsley that Raum For Everyone was the answer to all of our prayers?" He removed a tiny bottle of hand sanitizer from his inside pocket and slathered some on his hands. Lou glanced up at his forehead and registered the strange smooth texture of Brusk's skin. Was he wearing concealer?

Helen sighed. "I merely relayed your recommendation to Elmsley. He needed no convincing from me. Also, as you know, this whole—performance—is premature. The budget for Raum For Everyone isn't formalized until the board votes on Monday."

Brusk gave a patronizing chuckle. "The board consisting of myself, Tim Palgrave, Elmsley, and—after Monday—His Royal Highness."

"The prodigal son returns." Lou couldn't help herself.

Brusk shook his head slowly, as if he pitied Lou's naïveté about world affairs: "I realize you traffic in hyperbole, Ms. McCarthy, but I've worked with the crown prince and his family for almost a decade. I assure you the Saudis aren't the monsters the mainstream, and dare I say *racist*, media would have you believe."

Lou had heard enough. She excused herself, leaving Helen and Brusk to catch up and self-congratulate on their joint victory. She needed to find Charity and figure out a new plan, but first she needed a very large drink.

Fantastic. Lou reached the drinks table at the exact same moment as Elmsley Chase's girlfriend, who'd apparently had the same idea. They both paused as they saw there was only one glass remaining.

"Please," said Lou, barely able to hide her contempt for yet another collaborator in the destruction of the universe. "Your boyfriend is paying for it, after all."

"Actually I'm pretty sure Prince Bonesaw is picking up the tab." Meredith tipped her head in the vague direction of where the prince and Chase were standing.

Lou's eyes widened. Had she really called him Prince Bonesaw? "You're not a fan?"

Meredith gave a lopsided smile. "A fancy suit and a TED Talk doesn't make him less complicit in his father's crimes. My dad worked for Amnesty International for most of his life. He must be spinning in his grave. Or, I guess, his urn. Can you spin in an urn?" Lou heard it now: the slur in Meredith's speech. She'd been hitting the champagne pretty hard. Who could blame her?

"*Rattling* in his urn?" Lou felt immediately terrible at her attempt at gallows humor—joking about your own dead relatives is one thing; joking about someone else's . . . But Meredith didn't seem offended. She laughed a loud tipsy laugh. Two women brought together by a common desire to be as far away as possible from everyone in this room, but unable to leave. Meredith took the sole remaining glass of champagne and handed it to Lou. "Meredith Maitland."

"Lou McCarthy."

"I know," said Meredith. "I gave Elmsley so much shit for what he did to you at Raum One. He forgets sometimes that his douchebag CEO act has consequences."

"No fucking kidding," said Lou. "Still, he seems to be doing OK." She gestured toward the opulence of the room, and the ugliness of the art on the wall.

Meredith didn't take the bait, so Lou added, unnecessarily, "And thanks to tonight, he'll soon be doing *really* OK."

Meredith opened her mouth to speak, but then closed it again, as if she was trying to decide whether to confide a huge secret. She took a half step toward Lou—so close their noses almost touched. "Have you asked Elmsley why he so desperately wants to take Raum public?"

Why would she? "He'll make about a hundred billion dollars. Seems like a pretty good reason."

Meredith smiled. "Actually he won't. All of his IPO proceeds are going to his new philanthropic foundation." She said this like it was common knowledge.

Lou took a step back, almost colliding with the Belgian chargé d'affaires. "What foundation?" The words Elmsley Chase and "philanthropic" barely belonged in the same universe.

"The Ramsey Chase Neuroblastoma Research Trust. The biggest endowment to research childhood cancer in history. His legacy." Meredith laughed again, as if she found the idea of Elmsley Chase donating every penny of his personal wealth to cure the cancer that killed his younger brother at age fourteen just as unbelievable as Lou did.

"You're not serious?" Lou had heard Elmsley describe Ramsey in TV interviews as his inspiration, his conscience, his guardian angel. But the idea that Chase would actually donate his IPO windfall to *any* good cause was an obvious lie.

A waiter strolled by and Meredith tried, unsuccessfully, to flag down more champagne. "Elmsley and Ramsey were inseparable growing up. They had to be. Their dad was always working and their mom was a total social butterfly. Kids like me dreamed of one day going to the Olympics, but according to his mom—who is a sweetheart, by the way—Elmsley and Ramsey hid in their rooms for hours playacting as CEOs. Big-shot businessmen like their dad, you know? The two of them had this shared dream that one day they'd start a company together and it'd be so successful that they'd get to ring the opening bell at the Nasdaq." Meredith looked around, and lowered her voice. "That's all he's ever cared about: standing on that stage and ringing the opening bell in his brother's name. It's what drives him." She stared wistfully over Lou's shoulder. "Like he can't rest—can't enjoy life—until he's rung that fucking bell."

Lou scrambled for the right words. "That's insane . . . I mean . . ." She couldn't finish the sentence, or the thought. She knew what it meant to idolize a parent, and how much a stupid promise could mean to a kid. But she also knew how little those same promises meant to adults . . .

"It's only crazy if you believe a man like Elmsley isn't capable of doing something out of love, or loyalty. Which I guess would make me . . . what? A trophy? A prop? An idiot?"

Lou scrambled to backtrack. "I don't think you're a trophy. I've seen the way he looks at you." Honestly, Lou couldn't remember if she'd ever seen Elmsley Chase look at his girlfriend.

"It's OK," said Meredith. She plucked the glass out of Lou's hand and took a swig from it. "Do you mind?"

Lou shook her head. "Please."

Meredith regained her original train of thought: "For what it's worth, Elmsley has written a bunch of data-protection clauses into the deal—the Saudis get the Raum Bands, but Elmsley keeps control of all the data. He'll make sure there's no way the prince and his dad can use Raum's technology to spy on their citizens."

Lou gave an angry laugh. "But he's fine when his rapist CTO uses it to stalk his victims."

Meredith rolled her eyes. "Alex? I seem to remember someone tipped off a journalist about him."

"Yeah," said Lou, "Helen Tyler. To set me up."

"And remind me who Helen works for? She could have set you up a thousand ways, without exposing Alex."

Lou almost replied that Helen worked for the board, not Elmsley. Then she remembered Helen's $100 million side deal. "You expect me to believe Elmsley *wanted* Alex Wu to be outed as a rapist? That he—"

"Is actually a good man who only plays an asshole on TV? Hates that everyone he hires turns out to be a scumbag? Wants to use his IPO money to help make a difference? You don't get to build a half-trillion-dollar company without working with the occasional monster. He's promised that after the IPO he's going to spend his life and his money to undo . . ." Here she stopped herself from saying the obvious. *All the damage that Raum has done.* "Like Bill Gates with malaria."

Lou didn't know how to respond. She knew Meredith needed to believe all this shit about the man she loved—God, how she understood that— but Christ.

"Maybe one day you'll get to know the real him. The guy who feels terrible that we had to postpone our weekly Netflix date to host this bullshit." Meredith drained her glass. "He's promised me a redo tomorrow, and I know he'll be there. He always keeps his word."

Lou was saved from gagging at Meredith's description of billionaire date night by a small huddle of bodies rushing past, almost knocking them off their feet. She turned just in time to recognize Elmsley Chase, the crown prince, and Helen Tyler disappearing down a hallway, trailed by one of the prince's bodyguards. Charlie Brusk was following a few feet behind.

As Brusk passed the table where Lou and Meredith were standing, he slowed down just enough to say to Meredith in an out-of-breath half whisper, "Elmsley asked if you could keep the guests entertained. There's been a . . . situation." Lou felt a chill. Had Brusk really glanced at Lou as he said the word "situation"?

Meredith gave a confused, tipsy nod and Brusk headed off down the hallway. Lou watched them go, then turned back to Meredith only to find she was already across the room, intercepting a waitress to get another drink.

Lou didn't hesitate. She walked as fast as she could down the hallway, without quite breaking into a run. She stopped at every closed door, listening until finally she heard Elmsley Chase's loud voice. Lou gripped the handle and opened the door just a hair, freezing when it responded with a loud creak. She held her breath, but Elmsley continued to shout. Through the crack, she now saw that the group had passed all the way through the room and out through a set of patio doors onto what must be a balcony. She pushed open the door wider and slipped inside.

The design of the bedroom echoed that of the house's entryway—a jarring combination of oak-paneled walls, glass shelves, and very little furniture. The only hint of the room's purpose was a steel-framed four-poster bed covering most of the floor space. Yet more bad art lined the walls: garish watercolors of Bay Area landmarks clashing with the severity of the oak and glass. Lou crept her way closer to the balcony. "My information was very clear." She could hear Prince Bansar now, his unmistakable accent tinged with anger. "This . . . person who calls himself Fate is responsible for the death of your CTO, and maybe the deaths of several other men. His intention is to sabotage the IPO and maybe even destroy Raum itself."

Lou froze. The prince knew about Fate! He was using male pronouns, thank God, so at least Charity was safe for now. Lou's optimism was quickly dashed as she heard the words "Redwood Hotel" and "base of operations."

Charlie Brusk spoke next. "Excuse me for asking, Your Highness, but who is your source for this information? Is he reliable?"

The prince dismissed Brusk's question. "That is not important. What matters is that my security team are already closing in on this saboteur. My father has authorized his full resources. He will not tolerate the failure of this IPO."

Lou could hear the tremor in the prince's voice. This wasn't anger; it was terror. He knew how the king would react if the IPO collapsed.

"I don't give a shit what your dad will tolerate." Lou heard Elmsley Chase again—a man who refused to take orders in his own house. "Your people can investigate, but if they find anything, they call me first. The IPO is back on track and *I* won't tolerate another scandal because one of your people goes rogue." He must have turned to Brusk, because now he added, almost wistfully: "I mean it, Charlie. You know how important this is to me."

Lou remembered what Meredith had said about Elmsley's promise to his younger brother.

"We will keep you informed," the prince cut Chase off, in a tone that somehow managed to sound both dismissive and deferential.

Lou had to go. What if Charity was already at Raum One, planting the fake data? Lou had to warn her she was walking into a trap.

Her panic was interrupted by the sensation of her phone vibrating urgently in her pocket. She fumbled for the handset and felt a wave of relief when she saw the message from a withheld number. *Opposite the Four Seasons. One hour. —C.*

81%

LOU RACED DOWN the concrete steps, not daring to look back as she passed the line of idling black SUVs and vRaums snaking down the cul-de-sac.

She set off in the direction of Raum One and ran for almost a mile until she finally saw a cab—an actual yellow taxi—driving toward her. Empty, like almost all the cabs in the city. She dived in and gave the driver the address of the Four Seasons.

Now she pulled out her phone and opened the *Wall Street Journal* app. Miquela Rio's story was already live. *Raum For Everyone pledges billions to bring Raum's algorithm to the world.* Social media was exploding, too, at news of the free Raum Band: bankers and tech pundits cheered yet another bravura performance from the greatest Disruptor of all time, while human rights advocates howled with outrage at what was clearly a way for authoritarian regimes to track their citizens. The first response to the tweet announcing the story was from Tommy Paphitis. A single word: *Awesome,* accompanied by an emoji of some confetti.

The cab turned onto Market Street and Lou asked the driver to slow down. She slid lower in her seat as they crept past the small plaza outside Raum One. Three black SUVs—the same model she'd seen outside Elmsley's house—were parked in a No Parking bay, hazard lights flashing. A man in a black suit—who might easily have been the brother of the prince's bodyguard from the party—was waving a diplomatic passport in the face of a furious-looking SFMTA parking cop. Lou prayed that Charity was already long gone.

The cab pulled up outside the Four Seasons, and Lou hurried through the revolving doors. Upstairs she found her mom still in Helen's kitchen, poring over yet another binder of potential Claude Pétain suspects.

"How was the party?" Her mom asked this without looking up from her binder.

"Little weird," said Lou, trying desperately not to have a full-blown panic attack. "Where's Carol?"

"On her date with Detective Martinez."

"Jesus." She'd told them both to stay indoors, even before Saudi intelligence officers were roaming the streets looking for anyone involved in sabotaging Raum's IPO.

Her mom raised her hands as if to say *Whatareyougonnado?* "She flew all this way to help me find a psychopath. Least I can do is help her get laid. I have Martinez's cell number, and I promised them both that the first sign of a mob, I'll call SWAT."

Lou slumped down on the stool on the opposite side of the counter. "I'm really sorry I got you into this, Mom."

Her mom closed the binder and pushed it away from her. Then she took hold of Lou's hands. "You didn't get me into anything. Elmsley Chase got us both into this when he hired a rapist to work at his company, then punished you for writing the truth. I seem to remember a certain fifteen-year-old girl once telling me that she wasn't going to feel bad for telling the truth about . . . remind me the rest?"

"A fucking asshole who wasn't worth the shit on your shoes." Lou turned her head away as she remembered the teenage fight with her mom. The biggest they'd ever had. Her dad had called for the first time in months, begging her to come visit him in South Carolina. He was sick, his girlfriend had thrown him out, and he was living in a Motel 6 in Richburg. Her mom had encouraged her to go, and Lou screamed at her, accused her of falling for his lies all over again.

I won't feel bad for telling the truth. What a fucking hypocrite.

Through Helen's kitchen window, she could see the shimmering lights of the city, and the peak of Coit Tower piercing the fog.

"What if it wasn't the truth?"

Her mom squinted across the table, confused by the question or perhaps the sudden intensity with which her daughter had asked it. "About Raum?"

Lou shook her head, tears already forming at the corners of her eyes. She had been putting off this moment for twenty years, but had finally run out of road.

"About Dad." Any minute the prince's men could kick down the door, drag her off to torture her about Charity. She couldn't bear to hear her mom praise her as this fearless truth teller anymore. It was all bullshit. She'd been lying her whole life. "The house in South Carolina. He said it was for us."

She felt her mom squeeze her hands tighter. "He was a liar and a cheat, Lou. He stole all our money to buy that house for him and his . . . mistress. He admitted it in the divorce."

Lou was suddenly ten years old again, shuffling downstairs. Her dad on the telephone, talking to the realtor. Her heart bursting with love as she heard him talk about move-in dates, and floor plans and security deposits. It was really happening. Now she was crouched on the bottom step as her dad asked about the yard, and the grill, and the play swing: *Oh! That would be just perfect for . . .* She was about to rush over and squeeze him so tight, to thank him for keeping his promise. Then she heard it: a name that wasn't hers. She knew only one girl named Milly, her elementary school teacher's daughter. And now her world had fallen apart; she was curled in a ball, head pressed tight against her knees. The sound of her mom's key in the lock and her dad cursing as he quickly hung up the phone.

Click.

Lou was twenty-nine again, her mom still looking at the daughter who risked everything to protect her. And, just like all those years ago, she knew what she had to do.

She pulled her hands free from her mom's grip. "You don't understand. He told me the house was for us. For me and him. We were going to leave you."

She tried to explain herself, but the confessions came in sobs and gulps. "You were always working. And when you weren't, you were either sleeping or yelling." Back then, Lou didn't know why her mom was mad with her dad all the time or even what a drunk was; she just knew her dad was there when she came home from school, always sitting on the couch with a beer, waiting to hear about her day. On the weekends he let her go to PG-13 movies, and trusted her to play in the park while he "ran errands." It was her dad who'd taken her to the woods and taught her to hold a shotgun, for her own protection, even though her mom had banned firearms from the house. That dumb fucking rhyme that still haunted her.

Never, never let your gun / Pointed be at anyone . . .

Now she watched her mom's face as she processed the secret Lou had held for almost twenty years: the real reason she'd run to her dad's truck that night, unlocked the gun box with the keys he kept on the visor, and carried the shotgun back toward the house. She always knew her mom didn't love her, but now she knew her dad didn't either. She wanted him gone. If Carol hadn't shown up when she did, she'd probably have banished them both. Or worse.

Afterward, once her dad had packed up his truck and driven off down the driveway, her mom held her and said she understood. Lou was upset that her dad was cheating—any kid would be. And to leave a gun where a child could find it! Carol came up with that dumb nickname: they'd always be safe with Lou the Terminator around. Lou the truth teller.

And Lou had gone along with it—adopted this new understanding of the world as her superpower. She knew everyone was a fucking liar. A bullshitter knows a bullshitter.

Finally her mom spoke, her voice quiet and shaky, her eyes red. "I knew he was poisoning you against me. While I was working all those hours to pay his debts." Lou had never seen her mom cry before.

"Then why didn't you throw him out?" Lou didn't mean the question to sound so accusatory, but it was one that had burned in her for years, even as she'd come to realize the truth about her mom. Why did she have to be the one to pick up the gun? Why was she the only one who ever did anything?

Lou saw her mom's jaw tighten. "I knew how much you loved him. I wasn't going to take that away from you, so long as it was only me he was hurting."

"Even though you knew he was going to take me away?" But Lou understood now. "Because you knew he wouldn't."

Without saying another word, her mom stood, walked around the counter, and pulled her daughter into the tightest hug of her life.

Lou gripped her back, tighter still. "I love you, Mom."

Her mom stepped back, hands grasping her daughter's shoulders. "Listen. Me, Carol, and Martinez are going to nail this Pétain bastard. And whatever drama is written on your face tonight—"

Lou started to explain about the prince, but her mom silenced her again. "I don't need to know. It'll only scare the shit out of me. Just promise you won't try to handle it alone: your buddy Helen has money and power, and you want a person like that on your side. Don't count her out just because you hate Raum, OK?"

"Mom . . ."

"OK?" She was squeezing Lou so tightly now that Lou thought her ribs might crack.

Lou nodded against her mom's shoulder. It was Charity, not Helen, that she needed to work with to have any chance of getting out of this mess. Assuming the prince's men hadn't already found her. "Shit, what time is it?" Lou pulled herself free and raced through the connecting door into the living room.

Her mom called behind her: "A little after ten."

Lou pressed her face against the tall window and looked down onto Market Street. Fuck. Standing in the doorway of the cell phone store opposite, illuminated only by a strobing streetlight, was a tall figure, dressed in a long brown coat with a high collar. She hugged her mom one last time and rushed toward the elevator.

By the time Lou made it across Market Street, Charity had stepped back into the doorway, half-hidden in the shadows, her brown trench coat buttoned to the neck.

"The Saudis know about you. They're waiting at Raum One." Lou's warning echoed in the doorway.

But Charity didn't respond. She just stood staring over Lou's shoulder, until finally: "We're so fucked." She shouted this to nobody in particular.

Lou heard a yell from across the street and spun around. A skinny woman in a torn and stained ball gown that had once been red was screaming at a wall. Lou turned back to Charity. "Do you know who tipped them off?"

"Who did you tell about our meeting at the Redwood?"

Lou was shocked by the accusing note in Charity's voice. "Why would I tell anyone?"

"Not even your mom?"

Lou felt a flash of anger. So much for being on the same team. "Have you seen Claude Pétain's latest video? He's issued another fucking red notice against them. I know you know who he is."

Charity grabbed Lou's arm and pulled her farther into the doorway. "I swear to you, Lou, I have no clue. But I can handle him."

"Bullshit. You used his mob to scare me, so I'd have to stay with Helen."

Charity puffed her cheeks and exhaled slowly, her defensiveness evaporating. "I know how to manipulate him, but every time I think I've figured out his identity, it's another red herring. That's how I'm sure he's working with the Saudis—he's too well protected. It's pretty ironic—his racist supporters would go apeshit if they knew the truth."

Lou pulled her arm free from Charity's grip. "What's our next move? There has to be another way to bring them all down."

She thought—hoped—she could see the brilliant woman's brain processing all the possibilities. A human version of her own algorithm. But the next time Charity spoke, her voice was drenched in sadness. "They've won, Lou. It's over."

Lou's anger flared again. "You don't get to decide that."

Charity jerked backward, instantly defensive again. "Do you have a plan? Even if I could get inside Raum One and plant the fake data, nobody will care after this Raum For Everyone bullshit."

So that was it? Charity was just going to give up. This person who, from the ashes of the worst day of her life, had built an algorithm capable of flattening the Silicon Valley patriarchy, of giving men like Elmsley Chase and Charlie Brusk and Prince fucking Bansar exactly what they deserved. Who . . . *Oh.* Lou heard herself gasp as the thought struck her.

"You told me your algorithm could fit on a USB stick, right? You just connect it to a data source and it basically works itself?"

"Yes, but . . ."

Lou wasn't here for "yes, buts." "So if we could plug it directly into Raum's database, wouldn't it just . . . do its thing?"

Charity tilted her head. "Its thing?"

"You know what I mean. You told me you'd designed the algorithm to figure out what men like Alex Wu and Elmsley Chase want, and then give them what they deserve. So if it could see inside Raum's corporate server, how badly Elmsley and Brusk and Palgrave need this IPO, then wouldn't it . . . do its thing? Figure out how to stop them?" She anticipated Charity's next objection. "You can't get into Raum, but I still can."

Charity stayed silent just long enough for Lou to realize how stupid her suggestion sounded. But then . . . in a quick motion, she dug her right hand into her coat pocket and removed something silver and rectangular, pressing it into Lou's hand. Lou's fingers instinctively closed around the object. It was a USB stick.

"Are you fucking kidding me? You knew I was going to suggest that?"

Charity shook her head. "Would you believe the algorithm did?"

Lou laughed. "No, I wouldn't." Although, honestly, at this point she had no idea where Charity's brain ended and the algorithm began. She looked down at the stick and noticed four numbers written in black Sharpie, along with a small round circle.

"What's 1414?"

Charity smiled. "The melting point of silicon." She waited for Lou to put the USB stick in her pocket, then continued. "Just insert it into Ten's workstation. It'll seem like nothing's happening, but it is."

Lou nodded. "Do I need his password?"

Lou didn't understand what Charity said next. At least not until she said it for a second time, more slowly. "G'day Holly." Then she added: "Capital *G*, Capital *H*, at sign instead of the *a*, zero instead of the *o*."

Gd@yH0lly.

Another theory confirmed. Poor Ten. "Can you get him out of the office?"

Charity pulled her collar tighter against the cold. "I think it's time Holly paid a surprise visit from Australia. A date somewhere far enough from Raum One."

"He really likes you . . . I mean . . . he really likes her. The person you've been pretending to be."

Charity looked down toward her feet. "Everyone is pretending to be someone." She extended her hand again and this time she was holding a small cell phone. "A clone of Tim's phone. You'll need it for the two-factor authentication. Password, security code from the cell phone, then wait thirty seconds for the algorithm to upload."

Lou took the phone and shoved it in her pocket with the USB. "Thirty seconds? That's all?"

Charity gave a snort of laughter. "The whole algorithm is less than two gigabytes. Were you hoping for a creeping progress bar like in the movies?" She threw her arms up in mock alarm. "The security patrol will be here any minute!"

Lou wasn't amused. "I'm not worried about shit that happens in movies. I'm worried about getting chopped up by the crown prince's dad. Y'know, like in normal fucking life."

Charity laughed, and even Lou found it hard to keep a straight face at the absurdity of it all.

"OK," said Lou, turning toward the street. "I'll go now. Message Ten and tell him you just landed from Sydney or whatever."

Charity grabbed her arm again. "Not tonight."

Lou raised her hand. "I'm not going to argue."

"I'm not arguing—I'm trying to stop you getting yourself killed. You need to leave Helen's apartment first thing tomorrow morning. Spend the day strolling around town, go to the park, climb Twin Peaks, you get it?"

Lou had seen enough spy movies. "Any sign of a tail, abort. I get it."

"This is fucking Saudi intelligence, Lou. If they're tailing you, you're already dead. This is just about improving the odds." She paused, and gave Lou what was presumably supposed to be a reassuring smile. "Eight o'clock. I'll make sure Ten is waiting for Holly up in Wine Country. When you make it to Raum One, go to the rear service entrance. There's a guard there called Mac who occasionally does favors for me. Tell him Kaitlynn sent you."

"Kaitlynn?"

"Kaitlynn."

"And I'll meet you back here when it's done. Same time?"

Charity nodded. "Ten o'clock."

Then, before she could say any more, Lou was out of the doorway and halfway across the street, back toward Helen's apartment.

She had barely made it twenty feet—dodging Saturday night traffic in the middle of Market Street, clutching a USB stick containing the world's most badass algorithm and an illegally cloned cell phone, the possession of either of which was certainly a felony—when Lou realized she was being watched. Standing on the curb, outside the Four Seasons, wearing a $10,000 jumpsuit and with an expression of absolute fury on her face, was Helen Tyler.

84

"WHAT EXACTLY DO you expect me to say?"

The two women were back inside the Four Seasons, but Helen had refused to let Lou back up to the apartment until she told her everything.

There was no point in holding back. Helen had seen her talking to Charity and filled in the blanks with what she'd just learned from the Saudis at Raum One. Tim Palgrave's girlfriend. Fate. The Four Seasons. The only thing missing was why. So they sat on a pair of leather armchairs, tucked into a far corner of the private residence lobby, as Lou described it all: her meeting with Charity at the Redwood, the true history of the Raum algorithm, and now her plan to install Charity's own version of the code on Raum's server in the hope-against-hope that it could some-how figure out how to bring down Raum's IPO, just as it had destroyed Alex Wu and Joe Christian. Throughout all of this, Helen's face stayed entirely placid, her eyes fixed straight ahead like a court stenographer's, until finally . . .

What exactly do you expect me to say?

What *did* Lou expect her to say?

"I want you to tell me the truth. Did Elmsley really promise you a hun-dred million dollars if you helped him keep his job until after the IPO?"

Helen's expression betrayed no surprise that Lou knew about her side deal. "I suppose Miss Jones also told you why Elmsley is so keen to keep his job?"

Lou nodded. "His brother." Although it had been Meredith, not Char-ity, who had told Lou about Elmsley's vow to ring the Nasdaq bell in memory of Ramsey.

"Then you understand why I agreed. I help Elmsley fulfill this one harmless dream, and I retire with a hundred million dollars. Do you know how much good I can do with that kind of money? Plus what I'll make from my black widow routine afterward. Ironically, Charity Jones was at the top of my list for a payout."

Lou nearly fell out of her chair. "You . . . *knew* about Charity?"

Helen raised her hand. "I didn't know exactly what happened between her and Alex, but I knew there had been a third creator of the algorithm, yes. I told you, it's my job to know things. I thought she might be my ticket to tanking Raum's stock after the IPO."

Lou started to interrupt. Rape wasn't something that happened *between* two people. But Helen got there first. "A poor choice of words. I knew Miss Jones had been written out of history, that is all. Certainly never in my wildest dreams did it occur to me she might be Fate. To my shame, I didn't even make the connection when Joe Christian started yelling about a charity." She paused. "It does, however, explain why I had the damnedest job tracking her down."

Lou gripped the arms of her chair, the leather firm below her fingertips. "So why all the secrecy? I could have helped you look for Charity." She hesitated as she realized. "I mean look for her on purpose."

Helen gave Lou a side-eye that said people who live in glass houses shouldn't throw stones. "My deal with Elmsley was predicated on him keeping his job until after the IPO. I needed your help figuring out who was trying to stop it happening. Would you have agreed if you knew the company's true origins?"

Lou conceded the point. "But now I *do* know—and you're right, I won't be complicit in helping Elmsley or anyone else profit from Charity's work. If you really want to get justice for her—real justice—then we have to help her take Raum down. Not after the IPO. Now. No more fucking billion-dollar paydays for rapists and their apologists."

Helen sighed. "I agree."

"So you'll help me? Or at least not try to stop me?"

Helen took a slow breath. Lou recognized the look immediately. The same look Carol used to give her when she babysat Lou as a child—weighing up whether to allow her a second cookie, or to stay up an extra hour after bedtime. "What's my alternative? To hand you over to the prince's men? I could lecture you about the danger you and Miss Jones are putting yourselves in, but . . ." She gave an exasperated shrug. "What do you need me to do? Specifically?"

There was only one thing Lou needed. "I need your access key card. Charity says she can get me into the building, but I want a plan B. And if Elmsley or anyone else asks where I am tomorrow, you need to cover for me."

Helen nodded. "It would be my pleasure."

85

LOU WENT STRAIGHT to bed, not expecting to sleep. She crashed hard and fast, her near coma punctuated with waking nightmares of death squads and algorithms and Alex Wu, Joe Christian, and Charlie Brusk tumbling onto ice sculptures or leaping in front of trains. She dreamed about Charity and Helen too, her subconscious brain conflating them into a single blurry person whom Lou had sworn to help bring down Raum.

Lou only knew for sure that she'd slept when suddenly it was daylight. She grabbed her phone, panicked that she had missed her alarm—but it was only 6:55 a.m., five minutes before her intended wake-up.

"Sorry to startle you." Helen was standing at the foot of the bed. "I'm afraid we've been *summoned.*"

"Summoned?" Lou sat up, still groggy from sleep.

"The prince has sent a private investigator to Raum One. He wants to interview us." She delivered this terrifying news so breezily that Lou couldn't believe she had heard her correctly.

"It's nothing to worry about," Helen continued. "Bansar needs to show his dad he's doing everything he can to find . . . you know who." She placed a porcelain cup of coffee on the bedside table. Then she began assembling Lou's outfit from the small piles of clothes scattered around the floor of the bedroom. "I suggest we go in, plead ignorance, and then get the hell out of there."

Lou jumped out of bed and started pulling on her jeans. "Shit, shit, shit."

She felt inside her pillow and confirmed the USB stick and cell phone were still where she'd stashed them. Then she finished dressing and dragged a brush through her hair as she walked into the kitchen.

"Do you think we should try to warn her?"

Helen turned on the coffee grinder—without first adding any beans—then lowered her voice to a near whisper: "Are we having second thoughts?"

Lou shook her head. "I slept better last night than I have in days."

Helen turned off the grinder. "Excellent," she said back at her normal volume, and with a crisp clap of her hands. "Then let's go and chitchat with some monsters!"

A brisk, petrified walk later, Lou and Helen stepped through the security barriers and into the lobby of Raum One. Lou spotted Landon by the elevators, talking with a man in a dark gray suit. The man had the same piercing brown eyes, neatly trimmed black hair, and sharp cheekbones as all the other members of the prince's entourage. "Miss McCarthy, good morning, you will come with me?" The man didn't say a word to Helen. Hadn't the Saudis summoned them both? Between that and the presence of Landon—who appeared only when violence was anticipated or required—Lou suddenly felt an overwhelming urge to run. But run where?

Landon raised his hand to the man, and spoke to Helen. "He wants to do this upstairs. I've already told him—"

Helen shook her head. "We'll talk in our conference room." Her tone made it clear this wasn't a negotiation. "I'm sure that will be satisfactory to the prince. I assume he wishes the investigation to remain discreet?"

The guard started to interject. "My instructions—"

Helen gave one of her tight smiles. "Are of absolutely no relevance. Miss McCarthy works for me, and I report directly to the Raum board, not to your employer." Lou was impressed at Helen's ability to make the word "employer" sound like an insult. The way she'd subtly reminded the man that the prince no longer had a board seat was ice-cold.

The guard tried again, but Helen continued. "I'm perfectly happy to get Charlie Brusk on the phone if you're uncomfortable answering to a woman?"

Two minutes later, Lou, Helen, Landon, and the man in the sharp suit were sitting in the conference room, in silence, when a second man, this one dressed more casually in a blue T-shirt and jeans, sauntered in, carrying a slim manila folder. He wore a brown leather Raum Band on his wrist. "I apologize for keeping you waiting," he said, "and for the misunderstanding with our security team. They can be a bit . . . what is the English phrase? Pot-faced?" He gestured toward the man in the dark suit, who, taking his unspoken orders, stepped outside and closed the door.

"It's po-faced," said Helen, "as you know perfectly well, Alastair." She stood to greet the man in the blue T-shirt, and Lou thought for a bizarre moment that she might hug him. "How long has it been? Twenty years?"

The man in the blue T-shirt seemed flummoxed until, slowly, his frown gave way to a shocked smile. "My God, Helen . . ." His accent was suddenly, and entirely, British.

"As you live and breathe," said Helen. "LSE rowing team, victorious team of—"

"Nineteen eighty-nine! Good heavens. If I'd known you were working here . . ."

"Likewise, likewise. Small world. Now, shall we break out the thumbscrews?" Was this why Helen had seemed so calm at the prospect of being interrogated? What the fuck was this world where everyone in a position of power seemed to have gone to school with everyone else?

"No thumbscrews necessary," said Alastair, as he flipped open his folder and extracted a small stack of papers. From his jeans, he produced a silver fountain pen. "Miss McCarthy, thank you for meeting with me today. I believe you are already aware of the circumstances—it has come to our attention that Alex Wu's suicide may not have been a simple case of depression, and that a person or persons unknown may have been working to sabotage Raum's IPO. I also gather you and Ms. Tyler—Helen"—he smiled toward his old friend—"have been following a similar line of inquiry on behalf of Raum's board. My hope is that we might pool our information, so that His Royal Highness may receive a full report." He turned to Helen. "If that would be agreeable?"

Helen nodded her assent, and Alastair turned back to Lou. "You paid a visit to the Redwood two nights ago?"

Faced with no alternative but to play along with this deadly charade, Lou began telling the story they'd rehearsed on their short walk to Raum One. "Helen and I were looking into an apparent attempt to blackmail Martina Allen's husband, Thomas Calder. There was a video that appeared to have been shot at the Redwood."

Alastair nodded and steepled his fingertips in front of his mouth. "So you went to the Redwood to investigate this video."

"I went to the bar to see if I could find any of the three women featured in it." So far, so true.

"And did you?"

"No."

"Who did you see?"

Lou felt her foot bounce under the table. "I saw Brett Palgrave—Tim Palgrave's son." Then, as if an afterthought: "I also ran into a woman I'd met at Raum One a few nights earlier. A friend of Brett's father."

Alastair considered this. "They were together? This woman and Brett Palgrave?"

Lou shook her head. "I don't think so." So far, she had been careful to tell the Saudis only what they could have seen by checking the bar's security tape. Charity had deleted the footage from the gift shop and the hallways. Lou hoped Saudi intelligence hadn't gotten to it first.

Alastair uncapped his fountain pen and underlined something on his papers. "And you didn't pass on this information to Mr. Palgrave? That you saw his girlfriend at the Redwood with his son."

Lou tried to appear calm and eager to help even as her heart threatened to burst from her chest. "Brett was drunk, and close to getting kicked out. The woman was at the bar, and I just said a quick hello."

Lou hesitated, just for a fraction of a second as she realized the security tapes would show a much longer conversation between her and Charity. Before Alastair could seize on the discrepancy, Helen cleared her throat. "I think I can add some context here, Alastair. When Lou saw the woman with Tim at Raum One, it was clear that she was . . . well . . . a paid companion, isn't that right, Lou?"

Lou nodded. "I wouldn't want to embarrass Tim."

Alastair recapped his pen. "Yes, Mr. Palgrave has acknowledged being less than . . . discreet with his private affairs. And I understand you also went to visit the wife of Joe Christian from Grintech?"

Lou was blindsided. How long had the prince's men been watching her? "Amelia has nothing to do with any of this."

"And you know this how?"

Helen shot Lou a look, but it was too late.

"Because she works in a fucking dress shop to keep her kids in school because her asshole ex-husband couldn't face the consequences of his own decisions." Lou stopped herself. "I thought the two suicides might be connected, but I couldn't find any proof to back that up."

"OK, are we done here?" Helen sprang to her feet. "I assume you don't think we are somehow in league against Raum? Lou is only here because I hired her, and I'm only here because His Highness's good friend Charlie Brusk hired me."

"One last thing, just for completeness." Alastair reached back into his manila folder and extracted a large color photograph. "This is the woman you met at the Redwood Hotel?" He slid the photo across the table. It was an enlarged headshot of Charity, possibly a passport photo. Lou thought she might throw up.

"I think so," said Lou. "I don't have a great memory for faces."

"And you have never spoken with her except for those two occasions?"

Lou shook her head.

"Yes or no, please, Miss McCarthy." He stared right into her eyes as he asked this.

"No."

"And is there anything else I should know about the killing of Alex Wu?"

Lou feigned confusion. "Alex Wu committed suicide."

Alastair gave a wistful smile. "My mistake."

He replaced the photo and papers in the folder and stood to leave. Then added, seemingly as an afterthought: "While we continue our investigations, Mr. Chase has agreed it would be best if your employment were to be terminated."

Helen spun around to face Alastair. "Excuse me? Lou works for me, not Elmsley . . ."

Alastair gave a placid smile. "Mr. Chase has asked me to thank Miss McCarthy for her service to the company." Now he turned to Lou with the same shit-eating smirk. "You will be paid any outstanding fees for your services. Any personal possessions you have left in the building will be sent to you shortly."

"This is ridiculous," said Helen. She pulled out her cell phone and began jabbing at the screen.

Alastair was already standing by the doorway. "Mr. Chase is in an important meeting with His Royal Highness all afternoon. I'm sure they would not welcome the interruption." He left the threat hanging.

Helen turned to Lou, frustrated and temporarily defeated. "Why don't you go and have a bite to eat? Watch some daytime TV. We'll talk when I get home later."

Lou nodded slowly. "Fine."

"Fine," said Helen. Now she pointed toward a hook behind the door. "Don't forget your coat." Then to Alastair: "I assume that doesn't count as a possession? Unless you'd like her to freeze to death?"

He nodded and Lou took Helen's trench coat from the hook and carried it with her out of the door. Only after she was well clear of Raum One did she dare slip her hand into the coat pocket and confirm the presence of Helen's security swipe card.

LOU ARRIVED BACK at Helen's apartment, knowing exactly what she had to do. Which didn't make it any less terrifying.

She went first to her bedroom, where she grabbed a cream *New Yorker* tote bag—into which she stuffed a handful of Helen's T-shirts and a green baseball cap. Next, she switched off her phone and removed the SIM. She hesitated, staring down at the tiny gold card.

Are you sure you want to do this?

Y/N

She slipped the SIM into her back pocket and dropped her now useless phone into the tote bag. Then she moved to the bed and retrieved Palgrave's cloned cell phone from inside the bottom pillow where she'd stashed it, along with the USB stick labeled 1414º, wrapped carefully inside the slip of yellow legal paper on which she'd written Ten's password.

She thought about Ten. Any minute now he would receive the best IRC message of his life. His true cyber-love Holly had flown from Sydney to California for a surprise visit! She imagined him changing into a clean T-shirt, free of Monster Energy stains, and excitedly ordering a vRaum to take him north to Sonoma—almost two hours in traffic. Nobody deserved that kind of heartbreak; but, in the grand scheme of things, he was getting off easy.

Lou slipped the paper, the cloned phone, and the USB stick into her other pocket, grabbed a small pile of cash from the bedside table, and headed out into the city.

88%

Six and a half hours later

THE CLOCK ON the Ferry Building ticked past seven p.m. Lou had been walking all day. Her feet ached, her lower back was screaming in agony from the hills, and her bag filled with T-shirts had somehow tripled in weight. She'd crossed the city from Union Square to Sutro Tower, from Golden Gate Park to the ballpark. She had sipped coffee in the Castro at a café called Squat and Gobble, and stopped to take in a free Mondrian exhibit at the MOMA, where she'd used the bathrooms to change into her third shirt of the day. She had eaten lunch at a burrito truck under the freeway bridge at Thirteenth Street, she'd pretended to read Camus at the Mission Library, and now, hair pulled under Helen's green baseball cap and wearing yet another T-shirt (commemorating a cancer-related charity run), she was almost back where she'd started.

In all that time, she hadn't seen so much as a hint of a tail—no sharp suits, no square jaws, no slicked hair or earpieces. Maybe Alastair had believed her display of innocence or—the thought stopped her dead in her tracks—what if they already knew where she was going? All these hours spent trudging around the city, changing clothes in public bathrooms, jumping at the sight of her own shadow . . . what if they were just waiting for her at Raum? Her phone was still inside the paper Walgreens bag for which she had traded her *New Yorker* tote, the SIM still stashed in her pocket. She couldn't risk checking in. The only thing she could do was stick to her plan and hope that if anything was wrong, Charity or Helen would find a way to warn her.

Lou leaned over the safety barrier that marked the frontier between the city and the vast expanse of water that composed the San Francisco

Bay. The sun was setting and the lights of the Bay Bridge twinkled through the fog. She gripped the wooden barrier with both hands, slowly inhaled a lungful of salty air, and felt strangely at peace. It was almost time. In less than an hour, she would go to Raum One and log on to Ten's computer and upload the contents of Charity's memory stick to Raum's intranet. Thirty seconds later her privilege-and-patriarchy-busting algorithm would be trawling the company's deepest, darkest secrets—the hopes and fears of its board members, including their dearest wish of all: for a multibillion-dollar IPO. Then it would figure out the best way to take it all away from them. To push Ctrl-Alt-Delete on the most powerful industry the world had ever known.

And after that?

After that was another world.

With her back to the city, Lou didn't notice the man in the blue Public Works coveralls, watching her from inside an unmarked white van at the curbside. The man, unlike the members of the prince's personal security team, was blond, and American. He had been supplied by the Saudi embassy from a roster of contractors used for precisely this kind of job. The man stared at Lou just as she stared at the commuters disembarking from the ferry. With scant consideration for parking tickets, he slipped out of the van and waited for Lou to make her next move. For six hours he had been following her, on foot and in the van, and so far as he knew, she hadn't even suspected his presence. With night falling, he knew that if she was planning to meet someone, it'd likely be soon.

The Ferry Building clock ticked past 7:35. It was time for Lou to move. She would take one last detour—crossing Market Street underground via the BART station at Embarcadero. This was something she half remembered from an old British spy show: a "choke point." Lou's plan was to wait at the bottom of the stairs, to see if anyone followed her. Then she would go back up to the street and repeat the same test. Only then could she know she was in the clear.

She hadn't even made it halfway down the stairs into the station when she caught a glimpse of a man in blue coveralls, reflected in the concave mirror above the entrance. Her heart quickened as she recognized the man's face. She was sure—absolutely certain—that she had seen the same man smoking a cigarette outside the MOMA two hours earlier. His face had reminded her of her high school history teacher back in Atlanta. The resemblance to Mr. Davis was so striking she'd almost waved. The man certainly didn't look anything like the Saudis she'd seen at Raum One, which Lou now realized was exactly the point.

She kept walking, slowly, down into the ticket hall, but instead of waiting and ascending the same stairs, she broke into a sprint—past the Clipper machines, across the tiled floor of the station, and back up through the exit onto the other side of Market Street. She doubled back toward the Ferry Building, ducking past irritated commuters and almost crashing headlong into a one-legged man in a wheelchair. She dared not look back, but could sense the man in the coveralls close behind her. Without slowing down, she reached into her Walgreens bag and grabbed her phone, shoving it into her pocket. Then she dropped the bag and its stash of T-shirts into a trash can. This gave her the extra burst of speed she needed. She was almost back at the Ferry Building, with just one street—the wide Embarcadero—separating her from the maze of shops and restaurants inside of which she could find a place to hide. As she reached the roadside, she was relieved to see the first crossing light was already flashing. She sprinted out onto the road, weaving past tourists and yet more commuters.

And that's when she heard it. The squeal of brakes and a sickening crunch. Then screams and shouts for help. A self-driving vRaum had come speeding through the red traffic signal, clipping the curb exactly where Lou had been standing seconds before. Now she saw its real target. People were running and shouting into cell phones as the man lay sprawled on the road in front of the car, which had a shattered windshield but otherwise seemed undamaged. The man was not so fortunate; a pool of blood was already forming around his head, matting his blond hair and staining the shoulders of his coveralls brown.

THE DIGITAL CLOCK projected onto the side of Raum One showed 7:53 p.m. when Lou reached the building's rear delivery ramp, still freaking out at watching yet another man die by Charity's invisible hand.

At the base of the ramp, Lou saw a metal door marked NO ADMIT-TANCE. It was the only regular-sized door in the building's vast mainten-ance bay; all the others were designed for trucks, loading and unloading the tons of daily supplies required to keep the huge building operating at maximum efficiency. It was also the only door with any kind of access system: a key-card swipe panel with a blinking red light.

Lou pulled Helen's security pass from her back pocket and waved it against the black square. There was a loud buzz, but the light remained resolutely red. Lou held her breath, but when the cavalry didn't appear, she waved the pass a second time. Still nothing.

She was about to head for the front door when she was startled by a cough from behind her. She spun around and came face-to-face with a short, balding man in a white T-shirt and baggy jeans, a Raum mainten-ance ID around his neck and a basic-model Raum Band on his wrist. "Hey," blurted Lou. "I'm trying to get to my office. I got locked out." She held up Helen's swipe card as if somehow that would make her ridiculous lie seem more believable.

"You must be Lou," said the man, extending his hand. "I'm Mac. Kaitlynn said I'd find you here." Lou was confused until she remembered that Kaitlynn was yet another of Charity's pseudonyms. She took Mac's extended hand and shook it as he added, "Sorry to leave you hanging. I was taking a piss."

Mac opened the metal door with his own swipe card and wished her an ominous "Good luck," before heading off back wherever he'd come from. How much did he know about her plan? Enough to think she might need luck on her side.

Lou passed through the door and emerged into a bare white maintenance hallway. The floors, walls, and ceiling were all painted stark white, with a solid strip of yellow on the floor as a guideway for the robotic engineering carts that shuttled back and forth between the delivery docks and the various parts of Raum One: the self-driving-car labs, the Raum-Service test kitchens, the employee dining rooms. This must be the same hallway through which Joe Christian had passed on his way to see Alex Wu the night they both died. Was it always this empty?

Lou jogged down the hallway until she reached two sets of polished chrome elevator doors. A camera stared down from the ceiling, although there was no light to indicate whether it was recording. Lou adjusted her posture. If she was being monitored, she wanted to seem as relaxed as she possibly could—a Raum employee heading to her office, or an assistant running an errand for her boss. She inhaled slowly and pressed the elevator call button. Still no response. She felt a spike of panic and jabbed the button again. Then she noticed another swipe panel, helpfully positioned on the wall opposite. She waved Helen's card over the sensor and allowed herself to exhale as the elevator doors *bing*ed open. So far, everything was exactly as Charity had promised. No security and no Saudi investigators in sight. Lou reminded herself that she still hadn't done anything wrong. Not yet.

Emerging seconds later on the basement level, Lou was again discombobulated. The elevator in the main lobby opened right alongside Helen's conference room, but this one had deposited her on the other side of the building. To reach Ten's sanctum, she'd have to cross through two open-plan offices. This being a Sunday night, the building should be relatively quiet, but that also meant she'd stand out even more starkly if anyone was monitoring the security cameras.

Lou passed quickly through the first windowless office, where during the day Raum's finance admins toiled on expense reports and other thankless tasks. Tonight the space was entirely empty. The admins had

already headed off kitesurfing or vaping or whatever Raum's employees did with their weekends. She wasn't so lucky when she reached the
second office: an elderly cleaner hard at work vacuuming under a desk.
"Buenas noches," murmured Lou. The woman gave a weak smile and kept
vacuuming as Lou strode past the bathrooms and the small kitchen and
snack nook, before she finally arrived at the door to Ten's office.

Lou stood, paralyzed. This was the point of no return, the end of
plausible deniability. Were the prince's men waiting behind the door?
Had Charity's plan to lure Ten away failed? Would the USB stick work
as Charity had promised: uploading the algorithm and connecting it to
the right data sources on the server? Did technology, or life, ever run so
smoothly?

But she had made her mind up long ago. She had promised Charity,
and her mom, that she'd do what was necessary. Fearless Lou. Lou the
Terminator.

She took another breath, then gave a gentle tap on the door. She listened for a response and when none came, she pushed open the door and
stepped inside.

90%

TEN'S OFFICE WAS dark, the only light coming from the glow of a screen saver. No Australian surfer girls this time, just a flock of silver-and-orange toasters flapping ironically across an inky background. Lou stepped carefully across the floor, lifting her feet and setting them down gently so as not to crush any errant drones, although this time there were none. She reached Ten's desk and slid her hand into her pocket to retrieve the clone of Palgrave's phone, along with Charity's USB stick, still wrapped in its yellow paper. She set the USB carefully on the desk alongside the paper. As the wall clock ticked to 8:05 p.m., she pressed the side button on the cloned phone and watched—her heart waiting to beat again—the device power on.

Then she froze. Had Charity said to insert the USB stick first, or Ten's password? Surely the algorithm couldn't be uploaded until the machine was unlocked? No. The algorithm obviously went in first, before the computer woke up and connected to the network. Stick first, then password. Obviously.

Lou picked up the USB and closed her fingers around the cold metal. She couldn't risk wasting another second, dithering about which order to do things. Surely the world's smartest algorithm couldn't be foiled by a former journalist in the midst of a panic attack. Lou located an empty port on the main computer tower next to the monitor and slid the stick home.

She suddenly thought about the cleaner and cursed herself for once again underestimating a woman based on her appearance, and job. Of course the woman would have alerted security about the badgeless intruder roaming the halls. She looked back at the door and waited for the men with guns to burst in. But the only sound Lou could hear was the low hum of a cooling fan deep inside Ten's computer.

With a shaking hand, she reached for the mouse and nudged it ever so slightly to the right. The computer whirred into life and the toasters were replaced with a familiar-looking Raum intranet log-in box. A drop-down menu, preselected with the username WheelerT@raum.com. Lou clicked on the drop-down menu, and Ten's email address was joined by an alternative username: *superadmin*, with a space for a password. She stared at the blinking prompt.

8:07 p.m. At that moment, a hundred miles north, in Wine Country, Ten Wheeler would be sitting at a restaurant table, waiting for his Australian cyber-love to show up for their first date. How long would he wait before he realized he'd been stood up? An hour? Two? He was about the only person Lou *didn't* have to worry about right now.

Very, very slowly and carefully, she typed Ten's password. *Gd@yH0lly.*

Then she waited, counting slowly in her head. *One . . .Two . . . Three . . .* There was no progress bar. No 0s or 1s filling the screen as the code transferred from USB stick to server, and set about its seismic task. Nothing to indicate that anything whatsoever was happening, except for the slightest whir of a hard drive and the very briefest flicker of a prompt window, which instantly vanished again. Charity was right: the process of bringing down the patriarchy was frighteningly anticlimactic. Either that or the USB stick wasn't working, or she'd inserted it too soon.

Fuck fuck fuck. Lou remembered Palgrave's cloned cell phone. She glanced down, and sure enough, she saw a prompt flashing on the device: *Confirm access to RA_2378?* And then two options, *confirm* or *breach.* Breach! Lou felt a swell of nausea. She hadn't thought to ask Charity if Palgrave's was the only device that received these security alerts. Had this exact same message just appeared on Elmsley Chase's phone? On Brusk's? Or the real version of Palgrave's handset?

Her whole arm was shaking now as she tried to click the *confirm* button on the phone's small screen, and it took her three careful attempts not to accidentally hit the *breach* option. *For God's sake, Lou. Focus.*

Eventually her finger found its target, and Lou sighed as Ten's computer briefly flashed some kind of confirmation message. The computer fan was noticeably louder now, and a tiny blue LED was flashing on the end of the USB stick, in short bursts.

After a few more seconds, the light turned solid blue. Was it done? The answer to that question came seconds later with the arrival of a new prompt window, displaying the single word *Done*. Lou took a slow breath in, then out, trying to calm her pulse and stop her palms from getting any more slippery with sweat. She pulled the USB stick clear of the computer—but as she did so, the prompt vanished, revealing a second one underneath.

I'M SORRY.

Lou stood, eyes fixed on the screen. Had she imagined it? The gray box and the message it framed had disappeared from Ten's monitor the moment she'd extracted the USB stick.

I'M SORRY.

What the hell did that mean?

I'm sorry, but your attempt to install Charity's algorithm was unsuccessful?
I'm sorry, but the Saudi intelligence services are on their way to kill you?

There was no time to find out. Lou shoved the USB stick back into her pocket, followed by the cloned phone. Then, acting on impulse, she used the sleeve of her shirt to wipe down the keyboard and mouse. Finally she examined the desk, to make sure everything was where she had found it. Thank God she did, because now she noticed the piece of yellow paper still sitting where she'd left it. She snatched it up and as she did, she noticed something even more alarming about Ten's desk. It was tidy. The clutter she'd seen there before—the desk toys and personal knick-knacks—was all gone.

Her eyes flicked around the office. The photo of Ten Wheeler standing with Steve Wozniak had vanished too, leaving just a single nail jutting from the wall. The hook where Ten's hoodie always hung was empty. The pile of notebooks that had been next to the door was gone.

Dread coursed through Lou's body as she realized: Every one of Ten's most valuable possessions was missing. He wasn't coming back.

91

LOU RAN. THIS time she didn't bother with the service corridors but raced straight to the main elevator, then sprinted across the lobby and out onto the plaza. Without pausing for breath, she kept running down Market Street in the direction of the Four Seasons.

Why was she running? She didn't know. All she knew was everything felt very wrong. Ten was supposed to be at dinner with Charity, so why had he cleared out his office? For that matter, where were the Saudis? Earlier the lobby and the front plaza of Raum One had been swarming with the prince's security men, and now—less than an hour after the man tailing Lou had been crushed under a vRaum—they were all just . . . gone?

It must be almost nine o'clock. Her plan had been to wait in the twenty-four-hour Coffee Express near the Four Seasons, giving her a clear view of the doorway where she'd agreed to meet Charity at ten. Now, though, that seemed way too close for comfort. Her instincts proved right when Lou approached the Four Seasons and saw the flashing blue lights of three police cars parked outside. Lou stopped running, but only for a second. She thought about the man hit by the vRaum. Did the cops know Charity had killed him to protect her? Why else would they be here?

She turned on her heel and raced away in the opposite direction.

What the fuck was happening? What the actual fuck.

"Lou, thank God, are you OK?"

Carol's voice on the end of the phone sounded frantic. Lou had reached the badlands, not far from where she'd been attacked by Pétain's mob just a few nights earlier. This time, though, she had opted for the (she hoped) safety of the floodlit Tenderloin Children's Playground. It was a favorite hangout of sex workers and their johns, but tonight Lou had the small patch of grass to herself. She had reassembled her cell phone and called her mother's number. It was Carol who picked up.

"I'm fine, I think. I was just at the Four Seasons . . ."

"Oh my God, she's at the Four Seasons . . ." Lou heard Carol passing this information along, presumably to her mom.

"I'm not at the Four Seasons. I'm—"

Carol interrupted. "Don't tell us where you are, Lou. Pétain's psychos showed up at Helen's place. Didn't you see any of this online?"

Lou felt herself go numb. She had been so focused on avoiding the Saudis that she had barely thought about Claude Pétain and the threat against her mom and Carol. "Are you OK? Is Helen with you?"

"We're fine. Helen's here—just a bit shaken up. One of them tried to get into the apartment . . . She whacked him pretty good. She thinks she broke her finger. But you should have seen the other guy."

"Let me talk to Helen."

Lou heard the sound of someone fumbling with the phone, and then Helen's voice, calm and aloof as ever.

"Lou? Everything's under control here—we're with Detective Martinez. Where are you?" Lou heard someone yelling in the background—a man. "Ah yes, right, don't answer that. It seems Pétain's mob may have gotten access to our cell phones."

Lou clutched her own handset tighter. Pétain's surveillance network had found her once—the other night in the Tenderloin—and it wouldn't be long until it found her again.

"Listen to me. You need to switch your phone off. Martinez too." She wanted to tell Helen that she'd installed Charity's algorithm on Raum's server, and that somehow it'd figure out a way to make everything OK. But she couldn't—not least because she had no idea if any of that was true.

"I know," said Helen's exasperated voice. "But your mother refused until she knew you were safe. You need to get to a police station. They'll reach Martinez, and get you to safety."

Lou started to protest, but thought better of that too. There was no sense trying to negotiate. "Promise me you'll stay with them both until I get there. I mean it, Helen. Don't let them out of your sight."

"You have my word, but do please hurry." The line went dead.

92

LOU COLLAPSED ONTO a metal bench, her entire body on the brink of shutting down. Her mind was reeling—from guilt and anger that once again Pétain's mob had almost killed her mom and Carol, to relief that it was them, not the Saudis, who had shown up at the Four Seasons. Not that it made much difference: the mob had arrived at Helen's front door right after the prince's man was hit by the vRaum. An eye for an eye.

Lou held down the power button on her phone. If they were monitoring the device, then she had to stay off-line until after she'd found Charity and confirmed whether the algorithm had successfully made it onto Raum's server. She had no idea how it worked; how quickly it would start making things right.

Lou jumped up from her bench. Was she already late? She couldn't see a clock, but what she did see was a dark figure sprinting toward her from across the park. It was a woman, wearing tight black running pants and a black fitted T-shirt over broad shoulders, and a black baseball cap. Her gait was definitely more like a jogger's than a homeless person's. A woman jogging through the Tenderloin? Lou squinted into the darkness as she got closer.

"Charity?"

A second later Charity Jones was by her side, panting and eyes wide. "It's Ten," she said when she finally found enough oxygen. "They've got Ten."

Then without another word of explanation, she grabbed Lou's arm and dragged her across the park.

93

"WE SHOULD BE safe here."

Charity dragged Lou two full blocks through the Tenderloin until they reached a dark gray vRaum—or what was supposed to look like a vRaum—parked across the street from a shuttered Holiday Inn, its hazard lights flashing and engine running. She jumped into the driver's seat and indicated that Lou should sit in the back, like a passenger waiting for her ride to begin.

Lou felt anything but safe. "You said they've got Ten. Who?"

"Prince Bansar and his goons." Charity was still hyperventilating, forcing the words out between gasps. "They've taken Ten to his boat in the Marina."

Lou was hit with a wave of adrenaline, and sheer panic. She thought back to Ten's office: the missing stuff, and the weird message on his screen.

I'M SORRY.

"I don't understand. He hasn't done anything wrong."

For a long time Charity stayed silent, staring straight ahead through the windshield. Then suddenly she was pounding the steering wheel with both fists. "He went to them. He fucking went to them. Fucking fucking stupid stupid men with their fucking white-savior bullshit."

Lou leaned forward between the front seats and grabbed Charity's shoulder. "You need to tell me what's happening."

Charity gave a long, slow sigh. "He told them about Alex Wu, and Joe Christian, and Tyrus Weber, and the algorithm."

Lou opened her mouth, but no words came out. Ten had ratted them out. This was the end of the world. "Why would he do that? They'll kill us. They'll kill all of us."

Charity shook her head. "You're not listening. He told them *he* was Fate. They came to Raum One to interview him. When they asked him about Fate, he broke down, admitted it had been him the whole time."

"Why the fuck would he do that?" But Lou knew the answer. "Jesus. He was protecting you."

I'M SORRY.

Charity nodded. "He knew the algorithm as well as I did. He must have recognized the patterns."

"And the victims," said Lou. "Wu, Christian . . . I asked him about Tyrus Weber."

Charity thought for a moment, then slammed the steering wheel again. "Fucking idiot. Now they know about my version of the algorithm, and they think Ten has it. Raum's infosec team has locked down his computer, cut off his superuser access."

"Locked down? So I just uploaded the algorithm into . . ."

"An empty, air-gapped workstation—disconnected and firewalled from anything useful. Thanks to Ten, we're completely frozen out."

"Fuck," said Lou. "How do you know all this?"

Charity handed Lou her cell phone. It was open to an app she didn't recognize: a black screen with an orange speaker icon and two buttons below it, with the icons for record and play. Some kind of audio-recording app.

"I sent him a gift—from Holly. It had a listening device inside."

"The kangaroo." Lou remembered the key ring Ten had shown her from his Internet girlfriend. It *was* a bug! Lou made a mental note never to doubt her paranoid hungover self again.

Charity wiped her eyes. "He told you?"

"He didn't have to. What did you hear?"

Charity hit the play icon in the app, and the phone's speakers began blaring the sound of rustling. After a couple of seconds, the rustling stopped and Lou heard voices. Two men, maybe three. One of the men had a British accent—Alastair, perhaps—and the other sounded Middle

Eastern or perhaps Eastern European? Lou was not good with accents. The third voice, though, was very clearly that of Prince Bansar. He was speaking in English.

"An algorithm that can kill a man without leaving a trace. My father will be very impressed to hear about his." Lou winced as she heard a scream. Then Bansar was speaking again: "I absolutely detest violence, Mr. Wheeler. My father, on the other hand, has only two interests: money, and killing people who take his money. Once we reach Riyadh, you will tell him how to access your algorithm and beg that he lets us both live into old age."

Another scream, this time inches from the microphone. Lou winced. Ten was giving his life to protect Charity.

"Your Highness . . ." Lou recognized another voice—the man Helen had called Alastair. But whatever he said next was drowned out by more rustling and then, almost imperceptibly, a new, much quieter voice: hurried and whispered, almost like a chant. Then came another clattering sound and the recording ended.

"What was that last part?" said Lou. "It sounded like Ten."

Charity jabbed at the phone's volume button, then swiped at the screen. The audio began playing again, far louder, and isolated to the chant. "The *Oppulous*. Marina. The *Oppulous*. Marina." Ten whispered this same series of words three more times before the audio went dead.

"He must have known you'd be listening." Lou wondered how long Ten had known that Holly was actually Charity. Had he really only figured it out when Lou had asked about Weber?

Charity didn't respond. "I checked the prince's flight manifest. His plane is due to leave for Paris at two a.m. We have to stop him."

Four hours. They still had time. "We can call the FBI. I have a source in the San Francisco field office. An American citizen has been kidnapped, and is about to be taken out of the country."

Charity turned toward the back seat again, tears streaming down her face. "Even if they believed us, we both know nobody in the government is going to touch the Saudi king's son. Even his least favorite one."

Lou's brain was racing. "Then we call the king. We can play him that recording—his own son calling him a murderer. That won't play well on CNN."

Charity actually laughed at the idea. She lifted her thumb and pinkie mockingly to her ear. "Oh hi, Your Majesty? This is the woman who's trying to blow up your Raum investment. I'm here with a journalist, and we just wondered if you could ask your son to release our friend tied up on his boat."

Lou was in no mood to be mocked. She'd known Ten for only a few weeks, but he *was* her friend, and he used to be Charity's too. "I don't hear any better ideas. Where's your algorithm when we need it? I assume the USB wasn't the only copy."

"Off-line," said Charity flatly. "The only reason Ten is still alive is because the prince thinks he wrote this awesome code that can cause men to throw themselves off buildings. The ultimate cyber weapon to take home to Daddy. How long do you think the king will have to torture Ten till he admits he lied, and leads them to me? I can't risk them getting hold of it."

Lou knew she was right. "I can call Miquela Rio at the *Wall Street Journal*." She dismissed her own suggestion. "They know we won't go to the press, because Miquela will want to know why they kidnapped Ten. That's a story we *really* don't want her to tell."

Charity nodded. "Elmsley Chase will get his fucking IPO—which is all he cares about—while Ten ends up in a shallow grave in the desert."

For the second time in as many nights, Lou could hear total defeat in Charity's voice. After all her work, and right on the verge of victory, Ten had brought it all down by trying to save someone who didn't need to be saved. And this time there could be no algorithmic Hail Mary. She felt her throat constrict as she realized the king wouldn't stop with Ten, especially when they figured out he didn't even have the algorithm. She imagined Claude Pétain's mob descending on her mom and Carol. Then they'd come for her, and Charity.

Except. Lou heard her own words still echoing in her head. "That's not all he cares about." She thought back to a conversation she'd overheard at Elmsley's house, between Chase and Brusk. *I mean it, Charlie. You know how important this is to me.*

"Elmsley?" Charity's face was a mask of confusion.

"I met his girlfriend last night, at the house party. She told me he's obsessed with the IPO because of a promise he made to his brother. Apparently they always dreamed of creating the world's most important company and taking it public."

Charity laughed. "That might be the whitest dream I've ever heard."

Lou laughed too. "But it gives us leverage. I guarantee no part of that weird fraternal fantasy involved kidnapping Ten Wheeler, or aiding and abetting a murderous Saudi king. If Elmsley really is doing all of this for some weird promise he made to his brother, then he's not going to want it tainted by any of *this.*" She gestured toward the recording still open on Charity's phone and waited to let this revelation sink in.

"Let me get this straight." Charity practically hooted in response. "You think you can convince Silicon Valley's biggest asshole to help us rescue Ten because it's the right thing to do? He's just supposed to forget that Ten admitted to killing Alex Wu and trying to destroy his IPO? Or does your plan involve throwing me under the bus too?"

Lou took a breath. Snapping back wouldn't help. "I know it's hard to believe, but when he understands why you targeted Alex Wu; realizes his whole company—his whole dream—is built on *your* algorithm . . ."

Charity couldn't hold back anymore. "Are you out of your damned mind? You're going to tell him *everything*? Because you think he *might want to help.* Jesus fucking Christ. Maybe he'll voluntarily give up his IPO too."

Lou raised a hand. "He can have his dumb IPO. We'll promise him no more Fate, no more sabotage, no more surprises—all he has to do is convince the king to let Ten go."

Charity interrupted again. "So we save Ten, but Elmsley gets his IPO and the bad guys win again. Fuck that. I've spent years studying these

assholes, and I know the only way they change their behavior is if they
lose."

"That's not true," said Lou. "Alex Wu, Joe Christian, Tyrus Weber—
you took everything from them and they still didn't change. You said
yourself, your algorithm doesn't force men to behave differently—it just
makes them face the consequences of their own choices."

"So?" Charity had at least stopped yelling, and seemed to be listening.

"So, Charlie Brusk covered up for Alex back at MIT. Elmsley never
knew the truth about Alex Wu or the algorithm. He never got the chance
to do the right thing. Maybe if he had, Alex would be in jail right now,
and you could be CTO of Raum."

"I never wanted to be CTO of Raum."

"Fine, but that should have been your choice." Lou shrugged. "Maybe
you're right. Maybe Elmsley would never have bought your algorithm if
he knew it was built by a woman. Maybe Meredith is totally wrong about
him, and the whole Ramsey story is PR bullshit. But your algorithm
would give him the choice."

"So we should give him the choice?"

"First we give him the facts, then the choice. He can save Ten and get
his IPO, on our terms. Or he can turn us in to the FBI or the king and
have our blood—and Ten's—on his hands. Either decision will have consequences, for him, for us, for the promise he made his brother."

Charity tilted her head, weighing up the logic of Lou's plan. "What
are our terms?"

"You tell me." Right now all Lou wanted was for her mom, Carol, and
Ten to be safe.

Another long pause. "He quits. Right there and then on the IPO stage.
He rings his little bell, then says, "'You know what, I'm out.' And then
he turns to the board, and every predatory asshole at that company . . .
'Guess what, bitches, y'all are out too.'"

Charity must have seen Lou's eyes widen. "I'm not even close to done.
After he quits, he can give half his money to whatever charity he needs to
set up for his brother, but the other half he's going to invest. In women.

In people of color. Only in companies run by folks like us. Not a single straight white cisgender fucking bro piece of shit." She paused. "You need me to go on? My list is ten years long."

Lou hesitated. Was Charity expecting her to object to any of this? Because she had a list of her own: "And to Stanford," said Lou. "An endowment, or bursary fund, or whatever it's called. For women in computer science. But the school only gets the money each year if as many women graduate as men."

"Yes!" Charity clapped her hands in emphasis. Then her face fell. "You know Elmsley is not going to go for any of this shit, right? They never make the right decision. Ever."

Lou reached down and switched off the hazard lights. "You've done the hard work. You've gotten us to the brink of changing the whole world. Now it's my turn. Your algorithm chose me for a reason, didn't it? I sure as hell didn't ask to be here."

Charity put the car into drive. "None of us did."

Lou sat in silence as the fake vRaum hurtled up toward Nob Hill and on to Pacific Heights. For all her bluster, she had no idea if her plan would work. It was a nice fantasy: that when faced with all the facts, Elmsley Chase would be convinced by the memory of his dead brother to do the right thing. To call the Saudi king and demand he let Ten go, then stand on the IPO stage and admit that his company was built on theft and rape and misogyny and God knew how many other crimes. Maybe Meredith Maitland believed all that stuff about Elmsley wanting to do the right thing. But what reason did Lou have to think it was true? Her mom's words about Helen echoed: *She has money and power, and you want a person like that on your side. Don't count her out just because you hate Raum, OK?* Could the same possibly be true about Elmsley Chase?

There was another problem. Lou's whole plan depended on Elmsley Chase agreeing to meet her. She could call Helen for help, but not without tipping off Pétain's surveillance network. Then she remembered what Meredith had told her—how she and Elmsley had been forced to postpone their Netflix date night for the Raum For Everyone announcement.

She pictured them tonight, snuggled up on their couch binge-watching whatever the hell billionaires binge-watched. How would he react to being disturbed by a frantic former journalist ranting about algorithms?

Not well.

And so now, as they hurtled toward their destination, Lou decided to risk one last roll of the dice. She pulled out the cloned cell phone—the duplicate Charity had made of Tim Palgrave's device. She switched it on and scrolled through Palgrave's contacts until she found the name she was looking for. Then began to type out a message.

94

AS THE CAR rounded the corner into Elmsley Chase's cul-de-sac, Lou was relieved to see the security tents from the previous night were gone, along with the guards.

"Wait for me here," she said, opening the car door before Charity had even had a chance to stop fully. "If you see the prince's men arrive or anyone carrying out a body bag, then . . ." Then what? "Go find my mom and Carol and get them somewhere safe, OK?"

"This is insane. You're going to get yourself killed." Lou felt Charity's hand on her leg, but they both knew there was no other option.

Lou ran toward Elmsley Chase's home, slowly up the stone steps, past the two stone lions, and pulled the heavy doorbell chain. Then she prayed—to God, to the universe, to anyone who was listening and might have the power to grant her wish.

In the distance Lou could hear the sound of a police siren, but otherwise the neighborhood was silent. She glanced again at the Roman numerals carved into the stonework next to the doorbell. *MM.* The year 2000. "Fuck," Lou whispered to herself as she realized her mistake, just as the door swung open.

"Oh!" Meredith Maitland was clearly confused as to why Lou McCarthy was standing on her doorstep at eleven p.m. "Elmsley isn't here. He just got called to a meeting."

"I know," said Lou, allowing herself to take a breath. The text message she'd sent from Tim Palgrave's number had done its job. "It's you I wanted to see."

A few minutes later, Lou and Meredith sat facing each other in the library of Elmsley's town house. Or rather the room was obviously intended as a library—with towering oak bookshelves running along three walls, a writing desk, and three large comfortable armchairs that sighed gently under their weight. The only thing missing was any actual books. Every shelf was bare.

"You wanted somewhere private. This is private. Now why are you here?" Meredith's voice echoed around the empty room as she spoke. Her demeanor was of a woman conflicted: as if she didn't have time to listen to what Lou had to say, but was desperate to hear her say it.

Lou spoke slowly, and calmly. Even if Elmsley realized right away that the message from Palgrave was a fake, it would still take him at least half an hour to get home. Lou had enough time to make her pitch. First she would convince Meredith; then the two of them would persuade Elmsley. Partners.

"First, I owe you an apology."

Meredith seemed genuinely surprised. "For what?"

"The other night when I was here, I made a comment about this being Elmsley's house."

"I don't remember. I was pretty drunk."

"You weren't that drunk," said Lou, "but I made the same shitty assumption everyone makes about the partners of successful men, and I'm sorry." She pointed downward, in the general direction of the front of the house. "Your initials are literally carved in the wall. *MM*. I thought it was the year the house was built."

Meredith waved the apology aside. "I get it. I'm the gymnast who started a social network for dogs. Who's more likely to be the one who pays the mortgage on this place: the woman whose company made six hundred and fifty million dollars last year, or the man who burned through four hundred million and still thought it would be good PR to take only a dollar salary like Steve Jobs?" She rolled her eyes at the thought. "I told him he can repay me after the IPO."

Lou took her cue. "I need to tell you something about the IPO, and it's going to sound insane. All I ask is that you hear me out. I promise at the end it will make sense."

"That's quite the opening gambit." Meredith leaned back in her arm-chair. "OK, I promise I won't kick you out till you're done."

And so Lou told her the story, just as she would have written it for the *Herald*, or the *Wall Street Journal* or the *New Yorker*. The true story of the algorithm that had become the heart and soul of Raum.

The only part she edited—just slightly—was what exactly she and Charity had planned to do inside Raum One. In the revised version, there was no faked data or USB stick: Lou had only been looking for evidence of fraud inside Raum, but hadn't found any. Raum was a horrible com-pany—she still believed that—but Elmsley Chase wasn't a con man.

Meredith Maitland listened in silence. Barely blinking even. The only time she did react was when Lou explained how Ten Wheeler had turned himself in to the Saudis to protect his old friend and teammate, and they had less than four hours to save his life. At that, Meredith quietly stood up and walked over to one of the library's huge windows, pushed it open, and took in a lungful of air, then returned to her seat.

"Elmsley didn't know about any of this?" The look of hope in her eyes was unmistakable.

"He had no idea. Charity says Charlie Brusk used his position at XXCu-bator to pay off the witnesses. Joe Christian and Tyrus Weber. He was sure if Elmsley knew the truth, he would have freaked out and refused to buy Alex and Ten's company."

"And what do you think?"

"I think the Elmsley Chase you described to me—the one who built this whole giant company to keep a promise he made to his brother—wouldn't want his legacy to be built on technology stolen from a rape victim."

"Rape survivor. And of course he wouldn't." Meredith stood and walked over to the writing desk and, after fiddling with the lock, pulled open a slim drawer: so slim that at first Lou thought it was a shelf. In fact, it was neither a drawer nor a shelf, because now Meredith removed it entirely from the desk and handed it to Lou. It was a child's drawing, housed in a slim wooden frame.

Lou examined the chunky blue and red shapes: two rudimentary blue stick figures, standing on a red rectangle. One appeared to be holding a briefcase, the other some kind of trophy. Then Lou saw the caption, scribbled in green crayon. *Elmsley and Ramsey, co-CEOs of RamEl Corp (world's richest!!!).*

"His most treasured possession." Meredith gave a tight smile and closed her eyes.

Lou handed back the picture, and Meredith returned it to its hiding place in the desk, with a click. "I'll talk to Elmsley as soon as he gets home. He'll call the king . . ."

They were both startled by the sound of a door opening behind Lou. "Like fuck I will."

Lou spun around to see Elmsley Chase framed in the doorway, his face red with anger. She had no idea how long he'd been standing outside, listening to their conversation.

"If any of that bullshit was true, then you would be talking to the cops, not showing up at my house, sending spoofed messages . . ." Chase stepped farther into the room, waving his cell phone. The fake text from Palgrave's number was still visible on the screen.

Lou tried to explain, but Chase wasn't done. "You just admitted you and your friend tried to destroy my company. Now you want to implicate me in a kidnapping?"

Lou jumped to her feet, but Meredith reached over and put her hand on his shoulder. "Elmsley," she said, as if soothing a child. And then again, more firmly. "Elmsley."

The repetition was like a magic spell. Elmsley Chase stopped yelling and stared at his girlfriend for what seemed like a full minute before he spoke again. "You believe this?"

Meredith didn't hesitate. "I do." Then, staring straight into his soul: "So do you."

Another long pause, before: "Fuck." Elmsley slumped into the third armchair. "Fuck."

"I'm sorry," Lou said in a whisper. And she was, because the Elmsley Chase hunched in that chair may well have been a different species from the person she'd seen just a week earlier, striding onstage, ready to announce his world-shattering IPO. He was a man defeated. A man exhausted. A man who must surely have sensed karma—fate!—snapping at his own heels but, until this moment, had no idea why.

"So how do we fix this?" His eyes were red. "What am I supposed to tell King Faisal?"

Lou had her answer ready. "The prince has diplomatic immunity, but his father can take it away. Call him and tell him Bansar has kidnapped your best engineer because of some deranged conspiracy theory. He's going to derail the IPO and cost the kingdom billions, unless Ten is released unharmed."

Elmsley nodded, still without looking up. "Lie to the most dangerous man on the planet. No biggie."

Lou shook her head. "It's not a lie. If they let Ten go, Charity will stop trying to sabotage the IPO." She glanced toward Meredith. "We didn't realize you were doing it for Ramsey."

Elmsley's head jolted up. "Don't say his name." Then added softly: "Please. Not like this."

Lou understood. "Charity has given me her word. No more Fate."

"And in return?" It was Meredith, not Chase, who asked this question.

Again, Lou had her answer ready. "You said Elmsley wanted to use his money and his influence to undo the damage that Raum had done to the world."

Meredith tried to object, turning to Elmsley. "I didn't—"

Lou was quick to clarify. "She didn't use the word 'damage.' But I knew what she meant. Can you imagine a more powerful way to cement your place in history than to stand on the Nasdaq stage, right after ringing the bell, and to . . ."

Elmsley completed the sentence. "To quit. I get it."

Lou continued her pitch. "To send a message that you know the next generation of companies like Raum won't be built by people who look like you." She paused for effect. "I assume you'll be angel investing in companies after the IPO?" This was the standard playbook for post-exit founders—to spend some of their hard-earned billions backing the next generation. Which usually meant the next generation of bro founders just like themselves.

"He will," said Meredith. "In companies that are very, very not like Raum." She turned to Elmsley for confirmation, but he was already tapping the screen of his cell phone, making the call that would hopefully save Ten's life, and his own legacy.

95

LOU HURRIED OUT of Meredith Maitland's front door and was relieved to see Charity's car still parked in the same spot.

Lou had heard only one side of Elmsley's call with King Faisal, but it was clear from the way he held the phone away from his ear that Prince Bansar had dropped another few thousand points in his father's estimation. His Highness promised that Ten would be released within the hour. Meantime, the wood chipper was no doubt standing fueled and ready to welcome home the prodigal son.

Now they could only wait and hope. Would the prince really set Ten free and board a plane home to Riyadh, knowing it might be the last flight he'd ever take? Before Lou left, Elmsley had promised to call every legislator in his address book to make sure there was nowhere Prince Bansar could run. No doubt Helen would do the same.

Lou pulled open the car door and clambered into the passenger seat. "We did it," she said. "The king is ordering Bansar home."

Charity was sitting in the darkness, staring at her phone. "We're already too late." She turned the screen toward Lou, who saw a chain of text messages. "Tim Palgrave just called Charlie Brusk and asked to borrow his private plane. Charlie said he sounded frantic."

Lou felt a chill. "When did this happen?"

"Ten minutes ago. Probably right after Elmsley spoke to the king. He's going on the run, and taking Ten with him."

"And *Tim Palgrave* is helping him?" Lou had always assumed Brusk was the Saudis' inside man on the board. But then she registered what else Charity had said. "Charlie Brusk *called you* to tell you this?"

Charity sighed. "Can we talk about it later? Charlie told Palgrave his plane isn't available, but it won't be long till he finds another option. We have to get to the Marina before they leave."

Charity reached to put the car into gear, but Lou put out her hand and stopped her. "No, we can't talk about it later. Why would Charlie Brusk be calling you to tell you about the prince's travel plans?"

Charity shut off the ignition and gave a long, frustrated sigh. "Because he works for me, OK?"

"Works for you how?" Lou spluttered her response. Charlie Brusk—the man who had covered up for Charity's rapist, had funded Christian and Weber, funded every toxic startup in the Valley . . . was on Charity's payroll?

Charity sighed. "It's really more of a strategic partnership. I told you the women at the Redwood give me investment tips. Sometimes I pass them along to Charlie, and in return he gives me information I need. Like, for example, warning me when Tim Palgrave is about to skip the country. It's useful to have a front man."

"He knows you're Fate? What you did to Alex Wu, and the others?"

Charity held up her palms. "He knows exactly as much as he needs to know. And he definitely knows what will happen if he ever stops being useful . . ."

"Useful like dragging me to XXCubator, then pretending to be one of your victims to get me away from Amelia Christian."

Charity shrugged. "The prince's men were already digging, and I didn't want you leading them to the Stanford–MIT connection before we'd had a chance to talk."

"And the rash on his forehead?"

Charity rubbed her own scalp. "That was real. I sent him the same stuff I found in Joe Christian's apartment and told him where to put it. He was not happy, but he did as he was told."

Lou had so many more questions, but Charity was clearly done explaining herself. "Are we going to do this all day? Ten is about to be put on a plane to the Middle East."

"Fine." They could argue about this later. "So what's Tim Palgrave's angle here? Why's he helping Bansar escape?" A possibility occurred to her, and she felt her heart pounding again. "Shit . . . what if Palgrave is Claude Pétain?"

Charity raised her hand. "Tim? Be serious. He can't set a VCR."

But Lou *was* being serious. "Pétain is obviously close to Raum. Someone with a vested interest in defending the company against critics and journalists. What if Palgrave joined forces with the Saudi intelligence services—got access to all their surveillance tech—and created this Pétain character to do their dirty work? We all think he's so dumb. Do you really believe that shit about him accidentally investing in Raum because he thought it was a sweater-vest company?" Then she added, pointedly: "If you give people something that fits in with their prejudices, then they just stop asking questions. Isn't that how it works?"

Charity ran a hand through her long hair. "And now Tim's getting the fuck out of town too, with his buddy the prince? They know the jig is up."

Lou thought she was going to say something else, but she just pressed the ignition and gunned the car in the direction of the Marina.

96

"SO WHAT'S OUR plan?"

Charity shouted this over the roar of the car's engine. Even with her terrifying driving, it would still take them twenty minutes to reach the Marina, where the prince was holding Ten. Lou had spent the drive staring silently out of the window, trying to figure out how the fuck they could stop the prince fleeing with Ten. She also couldn't shake the notion that Tim Palgrave might be Claude Pétain. *If you give people something that fits in with their prejudices, they just stop asking questions.*

Ohh. Lou jerked her forehead away from the cold glass. "I know how to stall Prince Bansar, and take down Pétain. Assuming I'm right and he's really Tim Palgrave." She pulled out her cell phone. "I need to call my mom."

"Your mom?" Charity jerked the wheel to the left to avoid a cyclist.

A moment later, Kerri-Ann McCarthy answered. Of course she hadn't switched off her damn phone. "Mom, it's me. Where are you?"

"We're still with Martinez. Where the hell are you?"

"I'm safe. And I know how you and Carol can catch Pétain."

There was silence at the other end of the line. Then, "Lou, you need to come here . . . There's shit all over the Internet telling his crazed fans how to find us. They know where we're going before we even get there."

Lou squeezed the handset even harder. This was exactly what she was counting on.

"Mom, you need to listen carefully. You, Carol, and Martinez need to come to the Marina. The part where the crazy-expensive boats are moored, OK? There's a yacht there called the *Oppulous*. Opp-u-lous. Don't ask me why. I'm headed there now."

Lou heard her mom take a breath. "You want me to bring Pétain's psycho mob to the Marina?" She was clearly saying this for Martinez's benefit too.

"Right—but stay out of sight. That's really important."

"Why?"

Lou didn't have time for questions, and she didn't know who was listening. "Just tell Martinez to have his SFPD friends standing by. SWAT, the bomb squad, the more the merrier. Anyone who wants the chance to arrest Pétain and his buddy Prince Bansar."

Kerri-Ann had put the call on speaker, because now Martinez's voice burst in. "Are you shitting me? That asshole has immunity. My captain—"

"I am shitting you not," said Lou, hearing Helen's voice in her own. "And in about half an hour, someone at the FBI is going to get a call from *his* boss telling him that the prince's immunity is lifted and he's wanted in connection with a kidnapping. Tell your captain you can get a jump on the feds."

Lou heard Charity laugh from the driver's seat. "A jump on the feds. Shiiiiit."

Lou knew the risk she was asking her mom and Carol to take. But she also knew they had to end this, now. "I don't want to put you guys in danger."

Her mom didn't hesitate. "A ten-year-old girl pointed a shotgun at her own father because I wasn't there when she needed me. You think wild horses are going to keep me away from that sailboat? Just promise you won't get yourself killed before I arrive."

"I promise." Lou could already see the masts of the Marina in the distance. "OK, I have to go. You just need to get here as fast as you can, and stay out of sight. The *Oppulous*. OK?"

Silence. Her mom had already hung up. The woman was incapable of saying good-bye.

Now Lou turned to Charity, who was navigating the car through the tangle of roads around the Marina. There was just one more thing she needed to do.

"That trick you pulled with Martina Allen and Elmsley's teleprompter— the fake *Politico* page with the photos—can you do that again?"

"Now?"

Lou realized the ridiculousness of the request, given Charity was currently negotiating a narrow concrete jetty at sixty miles an hour. "I mean, can you create a fake news story that's only visible to certain people in this area?"

Charity shook her head. "Not unless they all happen to be on the same network. At Raum I had to spoof a whole cluster of cell towers. It took hours to set up."

This was not the answer Lou was hoping to hear. "Remember what you told me outside the Four Seasons—that Pétain's racist followers would go apeshit if they knew he was working with King Faisal?"

Charity didn't even try to hide the doubt in her voice. "That's our plan? To lure Pétain's mob of racists down to the Marina in the hope they'll just spontaneously attack Prince Bansar?"

"I don't need them to attack him. I just need the prince to think they might."

There was plenty more to Lou's plan than that, but she didn't have time to explain. She still had to figure out how to convince the mob to do what she wanted, and her best idea—Charity's fake-web-page trick—was off the table.

That left only the nuclear option. Lou took out her cell phone and typed in the address of the *Herald*'s website. A few taps later she reached the log-in screen for the paper's news management system. She carefully entered her old username and password, hoping beyond hope that the technophobic Stephen Camp hadn't gotten around to deleting her account. Another few seconds passed and her wish was answered.

The *Oppulous* was easily the largest vessel in the Marina—towering three stories above the waterline, with four masts, and a forest of communications equipment. Not quite a megayacht, but still formidable in size and shape, it looked like a scaled-down model of the mammoth cruise ships Lou had seen docked at the Embarcadero, bound for Mexico or Hawaii. They pulled up alongside the bow and Charity turned off the engine and darkened the headlights.

"You really think this will work?"

Lou had no idea. She took another glance at her phone and satisfied herself that the "newsshort" she had just hurriedly typed directly into the *Herald*'s News Management System was still sitting in its drafts folder, ready to go live. For the first time in her life, she had written a story she knew to be totally, 100 percent false. And worse, she'd written it by breaking into the website of a newspaper she no longer worked for.

At this moment, though, none of that mattered. It was Lou's best chance of saving Ten's life, and maybe all of Silicon Valley too.

Her finger hovered over the publish button.

Wait. She turned to Charity. "Do you have a photo of Ten?"

"Like a headshot?"

Lou nodded. "Something recent. Something that looks like he usually . . . you know."

Charity scrolled through her phone and a couple of seconds later an attachment beeped into Lou's inbox. The image was a selfie: tightly cropped and showing a beaming Ten, sitting in his office chair, wearing his trademark stained black T-shirt. The only difference from his usual appearance was—Lou could hardly believe it—he seemed to have combed his hair.

Two clicks later, Lou had added the photo to her story. Now she stared at the all-too-familiar question flashing on her cell phone screen . . .

Are you sure you're ready to publish?

Y/N

Click.

Lou was first out of the car, with Charity following closely behind. They looked up and down the jetty and saw no signs of life. The *Oppulous* was similarly, eerily silent, with just a single light shining from a window on the middle deck.

They walked quietly to a ladder that rose up the smooth side of the yacht, buffered by two narrow guide rails. Lou grasped the rails with both hands and began to climb aboard. She heard the clanking of metal as Charity followed behind.

A shout, somewhere in the distance. Lou froze, still halfway up the ladder. It was probably just a drunk, because a moment later she heard a bottle smash.

Lou scrambled faster upward until she finally reached the main deck. Then, without stopping to consider the danger, she gently pushed open the main boarding door.

Right away she heard shouting.

"With deepest respect, Your Highness, this is highly irregular." It was Alastair, the man who had interrogated her at Raum One.

"How dare you question me? You will do as I say." The prince sounded frantic. Were they already too late to save Ten?

Lou pushed the door open wider and stepped inside the *Oppulous*. She found herself at the top of a wooden staircase leading to a single, low reception room. The space was dominated by a long mahogany cocktail bar on the opposite wall. To the right of the bar, cloaked in almost complete darkness, was a small seating area furnished with a leather sofa and what seemed at first to be an oddly shaped beanbag. She couldn't see either Alastair or the prince, but as her eyes adjusted, Lou realized that the shape was not a beanbag, but the huddled form of Tenrick Wheeler. She could see him moving, thank God, struggling against some unseen restraint.

Lou turned to Charity, who was still behind her on the steps, and whispered a quick description of what she could see.

"It is of no consequence. I shall do it myself," the prince was yelling again. "You can remain here and answer to the American authorities."

Without saying another word to Charity, Lou strode down the wooden stairs into the reception room.

The shouting stopped. Lou saw the prince now, standing to the right of the steps, dressed in his habitual white robes, and dripping with sweat.

Alastair stood next to him, and both men whirled around to face the interlopers.

After a moment's shock, the prince raised his hand and swept it toward the room—a bold and exaggerated gesture of welcome. "Miss McCarthy, what a pleasant surprise." His voice was more sinister, and British, than ever. If he noticed Charity standing behind Lou, he didn't mention her. Instead he barked a crisp command in Arabic, and two guards emerged from the gloom and leveled their handguns at Lou and Charity.

"Your dad sent us," said Lou. "We're here for Tenrick."

She looked across the room at the huddled shape. Ten had hauled himself up to a seated position, and Lou could see his face was bloodied, his shirt soaked through with sweat. "Lou? Shit, you shouldn't be here." Then he stopped, and let out a low moan—a sound somewhere between anguish and alarm.

"Hi, Ten," said Charity. "It's been a long time."

"Not that long," said Ten, nodding toward the stuffed kangaroo still lying by his side.

"Shut up," ordered the prince. "I don't know who any of you people are, or why you are here, but this vessel is Saudi sovereign territory." He reached into a pocket hidden deep in his robes and pulled out a silver pistol. The guards seemed almost as shocked as Lou, but kept their own weapons leveled at the interlopers.

Lou took a step back, instinctively blocking the prince's view of Charity. She was about to pass out from terror, but knew she had to keep talking. She turned to Alastair. "He hasn't told you? This isn't Saudi territory, and none of you has immunity. The king has ordered Prince Bansar home." Lou had no idea if that was technically true, but all she needed at that moment was for Alastair to believe it. And judging from the way his eyes flicked toward his boss, he did.

"Don't believe what she says." The prince was yelling again.

Charity stepped from behind Lou. "You don't have to believe a damn thing. Just call the king and ask him. And if we're lying, you boys can go ahead and shoot us." She directed this challenge at the prince's body-guards, who were also looking uncertainly toward Bansar.

"Your Highness, if what they say is true . . ." Alastair spoke the words carefully.

"No," shouted the prince, sweat pouring from his brow. He was still holding his pistol, which he now leveled at his lead investigator.

Alastair seemed strangely unfazed. Slowly, he reached into his pocket and pulled out an iPhone.

"You will not make that call!" The shout was followed by a gunshot and a surprisingly feminine scream of pain. Alastair grabbed his side, a corona of blood quickly spreading around his palm. He shouted another command and the guards turned to point their weapons at the prince.

Lou needed to run—she knew that—but her legs refused to move. "You guys should just go," said Charity to the guards, as if offering simple career advice.

The larger of the two men muttered something to his partner, and—guns still trained on their former boss—they walked quickly toward the door of the yacht. And then they were gone. With one last curse, Alastair dragged himself behind them.

Now there were four. The prince, Lou, Charity, and Ten. Only one of them was armed.

"You don't have to do this," said Lou. "If you leave now, you might still get out of the country before the FBI shows up. All we want is Ten."

Before the prince could answer her, Lou was startled by the sound of footsteps behind her. She spun toward the door, and Charity did the same, to see the shape of a man filling the doorway, blocking their escape.

That was when they realized the horrible mistake they had both made.

The man was tall but schlubby, with greasy hair and a messy goatee. He was dressed in an ill-fitting, but clearly expensive, blue pinstripe suit and a pink pastel shirt. *"Bonjour à tous,"* said Brett Palgrave, only son of Tim Palgrave. Then, noticing the pool of blood on the floor, with drips leading toward the doorway: "Holy shit . . ."

Time seemed to freeze. Lou had been right about Claude Pétain being a Palgrave—just the wrong Palgrave.

"A pathetic loser with Daddy's money who resents women," Lou snapped. "I should have figured it out sooner."

Palgrave stared at Charity. "I know you," he said slowly. "*You're* the one who has been trying to destroy Raum? A Redwood whore?" He took a step forward and Lou thought for a moment he might take a swing at Charity. But Ten must have somehow dragged himself to his feet, because now he came hurtling across the deck, hands still bound behind his back, his full bulk barreling toward Brett Palgrave. Lou and Charity were only just able to jump out of the way as Palgrave raised his hand and pushed Ten away as hard as he could. The big man crashed down to the floor with a sickening thud.

"Enough!" cried the prince from across the room. "We have to leave, now."

"My father is on his way," said Palgrave, his tone pleading. "He's finding us a plane."

The prince waved the words away. "We go now, with or without him."

"What about these two?" said Palgrave.

The prince gestured with his pistol. "You wait outside, and leave them to me."

Lou felt her knees buckle, but she was somehow able to stay standing. "I wouldn't go outside if I were you, Brett. Unless you want to run into my mom and her friend. You saw what they did to your boy in Atlanta."

Palgrave hesitated, but just for a moment. "Your *mom*." He said this in a mocking, singsong tone that Lou recognized from his Claude Pétain videos. "I hope for your mom's sake, she is nowhere near here." He switched to Pétain's fake French accent. "My followers are tracking her every move. If she's here, they won't be far behind."

"That's the basic idea." Lou gave a broad smile, which she hoped concealed the true depths of her terror. "Remind me, Charity, how do Claude Pétain's followers feel about Black and Brown people?"

Charity responded as if quoting from an academic paper: "About the same as they feel about women. They believe we are . . ." Here she mimicked Pétain's stupid accent: ". . . violent savages who should all be—quote—driven from these shores and forced to live on our own fetid island in the middle of the ocean."

Lou turned back to Palgrave. "I was just wondering how those same followers will react when they get here and find the prince holding their hero Claude Pétain hostage. Threatening to fly him to Saudi Arabia for God knows what sick reason."

"I think they'll burn this fucking place to the ground," said Charity.

The prince interrupted her, turning toward Palgrave. "What is she talking about, holding you hostage?"

"I'm sorry," said Lou. "But I'm sure I don't know who this doofus in the expensive suit is." She gestured toward Ten. "I was talking about Claude Pétain here."

She took her phone from her pocket, reading from the story she'd written minutes earlier. "Exclusive to the *Herald*. Police in San Francisco are investigating reports that Claude Pétain—the pseudonymous alt-right Internet troll who recently declared a cyber holy war on women and people of color—is being held hostage on a yacht belonging to Saudi crown prince Bansar bin Faisal. The claims, which were made via anonymous postings on dark web bulletin boards, allege that the prince was angered by videos made by Pétain attacking his father, King Faisal. In a now-deleted post, the famed Internet provocateur revealed his identity as renowned engineer Tenrick Wheeler and pleaded for his supporters to rescue him . . ." She turned her screen so Palgrave could see Ten's photograph below the headline.

Ten seemed bewildered, but then he forced a bloody smile. *"Bonjour à tous,"* he said in a stunningly bad French accent.

Prince Bansar erupted again. "There will be no mob, no burning. Nobody is coming to save you. Nobody will believe this man is Claude Pétain."

But Lou saw Brett Palgrave glance toward the doorway, presumably imagining what Pétain's crazed supporters would see if they stormed the yacht.

What they'd see was exactly what her story had described: the prince, holding his smoking gun, standing over a bloodied Ten Wheeler, who fit the exact profile of Pétain.

Palgrave took out his own phone and swiped frantically at the screen, verifying that the story Lou had read was real. And it was. No fake cell phone towers this time.

There was just one thing missing: the actual fucking mob. All Lou could hear outside the yacht was silence. And now, much closer, a click.

The prince had cocked his pistol and was now holding it to Charity's head. Lou had played her best card. She was out of ideas.

The prince took a step forward, dragging Charity with him.

"Wait," Ten shouted, "listen."

And yes, now they could all hear the distant shouts and crashes of a mob. Another smash of glass, much closer now. The sound of shouting. About fucking time.

More shouts, much closer. Something had slammed against the upper deck of the boat.

"It's your decision," Lou shouted to the prince. "The only way we're going to be able to hold them off is if Claude Pétain walks out of here—alive—and explains it's all a mistake. You think you can walk out of here, Ten?"

"I think so," said Ten, struggling to bring himself upright.

Another smash, and the whoosh of something igniting. Now Lou could hear the sound of a siren. "That doesn't sound good," said Charity, still resisting the prince's grip.

Palgrave made for the door and then stopped, oscillating back and forth between the doorway and the room. A confused, trapped rat.

Sirens. "Think fast, Princey. Ticktock." Lou was almost starting to enjoy this.

Ten stumbled a couple of steps forward. And then shouting toward the door: "Help me, *mes amis*! I'm in here!"

The prince released Charity and shoved her toward the staircase. Then he turned to Palgrave. "Do as she says. Get these animals away from my boat."

"Go," Palgrave whimpered to Lou. "Please go."

"You too," said the prince to his now useless underling. "All of you."

Lou and Charity grabbed Ten's arms and helped walk him toward the door. Palgrave followed behind, trying to shield himself behind the women.

They emerged onto the deck and were immediately blinded by a floodlight, shining up from the jetty. In the darkness beyond, Lou could barely make out the speckle of blue and red lights, emanating from scores of patrol cars, SWAT vans, and a long eight-wheel "mobile control center." And thank God, because behind the lights she could also see the mass of furious bodies that made up Claude Pétain's mob of supporters being kept at bay by two lines of police.

"SFPD," an amplified voice boomed from somewhere behind the spotlight. "Move slowly down the ladder, one at a time."

Lou and Charity moved in unison, grabbing the pathetic hunched figure of Brett Palgrave and pushing him ahead. He climbed slowly down the ladder. "That's Claude Pétain," Lou shouted to the line of cops. She was afraid he might still run—that the police might believe her fake story about Ten and let the real Pétain escape.

Sure enough, before Palgrave's feet had fully settled on the concrete, he was moving again—sprinting across the jetty toward his crowd of followers. He would have made it, too, had he not felt compelled to declare a preemptive victory. He easily passed the confused line of cops—who stepped aside in deference to the white man in a tailored suit—then raised both fists in triumph . . . *"BONJOUR À TO—"* before abruptly crumpling to the ground with a bestial shriek of pain.

"*Bonjour à* fuck you," shouted Carol, as she delivered a second blow to his balls with her aluminum baseball bat. She almost scored a third hit, but now two huge men dressed in SFPD riot gear grabbed Palgrave by both arms and slammed him flat. Lou caught up just in time to see the larger of the two men push his knee into the base of the whimpering Palgrave's spine, securing his hands with a plastic cable tie. Lou grabbed the bat from Carol's hand and in a smooth motion tossed it into the dock.

A few moments later Lou, Charity, and Ten found themselves left standing on the jetty. A few of Palgrave's trolls had staged a pathetic last stand—hurling plastic water bottles and street trash at the cops before being herded into a fleet of police cars. The rest had dissolved away, back to their basements or day jobs. Ready for the next super-troll to pique their attention and stoke their resentments.

An SFPD medic tried to dress the gash on Ten's head, but Charity waved him away and took the gauze and wet wipes herself. Lou watched as she dabbed tenderly at Ten's forehead and he tried unsuccessfully not to wince. The tears flooding down his cheeks told their own complicated story. "I'm so sorry. I'm so, so sorry," he was saying. Her work complete, Charity dropped her bloodied wet wipe, and the two old friends embraced for the first time in a decade.

Lou found her mom standing a few feet away staring into the bay.

"Where did Carol go? Tell me she didn't get arrested."

Her mom laughed. "She went with Martinez, but I'm pretty sure I didn't hear any Miranda rights." Her smile dropped. "How are you doing?" Then without waiting for an answer, she put her arm out and pulled Lou into a hug.

"Long week," said Lou, squeezing her mom tightly. "I'm just glad you're here."

"I'm glad too. It's not every day a mom gets to see her daughter foil an international kidnapping *and* expose the world's most famous troll."

Lou felt her phone buzzing in her back pocket. Without releasing her grip on her mom, she pulled out the phone and glanced at the screen. She was surprised to see a notification from the *Herald*'s internal messaging system, until she realized she had forgotten to log out after posting her fake story about Ten being Claude Pétain. She mouthed a quiet *Shit* as she saw the name Stephen Camp in the "from" line of the message.

What was the worst her old boss could do to her? Yell at her? Sue her? Her fake story had saved a man's life. And whoever had to write the day two correction—Tommy probably—would surely get a hell of a scoop.

She clicked open the message.

Does this mean you want your job back? —SC

Lou stared at the question as a second notification appeared.

It's yours if you want it.

Did Lou want it?

Y/N

She stretched her thumb across the on-screen keyboard to type her one-letter response, then tucked the phone back into her pocket.

Suddenly from across the dock there came a loud roar and the sound of rushing water. Lou and her mom turned to see the *Oppulous* had started its engines and was slowly—very slowly—chugging away from its moorings. Some of the men in windbreakers were yelling into their phones, while others were rushing toward cars and vans. A helicopter had appeared overhead and now activated a dazzling spotlight, trained on the yacht's upper decks.

Lou's mom raised her hand to shield her eyes from the spotlight. "How far do you think he'll get?" They could make out the figure of the prince piloting the craft slowly across the basin.

"Oakland, maybe," said Lou. "Though if he's smart, he'll turn back around and . . ." She interrupted her own thought with a laugh. "If he's smart," she repeated, shaking her head at the notion.

Her mom laughed too. "We haven't met a smart one yet, have we?"

Then Lou and her mom stood, arm in arm, watching yet another powerful man make the worst decision he possibly could.

ACKNOWLEDGMENTS

In 2014, Ben Smith, the (then) editor of Buzzfeed, reported that an executive at Uber had threatened to spend $1 million to hire a team of ex-journalists to dig up dirt on technology journalist Sarah Lacy after she publicly criticized the company's treatment of women. The incident made me wonder: What kind of reporter would ever go to work at a tech company to smear other journalists? And so the idea for this novel was born.

This is my first work of fiction, and there are a lot of people without whom it could never have been written.

The first is Lisa Cron who taught me literally everything I know about the craft of storytelling. Everyone should be lucky enough to have so brilliant and patient a coach. The next is Jim Levine at Levine Greenberg Rostan. Jim championed this book from the very start and, without his enthusiasm, I'd likely have quit when the going got tough. Similarly, Rick Horgan at Scribner who, despite not actually acquiring the book, came close enough to make me feel like I might be on to something.

Thanks to Rich Arcus, editor par excellence, who – amongst a thousand other things, including coining the title '1414°' – suggested that I make my fictional tech bros slightly less terrible, and thus more believable (ha!). To my copy editor, Michele Alpern, and proofreader, Sara Magness, whose incredible attention to detail saved me from myself many times. Any errors that remain are my won.

Eternal gratitude to my friends and trusted readers James Aylett, Veronica Irwin, Fran O'Leary, Nathan Pensky, and Dan Raile for their insightful and immeasurably helpful feedback on the manuscript.

Most of all, thank you to Eli and Evie for the hugs and games of hide and seek. And to Sarah Lacy – scourge of ridesharing giants, and the love of my life: This book is dedicated to you.